BOOK ONE IN THE UNITY SERIES

GLIMMER
AND
BURN

LUCI BRIAR

ISBN: 979-8-9993752-1-6 (Paperback)
ISBN: 979-8-9993752-0-9 (E-Book)

Book Cover by Miblart

First edition 2025

Dedicated to Luci Hammerhead-Cheese, my daughter's suggested pen name, who would exist if I were a touch braver.

CHAPTER ONE

A WANING MOON LIT Miranda's clandestine path through Legacy Park. The Fells sat just beyond the sculpted greenery and meticulous lawns. As she neared the border of the park, movement rippled between the row buildings and voices carried on the breeze that disturbed the empty stillness. She was crossing worlds, though it was just a few acres of lawn that separated them.

Lantern flame feathered the edges of shadows as Miranda breached the boundary between the upper-class nobles of the Garrison and the Fells, where, despite the late hour, beings of every race mingled freely, prostitutes propositioned passersby, and drunks slumped on stoops. Revelry danced with vice as fae embraced humans and immortals fed on willing hosts.

Miranda wore a black cape and long gloves, hoping to become another shadow tonight. She had put great effort into concealing every feature society had come to admire in their "princess," or so she had been dubbed by the nobility. She actively hated the epithet and the image it evoked of her as some perfect reflection of society's ideal. Her golden curls were scrunched under a raven wig. The charming olive brown dimples of her smile were buried under salacious amounts of rouge and her features smothered in heavy kohl and colored powder.

Her body, however, she flaunted. Charm was going to be her weapon tonight, a real-world test of all the training her mother had drilled into her as a child. Though, that training had been meant for tea parties and social gatherings, not subterfuge.

Head down, Miranda navigated the unfamiliar streets until a body fell across her path.

A great *oof* of air left the fae's lungs as he hit the ground, his hair not quite concealing the pointed tips of his ears. Miranda froze as a woman with small, fine pointed horns and purple skin rummaged through the unconscious fae's pockets. The thief locked gazes with Miranda for a heartbeat, her one iris red and the other a pale blue, before she leapt from the scene and disappeared around a corner. A demon. A rare sight outside Demon Row, their refuge in the city.

Heart in her throat, Miranda reached down for the fallen fae and checked for a pulse. He was alive, at least, just unconscious. In a moment of hesitation, she nearly caved to her parents' constant conditioning of honor and integrity. A guardian was bound to the service of those in need. But, right now she masqueraded as a human and her mission required she not give her power away needlessly.

With no other recourse, Miranda gingerly maneuvered the fae against the rough brick of a building. She brought a specific amount of money and couldn't afford to lose a single coin. Still, she slipped a copper piece into his pocket. Tucking her shaking hands into her cloak, she side-stepped the victim and pushed on.

She did not typically run around the Fells in a dress reminiscent of a prostitute, though her costume was carefully hidden beneath her cloak for the moment. Her sister needed rescue, but Miranda was the only one who *knew* that she needed rescue. Their parents, society, Cordelia herself were all blind to the very real danger they faced.

Enveloped in the vibrant hum of the Fells, she let her hood of black velvet fall to expose her face and grant her a better field of vision. A scent lingered in the air, grease and spice. Fried foods sizzled in carts as vendors prepared orders. The gutters of the dirt streets were damp and sludge collected in the corners. Bins were overfull of trash, mountains collecting at their base and haloed by flies.

Unity was broken into distinct districts, remnants of its original segregated design before it was rechristened Unity, in honor of a more unified ideology. The Garrison was home to the humans and guardians, where she had grown up mixing with the elite of the city's inner Ring. The Fells held no distinction of its own, where the morally disinclined gathered in a melting pot of debauchery and vice.

This was not Miranda's first time venturing beyond her backyard, though never so far. Growing up, she'd been curious and drawn to the unfamiliar, to adventure and the promise of something new. Yet, her knowledge of the Fells' twisting streets was not extensive and she needed precision tonight. Miranda had studied her father's maps of the city so she could find her way quickly and efficiently. She only lost her way once, trying to orient the bird's-eye-view map with her first-hand view walking the actual streets. Her destination: a pleasure club of some renown, sat on the northern most edge of the Fells, near the border with Demon Row.

The Black Heart was not the most popular club in the Fells, but the most notorious. One could truly "escape from the world" there, as the slogan went. The sign was visible the moment she entered the street, with flocks of people milling about the doors. Patrons coming and going. Workers hoping to take advantage of the crowd for some easy scores.

A place of secrets. The shuttered windows and large black doors concealed the activities of its patrons. One didn't advertise going inside and Miranda hoped no one recognized her. If her parents found out she was here...well, their disappointment would be the least of the consequences.

"'Ello, darling. You look a might nervous." A woman ambled closer and Miranda steeled her nerves. She would not flinch. She would not show any weakness. She was a guardian, after all, and she could more than handle herself.

"Meeting an old boyfriend," Miranda lied, her smile lopsided and her posture relaxed. Blend. She needed to blend. That meant not being intimidated or showing hesitation. She had to be confident or someone was going to figure out that she didn't belong here and decide to test if she were easy prey.

The woman, her face narrow and a slight point to her dark ears nodded in understanding. "Oh, honey, we've all been there. Best o'luck to you." With a wave of her hand, she left Miranda to her business.

With a deep, silent breath Miranda climbed the five steps to the Black Heart and pulled on the doors. Raucous music, laughter, and the clashing scents of perfumes and sweat assaulted her as she entered. Low lanterns encased in specialized glass emitted different spectrums of light in the grand foyer, creating deeper shadows and illuminating other colors. There were bodies everywhere, some clothed and upright, others in various stages of undress and intimate positions.

Miranda's eyes skimmed over the writhing bodies, and though she liked to think herself immovable, a hint of red colored her cheeks. She fought *not* to hear the grunts and moans undercutting the small orchestra on the stage. Archways opened to other rooms, with other sorts of activities. She clenched her jaw as she moved with grace toward the archway farthest to the left. The gaming room.

Her informant instructed her to meet here. Getting this chance had been a lucky break and she was running out of time. Her sister's wedding was in two short months and if Miranda had any hope of stopping it, she needed outside help.

In this room, the music was quieter. The flicker of lanterns was a touch brighter and warmer in tone. They lit rows of felt tables where people sat in the midst of various games. Cards. Dice. Knives. The scent of alcohol and tobacco smoke was stronger here. Miranda wove through the tables until she found the one in the far corner, near the potted bromeliad. As instructed, she sat and waited.

She scanned the faces around her, women in heavy powder laughing and drinking. Men either serious and stoic in their games or boisterous and handsy. A kaleidoscope of eye colors, dull or luminous. Smiles bared fangs. Pointed ears jutted from various hairstyles. Smoke collected above their heads like an ominous fog. A waiter with a jagged set of horns offered to take her order. Miranda politely declined and returned to scanning the room. A pair of eyes caught hers, pulling her attention from her task.

Even from afar, with the waft of smoke and flurry of activity, there was no mistaking the striking blue of that gaze. It captured her, as she was unmistakably the focus. The man appeared human, though she would bet anything that he wasn't. And he moved closer, snaking through tables toward her.

Miranda tensed. Was *he* her informant? She prayed to the Divine her staring hadn't been perceived as a threat or suspicion. She shifted her thoughts from his appearance to a more analyzing stare.

She had never seen her informant in person, so it was hard to be sure, but as the stranger moved closer her focused study never wavered. He was not wearing a cravat or coat, just an elegantly embroidered dark red vest atop a black shirt. The top buttons were undone, which may have been normal for the middle of the night in a pleasure club in the Fells, but was not for her. And he was handsome. And worse, it was clear from the swagger in his step that he knew it. Arrogance was the worst sort of vice and Miranda bristled well before he reached her.

He stopped near her table and gave her a small bow of his head.

Miranda huffed and looked pointedly away, though her pulse raced. She returned the nod with feigned ease.

"May I help you?" She offered, a curt edge slipping through her intention for civility.

His smile was pure sin, and the slight tilt to his head was the only acknowledgment of her tone. "I'm not certain, love. What sort of game were you hoping to play?"

Game? She glanced around her, getting her bearings again. He hadn't used the agreed upon signal phrase, which meant he was just some charming scoundrel showing interest because her dress was low cut. Her ability to hide her annoyance began to wane.

"Actually, I'm waiting for someone," she replied, no longer hiding the bite from her tone. She should be more diplomatic in her response, angering the wrong sort could cause an incident. But Miranda had always done poorly in etiquette class and hiding her emotions was not so easily done. She did, however, refrain from adding a snarky 'now leave me alone' to her statement.

"Is that right?" he said, all easy grace and nonchalance. Except that every fiber of her being was humming. Maybe it was the club affecting her, what she had seen in the other room, but she did wish he was ugly. His jaw showed a hint of stubble, raven hair cut so that it just covered his ears yet was roguishly styled, and his blue eyes lured her like a song until she might forget why she was here. He radiated all the wrong sort of energy that screamed 'danger' and 'trouble' but whispered 'you'd like it.' It was a hard combination to ignore. If she were not on such important business, it might be fun to show him exactly who he was attempting to seduce. Knock that smile off his face and give him some genuine shock if she oh so easily kicked his legs out from under him.

No. Miranda tore her gaze away, determined to keep her wits. She refused to smile, he'd only mistake that for encouragement.

"Evening," another voice said, from behind her, deep and gravelly. A second man approached her table and offered a quick sort of smile before continuing, "Is it whist or poker? Cause I've a mind for backgammon." He tipped the edge of his peaked cap.

Miranda froze. The signal. Then she took a quick, deep breath. Though her bearings were shaken, she could still recover. She had to recover. She wished with all her energy the handsome distraction would leave and not continue to make this harder. As amusing as it would be to throw him on his ass, she did not want to make a scene and scare away her only chance at saving her sister.

Instead of leaving, the Handsome Distraction seemed cheerful. "Wonderful, backgammon it is." He pulled out the chair next to her, and she caught a scent that made her head spin before it was overpowered by alcohol. Was he drunk? She was too green to really tell and he seemed to hide it well. No slurring. But why was he sitting down with her?

"Excuse me, this is a private—" She began to protest, but the informant interrupted.

"Drake stays. At my request." His words were final, spoken with the ease of authority of someone who wielded great power.

Her pulse spiked, she had a plan and now he was changing it. She considered that they intended to jump her and take her money, her prize merely a lie to lure a gullible noble from the safety of the Garrison.

She could take one of them, but two? And if they were not entirely human, as she suspected, then even one would be difficult. She adjusted her posture and chair, disguising the movements as unease, but she was tensed to retreat. There was a path to the door with a few chairs pushed out, but no patrons to get in her way. Hopping a table would be no challenge, to get something solid between her and them.

Her informant sat opposite her. He was good-looking in his own way, a more haunted and dangerous sort of way. He wore simple clothes made of rougher fabrics, though he exuded control and power. If the handsome stranger had disoriented her, this one had her on edge. He appeared entirely human except that his eyes were black and gold, with no trace of white. He was a grimm, the hybrid child of a demon. Guardian's shared blood with the Divine, but grimm shared the blood of the Infernal, deity of destruction and chaos. There was not nearly enough known about grimm, but the stories, whether fantasy or truth, were the stuff of children's nightmares.

The informant's gaze shifted easily between her and the handsome stranger, Drake—whose body language suggested he was as thrown as herself. That was promising, it suggested they weren't working together. The informant slouched casually in his chair, pulling out a pack of cigarettes which he tapped in a slow pattern on the table before speaking. His manner as easy as if he were relaxing on a beach. It had to be intentional. He knew he changed the game having them both here and he didn't care.

"So," he started as he popped a cigarette free and lit it, "I've found myself in the most interesting of situations where the noble daughter of a prominent guardian family and the recently-restored bastard half-blood son of a noble have a shared interest in information I possess."

Miranda's nose flared as she cast a look next to her, glad to see the devil-may-care look had disappeared from Drake's face. His features were stern, jaw clenching as he stared down the informant.

"I know you, too," Drake said, his voice less lyrical than before, deeper and filled with warning. "Thaddeus Wraith."

Miranda blinked. It couldn't be...

Wraith responded with a small smile, more a quirk of the lips, and took a hit from the cigarette. "Very good, Lord Drake. And it's Teddy, please, I'm not as scary as the papers make it seem, yeah? But my identity isn't the problem here, is it?" He didn't pause long enough for a response. "Now. I've something the two of you want and that's got me thinking. How valuable is it to you?"

"You promised that information," Miranda interjected more forcefully than intended and she was proud of herself for not backing down when Wraith's molten eyes focused on her. "I brought the agreed upon amount," she pressed.

Wraith was infamous throughout the city. The leader of an organized crime ring that expanded throughout the whole of Unity. He didn't work in the city's underground, he *was* the city's underground. Whispers about him often used the derogatory term 'imp' but until now she was never certain if that was because of his lineage or his preference for brutality that demons often shared.

"Yes, well, Miss Wilde, this is business," Wraith stated, pausing to take another drag of the cigarette, "And in business, I favor the highest bidder. So who wants to place the first?"

This was not how it was supposed to happen. She was not supposed to be in a bidding war, she already agreed to a price and she only had so much at her disposal. But she was not going back empty handed. She would win at any cost. Cheating and underhanded tactics were not off the table, which was a hard choice for a guardian, but Lord Drake made the choice for her the moment he appeared and ruined everything.

Devin Drake uncurled his fists. A second bidder was not what he and Wraith had agreed upon, but Devin was hardly surprised by the underhanded move.

Wraith was the unofficial leader of Demon Row. The Butcher of Barret. The Lord of Crime. It was rumored Wraith himself was a grimm, a fact now glaringly obvious.

The man's eyes were otherworldly. The whites were entirely black with bright, almost glowing gold irises. His body was draped like he were lounging in the safety of his home, smug and at ease. Devin found it harder than most to trust demons, having served in the infamous Demon war. Seeing their brutality first hand did not exactly endear him to their plight.

This was *his* club, damn it. Wraith was the outsider here. Devin had security everywhere, knew every secret corner, every brick. He was not about to go making the wrong sort of enemies, but he wasn't going to be played with on his own property, either.

"This isn't how we do business," Devin said, keeping anger out of his voice. Yes, he wanted what Wraith held. It was the first step to ending the revenge that had festered in him for the last sixteen years. He had no clue what a noble woman would want with information about a corrupt alderman. He didn't care. For all her pretty face and pleasing assets, she was not what he was truly after tonight. He intended to charm her into vacating this corner of the room so he could meet Wraith privately. He hadn't known she was to be his competition.

"Then we won't do business." Wraith shrugged before flicking his ash into the ashtray. "It makes no difference to me, I've plenty of means to get money. Your little vendettas against Yarrow Graves matter very little in the grand scheme of things." Wraith gestured with his cigarette before setting it in his mouth and taking a hit. "So," he let the smoke drift from his mouth, "what'll it be? Am I taking my business elsewhere? Time is money, I don't much care for wasting it."

Devin entertained the idea of calling in his security to handle Wraith. There might be fallout, Wraith was a powerful figure, but it would be worth it to forgo this insipid charade. Now that the club was flourishing, Devin could finally pursue what truly mattered. Ending the life of Alderman Yarrow Graves. However, in the past year he'd accomplished very little. Graves was too well-connected, too clever, and practically untouchable beneath the armor of societal adoration. Devin couldn't get within earshot of the man, let alone close enough for bodily harm.

Wraith had turned his first lead in all that time into a farce. Still, even Devin knew not to push Wraith too far. Crossing Wraith would be suicide.

Devin considered the woman beside him, Miss Wilde. No doubt one of the daughters of James Wilde, the guardian Alderman. He couldn't recall her name at present. Something with an N or possibly M. She had captured his attention long before she had found herself in the seat he reserved for this meeting.

Dressed in flattering scarlet, raven hair—he suspected was a wig—and thick make-up wasn't enough to hide the ferocity in her gaze. She had been both unsure and yet confident as she passed through the first room of his club. Most noble ladies wouldn't have made it that far. No refunds, unfortunately, for weak constitutions. Yet, Miss Wilde had pressed on, though so clearly uncomfortable.

She made little effort in hiding her contempt for him. He hadn't spoken two words to her before she'd decided she disliked him. Under different circumstances, he'd amuse himself with instigating her anger. Now, of course, he knew she had been on a mission to gather the information he sought for his own ends. That made her an obstacle. A gorgeous, alluring obstacle, but no less in the way.

Even now, she radiated anger. She was incredibly easy to read, though he guessed she would not like that about herself. Still, he wasn't sure if he could outbid a noble. Devin was by no means poor, but he wondered if his view of poor matched the Lady next to him. Would he need to dip into the club's funds? Jack Hale, his manager, would moan about the irresponsibility for months and Devin might have told Jack to fuck off, but it was Jack's management of the Black Heart that left Devin free to hate his life and drink his past away, so he allowed the man more liberties than he might otherwise.

But he wanted this information. All other attempts to get close to Graves had failed, now he was hunting for leverage against his enemy, a level of espionage he had not resorted to lightly. Whatever Miss Wilde's reasons, Devin had his own revenge to think about. If he couldn't avenge his fallen comrades what was the point?

Miss Wilde's gaze kept shifting toward him, trying to read him, but he kept his demeanor neutral. He wouldn't let her see his desperation. And from the looks of it, she had not planned on a bidding war, either. Maybe he could outbid her without having to siphon off the club. He was, technically, a lord now and had his own money to use. But would it be enough to outbid Miss Wilde?

Wraith worked his tongue along the back of his teeth, watching them closely. He was still at ease, body draped over the booth, but growing bored. "I'll tell you what, let's make this a bit easier." He reached into his coat and drew out a piece of paper. He tore it in half and slid a piece to each of them. "We'll do a silent bid. Write down what you'll pay. Highest wins."

He handed Miss Wilde a pencil first. "Keep in mind, I'm not selling for less than what was originally promised. And if you want to outbid the other, might want to think of a nice large number. Understood?"

Miss Wilde nodded and hovered over her paper, obscuring Devin's view with her body. Her shoulder rose to the curve of a slender neck, to the base of her scalp where, now, he was certain she was wearing a wig. Golden strands curled out from the net of raven hair. Blonde, he knew it. Striking against the warm tones in her skin.

She folded the paper and offered the pencil tip first, her grip likened to holding a blade, as if she were prepared to stab him with lead. He plucked the pencil from her and her fingers instantly curled into a fist. Devin masked an amused smile with a cough and swipe of his hand. A viper ready to snap. Were they in different circumstances, he'd have gladly spent the evening teasing out her venomous strike.

Indecision wrestled in him for a moment. He was not going to throw this bid, not for her pleading eyes, not for a carriage of orphans. He tapped the pencil point on the paper, searching for a number.

When he finally bent to write—making a great show of obscuring *her* view with his shoulder—Devin got to the final zero and hesitated. One number might stand between him and his revenge...Devin threw the pencil down, folded his bid, and slid the paper to Wraith.

He might have lost the whole thing over that zero. And it was not pity or compassion that stayed his hand. It was self-preservation, pure and simple. He had to be economical. If he lost, maybe they could share. His grin returned. He'd enjoy sharing more than just information with Miss Wilde.

Wraith collected the bids. "Thank you for your business." He looked at both, smiling. Then his eyes moved to Miss Wilde. "Congratulations, Miss, you've won yourself some information."

She breathed as if she'd been holding her breath and nodded. "Thank the Divine."

"Payment up front."

Her face hardened. "I have what was promised, the rest can be arranged in two installments. Just give me the name and address for delivery." She slid her offering toward him and Wraith stared at her a moment longer.

"I expect you know what happens if you don't pay?" he said, the threat implied. "So let's just make sure we hold up our end, yeah?" He took the offered notes and handed her an envelope.

Devin followed the transaction. Revenge flared angry and consuming in his heart at the sight, so close to information that could ruin his enemy. He suppressed the urge to snatch it and have Miss Wilde escorted outside. He should have added that last zero. What an idiot. He would not make such a mistake again, no matter how enchanting the eyes.

"Good day, Mr. Drake," she said, mouth tight, and she booked for the exit.

Hold on a damn minute.

Devin rose and followed, catching her as she raced down the steps of the club and into the street. His hand closed around her wrist and she whirled, eyes like emerald flame. She moved with expert control, advancing, and driving him into a wall. She was strong. Inhumanly strong. So, Miss Wilde was a guardian. The sub-race of humans gifted blood from their Divine to make them stronger and faster, better agility and stamina. Advantages to help humans compete in a world of monsters. Except now, those monsters were neighbors and peers.

"Easy, love, I'm just here to talk," he said.

Her arm pressed against his throat to hold him in place. Her eyes were sparks of rage. There was a masochistic part of him that wanted to push her. To see how far he could rile her before she struck. To tempt. To find what buttons made her nose flare and her eyes assault. He had no doubt that she could land him on his ass if she wanted. And he would very much enjoy being on his back under Miss Wilde.

Devin clicked his tongue and laughed as he halted that train of thought. He nearly forgot she was in his way.

"What? Why are you laughing?"

"You'd kill me if I told you," he admitted freely.

Miss Wilde's arm pressed harder into his neck. "What do you want? I won. I get the prize."

"That you did. But I couldn't very well leave it at that, could I?" He smiled with as much charm as he could muster under the circumstances. She looked ready to cut his head off. Temptation still called to him. She was tantalizingly close. All he had to do was look down to notice her chest pressing the confines of her dress as she took quick, heavy breaths. But that envelope clutched in her other arm called louder.

"Why? It's not that hard," she prompted, innocently ignorant to the turmoil her anger was causing. Devin cleared his throat and swallowed down the innuendo *begging* to be shared.

"Perhaps I could explain if my throat weren't being crushed," he tried, adding a small cough for effect.

She rolled her eyes, but eased back, releasing him. Though, still on her guard.

"Thank you. That is much better." He smoothed his clothes, picked off a spec of dirt. They hadn't drawn much attention, the sort of crowd that gathered outside his doors were not the sort to bat an eye at a woman forcing a man against a wall. He noticed Jack over Miss Wilde's shoulder, wavering at the door and ready to intervene.

"What do you want? I have places to be," she snapped, unaware of how close she came to being outnumbered. He and Jack, a half-fae and an immortal, could easily hold their own against a guardian. Devin *could* have forced her to give him that envelope and be done with the nice guy routine. Or steal it from her, he was good with his hands. She wouldn't know until too late. But, alas, for all his faults and thwarting of rules, even scoundrels set limits. She had won, fair enough.

Devin studied her. Beautiful face twisted in steely resolve, but then that something deeper simmered in her eyes. Desperation? Why did she want this information, anyway? Perhaps her stakes were higher than he estimated. "You know that I want the information in your hand."

"Yes."

"Well, I thought perhaps we could work together. We seem to have a similar goal. Why not share? I can make it worth your while."

Her smile was anything but friendly. "I don't need any help and you have nothing I want."

"Ah, princess, but everyone needs help once in a while, no?" He leaned in closer, noting how she stiffened, but not altering his course until his lips were near her ear. "And, darling, everyone wants something." His arms maneuvered to keep her from retreating, placed to hold her arm if necessary. Devin did not make restraining unwilling women a habit, but this was a desperate situation and she was being needlessly obstinate.

"*Don't* call me princess." She spoke through her teeth, almost snarling with warning, and snatched her arm away before he could restrain it. Her movements were quick as a spark, her body a few paces away before he could blink. He put his hands up in a show of submission.

"Regardless, I think we can help each other."

"There's nothing I need from you," she said, voice stern. "I'm more than capable of handling things myself. Thank you for the offer. Don't touch or follow me again." And she turned on a heel and stalked off into the night.

Beautiful, but stubborn and rash. Fine. He had other ways of achieving his goal. He didn't need her.

Devin returned to the club and headed upstairs. Jack had retreated to the office, looking over accounts and only sparing him a few blatant looks over the pages. Devin went straight for the shelf of brandy.

As Miss Wilde fled, he'd started to see the pulsing flame of her aura. He tore off the cap and let it fall before tipping the bottle to his lips. He hoped he would never see the siren again.

CHAPTER TWO

M IRANDA HOPPED FROM HER window and into the familiar darkness of her bedchamber. She threw off her cloak and began to adjust the sconces on the wall until the shadows grew large with the contrast of light. She had training and tea with her mother in the morning, but she had resisted checking her prize the entire walk home—a feat drastically out of character.

Her hand plunged into her bodice and fished out the small blade concealed in her corset, one of several hidden just in case. Hands shaking, Miranda sliced through the plain seal and hesitated. There would be no going back once she read the contents. This document contained potentially incriminating evidence against her sister's fiancé.

Sneaking around the past few weeks, searching for a way to expose Yarrow Graves as the monster he was, had amounted to very little. She had her own story, but who would believe her over a respected political official? Any attempt to discredit Graves might look like petty jealousy over Cordelia's grand match while she, the older and more eligible sister, was overlooked.

She had to read the contents, she had to take that leap. But...perhaps she could do so with some friendly company.

Miranda pushed aside the clutter on her desk and gingerly set down the envelope. She tore off the cumbersome dress and undergarments in favor of her nightclothes. The red dress fought her as she tried to cram it under her bed, the skirts continuing to billow as air gathered in their layers. This dress could not be found in her wardrobe or there would be questions. The itchy wig followed, her hair once again free.

Once satisfied that the evidence of her trip to the Fells was hidden, Miranda retrieved the envelope and proceeded into the still hallways of her home.

She had made this walk a hundred times over the years, whenever Lydia came to stay for a few days. The guest rooms were a floor below hers and had their own hallways for privacy. Miranda knocked, waited for a reply, then opened the door expecting to find Lydia Foster, her best friend, asleep in bed. The bed, however, was untouched.

"Damn it, Liddy," Miranda whispered to the empty room. There was only one other place in the entire estate where Lydia might be at such an hour.

The Wilde estate held a quaint, cozy library. Not overly large or grand, a family of guardians prided themselves on physical pursuits. Miranda herself rarely visited here. Even as a child she was too busy getting muddy or finding bugs until she was old enough to practice swordsmanship on trees and shrubs in the gardens.

There were not many places to hide and, given the hour, only one source of light. A flame flickered around a shelf nearest the back wall of floor to ceiling shelves. As Miranda rounded the corner, she knocked straight into the mobile ladder.

"Divines above—" The soft curse preceded a high-pitched cry and a woman fell to the carpeted floor.

"Lydia!" Miranda reached down to help her friend. "Are you alright?"

"Not me, the books!" Lydia let go of Miranda and started collecting the books that followed her to the floor when she was thrown from her perch. "Thank the Divine, they're all intact." She gingerly brushed the cover of the final tome and set it in the stack with the others, the tower balanced on her arm and jutted hip.

Lydia Foster was a bespectacled woman with ebony curls that her poor maid had wrestled into a coiffure that had, no doubt, been neat and tidy this morning. Now it was barely contained with strands twirling their escape.

"Forget the books, are you hurt?"

Lydia looked up, blinking as if she had just realized Miranda was there. "Me? Oh, well, I suppose…" She wiggled her limbs. "All seems to be in order—oof." She rubbed her elbow. "Probably a bruise. Nothing to fuss about."

Miranda shook her head. "Never change, Liddy."

Lydia gave her a wide smile, her eyes blurred slightly by the special lenses in her spectacles. "I should think not. Not until I finish my book."

"Yes, I remember. The first historical context on demon culture." It would be the first because, at present, all literature on demons concerned their many transgressions against the other races or how best to kill them. The Demon War had ended sixteen years ago, but as the opposing force in the conflict, demons and their kin, grimm, suffered more prejudices than the other races. Lydia was obsessed with researching and learning about their languages and culture.

"I'm close, Miranda, I have pages of research. Notebooks full. My mother is quite displeased. She says my fingers are always stained with ink and ruining the china."

"Did you really need to research it in the middle of the night?"

Lydia pierced her with a knowing stare—or, rather, it might have been knowing. It was hard to tell exactly what Lydia's eyes were attempting to express. "I could ask the same of you. Your mother nearly caught you, by the way."

Miranda winced.

"Thankfully, I had already been to your bedchamber to see if you couldn't sleep either and wanted to explore the library with me, but you weren't there. Your mother found me just as I was leaving and I said you were out like the dead after we had spent the night talking."

"Thank you, Liddy."

"It's not a bother, but where were you?"

"I was getting this." Miranda revealed the envelope, and Lydia raised a dark eyebrow curiously.

"Yes...a lovely envelope, dear."

"It's what's inside, obviously. I just...I'm scared to open it."

Lydia's smile faltered. "Is this about your secret mission? The one you refuse to tell me about?"

"Maybe," Miranda hugged the envelope to her chest.

"Well, if you want my help opening it, then I think it's time you tell me what this secrecy is all about."

"Fair enough." Lydia was the only person in the world Miranda trusted with her mission. Not even Cordelia knew Miranda's true aim was to stop her wedding. "First, the information, then I'll explain."

Regaining confidence, Miranda opened the envelope. The paper inside was thin, just a single sheet, and Miranda leaned toward Lydia's candle.

These were not any sort of letters that Miranda recognized. She squinted, wondering if the light was playing tricks on her. The longer she stared, the more she realized she *did* know those letters, at least, she knew of their existence. Reading them, however, was impossible. "Blast it all, this is written in Faery."

The page creased as her fingers clenched. She saw and heard nothing save the hammering of her pulse working into a frenzy. Shit. All the work, the weeks of pooling allowance in secret, all of it amounted to a document that she couldn't read.

"I don't suppose you can read Faery?" Miranda offered the page to Lydia.

"I'm afraid not, no. I have been working on a translation of ancient Demonic, but...I suppose that's not very helpful."

Miranda leaned into the shelf, working at her bottom lip with her teeth and fingers. This was a nightmare. What use was a document she couldn't read? This might say anything.

"Oh, I know!" Lydia brightened. "Your sister's fiancé can read Faery, I'll bet anything. My mother is always going on and on about him." She adopted a mocking tone. "Cordelia is so lucky. He's just the sort of suitor you should be looking for, Lydia. Why can't you be more like the other girls, Lydia? You can be such a disappointment sometimes..." Lydia's voice trailed off and she looked down at her lap. "Anyway. Alderman Graves could translate it for you."

"I'm afraid that won't be possible," Miranda said, shoulders sagging in defeat. "My intent was to use this to expose Graves of crimes that would have him arrested."

Lydia opened her mouth then closed it, her nose wrinkled as she processed Miranda's words before saying, "But then, what would become of the engagement and wedding?"

"That's the point, Liddy. There can be no wedding." The words left Miranda's chest hollow, like a great weight had shifted and been set free. Though she planned to omit most of the details, it felt good to share her mission with someone.

"I don't follow."

Miranda's muscles locked as she said, "Graves is not a good man, Liddy. He's...well, he's a monster and I won't let him marry my sister."

"How on earth is Graves a monster? All I hear are his praises. My mother was furious that Cordelia was chosen when I am also human and a few years older." She shrugged. "I hardly care either way, but I suppose it would have been nice to secure a match that would end Mother's urgency to find me one."

Miranda rubbed her arms, though the room was a pleasant, tepid spring temperature. "He...well, he just, he's not...good. Promise me you won't forget that. He talks nicely, but it's all a lie."

"How do you know, Miranda? What happened?"

Miranda shook her head and closed her eyes to the rush of memories. She refused to let them devour her again, not here. She shook her head. "It doesn't matter. What does matter is that I keep him as far from Cordelia as possible. This information was supposed to do that."

"What about the books?" Lydia stood up. "This is the section on demons..." She pointed to a section of ten books and then let her eyes wander. "So then over here..." Her finger hovered in front of the spines as she read and walked, Lydia eventually found the books on Faery.

"Here we are. Which court?" Lydia asked.

"Um, well, Graves is Night Fae, so Night?"

Lydia passed over Summer, Winter, and Day until she found the singular book on the Night Court. "Ah. Seems you have even less literature on them than demons."

Miranda sighed. "My father always said they were the last to sign the accords, perhaps they aren't big on sharing their knowledge with outsiders."

"Is the faery language universal?"

"Possibly. Our lessons on the faery language included counting to ten and some colors. Damn it." Miranda bared her teeth and started to pace. There wasn't likely to be anywhere outside the courts themselves where she might find a translator. Fae and humans might be trying to coexist, but each race still kept to their borders. She was unlikely to find books to aid her in a translation and going to a person with this sort of information was out of the question.

Graves was beloved and duplicitous. She couldn't risk him finding out what she was doing. He controlled high society the way Thaddeus Wraith controlled the criminal underground. The first Night Fae to run on a campaign of tolerance and peace, he embraced every idealistic policy proposed in parliament. He was personable, charming. A fox dancing with his prey like equals.

Her prize mocked her. She shouldn't have waited until she was home, she should have checked the contents and thrown them back in Wraith's face as the mockery it was. She'd been so...distracted, so disarmed by that annoying—

Miranda stopped pacing.

"What is it?" Lydia returned the book she'd been skimming to the shelf and went to Miranda. "Did you think of something?"

"I may have," Miranda started, words forced through her clenched jaw. This was the worst solution imaginable, but if Miranda recalled enough of her mother's lessons it was possibly the only solution. "How much do you know about Lord Devin Drake?"

Lydia frowned. "The name is familiar...is he the one that inherited out of nowhere? Mother called him a half-fae who no one had any clue existed until Lord Warner died."

"That's what my mother said as well, it was quite the scandal last year." Miranda chewed her lip, thoughts returning to the club. He was only half-fae which explained why he appeared entirely human save the ethereal blue of his eyes.

"I suppose he might read Faery, but I don't see how that helps you." Lydia adjusted her spectacles. She was never without them, the lenses obscured her eyes so that it was hard to see where she was looking or the exact color, though Miranda had always assumed they were brown.

"Well...I was actually with him not hours ago."

Lydia's jaw fell open. "That's quite the scandal, Miranda. What were you doing with a Lord at such an hour?" Her pale cheeks flushed with color. "I wasn't aware either of you were even acquainted."

"We're not. And it wasn't like that, so please don't think I was out pursuing any sort of lascivious activities. Honestly, the thought alone is repulsive enough." As if to prove her wrong, her mind conjured the image of Drake's very handsome face as he whispered seductive words against her ear. She closed her eyes briefly, hoping to force him from her mind. "Repulsive. I'd sooner endure a hundred of my mother's eligible bachelors than his annoying flirtation."

Lydia looked ready to laugh, her lips forming a tight smile like she were holding it in. "That's quite the protest. I'm sure to believe you now."

Miranda narrowed her eyes. Lydia was not observant of anything outside of a page, so it was hard to say if she was sincere or placating.

"Anyway, I have reason to believe that he will help me."

"Are your cheeks red, Miranda?"

The words hit like a slap and Miranda hid her cheeks with her hands. "No, of course not. Why on earth would I be blushing?"

"Oh, you weren't. But you are now." Lydia giggled.

"I was merely caught off guard. Drake is insufferable. Full of himself. Arrogant." Miranda took a deep breath. "But he may be my only hope of translating this."

She couldn't very well go waltzing around Unity asking for someone to help her translate incriminating documents concerning Yarrow Graves. Ready to be done with this conversation and salvage what meager sleep she could before her full morning tomorrow, Miranda left Lydia to her midnight research and returned to her room.

She had expected to sleep soundly knowing she was that much closer to saving her sister from a disastrous engagement. Instead she tossed and turned, haunted by looping, unfamiliar letters and the most aggravating set of blue eyes.

Miranda awoke three hours later, bleary-eyed and fatigued. Her maid threw open the curtains to let in the first rays of morning. All her life Miranda had started her day with the sun. It allowed her to fit training into her schedule of studies, social engagements, and etiquette lessons. Even though she had outgrown most of her studies, Miranda could continue training until marriage.

"I'm not feeling well." Miranda groaned, turning over and pulling her pillow over her head.

Her maid, Yara, started making the bed around her. "Your parents will never believe that you are ill. Up you get. You've got training then tea with your mother and sister."

Miranda sat up. The only time she had missed a training session was when she'd been unconscious with fever. Perhaps she should have feigned oblivion.

A guardian must keep their skills sharp and practiced, it is the greatest honor and should not be fooled away.

She heard her father in her head, willing her upright. Not everyone was gifted with the Divine's blood so she must never be ungrateful. In truth, she favored training more than her other studies, just not when she'd spent all night sneaking around the Fells.

She shuffled from her bed and freshened up. Yara helped her into her training uniform and did her hair before sending her down. Her training uniform was form fitting and traded skirts for pants to aid maneuverability. Navy blue with white accents and gold filigree were sewn into the shoulders and lapels. It was one of the few exceptions to lady's fashion of heavy, layered dresses and corsets.

The training room was in the basement. A large space with no furniture, just cushioned flooring for rolls and melee. The walls held weapons for practice, though most guardians settled on one type for their proficiency. Since the end of the war, her father had taken to adding weapons from the other races to their arsenal. Faery daggers and broadswords. Demonic maces. They were crafted in unique materials, unlike the steel of human weapons. Moonstone. Tempered obsidian. Silver.

Miranda enjoyed practicing with them, learning their weight and balance. But she was partial to a sword. It was her father's choice of weapon and, as a child, she had longed to be as strong as her father. Her father was not there today, however, and only Master Thorn awaited her.

A no-nonsense teacher, Thorn ran her through her drills and stretches with barely a good morning. His only comment had been that she was tardy.

"In a hurry today, Miss Wilde?" Master Thorn asked as she fumbled through her stances. Training ended with a sparring match, and while Miranda had no trouble keeping up with her instructor at this stage of her life, today she was not herself. Her mind was adrift with the prospect of a reunion with a certain roguish asshole.

Miranda caught her breath. Thorn's sword hovered inches from her nose. "Yes, sorry, Master Thorn. I have tea with my mother later and got a late start. I...I slept poorly." Not a total lie.

He returned to a neutral stance. They bowed and he dismissed her for the day with a sharp reprimand that she get some proper sleep for next week. Miranda rushed to clean off the sweat and get dressed for tea, pants not permitted. It was nearly an hour before she headed into the parlor swaddled in layers of pale blue skirts. Her mother and sister were already sitting, but the tea and sandwiches had not yet been served.

She only had to get through tea before her time was her own. If Drake had inherited his father's estate, then the house was in the Garrison. She merely had to sneak into her mother's office and find the almanac that contained a list of the current peerage and their addresses. So long as she stayed in the Garrison, she needn't wait until nightfall. Though, she couldn't be certain that Drake would be home, there was no harm in checking.

But first...tea.

"Miranda," her mother addressed primly while Miranda offered apologies for her tardiness. "Sit," her mother instructed. "We were just discussing flower arrangements."

Miranda looked past her mother to her younger sister. They shared the same face shape, but her hair and eye color matched their mother's soft, pretty shades of brown, while Miranda took after father. Cordelia was only younger by a few years, but their lives had been invariably different. Cordelia was not a guardian.

Having the gift of the Divine's blood was considered a great honor. Not every human was born with the gifts it bestowed. Agility. Speed. Strength. It was said that they were gifted the Divine's blood millennia ago so that humans could compete in a world of magical creatures. The gift tended to run in families, passed from parent to child, but could manifest in any human no matter their lineage. Both Miranda's parents were guardians, even her mother, the prim and proper lady sipping tea with the utmost decorum could face an immortal in combat. But the Accords saw those days long buried. Now, there was peace and very little need for defenders.

"We picked out a lovely arrangement of everblooms and night lilies. I think it'll really highlight your sister's features and coloring," her mother commented. A servant brought fresh dewbaine tea and lunaleaf sandwiches, fae ingredients that they had started to explore after Cordelia's betrothal to a Night Fae.

Miranda wasn't partial to tea of any variety. She preferred the coffee that the watchmen drank at crime scenes or on patrols. Miranda pictured her mother's face if she asked for coffee. She smirked to herself and took one of the sandwiches, then piled a heap of them onto her plate. She forgot to eat in the haste of the morning.

Were this a marriage of love, Miranda would have been happy to share in the planning. She may not see herself at an altar, her personality had kept suitors at bay for years and was unlikely to change, she would have been happy for Cordelia. However, it was clear to Miranda that her sister held no regard for Graves and Miranda's own past with the monster soured her to talk of wedding planning. As their mother continued to comment on flowers and colors and arrangements, Cordelia wrinkled her nose.

"I saw that, young lady." Their mother sipped her tea. Cordelia straightened and shared a glance at Miranda that said, *mom is so annoying*.

"Aren't orchids out of season?" Miranda asked, sending a silent wince of apology to Cordelia who opened her mouth in silent betrayal. "I do agree, they are the perfect flower for Delia, we may have to push the wedding back a month to make sure we receive the best possible arrangement." It was hard pretending, forcing herself to be the model daughter, but it was never without purpose. Pushing the wedding back would buy her more time to ensure it never happened at all.

Lady Wilde smiled. "I'm so glad this wedding has had such a positive influence on you, Miri. It makes me hopeful that one day you may find your match."

Miranda fought the urge to roll her eyes. She wished her mother could see the change this wedding had had on Cordelia. Miranda had always been the overtly rebellious, troublesome daughter. Cordelia was a ray of sunshine, brightening any room she entered. No one else was as possessed of laughter and light.

None of that was evident now. It had been ages since Cordelia tried to sneak into Miranda's room late at night so they could giggle together or creep into the kitchens to swipe a sweet from the storeroom. Miranda had never been good at hiding her misdeeds, but Cordelia was a professional. Mother and father never suspected their sunny, sweet Delia. Only Miranda and a few servants knew that the sunny disposition masked mischief and deviance. Many a broken vase had been blamed on Miranda when Cordelia had been the true culprit.

"My lady, you have a visitor," announced their butler, Martin. With any luck this new visitor would distract her mother enough that she would be dismissed. Miranda swiped a few more sandwiches, holding out her top skirt to create a basket.

Lady Wilde overlooked Miranda as her attention went to the door, always the gracious host.

"Alderman Yarrow Graves is waiting in the foyer," Martin said.

Miranda nearly dropped her contraband, muscles freezing in place. Graves was here.

She began to return the sandwiches and didn't bother to brush away the crumbs as she let her top skirt fall back into place. She wouldn't leave her mother and sister with Graves. Not when she alone knew the truth of his character.

Her mother's posture and demeanor changed instantly, her smile more genuine as she said, "Please, show him in and make sure cook knows to send up another round of fresh sandwiches and tea for our guest."

Miranda's eyes moved to Cordelia, whose expression hadn't changed. How did no one notice? Her sister was not herself. Anyone who knew Cordelia could see it, why couldn't her parents? Or were they willfully blind to their daughter's feelings given that this was an 'ideal match?' For years, Unity had sought to garner harmony among the races. Ages ago—Miranda couldn't recall exact dates and numbers—half-races weren't tolerated, but scorned and hated. That was supposed to be in the past, and it mostly was, as far as Miranda knew, but there was still resistance to the idea. A marriage between a distinguished fae of the Night Court and a human was just the political move that her parents craved. It was for the greater good, after all. Their privilege meant they must serve as examples for others. The world would follow if they took the first steps.

Martin returned with Graves and everyone stood as he entered.

"Oh, Lady Wilde, my apologies. I was unaware you were in the middle of tea," Graves's voice was smooth as silk, jovial in a way that gave the illusion of good humor, and courteous to a fault. Miranda gave him the barest of acknowledgements she could muster given her mother's watchful gaze, but she would not look at him. Not directly.

"Nonsense, you are always welcome, Lord Graves," her mother said, "Please, do sit." She gestured toward a chair.

Cordelia and her mother shared the love seat and Miranda sat in an armchair farthest from the door. The room was meant to be inviting and was constantly updated to the latest trends in patterns and style. Currently, that meant wallpaper with floral patterns and soft, pastel colors of pink, green, and blue. Naturally, the furniture had been reupholstered to match.

"Thank you, Lady Wilde, tea would be greatly appreciated." Graves removed his top hat—the brim a touch wider and material not quite the same as a standard hat. This one probably blocked out the sun. Night Fae didn't burn or die in sunlight, but it was supposedly exhaustive and often led to headaches. "I'm here for business first, though, I find I quite miss my lovely betrothed's beauty after so long apart." He sent Cordelia a smile and her sister acknowledged the gesture with a mechanical 'thank you' and a dip of her head. "I was hoping to catch your husband, but he is not at home?"

"Yes, he had an appointment with Alderman North. I do hope I can offer assistance in his absence?"

Miranda narrowed her eyes. Graves was too smart to have miscalculated her father's whereabouts. He was playing a game. Manipulating everything to his whims. Miranda set down the sandwich she'd crushed in her fist, wiping away the crumbs before her mother could scold her.

Graves appeared to consider her mother's offer. "I'm sure it can wait. I'll admit to an innocent deception, speaking with Lord Wilde was merely a means to admire my lovely bride. It feels...much too long until our marriage." Now his sleazy gaze fixed on Cordelia. She shifted, but kept her posture because it was expected that she did not squirm. Couldn't her mother sense the unease? Cordelia had the look of someone attending their dog's funeral, not the glow of a happy bride-to-be.

Her mother laughed, a honed-practiced gesture and not at all a true display of amusement. "Now, now, Lord Graves. There will be plenty of time after the wedding." Her mother brightened. "Speaking of, I've been discussing with my daughter about the flower arrangements—" She must have mistaken his shift in expression for boredom at the tedium of wedding preparations because she quickly corrected, "Don't worry, I have no designs to pester you with details, but they will require shifting the date back another month. Those blooms are not in season quite so early."

Graves lifted his cup to his lips. He favored gold in his attire, gold trim, gold inlaid filigree, gold lining to his black coat. It matched the bright, luminous gold of his eyes. He was a Night Fae, with paler, almost ashen colored skin and grey hair neatly trimmed and styled close to his head, showing the prominent tips of his ears. The scent of his sickly sweet pomade overpowered if one got too close. He had been too close to Miranda once, a mistake he had not made twice.

"Well, I'm sure I'll be satisfied with whatever my lovely bride desires. What is a month, after all, when we have a lifetime ahead of us?" His words and manners remained cordial, though the muscles in his jaw were strained. The news had disappointed him. Why?

Miranda's heart was hammering like a sledge to heavy bolts. Why was he so eager to marry Cordelia? What was his plan for her? Miranda choked down a scream. Her limbs ached to flip the delicate tray and shatter the pristine china over the floor. Yet, she sat. Ankles crossed and her posture rigid. Her hands should be displayed softly on her thigh, but she had to tuck them in her side to hide the tremor.

"How generous, Lord Graves, I do hope it hasn't upset your plans overmuch," her mother continued, and Miranda nearly snorted. The change in date had upset *something*, but he wouldn't let his anger or true motives show here. Not before there were rings exchanged and a binding, legal contract holding Cordelia to him. "Isn't that comforting, darling? Any woman would be lucky to find a man with such gracious character."

Cordelia's smile bared teeth.

"Oh, please, you are being too generous, Lady Wilde. I am undeserving, I assure you." Everyone chuckled, but for endless layers of contrary reasons.

Graves's eyes slid to Miranda for the first time since he entered. She froze, ensnared by the same eyes that had haunted too many nightmares since last year. All the fight drained out of her and she was somewhere else, somewhere dark with an overpowering scent of pomade. She swallowed, but her throat was too dry and she had to cover her cough with a sip of room temperature tea. Or, rather, she had meant to take a dainty sip—habit with her mother present—but had gulped the contents of the cup in two swigs.

Lady Wilde's sharp eyes snapped to Miranda, but she would not scold her daughter in company, that would come later. Miranda re-

sisted swiping at her lips and picked up a napkin to blot the corners of
her mouth.

"Since I am here, Lady Wilde, and the weather is unaccountably
fair, might I take a turn about the garden with Miss Wilde? I feel we've
hardly had a moment to talk since the engagement."

Miranda leapt to her feet. "No."

"Miranda?" Her mother awaited an explanation for the outburst
with drawn lips and wide, accusing eyes.

"I mean...it's just..." Miranda was breathing too quickly to speak
clearly. "I only..."

"My dear, please sit down." Her mother spoke with calm authority.
Her mother was furious. Miranda would not live down this afternoon
quickly. "I do apologize, Lord Graves, my eldest does let her actions
run away from her sometimes."

"Oh, I don't mind." He smiled at Miranda, in appearance a show
of friendly understanding, but to her something much more sinister.
"The young are always given to flights of passion. I was no different
once, I'm sure."

Miranda's jaw locked as she lowered herself back into her seat. She
wanted to punch that fake smile off his face.

"Might the younger Miss Wilde and I take our walk?" He held out
a hand to Cordelia, who eyed it like it was made of snakes.

Her mother had to say no, but why would she? There was no reason
to deny his request unless one knew all the facts and her mother didn't.

"Oh, I'm afraid that won't be possible today, Lord Graves," her
mother said, taking Cordelia's hand and pulling her youngest daughter close. If Miranda didn't know better, she'd mistake the gesture
as protective. Graves frowned, visibly. He had not anticipated being
denied. Why did he want to walk with Cordelia? Did he want her alone
to...

Miranda closed her eyes as she attempted to fight the panic in her chest. Her mother had denied him. There was no further cause for alarm. She may not have done it for the right reasons, but her mother had saved the day.

"Cordelia has a previous appointment that I cannot cancel. We were just finishing our tea when you arrived and I'm afraid are already running behind." Her mother stood and Lord Graves was forced to rise as well. His grip on his hat kept shifting, and though he smiled, it was strained. He was short for a fae, matching her mother in height and losing an inch on Miranda.

She could easily beat him in a fight. It was an option that her dreams had indulged, more often than her waking mind. He was too well positioned to be attacked. Even now, completely unarmed and vulnerable in their parlor, he was protected by the conventions that frowned upon murder. If she were to strike him, the ramifications would be too perilous to navigate and would only create more problems. Still, it was a satisfying fantasy.

"Of course, Lady Wilde, I'm so sorry to have kept you."

"Not at all, Lord Graves. You are to be family soon. You must stop by whenever you wish."

He set his hat on his perfectly styled hair. "I may take you up on that, Lady Wilde."

Miranda's gaze did not leave him until he disappeared under the watchful eye of Martin. Only then did Miranda's chest ease enough for her to catch her breath.

"But, mama, what app—"

"Come now, Cordelia, surely I told you about the appointment with the...milliner." Her mother turned on her, "Do not think you have escaped, Miranda. We will talk later."

As the women quit the room, Miranda sprinted for her bedchamber.

"Miranda Olivia Wilde you will walk like a lady in this house. Unless you are hiding a uniform under that dress." Her mother's voice carried after her and Miranda adopted a controlled walk until she was far enough away that her mother wouldn't hear the thump of her feet.

She slammed her door shut and tucked her trembling hands into her chest. She itched to break something, to fight. Her breathing hefted her shoulders as she tried to calm herself for the grueling task ahead. If she wanted to be rid of Graves, she couldn't rely on her fists. A level of tactics was needed that she had never excelled at, despite years of training.

Still shaken, Miranda prepared to head out under the excuse of taking a turn in Legacy Park. It was still before noon and she hoped to catch Drake during luncheon.

She would have to tread carefully to get what she wanted. Drake was a known flirt and could be dangerous to her goals. After meeting him last night, she had witnessed how he might draw you in. That dangerous air about him that breathed of adventure and life. He was entirely too handsome, and there was something in the way his eyes locked with hers, that called to the part of her that craved challenge. And he *could* challenge her, she was sure. If she could just avoid being drawn in by his charm, his flaws would surely keep her senses in check. His reek of alcohol and exceedingly annoying banter. It would be easy to keep him at a distance if she just focused on his flaws.

CHAPTER THREE

D EVIN WOKE SOBER. A state he actively fought during his every waking hour.

The vivid details of his father's ancestral home spanned before him. The hand-carved inlay in the wood. The texture of the canvas that held the masterful brushstrokes of some famous painter Devin wouldn't know the name of, given his education had been rather less Upper Ring than his father's. It all legally belonged to him now. And while he actively fought to suppress and hide the fae part of himself, he openly detested his entirely human father.

His father's will intended the estate fall to Devin's human and legitimately born half-brother. However, his brother passed not even a few months after their father, leaving the estate in legal limbo until the next in line to inherit could be found. Too bad Devin wanted nothing to do with the place.

There was a brief time, when he was young and hopeful, that he might have sought to be part of his father's world. Devin quickly soured to that dream. Age had shown him that his father and all he stood for were nothing that Devin wanted for himself.

Then, fate's mocking hand had bequeathed him his seven-year-old heart's desire: the home of his father. But his heart no longer worked and these walls held more poison than promise.

Sober, awake, and tormented by an unforgiving sun, Devin grew more irritated by the second. A headache formed near his temple. Moonlight was his solace, thanks to his mother's Night Fae heritage, yet it highlighted his in-between existence. Not human enough for the social elite that sired him and spurned by the Night Fae because his mother had followed her heart to far from Court.

But the worst part of waking sober each morning was how his senses returned to their full clarity. A servant had shuffled past and he *sensed* her. Her urgency, her fear, her prejudice, it flitted toward him like the gentle brush of the tide, like scents he could see.

Devin growled as he rose to a sitting position on the overstuffed sofa. It was not meant for sleep. It was a decorative piece designed to impress important guests. Devin was creating uneven lumps in the cushions, since the good alcohol was stored in the study and he was usually too far gone to bother searching the labyrinthine hallways for a bedroom.

The vintage scotch from the previous night sat near his boots, still open. He scooped it up and started chugging. It burned, and he nearly sputtered twice—it was not the sort of drink one chugged, but he was desperate to go back to the haze that allowed him to pretend he wasn't half-fae. He got it down and let it settle. His stomach nearly protested his chosen breakfast, rolling with the threat of chucking the lot of it back up, but he kept it down.

Slowly, very slowly, inebriation began to dull his aura sight. His heightened awareness began to drift into a hazy fog. Another servant passed without the faintest hint of an aura. His fae gift was properly drowned once more.

He headed for the main hall and more servants scurried past. He sensed nothing, as it should be. Smothering his fae nature had been a necessity since childhood. The lingering prejudice from an eighty year war was still in force thirty-two years ago, when Devin's mother had fallen for a worthless aristocrat with no intention of allowing his fae proclivities to taint his ancestral seat. The whole unified races bit was recent.

Devin had never belonged to either side, but masking as fully human was safer than embracing the truth. Unity had been renamed at the same time as the war, and sought to mend those divides, to unify against the common enemy. Or, that was the hope and sentiment. In practice, people were still quick to judge and the habit was too ingrained.

Sure, burying a vital and unchangeable part of his person in alcohol for the better part of his life was not ideal. Or healthy. Or practical. And, yes, his self-loathing and untreated trauma did lead to a vice or two and was the root cause of his constant misery and desire to bury anything real with humor and innuendo. And, sure, the world was changing. Half-breeds were not so hated. Hell, even the grimm and demons were carved a section of the city as their own, and the war ended not even two decades.

Devin went to find some food, stopping to rifle through the mail only after he secured an apple. He stopped at a newssheet that contained a bunch of drivel about what the nobles were up to, nothing that truly mattered, and he would have tossed it with the others except for the name that stopped him: James Wilde. He had suspected Wilde to be the enchanting woman in red's father. It surely wasn't a common surname.

Absently flipping to the page, he skimmed until his heart skipped a beat. A party to celebrate the union of their daughter, the younger

Miss Wilde, to Lord Yarrow Graves and to honor Graves as a decorated hero of the Demon War. Graves. A hero.

He tore the paper to shreds and let the pieces scatter. Hero? What sort of lies was that bastard selling that Graves could get such a high standing family to believe absolute horse shit? Graves had blood on his hands. He was no hero. A sniveling coward who ran screaming at the first sign of trouble and got real soldiers killed.

Devin scrubbed at his face as he fought the tide of memories. So many dead. And it was all for nothing.

Breathing returning to a more neutral cadence, his thoughts drifted to his former comrades. The only survivors of the incident outside of himself and Graves, Rachel and Gideon, had become a sort of friendship built on shared horrors. Gideon had joined the Watchmen and where he went, Rachel was sure to follow. Devin hadn't heard from either in several months, but this sort of news would bring Gideon to his door. It was just a matter of when.

Damn it, he wished he'd stolen the information from Miss Wilde.

Though, none of this clarified what Miss Wilde intended to do with that information. Graves was to be her brother-in-law. Surely it was bad form to dig into the hidden corruption of the political figure about to marry into your family. Did she want blackmail? Perhaps she was of the few who knew Graves for what he was, a slimy coward who deserved little more than death.

"Sir?" Haversham, the family butler interrupted Devin's train of thought, and bowed, "There is someone here to see you, sir."

Devin frowned. "Why?"

No one had ever called on him before, not here at least. He'd taken a moment while brooding to wash the previous day off him and change his clothes, but he was no less ill prepared for visitors.

"She didn't say, sir, only insisted that it was urgent and that you would understand. She wouldn't give me a card."

She? Maybe Rachel sought him out about Graves? No lady of standing would call on him at any hour let alone...*what blasted time was it?* He hadn't a clue. He glanced around and decided he didn't care enough to bother pretending he knew the 'rules' of daytime visits from a woman so he sat down at the empty desk that had once belonged to his father. "Very well, let her in."

Haversham bowed and left.

Devin found another bottle and, this time, poured it into a glass before taking a sip. He no longer cared what he drank, so long as it was strong and instant in dulling his senses. When he turned, however, he realized he might be in need of those senses.

Miranda Wilde stood at the entrance to the study and he had guessed right the night before. Black was not her color. Now her hair was gold, held in a loose twist with wavy tendrils falling free. She was gorgeous. Stunning, really. But it was her eyes that captivated him.

Her beauty was there for anyone to see, but in her eyes, those green depths of intent and calculation hit him somewhere else entirely. Even now, showing up at his home unannounced and not a word exchanged between them, she was prepared to fight. The challenge and stubbornness. An unusual combination in a debutant. She was dressed plainly today, but no less flattering—and what the dress concealed his imagination was perfectly happy to compensate.

"Miss Wilde, to what do I owe the pleasure?"

She wrinkled her nose, holding an ungloved hand over her mouth. "Have you been drinking?"

Devin tilted his head. "This is my house. You're the one who shows up at an ungodly hour—"

"It's noon."

"—just to waltz in and criticize my drinking habits?"

She rolled her eyes, the unabashed annoyance drawing him in quite without his ability to stop it. "Obviously, that is not why I'm here."

"Then why?" He stood and sauntered closer, breaking the space that was considered proper distance in an effort to see her react. For all her beauty, this was merely flirtation for him. She was expressive and riling her was entirely too easy. He'd never take it further, that wasn't his game. Devin preferred to steer his intimate associations away from virgins and genteel ladies. Too messy. But it was fun to tease. "Is it to gloat over your outbidding me? Cause that is bad form, Miss Wilde."

"I don't gloat," she snapped, though she still hadn't told him why she was here.

"Then out of your depth, perhaps?"

"I can handle myself."

"I've no doubt," he said, laughing. Which made her bristle, her body squaring off as if to attack. Then her eyes dipped to his mouth and all games and jokes vanished.

What was she thinking? For a heartbeat, he actually wished he was sober. What color would her aura be? A smoldering red, most likely, but how much of it anger and how much something else? Fun and flirtation this may be, but he'd struggle with his decency if *she* offered. Honor was for men in society who needed to follow society's rules. As someone spurned from a place in that society he saw no reason for the rules to apply. He'd happily bend on his own lenient morals if tempted.

Not that she was likely to ever want to lower herself to a flirtation—or more—with the likes of him, but the look in her eyes had very briefly suggested she wasn't entirely blind to his charms. Did the lady protest too much?

She took a step back. "Enough. I came to offer you a deal."

"What sort of deal?"

"You want the information in that letter, so do I. However." She bit her lip, eyes wavering in their ferocity for the first time since she walked in. "It's written in Faery."

Ah. So *that* is why she was here. He went back to the desk and refilled his cup with water—he wasn't trying to drink himself into a stupor, but she didn't need to know what he was drinking—and downed the whole thing. Her exasperated huff and eye roll were highly amusing.

It didn't bother him that she knew he was part fae. The fact wasn't exactly hidden now that his name was out there for the world to see. He'd lost his right to privacy the moment his name appeared as heir to his father's house. Of course she would have heard. Her mother and sisters probably talked about that 'fae bastard' over their tea and biscuits. He had no reason to care that the information might influence her opinion of him.

"May I see the letter?"

She hesitated. Then, with a scowl and a sharp flick of her wrist, she flashed the envelope from the previous night. So fiery. "That's all until we have some sort of deal. How do I know you won't read this and then leave me with nothing?"

"I may be of a lower class than you're used to, but I'm more sporting than that. Besides, I get no benefit from hiding the information. You may do with it what you please, as I intend to do. So long as Graves suffers," he added with a smile.

Something crossed her features that he couldn't read, but she nodded. "Then as a show of good will..." She released the folder.

He opened it and turned the paper over in his hands.

The information was imperative to his goals, but so now was the possibilities Miss Wilde presented. Graves was marrying her sister—a loathsome and horrific thought, the poor girl—and that meant Miranda Wilde could provide him the opportunity to get close to Graves.

Close enough to run him through or poison his drink or punch until the breathing stopped, Devin wasn't picky about the means. It was in his interest to keep his association with Miss Wilde, though not in his interest to add more friction to this already heated mix by attempting any actual seduction. If he planned to use her for her connections, he'd have to behave.

He could handle the temptation. He'd been tempted before and resisted. All that was required was a more diplomatic approach and he could start by securing her cooperation in deciphering her information. Unfortunately, it was in a language that neither of them could read. A fact he opted to withhold for the moment.

"I'll agree to translate this on one condition." He said, leaning back and crossing his arms. Miranda's nose flared, her jaw flexing with the effort of some sort of restraint. But she said nothing so he continued, "We're in this together."

"What?" That broke her fury, her jaw finally relaxed.

He shrugged. "You need me and I want some assurance we won't be in each other's way again. As we both want the same thing, I see no harm in an agreement to work together."

Her fingers curled into fists, eyes adopting a malicious glint that tempted him to push just a bit further.

"I'm waiting, princess."

A silence settled. Electric tension hummed in the space between them. Miranda was poised to attack, her fists seemed to tremble with restraint. Their gazes held, despite the very real danger a guardian's wrath presented to his person. A thrill chased through him, igniting his body in a way he hadn't felt in ages. *Gods, this was fun.*

"Fine." She spoke through her teeth, turning her body away from him. "I agree."

Disappointment was not the sane response to a narrow escape at bodily harm, but it flared through him none-the-less. She wore her emotions in plain sight. He could see her reluctance. Her petulance. The sneer and half-glances were hardly anything new. Devin had been on the receiving end of such venom his entire life. He was notorious, after all. And a half-breed.

The barest slip of something more wasn't exactly new, either. His history sparked derision, but his looks often inspired lust. Miranda's eyes had wandered to his lips twice now, though he couldn't be absolutely certain whether it was for a kiss or a target for her fist.

"Perfect, then let's start with one very important question. A show of trust, you could say." Her jaw clenched once again, he worried she'd break a tooth. "What do you want with Yarrow Graves?"

Miranda should not have needed to hesitate; it was a reasonable question. Yet, there was something irritating about Lord Drake that spoke to the fight instinct drilled into her all her life. She took a breath. This was about Cordelia. Without Drake's help, she had nothing to go on and her efforts would be lost. Her sister would be lost.

She turned to him again, resisting the urge to roll her eyes as he coyly watched her like he knew a secret she didn't. His body was perched on the edge of the desk, completely at ease and confident she would cave. A muscle near her eye twitched, but her resolve was strong.

"He's engaged to my sister."

He frowned. "So I've read. It's newsworthy, apparently," he said in a tone that suggested he disagreed with its news worth, "What I'm curious about is what that has to do with *you*, Miss Wilde. Why are you interested in potentially incriminating information that will disrupt your sister's happy nuptials?"

"I love her," she replied.

For the first time, his mask of charming, insufferable rake slipped from his features. He met her eyes with a true expression, something earnest and real that vanished just in time to save her from getting lost. His eyes were dangerous. She'd lose her head…or more, if she weren't careful.

"He's not ensnared your good opinion as he has the rest of this city?" he asked, though his voice was calm she sensed he was holding back. She understood this sort of forced calm. Graves had wronged him, too. She wasn't sure how the two were connected, maybe something with their shared fae ancestry, but the two were enemies now.

"My opinion of him couldn't be lower," she spat, and instantly regretted the slip. Her tone had been too scathing. She revealed far too much.

Miranda sealed the thoughts of that night away, like she did every time they threatened to spill into reality. She could forget for a little while longer. Graves would be removed and she'd never have to spare him or his evil another thought again.

"I see," Drake said. Of course he did. She was too transparent. Stupid. Stupid mistake. He stood and moved closer in the span of a heartbeat. She must have been rattled because she hadn't adjusted her stance or prepared a defensive strategy. All those drilled in instincts to fight and defend, gone the moment her walls had threatened to fall to a very handsome rogue.

He was now close enough for her to catch trace iridescence in his eyes, the shimmer that made them luminous. Close enough to feel body heat and inhale the scent of *him*, not just the spirits—though the exact nuances were undiscernible at present. The sudden rush against her senses overwhelmed. Her mind nearly blank in response.

"I will do what I can to help you stop this wedding," he said, voice deep and even. It resonated through her bones and she fought a shiver.

"All I ask is that if the chance arises, you allow me to deal with Graves however I see fit."

Miranda looked into his eyes, reading his intent clearly enough. Without a word she nodded.

"Very well." His entire demeanor shifted and he gave her a wicked smirk. "Then we'll get started. First, I'm sorry to say I can't read Faery, either."

"*What*?"

He had the damn gall to look like this was a mere detail. Miranda ground her teeth. He had made her agree, made her *promise* to work together, without revealing his ability to read Faery. He was counting on her honor as a guardian to keep her word at any cost. She was going to enjoy proving him wrong. Nothing was more important than her sister.

"Before you attack me." He peered at her, head tilted. "Which I assume is the direction your thoughts were going—"

"Something like that," she seethed.

"Well, before you decide on how best to kill me, please consider I have other abilities to offer."

She crossed her arms, scowling. "Such as?"

"Such as, love, I know where you *can* get these translated. *And* not draw too much attention to the fact. If word gets out that a guardian noble is trying to unearth Faery secrets, of a respected alderman no less, who knows what could happen."

He handed the paper back to her and she snatched it close to her chest, securing it quickly in a secret pocket of her bodice. His eyes dipped, following the motion, and lingered a few seconds longer than she liked. She drew a knife, the flash of steel drawing his eyes to the more lethal parts of her anatomy—her hands—before returning to her face.

"Where can we get this translated?"

His expression soured.

Her patience was wearing ever so thin.

"The Night Court," he supplied.

Miranda's heart skipped a beat. "The Night Court? An actual Faery Court? There's no other place outside—""

"Nowhere else that I know or where I have…connections," he said, but she could read the omission in his tone.

Once again, he was not telling her everything. She eyed him as he avoided her. He took a few steps away, which at least freed her senses enough to think.

This room would have belonged to the late Lord Warner, his father. Bookshelves. Portraits. Decanters above the fireplace. A regal desk. All of it passed along to the next Lord through the ages, all of it distinctly human. She saw no trace of Drake here, given what little she knew of him, and for some inexplicable reason the idea made her sad.

Drake kept his back to her as he neared the desk. She wished he wore a proper coat. The loose fit of his shirt was too intimate, a reminder of how improper this entire meeting was, though she had no plans to leave until she got what she wanted.

"What are you not telling me?" She asked, hiding her flustered senses as accusation.

Drake turned to her finally, smile dazzling and fake. "Let's not make this difficult. We're on the same side, ultimately, and our working together does not require me to divulge my life's story."

She shook her head. "How can I trust you if you're hiding something?"

He shrugged. "Have to make that call for yourself, love. But right now, I don't know of another option unless you plan to waltz into the Night Court and kindly ask, or, in your case I'd wager 'threaten kindly' is more apt, that someone translate this. Which, will prove difficult for you, guardian or no, the Night Fae are not the accepting sort."

Miranda scowled. He had a point. "Fine. We'll go to the Night Court."

"Excellent. I'll see you this evening."

"This evening?"

"Something more pressing? Have another nightly rendezvous with sinister characters? The ideal and only time to visit the Night Court is night."

Miranda rolled her eyes. She'd never let her hesitation show to him. Even if she were terrified, the last thing he needed was more ammo to goad her with.

He nodded. "You might want to dress the part, too."

"What do you mean?" She snapped, almost reaching for her knife again.

"Only that you'll want to look like a guardian if we do this, and be ready for things to go south. I may have connections but the Night Court can be hostile in the best of circumstances. Graves is popular over there. You can fight, I assume?"

"I can handle myself." She countered. "And what's the point of your coming with me if we may still end up in a fight? I thought you had a connection." Never mind that she'd been trained to fight since she could walk.

"It is not my aim to get into a brawl in the Night Court. However," he crossed his arms over his chest, taking his time with his words like he was unbothered by schedules and appointments. Miranda glanced at the clock. Her excuse for leaving had been open ended, but if she were gone much longer then it might draw notice. "'Be prepared for anything,' that's what I always say," his tone implied he had never used the phrase before this moment.

Exasperated, Miranda crossed her arms. "Do you treat everything like it's just a game?"

"Of course not," he snapped with mock indignation, then his blue eyes darkened with suggestion and his voice dropped low enough to resonate low in her stomach, "There is plenty that I give my undivided and most sincere attention." He leaned that much closer, sinful promise corrupted his smile and made her body hum as he added, "Would you care for a demonstration?"

His spell held for a fraction of a second. For that moment, not a single violent impulse crossed the sudden jumble of her thoughts. She didn't move and, clearly, he had expected her immediate retreat because his smile dropped and suggestion turned to alarm as he held her gaze for one breath of genuine connection. And that was much worse than scandalous suggestion. Miranda forced the moment to end, refusing to connect to this man on any level other than to cause him physical harm.

"Lord Drake, you have...another, visitor." Haversham waited at the doorway. Drake swallowed as he took a step away from her, quickly, like *he* was the one retreating. It was Miranda's turn to smirk.

"How fortunate," Miranda said, meeting Haversham at the door, "I was just on my way out."

She stormed away, not waiting to be shown. As she barreled toward the front door, she passed a tall man with dark skin, cooled to an almost mauve color. Calm, soft brown eyes followed her for a moment. He wore gentleman's attire, but his pants were tucked into well-worn leather boots and stray threads escaped his coat. The directness of his stare gave her pause and he greeted her with a polite nod, though the rest of his body stayed inhumanly still. An immortal.

Miranda returned the greeting with a quick curtsy before thundering out the door. Her annoyance was too consuming for distraction. Once outside, however, she felt she could breathe again and took a moment to take in the cool air.

Another sleepless night awaited her. She'd have to find a way to sneak in a nap. She may have to skip supper in favor of sleep, but hopefully soon this would all be behind her.

Although...

Miranda frowned as she walked home. It wasn't far, actually, his home from hers. The great spire rose up to the south, a high, midday sun sitting almost on top, like a beacon. It had always put her at ease, the sight of it. She had been taught that Unity was formed when they erected the spire, that it was the first step toward peace. The lines between the races would finally end.

However, as she traversed glittering, grime free cobblestones and concrete, with clear pools gathering in the gutters, and newly updated gas street lights she couldn't help but notice the divide not only lingered, but was much larger than she'd previously assumed. The Fells were almost bleak in contrast. It reminded her that the world she'd grown up in was a façade. The illusion of an island from a varied and multifaceted world.

Miranda wasn't sure she wanted this mission to end. Yes, she wanted her sister safe and that monster removed from their lives forever, but what she didn't want was for this feeling to end. The scary, excited sort of feeling that comes with doing new and dangerous things. A sense of purpose and having to put her skills to a practical use.

Yet, she dreaded the future that awaited her otherwise. One day, her training as a guardian would stop and Miranda would continue on with her life. She would become a prim and proper wife. Become a mother. Manage a household. All her years of training sitting stagnant with no threats to combat. It was a time of peace, so what use was there for soldiers? That is the trajectory her life was expected to take. She would be just like her mother. A rusting tool left on a shelf while her skills at hosting tea and entertaining were expected to fulfill her until she could devote herself to motherhood.

But this feeling...this side of her, the side that had trained with swords and knives, was the part that screamed to be set free. It was that same part of her that took a perverse satisfaction from arguing with Devin Drake.

Yes, he was an instigator and a rogue, not the sort she should trust or have any prolonged partnership with, but the adventurer inside called for the challenge he presented. The conflict and mental sparring. It was invigorating, if annoying.

Logic and duty demanded Miranda ignore the small voice, that tiny part of her that wanted to argue with Drake again. Just for the rush of it.

The scent of Miranda Wilde lingered as she turned and stormed from his study. She must have washed recently as her soap was overpowering, even with his senses muddled he could pick up feminine notes of lilacs. It had been...a very long time since anything floral had lingered on him, near him, overpowering the musky office. A year of obsession had left very little room for distracting company.

He stood where she turned on her heel, not moving. Just breathing. And regretting every minute he did so.

She made it so easy to coax her ire that he wanted to do it all the more. He could never resist making a beautiful woman glare. However, he had not intended for her to look at him with such sincere longing that he was tempted to *actually* kiss her thus failing at resisting her temptation before they'd even begun.

Because a dalliance with Miranda Wilde would be doomed from the start. She did not belong in his world and he'd never be allowed in hers. There was also the glaring fact that she was, in all probability, an innocent and Devin was not the sort to deflower virgins when he never intended to linger till morning.

"Who is it, now?" Devin asked, finally scrubbing his face of the mess her candid green eyes had left him in. Haversham balked at Miranda flying past him and showing herself the door, completely unaware of anything beyond the breech of protocol.

The aging butler scoffed for a moment before clearing his throat and announcing, Jack Hale, Devin's club manager.

A business meeting he could handle. He instructed Haversham to show Jack inside.

Jack Hale was an immortal, their preferred name as opposed to the baser moniker 'vampire.' Society largely ignored their sect of the world, as their population was sparse at best, and there was a certain stigma attached to the race. The speculation around the Dark Vow required to start the change was damning on its own, but they would forevermore consume blood to maintain the gained invulnerability, strength, and immortality. In the early times, this meant that the other races were a food source. Now, immortals were quite neatly sustained through familiars and thralls. Suppliers were paid generous sums for small blood donations and laws were in place to keep them from feasting on mortals at their leisure.

Devin didn't care what drove a man to such ends and Jack certainly never shared, but the man was dependable and honest. Plus, good with numbers and accounts. That's all that mattered to Devin. Jack's past was his own business.

Jack entered the study, steps silent despite his wearing boots on a wood floor. He was a hair taller than Devin—a fact he regularly asserted—but similar in frame, yet gruffer in his manner and state of dress. Devin may shirk a button or two and some layers, but Jack's clothes were ill-fitting and disheveled.

"Another visit from Lady Miranda?" Jack asked, eyebrow arched.

"Lady?" Devin clarified, he'd been calling her 'Miss Wilde' since meeting her.

"It's *Lady* Miranda, but *Miss* Wilde since she's the daughter of a noble."

"How the bloody hell do *you* know the difference?" Devin hadn't questioned Jack's past, but being part of the gentry was too ridiculous to consider.

Jack wouldn't meet his eyes and Devin guessed the answer would remain a mystery for now. "What was she doing here, Drake?"

Devin laughed. "What can I say, I'm too tempting for even a well-bred lady to stay away long."

Jack's expression was unchanged, thoughtful and a bit sad. The man always carried a cloud of doom over his features. "That's doubtful. She was pissed as she ran out the door. Seems your effect is pissing off pretty women, rather than wooing them."

"Did you have a reason to be here?" Devin asked, as he took the seat behind the desk. He let his posture slump and leaned as far back as the chair would allow.

Jack's posture was worse than Devin's, a slight hunch to his frame as he attempted to make himself smaller than he really was. Devin was familiar enough to recognize self-loathing when he saw it. "Yeah, but if I've got to worry about an uppity lady making trouble for us I'd like to know about it now. Upper class ain't your usual type, Devin. They come with a whole mess of baggage. Rules. Laws. Her father would flay you alive just for looking at her."

"Obviously, I'm aware of the danger she presents. But there are...extenuating circumstances."

"Like hell. You want to get in her skirts. Or are you telling me *you* didn't notice that she was pretty?"

A surge of anger rose up his throat as Jack's rough voice called Miranda 'pretty.' He bit back a retort. Jack knew of his need for revenge, even of the bid war with Thaddeus Wraith, but Devin wasn't sure if he should disclose his...arrangement with Miss Wilde. He mused for too long and Jack's patience wore out.

"I don't give a shit about your personal life, Drake. I only care how it effects the club," Jack grumbled, though his actions said otherwise. He liked to complain and moan, but he never hesitated to help when needed. He'd picked Devin out of a few gutters, paid off debts, kept a store of liquor so Devin could drown his aura sight. The rough exterior was mostly show. "So tell me or don't, but if this effects business I'm done. I mean it this time. If your skirt chasing up the ranks brings hell down on the Black Heart then it'll be your mess to clean."

"Are you sure you've never considered a career in the theater? You excel at drama."

Jack never smiled and even now his frown only deepened.

"Fine, if I tell you, I need you to promise not to overreact."

Jack hung his head, hand over his face. "What the fuck did you do?" He fell onto the couch, sitting with his head in his hands. "Gods above, Drake, is it never going to be enough with you? I can't keep shoveling money into your self-sabotaging habits or paying off—"

"It concerns Graves," Devin interrupted.

"Fuck me." Jack laid back, stretching his legs over the arm of the couch. He stared at the ceiling with resigned frustration. He knew enough about Drake's past with Graves that he wouldn't stop him. On the list of things Devin hated, his father ranked third. First place went to Yarrow Graves, the man responsible for the death of his entire unit during the Demon War. Second, was himself, though he did not acknowledge this fact consciously.

"Miss Wilde and I have an arrangement to end Graves." He ignored Jack's groan. "We're heading to the Night Court tonight."

Devin was not keen to go to the Night Court. He had been there a few times when his mother was still alive, but if the rest of the world was slow to accept half-breeds the Night Court was archaic. Their welcome had been less than warm. As far as Devin cared, he didn't belong any more with fae than with the human elite.

"In fact," Devin picked up a pen and found a blank scrap of paper to write a note. "I need you to post something for me on your way out."

Jack sighed for half a minute.

The note was barely legible, but Kylin should be able to read it. Devin couldn't just waltz up to his cousin without some sort of warning. Devin sealed the note and held it out. Jack huffed as he stood to retrieve it.

"This ain't healthy, you know," Jack said as he snatched the paper and stuffed it in his pocket. "You can't bring back the dead with revenge. Past is past, nothing we can do. It's our job to suffer with it until we die."

"Because that sounds healthier," Devin responded drolly.

"Just count yourself lucky you can," Jack droned, his tone bleak. He stomped off, having neglected to talk about whatever he intended to discuss. He'd rant about it later, but for now, Devin wanted to be left in peace.

Devin had gotten very good at brooding alone. He had little to care for, aside from his club, in which he did take a certain amount of pride, but which did not fill any of the holes blown through his chest at the loss and neglect and abuse.

Oh well. Once Graves was properly rotting in the dirt, then maybe Devin would find some peace. And if not, then he'd be able to put all his energy into hating himself.

His eyes drifted closed.

And he saw her. At first it was fleeting. Just a passing thought of Miranda in her disguise, her olive skin barely covered by that red dress that flaunted all the right curves, leaving just enough to imagination. And he'd never been said to lack imagination. Decorum and respect, yes but his imagination was well up to the task of completing a flattering image of Miranda. Devin gladly embraced his dream, much more favorable than his nightmares, and allowed himself indulgences he wouldn't take while awake.

CHAPTER FOUR

D EVIN DEBATED WHETHER HE should attempt this mission
sober. He may need his wits about him and, though he was
loath to admit it, might need the help of his aura sight. He had not
been to the Night Court since he was a child, hand in hand with his
mother, cowering to sneers and whispers. Auras lashing out at the
sight of him with inky blots of disdain or disgusted muddy green, or
sharp, white hot arcs of contempt. His own family had refused to see
them, despite his mother's pleas. Her pulses of mauve shame and pale
yellow fear had made him feel helpless, scared when he should have felt
welcome.

He was not entirely sure how they would receive him now that
he was grown. Kylin, his cousin, was the only person to reach out
when Devin's mother passed. Not even her own sister had bothered
to check in. Kylin had held an ulterior motive, of course, hoping to
secure business for his trade when Devin's club had been starting out,
but he had not been openly dismissive or cruel. His condolences had
sounded genuine, at least. Their relationship was best described as
acquaintances who tolerated each other peacefully.

Devin took a drink.

Fuck it.

It would be hard enough ignoring the glances and whispers when he returned to the Night Court, he wasn't keen to brush the colors of their disdain across his eyes as well. Maybe the sight would be manageable if he had ever bothered to put in the effort of practice, but as it stood, auras were more of an onslaught than an advantage.

He dressed simply, black shirt and vest. Human fashion called for cumbersome coats and cravats, but he wanted freedom of movement. Three concealed knives, in case he was searched or lost one in a fight.

Outside was a cool night. Windy, but in a refreshing way. He was about to sigh and huff about how of course a 'Lady' would be running late. *What did a noble daughter care for times and schedules? Just leave him out in the—*

A lithe figure appeared beside him, nearly scaring the life from him. Her steps had been nonexistent, her presence like a shadow. She stood before him decked in black with curves cut perfectly against the brilliant moonlight.

Miranda.

This must have been her guardian uniform. Black from head to foot and no skirts, just blessedly form-fitting leather.

It was still the fashion for women to wear big, wide skirts and hide their figures save a few tantalizing peeks to better encourage trapping husbands. Even the women Watchmen, who wore identical uniforms to the men, were layered with branded coats and duty gear. Women in the Fells still wore dresses, though not as voluminous as the ones he saw in the Garrison. He'd never actually seen a guardian in uniform until this moment. Nothing about the shape of her thighs or curve of her hips was left to baser imagination. She would be a distraction.

Her golden curls were swept up in a bun at the base of her neck, loose strands catching in the breeze. She wore boots that hugged her calves and were practical with thick, flat soles. And that smirk on her face was almost sobering.

"Eyes up here, sailor," she scolded, albeit with a touch of humor. He was tempted to retort with something witty, but he kept his mouth shut. A witty response would delve much too close to bantering. Which bordered on flirtation. Flirtation was more fun when it was ill-received. And infinitely safer. His little overstep earlier proved that she was not as immune to flirting as she wanted to believe. He would need to behave tonight.

"Let's go," he said, turning away from her, so he didn't risk seeing every sway of her hips or the perfect shape of her thighs silhouetted against the lamplight. He had called a carriage for them, one of his plain coaches from the club. They wouldn't be able to enter the Night Court with it, but it would get them close enough.

The carriage sway was gentle and hypnotizing, the driver easily steering the horses through mostly empty streets. Devin knew why he was on edge, but Miranda sat just as rigid. Like she had a sword for a spine, though he noticed no weapons.

"Did you bring any sort of defense with you?" He ventured, as a weighty silence had descended between them. It would have been smarter to remain silent. Silence was better than the alternative, where her gaze burned and her tongue lashed and he felt alive for a few moments. But smart had never stopped him from keeping his mouth shut.

Her head turned slowly, eyes direct with confidence. There was a rigidity to her movements and a serene, controlled sort of power. Perhaps he'd been mistaken to think her stiffness meant nerves. She looked calm enough to cut the heart from his chest in front of his weeping family.

"I didn't think I'd be allowed a full sword. But I brought some security. Just in case."

Where? The fit of her uniform left little room for much else. He didn't see how she'd conceal a nail file, let alone a weapon of any consequence. The little devil of a voice in him suggested he search her and find out. He shifted, trying to be a gentlemen—for the moment.

"You suggested this might be dangerous," she continued, "So I came prepared." Her head tilted as she took in his appearance. "Are you concealing anything?"

"Care to check for yourself?" He quipped, unable to keep the suggestion from his voice or the glint from his eyes. Damn, he had slipped much too easily.

She was unamused, but not angry. Her lips were a patronizing smirk as she gazed out the window. "Keep dreaming."

"Oh, I have, Miss Wilde, and I'm woefully sorry that I hadn't yet seen this ensemble," he gestured with his chin. "Much less left to the imagination, though I think I filled in the details adequately enough for my purposes." His voice lowered with his intent and he was well rewarded when her smile vanished and steam practically puffed from her nose.

"Is it that you're unable to have a normal, decent conversation or do you choose to be an asshole?"

Devin shrugged. "Perhaps it's just you that brings out the worst in me, Miss Wilde."

She pointedly gazed out the window, arms crossed and her lips a harsh line. "I hope you'll at least be serious when we get there. If we fail because you think it's a joke, I'll kill you myself."

"Relax, princess, I've no intention of sabotaging our chances. I want this just as badly as you, remember?" He cleared his throat, hoping she didn't press him for his reasons.

"Will you stop calling me 'princess?' It's condescending and completely inaccurate. I'm hardly a princess."

"Hit a sore spot, have I?" He watched her huff and fidget, her eyes shifting to the other window, though they speared him quickly as they passed.

"It's...been a nickname that certain papers and gossip columns have used in the past. But it's not me. They call me princess because I'm pretty and my father is important. No one gives a damn about what I do or who I am. They'd call Cordelia that, too, but she's not a guardian so she gets a pass from the spotlight. And...recently the title has come off as more of a joke than anything."

"Why's that?"

She looked down. "I'd think it's obvious."

Devin floundered to catch her meaning. "I'm afraid not, love."

"My age? I'm nearly twenty-seven and yet," she gestured to herself, "Still no spouse. That's common knowledge. I'm nearing the prover-bial shelf; cause status and beauty weren't enough to compensate for my...flaws."

There was a crack in her confidence, a small fissure as she spoke about society's opinion of her. Devin wouldn't pretend to know how her world worked, the nuances clearly outside his understanding if a woman like Miranda could possess any flaw enough to make her un-appealing to marry. Provided the person was equally inclined toward matrimony, that is. Devin didn't count because while he had no wish to marry her either, it was not because of *her* 'flaws.' The vastness of their differences expanded in that moment.

"Sorry, love, I didn't know," he offered with sincerity.

"Please. Like I believe that you're sorry you hurt my feel-ings—which you didn't, by the way, it's just annoying." She refused to look at him, head cast at a strong angle to force her gaze out the window.

"Believe me or don't. I may not always play by a gentleman's rules, but I don't aim to be needlessly mean. I won't call you princess."

"Do what you want," she snapped.

He'd clearly poked too hard and now she hadn't just hidden behind her walls but locked all the doors and barred the windows.

It took another half hour before they reached the part of the city designated for the fae Courts. There was a shift in the energy of the air as they neared. Before the rename to Unity, the city had been divided purposefully and with clear, solid borders. A large stream curved its way through the streets, dividing the Courts from Unity so that only narrow footpath bridges could be used to reach them. No carriages crossed into fae territory. They disembarked and Devin ordered the carriage to meet them at the Night Bridge.

"If we're going to the Night Court, why'd we stop at the Summer Bridge?" Miranda asked.

Devin already felt heavier and they hadn't even crossed the stream yet. "It's better not to approach the Night Court from the human side. We'll be better received if we cut through Summer and Day."

He worked the tension from his shoulder, muscles clenching to keep him from entering. Pressing onward, he shuffled over the narrow, moss-covered bridge. The water below was crystal clear, winding down and out the southern border of Unity. Its source was in the Fey Wilds and defied natural law in flowing up higher ground, instead of down. There was some sort of magical fae nonsense that played with the current, but he couldn't remember what. At the end of the bridge waited the lush, verdant Summer Court. Devin stopped to check on Miranda, but she was crouched on her knees, petting the bridge.

"We don't have all night," he said and he attempted to keep the unease from his tone.

She pulled her fingers away from the plush moss and let her hands waft through fern fronds. A genuine smile warmed her face, alighting her eyes as much as the hues of the landscape. Still not enough to charm him to the fae side of the stream. Devin turned rigidly and continued moving while she caught up.

Fae embraced nature with their architecture, finding a balance between function and preservation. The trees were grown to be practical parts of the city, housing lights and glowing rocks. The pathways were carefully sculpted amongst rich grass dotted with flowers. Various springs and brooks trickled meandering courses through the unpaved paths, their direction not tamed or controlled. Heat radiated from sources he couldn't name, raising the temperature a good twenty degrees from the rest of the city.

A part of Devin was at home here, though he hated the fact. Hated that he felt calm around the natural beauty. That the twist of the water was soothing. Even being out at night felt invigorating, his body naturally attuned to the rise of the moon.

Magic was not something one wielded or controlled, not even the fae. It only existed in natural forms throughout the Realm. The fae were the chosen protectors of nature and so were more attuned to its magic than other races. That was the source of their gifts, of his aura sight. That was how they heated this court to unnatural temperatures and changed the flow of rivers. Or, that is how his mother had explained it. The specific names of the various stones and plants and elements and their multitude of uses he'd long forgotten.

"Wow, it's beautiful here," Miranda chimed quietly, taking in every detail.

"Yes, lovely," he mocked, not wanting to admit that he agreed with her. Though, a small voice in his head was extremely satisfied that she would find this place beautiful. Maybe she wouldn't reject his ancestry. Maybe she'd accept the fae part of him. He may not accept himself, but there was still a yearning in his chest for acceptance. Since he was a boy he'd subconsciously sought a place or people to call home. His mother had done her best, but the cold treatment from his father plus a young half-breed son and no home to return to had left her broken and depressed. And yes, he had friends who were polite about the subject, but that wasn't the same thing. If Miranda thought this place was beautiful then maybe…

Devin squashed that voice down hard. That was the fanciful fool talking. He couldn't trust a fanciful fool. Hoping that Miranda might accept him? That was the path to heartbreak. She was a noble's daughter and a guardian, even if she were polite or kind about his ancestry she'd never accept him for it. Not in any way that mattered to him. So there was no point in seeking it out or pondering what-ifs.

"Do all the courts look the same?" Miranda asked, breathless.

Had she truly never ventured past her garden gates? What sort of city promoted harmony and unity but then its social elite failed to venture from the familiar? He shouldn't be surprised she'd never been to a fae court. He was wise not to trust the fanciful fool. She had obviously been raised with the same prejudices that all guardians held for races they had once deemed dangerous.

"No, each court reflects the fae it represents. This is the Summer Court, which tends to be hotter and full of plants." He trudged on, wishing she wouldn't ask him about this. His stupid heart might mistake her curiosity for genuine interest or worse.

Miranda nodded, "Summer's attunements are flora, fauna, and earth, while the Night Court's are moon, water, and spirit."

"They teach you that at etiquette lessons? So you don't offend a Faery when dining together?"

Miranda's shrewd eyes landed on him. "We do learn about each of the races, yes, but I didn't do it for etiquette lessons. I've always loved learning about Faery lore and history. It's fascinating."

"Fascinating. I see. Like an animal that you can study?" His tone was unreasonably harsh. He knew it, but couldn't seem to stop it.

He wished they could just walk in silence. Coming here was painful enough without some guardian noble dangling hope in front of him.

"Okay," she stopped dead, forcing him to acknowledge or leave her behind. Which was tempting. "What is your problem? You've been an ass ever since we entered this part of the city. Why? Do you hate Faery or something?"

He smiled, not sure if she could detect his pain or not. "You could say that."

Her head cocked, confusion flitting across her face. "Wait a second, I thought you were part Faery? That's why I came to you in the first place," she said, brow wrinkled adorably. It was charming how she couldn't comprehend how those two truths could coincide. He hated Faery. He was fae. Really quite simple. He hated himself.

"Don't hurt yourself, love. It's not important. Shall we continue before dawn breaks and our chance to get into the court is lost for another day?"

Her frown didn't disappear but she followed without another word. Strange that he didn't feel better now that she'd stopped talking. He certainly did not want her to be curious about him, yet disappointment had settled in place of pain. And, if he wasn't careful, both would lead to heartbreak.

Miranda struggled to take in every detail. Beauty like this didn't exist in the Garrison. Even the finely sculpted halls or the masonry of the Spire didn't compare to a Faery Court. The Summer Court was woodsy and elegant, lush and warm. Delicate in appearance, yet it had to be strong to support the infrastructure of a city. It was still at the moment, save a few nocturnal creatures or the rustling of leaves.

"Did you grow up in this?" She asked, savoring the scents and otherworldly feel of such heat during a moderate spring. She wanted to name the floral and earthy notes in the air, but each plant was more foreign to her than the next. No azaleas or rhododendron in sight.

Devin's back stiffened, his pace slowing, though he didn't turn from his course. "No. This is the Summer Court, remember?"

"I meant in a court, not this one," she was too engrossed to comment on his tone.

"I wasn't welcome," Drake said, and he picked up his pace toward the edge of the greenery.

Ahead, two enormous, thick trees created an archway, their canopy's interconnected. On the other side was a different world. Miranda craned her head as they passed through the arch and into the Day Court.

A drastically different biome. Jagged rocks jutted up to form walls and sand-smoothed, rounded rocks formed homes, each layered in burnt shades of red, white, orange, and brown. Sand shifted underfoot and among the muted, desert tones were pops of brilliantly colored succulents. Giant variations with plump, rounded leaves or oily jagged curves or velvety elongated fronds. They walked on stone paths lit by molten rock, oozing a red-tinted glow.

Though the landscape here was harsher, dryer, there was an eerie stillness to the quiet. The court was completely, entirely empty. Summer had nocturnal animals and calm, but active weather. The Garrison, though it kept daylight hours, still had the odd patrolling Watchmen or cluster of moths over a street lamp.

Day was devoid of life. No moths. No crawling things or furry rodents. That one detail made the scene otherworldly, more than the heat or the sand. The sky wasn't as shrouded as in Summer and she could see the expanse of the night sky. During daylight, the sun would be merciless.

"Where is everything?"

She could hear Drake's sigh even with his five-foot lead on her. "Where is the Miranda who despised conversing with me? She didn't feel the need to ask every question that came to mind."

Miranda tore her eyes from the beauty around them, her temper flared, but she reigned it back. Mostly because it felt wrong to shout in such an eerily still place. "It was just a question."

Drake rounded on her, forcing her to stop or crash into him. His eyes were drawn, haunted, and there was no smile or glint of mischief. "And I don't know the answers. In case you missed it, I'm not exactly thrilled to be here. These courts are nothing but isolating cages to keep fae in and everyone else out. Why do you think they don't allow carriages or streets in here? Because the fae don't want outsiders poking around."

"But you're not an outsider."

His hand rested on his hip, the other scraping over his face. "I am not fully fae, Miss Wilde."

"But that doesn't matter anymore, the world—"

"It matters where we're going. In the Night Court, blood matters. The court that my genetics are attuned to doesn't want me and I can hardly go waltzing around in the Day Court with the amount of sun and glorification of daylight everywhere." He took a deep breath and it was the first time she had ever heard his tone neutral. The affect was unsettling. "If we can please get through this with expediency and less questions, I would be grateful."

"Fine, okay."

He turned to keep walking, but Miranda had a sour taste in her mouth. It wasn't long before they reached a break in the rocks that functioned as a doorway to Night Court.

Drake had stopped, eyes averted and tension coiling in his posture. He'd been on edge since they started, but now he seemed to be using great effort to hold himself together. What had happened to make him so uncomfortable in his own court? What made him hate himself?

She couldn't fathom how someone could hate who they were, especially when it was outside their control. He didn't choose to be fae any more than she chose to be a guardian. She didn't want to humanize the rogue, but the idea itched at her, nestled into her head and bothered her on his behalf. Still, she couldn't address it if he didn't wish to share. If he wanted to keep himself shrouded in mystery, she needed to let him.

"It's just up here," he said toeing at the sand. He crossed his arms, face set in a controlled mask of indifference. "Be on your guard. Night will be quite busy and we don't want to draw too much attention. Although..." His eyes raked up and down her body, though he lacked the drawl of innuendo his voice usually carried when remarking on her appearance. "It will be hard to hide." Once again, he made it all too easy to dislike him.

Miranda almost threw her hands over her chest, but she refused to rise to his baiting. Instead, she lifted her chin and met his roving eyes with a hard stare.

His responding smile was pained. "I was referencing your obviously guardian uniform."

"I'm sure you were," she challenged.

There was no normal spark of mischief in his gaze or feeling in his tone. "We should get this over with."

He turned away from her and she was surprised to find she was disappointed that he hadn't tried to flirt or shock her into anger. She'd volleyed and he let the serve sink into the sand. He continued without another word and Miranda was grateful that he couldn't see the pout on her lips as she followed him into Night.

Shadow lay heavy over the buildings and pathways. Smooth trees were integral to the structure of the buildings with black bark and gnarled, twisting, leafless branches. Mist lingered low in the streets, gathering in corners and deep places. The temperature dropped as they crossed and there were Faery everywhere.

Miranda raised her chin and walked with purpose. It wasn't likely they'd be attacked unprovoked, but her guard was still up.

There was something about the way eyes followed them. About the whispers that trailed behind. Drake's shoulders had tensed ever since they crossed courts. Were the stares and whispers directed at *him*, rather than her in her obvious uniform?

They waited for a group of fae to cross the footpath when one of the members locked eyes on Drake.

The fae wrinkled his nose like he had smelled something foul. "I told you this court is going to shit if the likes of him feels they can cross into our territory freely."

Drake kept his head down, remaining silent and still as he waited for them to move on. Miranda's mouth hung open, too stunned to react before the group had mumbled their insults and continued on their way.

"Hold on a damn second." Miranda pushed ahead of Drake, glaring at the rude fae retreating down the path. "What the hell was his problem? We didn't do anything to deserve that, I'm about to—"

She stopped when she saw Drake's face. He was a different person, looking even more ravaged than he looked back in the Day Court. Lips a tight line instead of a mischievous smile, his blue eyes drawn and empty instead of alight and seductive. "Leave it, Miss Wilde. You'll only invite trouble."

"But..." she huffed, not accustomed to someone being blatantly rude. In her world, you could be rude behind someone's back or when whispering with your friends, but never to their face. No matter how much they hated you, they would still smile and tip their hats. Her fists kept curling and uncurling. She was itching to chase that guy down and see how much he sneered with his face in a puddle.

"Their disdain was not directed at you," he snapped, "Your pride can remain intact and mine is not worth the riot you would undoubtedly incite if you retaliated. I assure you, love, I'm quite used to their derision."

Her heart broke a little. Not because she cared about *him*, so much as it was heartbreaking that *anyone* would think so little of themselves. He shook his head, tearing his eyes away from her.

"No need for pity, I assure you my confidence is no less humble than it was before." He smiled, attempting to placate her, she suspected, but it didn't reach his eyes and his jest had lacked the wit and charisma his quips usually possessed.

"Just stay close, we haven't much farther to go before we can be rid of this place." Drake started walking, slowing to make sure she followed. "Just up here is where we can find my contact. He's...an old friend of my mother's. He should be able to help us, though whether he wants to or not is another story. Just let me do the talking, if you please."

Miranda nodded silently, perfectly content to do just that. She could concede that she was out of her depth here. She fell into step behind him, eyes downcast.

Drake led her through smooth, onyx halls their surfaces shiny and glinting, until they reached a small courtyard. A gathering place filled with Faery. The air was sharper here, almost biting, and overpowered by a sickly floral scent. Miranda stayed behind Drake as he approached a fae leaning in wait against a column.

"Kylin," Drake's voice was quiet, he gave a tall, willowy man a nod, "It's been awhile."

Kylin's skin was cool ocher and offset the stark white of his eyes. A trail of tattoos glowed when they caught the moonlight in intricate patterns Miranda didn't recognize. Miranda glanced at Drake and noted his ears were short enough to be covered by his hair. She wondered if he styled it to hide the shape of them.

"Devin Drake. It *has* been a long time," Kylin's voice was smooth as silk, but somehow deadly. Miranda recalled from her classes on the races of Unity that Faery were all granted a gift associated with their court. Night Court Fae might breathe underwater, see auras, or grow stronger with the moon. Did Drake have a power? She wasn't sure how it worked with half-humans.

"This must be important if you're finally willing to work together."

Drake nodded as he replied, "Business has been doing well enough. And since you've been asking to expand your own trade, I'm finally able to partner with you as a supplier, *if* you can translate something for me."

Kylin narrowed his white eyes. "You are offering me an ongoing trade partnership, for a translation?"

Drake's posture was stiff, his distaste practically emanating from him. Miranda hadn't known he planned to offer something he didn't want to give. She would have felt guilty except that she had been the one to pay full price for the information in his hand.

"That's true, but this...it concerns Graves."

Kylin paused, glancing around. "Come with me." He led them into a private parlor, so the three of them were alone. Then his eyes finally found Miranda. "Why is she still here?"

"We're...business partners, for the time being. Miss Wilde and I have an understanding."

Kylin looked uneasy again, glancing around as if searching for enemies. "You know his influence here. You can't go throwing that name around and expect to get away without his knowing. He's the head of the Night Court, for solstice sake." Kylin swallowed, "I'm no supporter. He does what he likes and takes no heed of who he squashes. While quite a few of us are unhappy with his methods, he has enough of a following that no one dares cross him."

"This should prove promising in that endeavor," Drake held out the folder. "If you can translate it."

Kylin sighed, but took it and read it first, silently. His face was ashen when he looked back up. "I'm not sure how this will help you, but I'm sure it will get you killed if you're not careful. You, too, guardian."

"I don't care. I plan on saving my sister, whatever the cost," Miranda snapped.

"Sister?" Kylin asked, arching a thin eyebrow.

"Yes, Cordelia Wilde," Drake supplied, "I'm sure you've heard of her by now."

The name registered instantly in Kylin's face, how could it not? Graves was very publicly betrothed to Cordelia. Everyone knew.

"I see. Congratulations, I suppose," he offered, though the haughty tenor of his voice suggested he cared very little about the subject one way or the other.

Miranda narrowed her eyes. "You can take your congratulations and shove--"

"Can you translate this for us or not?" Devin cut her off, stepping between her and Kylin. He threw her a glare over his shoulder, and she hated being chastised by him.

Maybe she wasn't cut out for this sort of mission. Letting people talk to her however they wished was outside her capabilities. Her own mother hadn't succeeded in tempering her anger in twenty-six years.

Kylin watched the exchange with indifference, before saying, "It reads like an experiment. This is a list of items, equipment, tools, that sort of thing, but here," he pointed at the page, "It says: *final testing has proved successful. Subjects 1-15 did not survive the process, however, subjects 16-32 show promising recovery. We have identified the problem as a conflict with the fae's metabolism and the fae that survived have all shown favorable results in further tests, provided they survive injection. We can proceed with production on schedule."* Kylin stopped and handed back the paper like it was cursed. "It's signed. That's his mark on the bottom. And, if I'm not mistaken, this address is one of his buildings."

Miranda snatched it before Drake and set it in her pocket. "We have him, then," she said, heart racing. She was expecting the note to be bad, but not the casual account of killing fifteen fae for an experiment. Though she did not wish to delay her mission a moment longer, her conscience was tugging at the back of her thoughts.

"I imagine most of the subjects were willing volunteers. He's good at getting people to do what he wants, however dangerous. And, of course, we don't tolerate Watchmen in our territory, so there has been no outside investigation into these victims," Kylin said, clearly disturbed. "The Night Court tolerates Unity, as a kindness to the other courts, but Graves has been promoting a secret campaign about the fall of Unity. How the Night Fae will triumph as the true power of the city." His lips curled with distaste. "But killing his own kind to get there? He'd lose most of his support if this got out, not to mention the Watchmen would have to act, whether we like it or not."

"And if we expose this there's no way he'll marry my sister." Miranda grinned. "But how do we do that?"

"I don't know, but you better do it carefully and strategically. Don't let anyone know you have this and don't sell it to some paper or newssheet. You must outsmart him or he'll only find a way to cover his tracks. He is no fool."

"We'll be careful, thank you, Kylin," Drake said.

Kylin looked down his long nose at Drake, his smile strained. "Yes, well. You can make it up to me after you paid for your first shipment. Good night."

With that he left, slipping back out into the bustling streets.

Miranda worked her lip in her teeth while she considered what this meant. Her plan had been to figure out what she had and then turn it in to the Watchmen, but now they would need more. They had to make sure Graves never got the chance to cover his tracks. Then there was the experimentation itself. What was the purpose?

"Miss Wilde?" Devin's voice returned her to the room, he was already hovering by the exit, pacing. "We got what we came for, I'd like to see the back of this place."

Miranda rooted her stance. "We can't turn this in to the Watchmen. Not yet."

Baring his teeth, Devin returned to her side so they could keep their volume low. "Oh, and why's that?" Drake's tone was still clipped, still on edge. "It's not wise to linger here, even in this meager bit of privacy." He glanced at the walls like they were full of eyes waiting to turn them in to Graves.

"We have to find out what it's for," Miranda said, slow and calm. She was resigned to the idea, but she didn't like it. She had proof that Graves was connected to several murders, which was more than enough to serve her purpose. But...there was a greater evil at work. If she exposed the nature of the experiments, before Graves could have it hidden or destroyed—and he would as soon as the news was leaked—then they risked some other lunatic picking up where Graves had left off.

"Pardon?" he snapped, rubbing at his temple.

"The experiments. We have to figure out what they're trying to do first."

Drake laughed without humor. "I thought you wanted to end your sister's engagement then get back to life as normal."

"I do. I don't want to investigate this psychopath, but I don't believe we have a choice."

"We?" He shook his head. "No, *we've* gotten the translation. Now, *I* can use it for revenge. Your contributions are no longer required."

She crossed her arms, jaw tensing. "Then someone else continues his experiment and more people die."

"Listen, sweetheart, you may be cursed with a bloody conscience, but I hold no such qualms about letting nature take its course. I am here for one reason." He stared at her, resolute. Except, she wouldn't accept that he would let such atrocities slide.

"You can still do what you like with...*him*," she said, casting her eyes around to make sure they weren't being overheard, "All I'm suggesting is that we get at least some tangible information on his plan before we move forward. This could affect the entire city, you included. Your club, included."

She tried to appeal to his selfish nature, hoping that she could get him to agree. They could go their separate ways here, but he was the only other person who knew what she was doing and she feared that taking things a step further would require their continued partnership. She couldn't collect this information alone. It was her turn to manipulate him into agreeing to work together.

He shook his head, sighing. "I'm not a monster, I know that it's the right thing to do."

"Then why are you resisting me so much?"

"Because this is going to be dangerous and the last thing I need to worry about is babysitting."

Miranda stepped forward, nearly lunging. "Babysitting? I could level you without breaking a sweat. If anything, I'd be babysitting you."

Drake hung his head, his posture loosening.

She stepped away again, not expecting him to be defeated so easily. He hadn't even baited her since they arrived here.

"You do realize that this will make us a target," he said coolly.

Her heart squeezed. Did he care about her safety? Genuinely? She refused to believe he was trying to be noble and spare her from danger. He wasn't...he was an asshole. He didn't do nice things or *care*. Miranda's thoughts sputtered along with her attempt to retort.

"I see there is no arguing with you, since you're about as moveable as concrete. I want it known that I did try to stop you. Besides," he smiled, some of his humor returning and Miranda wasn't expecting how relieved she felt. "I was the one who duped you into working together in the first place. Reap what you sow, I suppose."

"Fine," she said, raising her chin in the air to hide her unease.

"Fine," he agreed, crossing his arms.

"I don't suppose you have a plan then, love?"

"I do, actually," she said, earning a raised brow in return. "My parents are throwing an engagement party. It's at his mansion in the Ring. I can get you inside. Then we can look around while he's distracted."

He laughed now, with more mirth than before. "*That's* your plan. To sneak into his heavily guarded home and rifle through his drawers?"

She rolled her eyes. "It gets us in his territory. All we need is a mention of what this experiment is about and then we get out of there and let the Watchmen take over." She paused, but quickly added, "Or you can kill him, I guess. Though in the middle of a ball is not ideal considering the amount of potential witnesses."

"And what about the address? I'm sure there's plenty of information to be gathered at the source."

"True, but I don't have an easy way to get into whatever this address turns out to be. I have a personal invite to his home, I think we should pursue that connection before we lose our chance. If we're discovered snooping at this building, we end up in his sights and there's no way we'd make it to his private office at the ball."

Devin rubbed at the back of his neck, some inner battle waging in his silence. Miranda bobbed on her toes, never good at waiting for others to catch up to her.

Finally, he said, "This is not a good idea. For a multitude of reasons."

"Oh? Name one."

"The first is me not killing the bastard while he cuts the cake."

CHAPTER FIVE

D EVIN HAD DONE A very good job avoiding soirées and fancy
gatherings of any kind since inheriting his father's house and
lands. It helped that society was hesitant to invite him in the first
place, but he wouldn't have accepted anyway. He grew up observing
from the outside, like the rest of the city. Grand balls. Fancy dinners.
Overnight excursions to private mansions in the country. Only rich
humans did those things.

Devin preferred his club and apartment in the Fells. It was grander
than anything he had growing up. Large, spacious. Long hallways that
led to rooms with purposes he never bothered to learn. It had been
furnished by the previous tenant, and he hadn't bothered to change it
except to buy his own bed in the master suite. It was the first time he'd
ever had a proper bed that belonged solely to him.

He was respected at the club, instead of the unintentional lord of
the manor. It wasn't in the nice part of town or frequented by high
society, but more citizens of Unity lived outside their social divides
than in, so his business was thriving. He often wondered why he chose

to stay in the Garrison, then, in this loathsome house with a history that wanted him erased from it.

Spite had a little to do with it. There was a sick sort of satisfaction in being here. With its stately furniture and paintings and heirlooms. All collected over the generations of the Warner—Devin kept his mother's surname—family. Imagine the solicitor's shock when his investigation into the inheritance led him to Devin's pleasure club. New laws created fewer restrictions about birthright and neither his bastardy nor his fae blood were reason enough to deny Devin. Now the entirety of Robert Warner's holdings belonged to him. A too large house, servants, and a noble title.

Devin couldn't decide what he planned to do with it all. Some days he wanted to burn the whole lot of it to the ground. Some days he wanted nothing to do with it, just sell it off and never think about it again.

Yet month after month he'd show up here for a few days. He let the steward ramble to him about the accounts and the staff and Devin would simply throw the funds where they needed to go and then amble about before leaving again.

He sat there now, not drunk but getting there. Alcohol had been the quickest, surest way to dull his sight.

Devin stared at the calligraphied page on his desk. True to her word, Miranda had seen to his invitation to the grand engagement party of Cordelia Wilde to Yarrow Graves. She must have bribed or begged her parents to allow the likes of him to attend. And Graves would see his name. Would he remember a lowly soldier? Would he remember threatening Devin, Gideon, and Rachel—the only surviving members of their unit—to keep his cowardice secret?

Devin took another long drink.

He still hadn't made up his mind about going. This was not what he signed up for when he agreed to destroy Graves. In fact, his attending a ball at the man's house was the very last thing he could have conceived. Devin wasn't sure he would be strong enough *not* to kill him. He wasn't sure he could look the man in the face or even breathe the same air without becoming violent. Miranda was right to protect her sister from Graves, her actions so far suggested she had first-hand knowledge of Graves's evil.

The thought turned his stomach and he pushed back from the desk, rubbing his forehead as he tried not to picture what Graves could have done to make her hate him so violently.

"Sir." The butler knocked and disrupted his dark musings. *What time was it?*

"Yes, Haversham?"

"There's a Mr. Gideon Blair here to see you," Haversham stated in that bland tone butlers used to hide any hint of an opinion or feeling in their words.

"Show him in," Devin ordered as he took another long swig of his drink then set it aside.

Gideon was a solid man with dark hair and an easy smile. He'd always been a bit of a skirt chaser, charming and flirtatious when he wanted to be, stoic and serious when he didn't. They might have been competitors if not for the perilous circumstances of their acquaintance.

He entered the room in full Watchmen uniform, dark pants and coat with brass trim and buttons. Rank and badge shined proudly on his chest and shoulders. It suited his build well, highlighting his muscles and power. Devin always wondered if Gideon didn't choose the profession because the uniform drew in women.

"Drake," Gideon said with a nod as he entered. He was powerful, even for a guardian, but was often too ridiculous for Devin to take him seriously.

"What do I owe the pleasure, Blair?" Devin reclined in his seat, though he knew exactly why Gideon was here. Devin kept his smile in place, despite his souring mood. He wished they were at the club, where Devin felt more in control, but he hadn't known Gideon would show up *now*.

"I've been busy," Gideon deflected, looking around. "Didn't think you'd stay at your father's home. I thought you hated him."

"I do, but the house is mine. Legally and all that, so until I decide what to do with the bloody place I may as well use it."

Gideon nodded. "And the idea of the former Lord Warner turning in his grave doesn't enter into it?"

"What brings you here, Blair? And without Rachel in tow? She finally wise up and tell you to go to hell?"

"I'm not her keeper." He adjusted his collar and Devin sensed that Rachel's absence was a point of aggravation. "Anyway, I'm working on something."

He meandered through the room, studying the titles of books on the shelf. Gideon stopped briefly in front of a portrait on the wall Devin could only assume was some long dead relative, he never bothered to study the family tree that had severed his branch.

Gideon continued to amble. He never could sit still. "I'm in charge of safeguarding this city and right now, I'm facing a few...obstacles. First, the crime lord Thaddeus Wraith and his enterprise. I'm determined to bring him down."

"Well, best of luck to you," Devin lifted his glass and took another drink. The buzz of the contents dulled his vision and smothered the color beginning to grow around Gideon's form. He could read people well enough without Sight, anyway. For example, Gideon was worried. He was frowning too much and he kept shifting his shoulders like he was itching to act, but couldn't.

Gideon's eyes snapped to him, following Devin's hand with the drink. He kept his thoughts on the subject to himself. "Second, a vigilante has popped up over the last couple months. The Rogue has been running around the streets stopping muggings or other small crimes. It's only a matter of time before the newssheets catch wind of it."

"Sounds to me like they're doing your job for you and you should be thanking them."

"Except, it's not their job," Gideon snapped, "And we can't have random citizens taking justice into their own hands."

Devin paused for a moment, not caring enough about the subject to argue. "You didn't come here to talk about Thaddeus Wraith or some nobody with an overinflated sense of justice. What is it you're here about?"

Gideon took a breath. "I was building to that. The third problem...is Yarrow Graves."

He met Gideon's eyes. A sense of understanding and shared hatred passed between them.

Gideon held some pathological need to be the hero. Like his self-worth hinged on his ability to protect others. That day in battle, he had gone back for the injured. He'd dragged corpses halfway to safety before realizing it was too late. Once returned to the mundanity of Unity, Gideon pursued the only career that allowed him to continue to be the hero.

Unlike Devin who had taken a decidedly less altruistic path in life.

Devin was barely sixteen when he enlisted, lying about his age for the access to stable food and shelter. But war was cruel, and it chewed thoroughly before it spit you out. The sight of anguished, murky yellow auras snuffing out one after the other had broken what little was left of his soul. He stumbled back to society emotionally stripped and more resentful than when he went in, but grit, luck, and a resounding performative charisma built his club, which was all he really needed to survive. Survive, but not live. With little to drive him except the festering wounds of society's treatment and then the emotional scars left by the war, Devin had poured what was left of his soul into the only worthwhile pursuit he had left. Revenge on Graves. After nearly a year he was the closest he'd ever been to achieving that revenge.

"What about him?" Devin considered telling Gideon about his plans to bring the coward down, but thought better of it. Gideon wanted Graves dead just as much as Devin, but given his career was not as free in his options. He couldn't go around murdering men he hated and he'd already shared his opinion on citizens taking justice into their own hands.

Devin, however, would end Graves's life or die trying. He only had to close his eyes to hear the screams again, to feel the hot spray of his comrades' blood across his face. If not for Graves's cowardice, the massacre wouldn't have happened.

Gideon smiled, but it didn't reach his eyes. He shoved his hands in his pockets, an old habit to keep from fidgeting. "I'm sure you've heard of the growing unease in the Night Court?"

Devin shrugged in response, he knew about it but only in the way everyone heard the whispers of hostility, and he wasn't about to share what he and Miranda had uncovered to a Watchmen, friend or not.

"I think Graves is organizing the Night Fae against parliament. I'm not completely sure what his goals are, and this is more of a gut instinct than anything. Officially, my hands are tied to the bureaucracy run by men who sympathize with Graves. We only know what we've picked up from the few patrols we send through the Night Court. Which, is getting increasingly difficult because there are no Night Fae in the Watchmen and no one else is queueing up to take that detail."

"We both know Graves is lower than the slime of the earth. What does this have to do with me? I don't know anything." Devin watched

Gideon's mouth close, a palpable hesitation, and Devin understood. "You think I have news because my mother was from the Night Court?"

"I was thinking of your club, actually. You're perfectly positioned to gather intel from all manner of race. I'm grasping here, I know, but I also thought it would be an excuse to check in. Make sure you hadn't drunk yourself to death yet."

"I'll keep an ear out for you, but that's the best I can offer. I won't disrupt business because you've elected to remain on the side of law and order when you could be helping me hunt the bastard down and end this by tomorrow."

Gideon rubbed at his temple. "While tempting, that decision was based on more than just me. My sister doesn't make the best choices, and since I promised to always be there for her, I can't go landing myself in jail. Plus, Rachel would have followed me." His eyes grew unfocused, distracted.

"Can't have poor Rachel ending up in jail, can we?" Devin was prodding weakness, he knew it, but that didn't stop him from voicing it. Gideon's flinch wasn't nearly as satisfying as Miranda's glare.

"You're an ass," Gideon said, voice low. "She said not to expect much in coming here. Guess I should have listened. You've got your drinks to wallow in, smother all the bad feelings."

"You should listen to Rachel." Devin's lip curled; his teeth bared. "She's got way more sense than you."

Gideon approached the desk and Devin wondered if he had pushed too far. He set his hands on the surface, glaring down from his higher vantage. "You're not—wait." His neck craned, eyes hardening as he snatched up the invitation Devin had stupidly left in plain sight. "What the fuck is this?"

Devin cursed under his breath then answered, "It's nothing."

"Nothing? This is an invitation to Cordelia Wilde's engagement party. To *Graves*." Gideon's voice thundered. He was seething and Devin couldn't blame him. He would be, too.

"When you're in my position you get invites to things." Devin shrugged as if the note were inconsequential. "It means nothing."

Gideon narrowed his eyes. "You're going?"

"I haven't decided."

"So, you're thinking about going where this weasel will be, not just in attendance, but in his very home? Were you going to mention this when I asked you about Graves?" Gideon leaned over the desk, using his height to stare down at Devin. "What are you planning, Drake?"

"For the record, yes, the plan was for you to remain ignorant. As for the details, it's best you didn't know," Devin replied, pointedly. He let the statement stand. Gideon continued to breathe through his nose, his posture stiff and his hands on the desk. He took the full meaning.

"If you do something stupid, I'll have to arrest you," he said quietly, meeting Devin's eyes. He knew there was only one reason on earth that would prompt Devin to attend a party with Graves in attendance.

Devin smiled. "You'd need evidence and a case to arrest me, Blair. I plan on giving you neither."

Devin was partially joking. He did not plan to murder Graves at the party. But he wanted to. He wasn't entirely sure he could resist should he find himself faced with the man himself. For Miranda's sake, and her sake only, he planned to allow the man to survive the night.

Gideon looked away. "You're right. It's best if I don't know." He stood up and straightened his uniform. He headed for the door. "Any information from the Night Court you can pass my way would be appreciated. And Drake?"

"Yes?"

"Get in a shot for me." Gideon left without another word.

Devin knew that Gideon was serious about arresting him, but he also knew Gideon wouldn't look too closely in any investigation involving Graves's murder. And now it was decided. Devin had to go to the party and he had to refrain from killing Graves on sight. Not an easy task.

Miranda had been prodded and handled until she was perfectly styled for her sister's special evening. She glided along the floor, the picture of society's princess. Poised and elegant on the outside while she entertained murder in her heart.

She and her family boarded the carriages Graves had sent. Only two women in full dress would fit in a carriage and normally each daughter went with a parent, but Miranda convinced her mother to let the girls ride together. Cordelia shuffled into her seat, staring out the window like rain had ruined her plans.

Cordelia wore pale yellow, a color that captured the blonde strands peeking through her brown hair. She was lovely, the picture of youthful beauty, but her face held a different story. Why could her parents not see the pain in their daughter's eyes? This would all be so much simpler. Miranda wouldn't need to be running around Unity at all hours with a dangerous rogue if her parents just disapproved of the match.

"Cheer up, Delia," Miranda said. Cordelia didn't move. "You know, I have a feeling that all will be right very soon."

Cordelia turned, so slowly her neck might have creaked. "Yes, of course."

Miranda bit her lip. She wanted to tell Cordelia her plans, to ease her sister's misery. But she couldn't. What if it went wrong? What if Cordelia wanted to help? She remained silent.

With nothing to say, Miranda looked at Unity passing by through the window. Her parents would never see what Graves was capable of, he knew how to hide his nature from the right people. Said the right words to assuage fear and doubt in his character. Filled the right pockets and whispered into the right ears, so that no one would question him. He projected a charismatic champion of unification.

This wedding would be the first mixed race union among the upper classes, which should have been a groundbreaking achievement. The union of such prominent lineages was hoped to act as the catalyst for others to start venturing further from their comforts, to explore the new and embrace the changes in Unity that had started almost eighty years ago with the war.

Her stomach twisted, nearly upsetting her lunch. She still hadn't told a soul, but her sister was not Graves's first choice. It was nearly a year ago when he'd sought Miranda as his match. Found her alone, as she was catching her breath from another overwhelming and stuffy ball she'd been honor bound to attend. He had been charming, almost kind. Drifting ever closer to her as he made polite conversation, despite the impropriety of their situation. They were alone in a dark area, without a chaperone in sight.

He'd made offers. Attempted to serenade her with promises of their unstoppable alliance. With the entire Night Court at his back, he simply needed a lady from the right social circles to increase his favor. Miranda was well on her way to being 'shelved.' One too many seasons with no trace of respectable suitors to show for it, certainly she would leap at the chance to have such an offer. A guardian from an honorable family would make a sensible alliance. She couldn't say exactly when his charms had faded. It was a gradual thing, the veneer falling with each polite refusal until polite wasn't enough. The tear of fabric still sent visceral shivers through her.

Miranda closed her eyes to the memories. Months of living in fear of retaliation, fearing what he would do to her for refusing his offers, for striking back. It was four months later that he announced his engagement to Cordelia.

To all the world, he seemed the besotted gentleman. Enamored with Cordelia enough to make his suit fast and plain. But there was a reason he'd done it publicly and announced his intentions to her parents, rather than ensnaring Cordelia in secret the way he had Miranda. Now no one could protest. Now, his true nature and intentions for Cordelia could remain hidden. He took away the choice to refuse.

She was at his mercy.

And Miranda was vibrating with anger, her nails cutting into her palms. She felt powerless. She had always been taught to attack a problem head on, to engage with her enemy directly, but this wasn't a brawl. And no matter how much she wanted to crush him in her hands, there was truly nothing she could do that was worth the consequences that would follow.

The sly smiles Graves sent her way at social gatherings. The way his eyes shifted to Miranda as he kissed Cordelia's hand. It turned her stomach. And she could only imagine what awaited her sister once a union was secured and she was tethered to him for life.

If Miranda's plans with Drake failed, she was ready to throw herself in the line of fire...to offer her own hand in her sister's place. If that didn't work, she would steal her sister away into the night and hide her where no one could hurt her. Neither of those options were ideal, but the alternative was unbearable.

They neared the house and entered the line of carriages waiting to be announced. Her heart raced as they inched closer.

It was a large manor, with dark vining plants that Miranda recognized from the Night Court sprawling up the gates and over the brick. They were in the Ring—named because it encircled the Spire which erupted menacingly from its center. Here homes were larger, grander, meant to hold the various alderman elected for the parliament or other prominent figures. Her father had a house here, if he wanted it, but he chose to remain in the family estate in the Garrison.

Graves's home matched no architecture Miranda was aware of, with twisting columns of ebony. Gargoyles snarling in lofty corners. Stained glass. And dark, smooth obsidian materials. His wealth and power were on full display as Miranda and her sister were helped from the carriage and escorted to a grand foyer of black and gold marble.

The ballroom was pure opulence, little domes extended the ceiling, making the room feel much larger despite being filled with people. A quartet played a haunting melody that filled the chamber, no doubt aided by the acoustics of the ceiling shape.

While still overwhelmingly human and guardian, there was the usual blend of races in attendance. The heads of fae courts, titled members of other races, or the respective alderman and their families.

Kieran North the Winter Alderman often attended balls and social gatherings, though he rarely did more than glower and observe like he was documenting the unusual habits of the upper class. He was punctual to a fault and usually left before ten, but easy to spot by the gap between himself and the rest of the partiers. A lone figure with ten feet of space on all sides.

Willa Shen, the Summer Alderman, was the first to dance and the last to leave. Miranda spied Miss Shen's intricately woven auburn hair as she hovered near the drink table, a cup in each hand. Lady Belladona Asche, a widow who turned immortal after her husband's passing, was currently married to the immortal Alderman. She liked to drink, gossip, and do as she pleased. Which made her either loved or hated, rarely in between. She was entertaining a growing mass of guests with a lively story. Her husband did not attend parties.

Drake's blue eyes should have been easy to find in a crowd of mostly humans, their luminous almost iridescent quality a stark contrast to, say Lady Merrin's human blue eyes. Miranda prayed he hadn't decided to stay home. She would never admit it, but she needed him. Without him here she feared she would lose her nerve. His presence made her more confident, since she refused to look weak in front of him. He made her want to shine. And she could use another person to help her get in and out unnoticed.

She bit her lip. And then there was the fact that he was attractive and full of roguish charm. The exact sort of charm her parents had always warned her about, but Miranda couldn't help but sway a bit to his magnetism. These thoughts were all safe in her mind. Tucked away and never to see the light of day.

Speak of the devil. Drake was already there, body slanted in a corner as he sipped at a Champaign flute. He looked pissed, but incredibly handsome. His clothes were fine and well-tailored to his body, dark velvets with splashes of deep maroon on his vest and cravat. His signature colors, it seemed, for she never saw him in anything but black and red.

Miranda's palms grew sweaty as her eyes lingered where they shouldn't. But, she reasoned, there was no harm in looking. She could hardly pretend she didn't *want* to look. He hadn't shaved the rough stubble along his chin, but he had taken effort with his hair. Parted to one side, less roguishly-tousled than normal. It still covered his ears, which made her chest ache, even if she was endeared by the display. Which was conflicting, since she was determined to hate him and would have denied the idea of Devin and endearing populating the same sentence if questioned.

She approached him slowly, suddenly self-conscious. At parties, her short-comings were always glaringly obvious. Men would ask her to dance and if she spoke they found her too aggressive, but if she said nothing they deemed her boring. She was rarely asked to dance twice.

She wished for the comfort of her guardian's uniform. She felt herself in it instead of at war with the person her gown painted her to be. But a uniform wasn't appropriate for a ball. Instead she wore a pale blue gown that billowed around her hips with a bodice that was both too tight and too low cut—her mother was desperate for her to attract the right attention.

Yara had styled her hair in an elegant coiffure, but she had plucked a few tendrils free to frame her face. She preferred the softer look it gave her features. She knew she could be intense and it had become habit to seek out ways of deceptively covering her harsher nature. She was not normally reduced to a blushing, self-conscious maiden.

But then Devin noticed her and her knees wobbled most annoyingly. Because his disquiet sneer transformed into a darker, more seductive grin once he spotted her. His eyes traced an unabashed trail up her body and his tongue licked absently at the corner of his lip, drawing her eyes and electrifying what had already been a potent moment. Miranda was not worldly. All she knew of desire and intimacy she learned through Lydia's fascination with research, the two of them passing books and even some illustrations in secret. But his eyes had her longing for things she couldn't define and a very base, impulsive part of her wanted him to teach her.

"Miss Wilde," he said with a slight bow. "It's a pleasure to see you this evening." His grin was slanted with mischief. He was attempting to play it off like she hadn't asked him here so they could spy on their host. He feigned casual poorly, and there was no mistaking his focus on her for anything less than lust.

He reached out for her hand, snagging it before she could protest and gently pressed his lips to her skin. The sensation flared up her arm like a wave, vibrating through her.

"If I'm going to play the part," he offered as he straightened. Her fingers slipped from his, lifeless and buzzing.

Miranda was rendered speechless. Behind them, the ball continued. Graves was here. They should focus on the task at hand. She should not be spending much too long staring at Drake like the only thing keeping them apart was sheer, barely restrained willpower.

Drake stood straighter, his eyes narrowed playfully. "Please don't tell me this is your first ball, Miss Wilde. I was hoping to follow your lead."

She shook her head, rattling the stupor from her brain. If she didn't get ahold of herself, this whole plan would fall apart. Miranda took in a deep breath and then released it slowly. She could do this. She just needed to remind herself that he was annoying and not at all interested in someone like her, not really. He liked riling her up, but he wasn't serious. Not with someone like her. Someone non-adventurous. With no experience. From her sort of family.

"No, of course not. It's..." she cleared her throat. "I've done this plenty of times."

"And surely I'm not the first gentleman to kiss your hand," He said, eyebrows moving suggestively. "Or am I just the first to make you blush?"

And *that* snapped her out of it. Leave it to Devin Drake to turn a romantic moment into one of exasperation. And he knew what he was doing when he kissed her hand, the cad. "Don't flatter yourself, it's just hot in here," she said.

Drake pulled at his cravat. "I can't argue there, it's bloody stifling in these clothes."

"In a few minutes the dancing will start and a lot of the focus will be here," Miranda started, "Graves will be expected on the floor, mingling with guests. We should be able to slip away at that point and find his office."

She made a few sweeps of the ballroom with her eyes, noting the layout and various exits. They were on the ground floor, but there was no telling how large this place truly was from the front. Not to mention if he had installed secret passages or rooms.

"He'll have guards throughout the estate." Drake sipped his drink to hide his words.

He did his own sweep of the room, keeping his body slightly turned so they didn't look to be in conversation. Though, Miranda found it hard to pretend that he wasn't still making her body tingle and antsy with tension. It was harder to imagine the whole room wouldn't notice all the tiny ways her body responded to simply being close to him.

Damn it. She was supposed to be above this. He certainly hadn't been this distracting before...but then, she also hadn't had contact with him in several days. She'd sent the invitation and a note, but dared not risk more and he hadn't attempted to contact her either. The days of waiting, with nothing productive to occupy her, she had unintentionally crafted silly fantasies involving Drake. Where she could take out her frustration and aggression on his person with fists or a weapon, but always eventually devolving into smoldering glances, hands brushing over her clothes, or even heated kisses that she could only imagine from pictures, rather than practice.

Excitement buzzed in her muscles and it was difficult to hide the restless fidgeting in her limbs as they conspired in secret. Devin kept his voice low, so that only she would hear him, the smooth cadence of his voice erupting in shivers up her spine.

"Graves is not an idiot and he knows he has lots of enemies, he'll not fill his home with people and leave valuable information unwatched."

The quartet shifted into the next piece. Couples flocked to the floor and into position, floating through steps drilled into them since birth. All eyes were on the dancers. Miranda's mother would be looking for her now, dragging a bachelor in tow to trap Miranda into a dance.

"Let's go," Miranda whispered and she scanned for her mother and Graves as she skirted the crowd for an exit. She was so distracted she nearly walked into a gaggle of gossiping aunts. A cloud of perfume smacked her in the face, each thick floral scent battling for dominance as the most garish.

"Oh, my dear, how lovely to see you again."

"How's your parents?"

"Are you very excited for your sister? Marriage is so wonderful. Graves is a great match."

Miranda smiled and nodded along, desperate not to be entangled by social etiquette and failing. She barely knew these people, only two of them she could recall by name. Yet they were relentless, barraging her with comments and questions and leaving no room to answer as they talked over themselves. She realized too late that she had lost Devin somewhere.

"I..."

"Don't worry, dear, I'm sure you'll get your own proposal...your sister's match will do wonders for your prospects. A connection to Alderman Graves can only improve your chances."

"Yes, you're not out of the running just yet. At twenty-three you're not quite over the hill."

"It certainly isn't your face that keeps them away, dear."

Now they were disguising their cruelty as pity. How very noble. And she was twenty-six, three years past her expiration date. Her mind spun as she tried to find an excuse to get around them. The last thing she needed was to upset elderly widows with little to occupy their time who would delight in drawing attention to even the smallest display of impropriety.

"Miss Wilde, there you are," Drake swooped to her aide, his arm sliding gracefully through hers and tugging her to his side.

Drake's effect was instant. The matrons turned their shoulders, lips sucking inward, and noses wrinkled in perfect unison.

"Lord Drake," the boldest acknowledged, though Miranda recognized the tone as begrudgingly polite. They would not overtly insult him at such a gathering, but his presence was not welcome. Was this truly some blatant display of prejudice? In the home of a Night Fae, were they really going to turn up their noses at Drake?

"We were just chatting with Miss Wilde," another continued, "I'm sure there are...others better served by your particular charms."

"The serving staff gather near the corners, dear, if you're more comfortable with their sort of conversation, as I can imagine the bolder topics of such a gathering would prove cumbersome."

Miranda's jaw hung open, too stunned to speak while they insulted Drake without batting an eye. It wasn't that he was a half-fae, they disliked him because he had been born poor. He bore it without comment, his smile fading with each word they threw at him.

"Actually," Miranda started, and the matrons all rounded on her, waiting for her to aid them in sending Drake away, "I'd rather talk with him than endure another second of your cruel backhanded comments."

The lady closest to her scoffed, putting a hand to her heart. "If you consider honesty to be cruel—"

"No, just you." Miranda hooked her arm through Drake's, reveling in their gasps of horror. "Lord Drake, you were saying?"

Miranda felt a warm flutter when his smile returned. "I was here for the promised dance, of course. If you're still up for it, Miss Wilde."

"The...what?"

He laughed, his humor returning as he squeezed her arm to his side. "Ladies, it has been a pleasure talking with you in spite of your callous wit, but then, the staff provide such intellectually superior conversation it's understandable you'd prefer the company of those...similarly limited."

He bowed and guided Miranda away, as the older matrons watched with open mouths as Miranda was whisked to the dance floor by the notorious Lord Devin Drake. They would have plenty to say tomorrow, but for now, they were speechless.

"What are you doing?" Miranda whispered as they joined the throng of dancers, next to a horned man with irises a molten red. She had stepped in on Drake's behalf, but she had not agreed to dance with him.

"I believe this is called a dance," Drake replied with a grin. "I thought you'd be familiar."

Her jaw sealed shut. She should walk away right now. She should not, under any circumstances, dance with Drake. His smile was too inviting. His manner too exasperating. His smell too intoxicating—*was he sober today?* Instead of spirits she caught the warm scent of leather and an earthy soap that muddled her already frayed senses.

He made her *feel* too much. Too much heat. Too much frustration. Too much longing. Instead of leaving, her body moved as it had been programmed. The steps committed to muscle memory.

They came together, paired off alongside the rest of the dancers. Drake's hand settled on her hip, his head tilted down.

How could he possibly know this dance? She found it hard to believe Drake could follow the steps drilled into her since she could walk, yet, there he was, leading her through the dance with the fluid ease of a natural. Her breathing grew rushed. Color rose in her cheeks.

The start of a smile threatened to commandeer her mouth but she resisted, for she refused to smile at Drake of her own volition.

"We should slip out before the song picks up," she whispered fiercely. She felt the gentle press of his hand like a candle flame, though there was no way for his body heat to coax through her many layers.

They swirled over the marble floor. Intertwined with dancers too absorbed in their own partners to notice how hard her heart was beating or how even the way he looked at her right now was somehow improper. He brought his face near her ear.

"Relax, love. We now have a clear path to the other side of the room." He spun her a bit harder than the dance required, breaking from the intended flow and closer to their goal.

Miranda shook her head, her fingers clawing into his shoulder. "You really need to stop touching me under the ruse of something else."

Heat flickered in his gaze. "Are you inviting me to touch you without a reason? Quite the bold assertion, but," his voice turned to silk as he dipped her backward then back up until she was flush against him in a flourish that was entirely unnecessary for this set. "I'd happily satisfy any desire you request, Miss Wilde."

She rooted her foot to the floor, halting his next step and he nearly stumbled. She expected him to get angry. Men always got angry when she showed aggression or asserted herself.

Devin laughed.

She continued to pout, but it was more of a stubborn purse of her lips.

"If I fall, I'm dragging you down with me," he said, sweeping her along, their feet moving in perfect step. One-two-three-one-two-three-one-two-three.

Miranda smiled. Their speed increased, and she was starting to have fun. Dancing, fun. She would not have believed it two minutes ago.

"If you think you can," she parried.

He was staring at her, not at the room. Neither of them were paying a wit of attention to anything outside of their arms, oblivious to the whispers that followed them, to the stares and shaking heads as Miranda mingled with the tainted. "Is that a challenge, Miss Wilde?"

Miranda swallowed. This was banter. Somehow they had started flirting. Her lips parted and she drifted in the exhilaration. Her mother insisted that dancing was the quickest way to judge if a man was suitable. Until now Miranda had not believed her.

She was caught up in the music, in the moment, lost in how easy it felt to move in step with him. Another spin toward the far end of the floor, but this time he had gently lifted her, her delicate shoes wafting across the floor. A laugh bubbled from her chest, forcing her lips into a true, beaming smile. The sort of genuine smile that refused to be anything but happiness.

Devin paused a step, but recovered smoothly. His gaze grew somber, as his grip on her shifted, almost like fidgeting. But that was impossible. What about her could have possibly made someone of his experience falter? Not her laughter or smile, that was too juvenile. Maybe the sudden shift had nothing to do with her.

His steps had slowed, his movements more stilted. She met his eyes and wished she hadn't. Her legs nearly stopped altogether. Then he licked his lips and *Miranda felt it.* Like a bolt of lightning in her gut that jolted through her limbs before settling low, low in her stomach. She chewed the corner of her mouth.

He stopped as the notes to the song died away and melded into another. They'd draw attention standing like this. If the whole room wasn't already aware of the scandalous dance she'd just experienced. She felt stripped to her core. Naked and exposed. Hot and shaky. Like she'd just done something extremely vulgar in public. And, for a moment, she didn't care or want it to end.

He cleared his throat, but didn't pull away. "I believe this is our stop," he said, a hint of something affecting his tone, voice almost gravelly. He cleared his throat again and began to loosen his hold on her. He stepped away.

Miranda let him slip through her hands. She didn't fight it. Her body felt like partially set gelatin. And slowly the sound of the ball grew loud again. Her ears rang as notes and the dull roar of conversation rose around her. They were near the far end of the room. Far from the assault of the nosy widows. Right next to a door that would lead further into the house.

Right. The plan. Her sister. Graves.

Miranda shook her head. This is exactly what she could not allow to happen. She stuck out a hand and balanced on the wall. Maybe inviting him was not a good idea. She couldn't be expected to do what was necessary when she felt like *this*.

"After you," Devin prompted.

Miranda pulled herself together. It was too late now. She gave herself a firm pinch on the inner part of her arm, hoping to ground herself in something real that wasn't the dream-like stupor of their dance. She huffed as they slipped from the ballroom. Hopefully, leaving whatever hovered between them on the dance floor.

Hopefully.

CHAPTER SIX

THE DANCE HAD BEEN a mistake. Devin held back as Miranda charged ahead to vacate the dance floor. Whispers lingered in their wake, narrowed eyes sticking to Devin as Miranda drew further from his tainted company. He briefly mumbled something about drawing attention and that they should separate to meet again once inside the secluded hallways that branched off the main ballroom.

Miranda agreed, her cheeks still red and a dazed cast to her eyes as she proceeded in the opposite direction.

Devin nodded his head at each gawking stranger, though it was getting harder not to grind his teeth or lash out. He'd been such a fool.

Once clear of onlookers, Devin found Miranda and she hastened to keep moving. The house was a labyrinth of identical obsidian hallways, and the shimmery surfaces sent reflections bouncing everywhere. It was not the sort of place one could navigate in a stupor. He narrowly avoided a wall several times thinking it was an open path. If they had any hope of succeeding, he needed to focus.

Yet, he was too torn for focus. One half of Devin was still dancing with Miranda, lost in the sea of possibility that had expanded before him when before there had been a straight and focused river.

The other festered in the bitterness of 'I told you so.' He didn't belong here and his association risked her reputation. Society was quick to turn, their opinions lost on a whim, and the scandal of involvement with Devin, no matter what honorary titles he now possessed, would seep into every relationship in his life. Which is why he was better off in the Fells. Amongst his own kind.

He wished his mother never taught him those steps. She taught him the quick, fluid steps to haunting fae melodies and the precise, sweeping ballroom dances that were expected at society parties. Dancing with her was of the few memories he had that didn't haunt him. When they danced, their loft hadn't felt so small and stifling. If he hadn't learned, however, he might have been spared all this doubt.

Because Miranda had defended him, she'd laughed with him, she'd ignored the voices and sneers and his heart yearned for hope.

Hope was dangerous. He'd learned to never trust a good thing over the years, it sooner came back to bite him.

The dance had changed everything. Exposed the risk of his feelings as well as showed him exactly why he had never attempted relationships with the nobility. It wasn't fair to expose Miranda to that sort of derision. She purported defiance and rebelliousness, but could she really handle the loss of her entire social structure?

Her laughter tore his swagger to shreds. Disarmed him in a way no other woman ever had. He should turn around now and run before she squirmed her little claws any further into his carefully crafted asylum of revenge and self-loathing. Or...

He could see just how far Miranda was willing to go.

Chasing her would have made him the worst sort of rogue. She'd risk her whole future debasing herself with a rake who could never offer more than what a night and a bed might allow.

Except, now he had danced with her. He'd held her in his arms and looked into her green eyes as everything shifted. As lust bloomed into more. As all his fears caught up with him, because in that moment he'd have happily ignored every voice of reason just to make her laugh one more time.

Devin tore his eyes from the back of her head. He needed to stop mooning and get his shit together.

"This place is a maze," Miranda said with a huff, "We're lucky we haven't been caught yet." She turned abruptly and they nearly collided. His face within inches from hers and more dangerous thoughts started tumbling through his head. What if he kissed her? If he leaned in and tested how far Miranda might be willing to fall with him?

Would she punch him?

Would she kill him?

Or worse, would she kiss him back?

He paused still close enough to feel each breath, lost in indecision. It took him much too long to step back.

"We should try a different floor," he managed, voice nearly cracking.

They found a set of servants' stairs, but a guard waited at the bottom. They huddled around the corner to avoid detection.

"If the stairs are guarded when no other room has been, the good stuff has to be up there," Miranda said.

"Of course," Devin agreed, so lost in his own musings he'd forgotten to consider the obvious. "He knows that people drift off at a party. He'd expect people to look for a quiet room or a dark corner. Nothing of value would be left where a couple could stumble upon it while knocking boots on the furniture."

Miranda's face twisted in disgust. "People don't really do that. It's...they'd incite scandal and ruin—"

"My dear Miss Wilde, I assure you that it is very much what people do. And often. And everywhere. In fact—" Devin paused and cleared his throat. He was really hurting himself more than her at this point.

"Well, regardless," she said, "We need to remove that guard. A distraction might work, though we don't want to raise any alarms. There's bound to be more up there so I can't just start knocking them *all* unconscious. We'll have to be selective." She chewed her lip as she thought.

Devin did his best not to look at her mouth. Tried not to imagine her teeth on his lips, biting gently, her breath shallow and full of want. How could he not want to coax a few forbidden moans from her? To show her that his mouth was good for more than just bickering?

He cleared his throat. Miranda was off-limits. The scent of her wafted into his face as she paced, trying to think of a plan. Divine above, there was no part of her that didn't tempt him. He wanted to taste the lilac on her skin, rip through her clothes and find all the crevices the scent lingered.

Infernal take him, he needed to stop.

He bit down on his tongue, hoping to quiet the riot in his veins. He was dangerously close to aroused and only careful control was keeping an erection at bay.

"I have an idea," Miranda turned on a heel and headed back toward the ballroom.

Devin kept his distance as he followed. Miranda stopped once they could hear the notes of the crowded ballroom, the background chatter and swell of music, but before they could see inside.

"I know someone who can help. You wait here and I'll get her," she instructed.

"Hold on, love," he grabbed her arm, but instantly regretted the action. They both paused, the dance still lingering between them. She swallowed as she carefully lifted her arm from his slack fingers. Devin took a slow breath before continuing, "Who is this person and how do I know they can be trusted?" He was choosing to be pragmatic instead of reflecting on the razor edge he was currently straddling.

"Of course, she can be trusted," Miranda scoffed, "Or I wouldn't have suggested it."

How was she maddeningly alluring one minute and infuriating the next? She'd stubbornly insist the sky were red if it meant disagreeing with him. "Not a team player, I see," Devin said.

"What is that supposed to mean?"

"It means that you are determined to be in charge, even when we haven't agreed to it. You may trust this person, but I have never met them and, as my stakes in this are just as high as yours, I'd rather not throw just anyone into our plans."

She had the audacity to roll her eyes. "This is hardly just anyone. Lydia Foster would never tell a soul anything. Honestly, she's more likely to forget what we're doing before she has a chance to let it slip." She crossed her arms and added, pointedly, "Unless you don't trust *my* judgment."

"In point of fact, I hardly know you, Miss Wilde," he retorted, resisting the urge to cross his own arms.

"I think of the two of us, *my* judgement is more reliable than yours."

"I beg your pardon?" He was truly offended. She had the nerve to say her judgement was superior when she was conspiring with the likes of him?

"Just..." she bared her teeth and, for a moment, he feared he'd laugh and set her off again.

"I suppose you won't let it go, then," he said.

She set her hands on her hips—or, rather, the billowing skirts that accentuated her hips—and snapped, "Do *you* have another plan for getting past the guard?"

He did not. "Fine," he relented," But we tell her as little as possible."

"Not a problem. She'll only want to hear as little as possible, anyway." Miranda left him in the shadows so they wouldn't be seen entering the ballroom together and sought out her friend.

Devin was quite content to sulk in her absence. Quarrelling had done little to temper his desire. If anything, it made it worse. Now, he not only wanted Miranda alone and wrapped in nothing but his arms, he wanted to see how she vented her anger with nothing to hide behind.

Miranda returned before his thoughts could dive too deeply into scandalous. A pretty raven-haired woman trailed behind her, her face soft and friendly, but her eyes were obscured behind round, blurry spectacles.

"Divine above, the stories weren't kidding, were they?" Miss Foster said, breathless. Maybe Devin had just hung around diverse crowds for too long, but there was something not entirely human about Miss Foster. He searched for the normal tells and found nothing. Except, he suspected the glasses hid her eyes the way his hair hid his ears.

"Lydia. Shh," Miranda scolded between her teeth.

"Miss Foster," he said with a bow, then he continued dryly, "We're in rather a hurry."

"Oh!" Miss Foster nodded and she adjusted her dress, twitching her skirts around awkwardly. Even Devin knew ladies didn't make dramatic shows of fixing their clothing in mixed company. "Sorry," she whispered as she adjusted her spectacles with the tip of a long, thin finger, "Just, uh, the material is—"

"Tell me you didn't hide a book in your dress," Miranda scolded.

"I'm afraid I can't," Miss Foster said with a sheepish smile. She adjusted her skirts again and three books hit the floor. They were small and thin, but still. Impressive.

Miranda covered her face in her hands.

"Well, you can't think I would be wasting my entire evening dancing," Miss Foster scoffed, "Honestly."

"It doesn't matter. I need you to create a distraction for the guard. Something...loud. Something that will lure him far enough away from the stairs for us to slip past."

Miss Foster nodded along. "Not a problem. I'm very good at making a scene."

"Not usually on purpose," Miranda mumbled just loud enough that he caught it as she pushed past him. He felt her skirts brush against his legs and he stepped back to avoid her plowing into his shoulder.

He and Miranda got into position just out of sight and signaled to Miss Foster, who gave them a very intentional thumbs up before casually meandering down the hallway toward the guard.

Miss Foster cleared her throat and drew the guard's focus. "Excuse me, sir, but is that a genuine Martinelli sculpture, or a reproduction?"

The guard blinked. "Uh...I couldn't say, ma'am, but you're not supposed to be in this part of the estate—"

"Oh, of course, obviously," she interrupted, "I was just fascinated by all these elaborate pieces. The theme is rather scattered, these two pictures are at least three centuries apart while the architecture of the building is clearly a nod to the mid-century modernist style founded by Calpernicous Dredge. That's not to say it's not truly lovely! These are amazing pieces and all the details throughout the home would put a museum to shame. I mean, the wainscoting alone reflecting the Faery Deviation Era is," she paused to take a breath before continuing to babble while the guard's eyes glossed over, "Masterfully crafted. I'd bet anything this is no Martinelli recreation. You know he used demonic muses in his work? From well before the war when that was still taboo. I've never been able to see one this close, in person, can I just get a closer look?"

"This is her idea of distraction?" Devin hissed, unamused. Unless Miss Foster's goal was to put the guard to sleep, he didn't see how this would accomplish anything.

"Just...give it a moment. Any second now..." Miranda watched the scene intently, awaiting something Devin couldn't sense.

Lydia had reached the sculpture in question, examining every surface with her eyes before reaching out with her hands.

"Ma'am, you're not supposed to touch that—"

Lydia jolted back, her hand nicking a corner of the sculpture. It wobbled dangerously in place.

"Here we go," Miranda whispered.

The guard and Miss Foster watched silently as the sculpture tipped and shattered against the floor.

"Oh, no. I'm so sorry." She bent to scoop up the pieces.

"Wait, don't touch anything." The guard left his post to attend to her. Devin and Miranda raced for the stairs.

"Thank the Divine!" Lydia's voice carried as they ascended to the upper floors. "It was a reproduction after all. You can tell by the cross sections here."

The hallways upstairs were not nearly as dark and laborious. There were a few guards patrolling, but the pair of them were able to time their movements enough to avoid detection.

Until they found a promising room with two guards outside it.

"Well, love, what's your plan?"

Miranda narrowed her eyes. "I thought I wasn't in charge anymore?"

He smiled. Even when he was conceding control to her, she still had to argue. "Fine, if you don't have an idea—"

"Shut up, I do have an idea. I'm going to take them out. Help me get close enough." She dragged him to her side, hooking her arm through his and then giggling into her hand.

Ah, he knew this ruse. The 'pretend we're looking for somewhere to swive but we got lost' ploy. However, he was hesitant to even pretend amorous intent with Miranda right then.

"Hey," the guards turned toward them, "You're not supposed to be up here. Keep all liaisons downstairs." The guard pointed to direct them away from the room.

"Oh, how embarrassing," Miranda covered her face quickly, pulling away from Devin dramatically. She was overacting, but it was a charming attempt. "I assure you, I don't normally do this sort of thing—"

The guard sighed. "Of course, ma'am. I'm sure your intent was entirely innocent. Either way, see that you find yourselves downstairs. These halls are off-limits. How did you even get past—"

Miranda struck like a viper, leaving Devin's side and striking once for the female guard's throat, turning her cry into a gargled gasp. In the same motion, Miranda caught the woman by the waist, twisted, and dropped to a knee as she took the guard to the ground.

The second guard only just recovered enough to open his mouth, intending to call for aid, but Miranda unsheathed the woman's dagger and threw it so the pommel hit him perfectly between the eyes. He collapsed as Miranda rolled and caught the dagger before it could clatter against the polished floor.

The entire attack was over in less than a minute.

Devin's mouth hung open. Miranda stood and brushed the loose strands of hair from her eyes. She adjusted the ridiculous dress back to its proper place. He knew she was powerful, but when he had joked about her besting him he hadn't ever truly meant it. Now, he wasn't sure he'd last two minutes against her. He cleared his throat and adjusted his own clothes, his pants growing uncomfortably constricting.

"Let's drag them inside so no one sees," she began to pull one by the ankles and Devin grabbed the other.

Once inside, he locked the door. Turning to the room, he found a stock of brandy and took a quick drink before dousing the guards so that they appeared drunk and not knocked unconscious. The alcohol numbed his Sight, but also worked to ease the unbidden desire that had abruptly flared again—after he had so carefully tempered his lust back when they were downstairs—as he watched her dispatch both guards single-handed.

Miranda was already searching, methodically opening every drawer and examining every shelf. Devin wasn't convinced they'd find anything of importance that way. Graves wasn't likely to have anything incriminating where anyone could find it by opening a drawer.

"Nothing," Miranda snapped, slamming another drawer closed. "This is all the sort of stuff in my father's study. Just business papers and boring shit. Nothing about experiments or the dead fae."

Devin searched the room from a distance, remaining in the center as his eyes swept over books and shelves and paintings.

"What are you doing?" She asked, annoyance clear in her tone. "Hello? Are you even looking?"

"Graves is a man of secrets, love. We're not looking for drawers or folders, we're looking for a secret compartment or a hidden door."

"That makes sense." She returned to searching the desk and he hovered just behind her, this time checking the bottoms and sides of drawers for catches or hinges, calculating the depth to see if it aligned with the outside. After several minutes, Miranda found a latch to a hidden drawer.

"He'll have a key or secret way to open it," Devin said, heart pumping a little now that they were on the verge of actual discovery. Being in a place like this, where worse than danger awaited if they were discovered, set him on edge.

"We don't have time for a key," she said, jamming her fingers in the seam of the drawer and pulling. It was the hasty option, sure, but now it would be difficult to cover their tracks. The board creaked and snapped open, thankfully not in pieces. It should close smoothly when they finished. Devin pulled his eyes away from the flexing muscles in her arms. She could break him in half.

"Well? Is it what you were looking for?" He insisted, as she lifted a drawing that diagramed the body of a Night Fae. It was a well-drawn figure, but distinctly scientific in nature with thin lines labeling various parts. Except, instead of arm, leg, or hand, it listed powers. Strength. Stamina. Speed. Reflexes. Above the figure was a picture of a single crimson droplet, the only colored part of the drawing.

Devin huffed, irritated. They'd already stayed too long. There was no time to keep looking.

Miranda, however, was silent.

"We can't linger any longer," he insisted, nearly taking her by the arm before thinking better of it.

"It's the Divine's blood," Miranda said, voice hollow. "Quick. We can't take this or he'll know it's missing."

Devin paused. That was impossible. The Divine's blood wasn't a tangible thing that existed. It wasn't bought or made. It only existed in...

Guardians.

Miranda grabbed a sheet of paper and a quill from the desk. Her hasty re-creation was...not as accomplished. When she finished, she stuffed the copy down her bodice and carefully arranged the drawer back together.

Voices outside the door meant their time was up, growing closer and clearly calling out for the guards passed out on the floor. Lydia's distraction had no doubt reached Graves's ears and he was cautious enough to make sure the rest of the house was clear. It was only a matter of time before he realized two guards weren't at their posts.

"What do we do?" Miranda asked, alarm clear in her face. There were no windows or other doors that he could see. They could hide, but even those options were limited. Under the desk, maybe, but both of them would never fit. He could tell her to hide beneath the desk while he faced Graves alone, but they'd use up all their time arguing about it. As he ticked through options, his mind plucked one out of the many. It was better than doing nothing.

Twisting so that he faced her, Devin closed the distance between them.

He guided Miranda back, forcing her legs against the front of the desk.

"What are you doing?" Her unsteady tone caught him by surprise. He had expected her to strike him or plant her stance so she wouldn't budge, not to easily cave while her eyes flitted over him like a rabbit caught in a snare.

"Hopefully, saving us from suspicion," he said, and he reached out for her cheek, but hesitated and pulled away. He saw no better way to disguise their true reason for being there, but kissing her was the last thing he wanted and the only thing on his mind since they started this.

Miranda's eyes widened, her alarm shifting to near panic.

"There has to be another way." She started to fidget, her shoulders heaving with each quick inhale.

Devin had prided himself that all these years of questionable morals, he'd never kissed a woman against her will. "Do you have a better idea, cause you've seconds to find it."

If dancing with her had shaken his senses, kissing her might do irreparable damage. Every muscle clenched.

There were footsteps outside the door. It would open any moment.

"Decide, Miranda, because time is up." He set his hands on either side of her on the desk, forcing her back even further, intruding on her space but never quite breaching it. Let them both be damned, he wasn't going to steal a kiss from her. If he kissed her, it would be because she wanted it, too.

She swallowed and looked at his lips, her body squirmed, and he let out an unintended breath between his teeth. He was standing too close to her and her dress was too damned big not to feel every swish and sweep of her skirts like a caress.

He took a calm breath in and out. It was his intention to remain a gentleman, or as much as he could given that he was suggesting they imply their purpose in that study was for him to fuck her on the desk.

Another calm breath. He needed to cool his blood, fill his mind with thoughts of dead puppies so he could keep from pouncing on her if she ever decided to initiate a kiss. Miranda was an innocent, as far as he could tell, and he wasn't about to kiss her fully erect and high on desire.

Not like this. Not here, where it was merely a ruse to cover what was about to become a very dangerous situation. That meant keeping the experience as chaste as possible, for her sake. He did not like victory so unjustly won and did not savor this. He did, however, want to know what her lips might feel like, even if it was brief.

The door handle moved. The lock only bought them a few extra seconds, minutes if whoever was there didn't have a key.

He closed his eyes, not proud of what he was about to do, but it was probably the only way the stubborn minx would cave. He dipped his face toward her, whispering just out of her reach, "Afraid you'll enjoy it?"

Her jaw tensed and her eyes locked on him with focused fury. He knew what he was doing by goading her, but he'd miscalculated how much that fire in her green eyes excited him. When her fist curled around his collar and she yanked, there was no amount of meditation that would cool the inferno in his veins.

At first, the crash of her mouth was harsh and rigid. She held his jacket in a fist and he froze as reality upended around him. It was more a show of force than a kiss, which he expected in part because everything with Miranda was a show of force. A battle. A fight.

But shit, he'd not planned on liking the brutality of her mouth. Excited by her yanking him down, body full of fire. Despite his honorable intentions he was raging hard and drunk with desire.

The door handle moved again, probably fitting the key in the lock, and she dived into the charade, parting her lips in frantic, passionate gasps. And...*what the fuck was happening?*

Devin had many faults. Vanity was up there. He knew he was handsome and desirable. Knew what women liked and had bedded enough of them that a kiss was merely a means to more enticing ends, a teaser that he'd often enjoyed, but rarely did more than get things moving. But *nothing* compared to kissing Miranda. He'd had whole nights of passion that weren't anywhere near as satisfying and arousing as Miranda's desperate, probing tongue against his teeth. Or her hands twisting into his neat lapels. Or, fuck, the *strength* of her dragging him closer, backward, on top of her as easily as she tossed the guards on their asses.

He braced an arm on the desk to keep his balance. Perhaps the door had opened, he couldn't hear anything above the roar of his pulse and her faint, almost delicate sighs of pleasure. He was fumbling—he, Devin Drake, whispered about in certain circles as *the* generous and unselfish lover—and he couldn't keep up with the onslaught of her passion. He expected chaste, maybe anger. Assumed she would become rigid with disgust.

In his wildest imagination, he had never anticipated Miranda Wilde to *eat him alive*. Enthusiastically. No part of her was rigid or disgusted.

She was liquid, melding against him. And he should have used his free hand to touch her, to find all the spots that made her breath hitch, to savor the chance to feel the soft, olive skin beneath his fingers without the risk of her attacking him for it. But he was pure reaction.

There was a resounding click of the lock just as she dragged her legs up his thighs and arched into him at an angle that would have finished him if they weren't fully clothed.

He groaned audibly into her mouth. The devil himself could have walked in that door and Devin would have told him to fuck off.

But it wasn't the devil. It was much worse.

"Well, well," A voice grated from the doorway, breaking the moment and Miranda's hold on him.

Miranda pushed him as she righted herself and he fell backward a few steps, his body heated and frozen at the same time. A riot of emotions kept him from acting on the dueling impulses to scoop up Miranda again and snap Graves's neck.

Graves stood with two guards next to him, his attire immaculate in ebony with gold embroidered designs. His eyes skipped over Devin and landed on Miranda.

"Miss Wilde," he said with venom laced in the words, "Imagine my surprise to find *you*, in such a state. And in my private office, no less. What a very curious predicament we find ourselves." Graves's cold gaze finally landed on Devin. "You look familiar, have we met?"

Miranda had seconds to size up the situation. While her face was still flushed and her lips still tingled. Devin stood in the center of the study, head angled with a singular focus. He was going to kill Graves right there.

She threw herself between them, slamming into Devin's chest and stealing his attention for a moment. His anger was palpable. The fury lingered like cold fire in the luminous blue of his eyes and he breathed with his entire body, but his mouth closed and he didn't push her out of the way.

Graves's glare, however, narrowed to pinpoint focus on her. Her fingers trembled, but she was able to bury them in the many folds of her skirts. It took all her strength to keep tears from springing to her eyes, but she refused to let him see her fear. She stepped away from Devin, but remained close enough to see him should he lunge.

"Miss Wilde," Graves said, controlled. "I admit I am quite shocked to find you in such a state. I thought you were beyond these sorts of temptations, if memory serves."

Devin's head spun to her, meeting her eyes with a wild sort of terror as if asking what Graves meant. She didn't flinch. She wouldn't. She coiled all her fear and trauma inward until all that remained was an emotionless mask. Hopefully it would be enough.

"I..." she started, but her tongue—which mere seconds ago had tasted Devin's mouth, a thought that sent blood to her cheeks—felt dry and stuck. She'd felt realms of sensations she'd never known were possible and now fear threatened to break her apart.

She continued, "Yes, I think I may have imbibed too much and...got carried away." She met Graves's eyes with a hard glare. She did not want to provoke him. Not in his domain with guards ready to do his bidding. But she couldn't resist holding up her chin with an air of defiance. Her message clear. She had just not wanted *him*.

Graves's styled hair had stark streaks of grey threading through the ebony and eyes that were luminous gold that offset the cold tones in his skin. The impression of him was a well composed noble fae, but that is not what made him threatening. He did not intimidate with his looks. It was his calm evil coupled with power that made him terrifying.

Miranda swallowed. "I didn't know this room was private."

Graves's look was droll as he glanced down at the still unconscious guards.

Miranda shrugged. "I was too preoccupied to notice your drunken guards. It seems you should hire more trustworthy staff." Her quip lingered in the air, filling the space to near suffocating. She wished she had paid more attention when her mother had babbled about choosing her words carefully.

"And you." Graves turned. "I should call you out for taking liberties with my soon-to-be-sister-in-law." Graves shifted his focus to Devin, and Miranda's heart nearly beat from her chest. "We have met, haven't we? In the war. Devin Drake, yes?"

Miranda held her breath.

"It's possible," Devin said through controlled enunciation of each syllable, "I try to forget those days."

Graves nodded. "Yes, terrible times. But, now the problem remains. What are we going to do about this situation?" He shook his head then bent to whisper to one of the guards, who disappeared. Miranda exchanged a look with Devin, their lie seemed to work.

"We'll take our leave," Miranda grabbed Devin and dragged him beside her, "So sorry for the trouble."

Graves blocked the only exit.

"You can spare a few more minutes," Graves said, his other guard waiting at his shoulder to ensure that they didn't try to slip past. "Given that your welfare is my responsibility—"

"My welfare is none of your business," Miranda snapped before clamping her jaw shut. She waited for his reaction, but his demeanor remained confident.

"It is when it's in my home. And what sort of gentleman would I be to let the pair of you wander off together? Tsk, tsk. That would reflect rather poorly on my judgment."

"We can't have that," Miranda said through her teeth.

"Miss Wilde, I am not the enemy. Though," His eyes pierced her for one singular moment like a jab of a knife. "We *will* have to discuss the real reason why the pair of you were snooping around my office. But this is not the time."

"We gave you the real reason," Miranda said, voice rising to a near frantic yell. She was never supposed to yell.

Graves simply smiled.

"Fuck," Devin's voice was low next to her, barely audible. Miranda tensed. "It's True Sight," he continued, "Graves can see lies."

Fuck. They hadn't a hope if he could see right through any excuse they could give. Miranda felt sick, her stomach rolling uncomfortably.

"Don't fret, my dear. Your animosity toward me is hardly secret. I'm not sure how you roped Mr. Drake into your vengeance," Graves's eyes dipped to where her arm was pressed into Devin's side, "Though I'm sure I can guess. Not above trading affection when it suits you, I imagine."

Miranda lunged. Her fist stopped inches from Graves's face, her arm straining. The guard had caught her wrist and they were locked in a stalemate. The guard was strong, even for fae. She couldn't move or shake his grip in the slightest. Miranda started to panic. Graves, however, gave no sign that her outburst bothered him. He made a flicking motion and the guard tossed her backward.

Devin caught her, but she twisted free of his touch. She had never been good at accepting defeat. Whenever her trainer had knocked her to the ground, she had just wanted to hit all the harder.

"Your father will be here soon," Graves continued, "Once I see you safely in his care, Mr. Drake and I can have a little chat about choosing a better location for his trysts."

Her father? A new sort of panic settled into her chest. What would he think of her now? Their story was she had come to this room with Devin to do wicked things. She couldn't tell her father the truth, either. That she intended to spy on Graves and stop his wedding to Cordelia. She was doomed either way but having her father think she was here to debauch herself was unsettling.

"Though I can't say I blame you," Graves continued, "Miss Wilde is quite beautiful. I was almost a victim of her beauty myself. A year ago. But it is clear to me now that her sister is the better match for me." His eyes casually settled on Miranda. "She's more compliant. Younger. More easily persuaded. Less...volatile. She knows what really matters in a relationship."

"And what's that?" Miranda asked, barely keeping her tone civil.

"Pleasing me," Graves said, staring straight into her so that his jovial air finally gave way to the sinister lurking beneath the surface.

Miranda resisted the urge to spit in his face, instead crossing her arms and attempting to keep from doing any further damage. Graves didn't know Cordelia at all. She was none of those things. She could be more headstrong and quick to fight than even Miranda, but he was right about her not having training to protect herself. Delia was still just a human and there was no way she could defend herself against a monster like Graves.

"Yarrow?" Her father's voice, from the hallway. "What's going on? Your guard came and pulled me from the ballroom. Something about Miranda?"

Graves finally stepped aside, allowing her father to enter. When his eyes found Miranda and then landed on Devin behind her, his expression swirled between anger and disappointment. This was humiliating.

"I'm afraid I caught them in the midst of some rather unsavory acts, James. But I arrived before any real harm had been done, thank goodness." Graves said, as her father straightened and assumed a stance Miranda recognized as one of authority. Legs slightly apart, hands behind his back, chin up. She hated when he stood like that. It meant she was going to be reprimanded.

"Miranda Wilde. I'm not sure what happened here, but we can discuss it at home. You will remove yourself from Lord Drake and find your mother immediately. Tell her you are to go straight home." He spoke to Graves, "I would appreciate your discretion in this," he wouldn't meet her eyes and it was killing her to think she disappointed him. "With any luck we can avoid scandal or, Divine forbid, marriage."

Miranda shook her head, hating the injustice of it all. Her father loved her, she knew he did, but he was so blinded by his own perceptions. He couldn't see that Graves was the evil one here. If he knew, if he truly knew what Graves had done to her then Graves would be in pieces. But she had never told him. Now...now he'd never believe her.

"Father, nothing hap—"

"We will talk at home, Miranda. Now please, step away from Lord Drake." Her father looked to Devin, "Who, I might add, I would be well within my rights to challenge over this. You can thank providence that you were not discovered by some gossiping debutante looking to one up a rival and with any luck, we'll avoid the altar, which if Drake's reputation is anything to go on, would be ideal." James took a deep breath, his anger simmering, but controlled. "I suppose it's to be expected when you weren't brought up in the right circles. Raised by a Faery mother, they'd have different standards of behavior."

Miranda's voice failed her. Her father's comment was unfeeling, incredibly rude and not something she'd ever heard from him before.

Her father gently pushed her from the room before she could speak. "Your mother. Now." He ordered.

"Thank you, James," Graves said, "I'll see to the management of Drake."

No. Miranda almost turned back, but then her father's voice stopped her.

"I think I'd like to speak to him myself, if you don't mind." Her father could be just as commanding as Graves and, with the wedding lingering between them, Graves did not want to piss off her father. "Outside. This isn't the sort of conversation for a civilized gathering."

Miranda prayed that Graves agreed. She slowed her retreat as she listened.

"Of course," Graves's voice was tight, like he was speaking through a fake smile. "I'll leave it up to you then."

Once assured Devin wouldn't be left to Graves's mercy, Miranda ran.

Maybe she was a coward, but she did not want to face her father again while Devin was with them. At least she knew her father wouldn't hurt him. Even angry, he was not the sort to resort to violence unnecessarily. She knew it was wrong to leave, but she felt like she was being ripped apart from the inside out, her body pulled in too many directions for one evening.

She found her mother with Cordelia. When their eyes met, her mother set down her drink and came to her side.

"What is it, dear? What's happened?"

"Father will fill you in later, I'm sure. Nothing I say will make a difference now, anyway. He sent me to find you," she took a deep breath, "And for us to await him at home."

"At home?" Her mother chuckled. "And be the first to leave the engagement party of our daughter? What is to be done with Cordelia? She can't leave early and we can't leave her behind."

"Oh, I don't mind, mother," Cordelia said, "It's a family emergency. I'm sure Lord Graves will understand."

Miranda hated the man's name leaving her sister's mouth. Cordelia threaded her arm through Miranda's. "Come mother, it is my party, and I shall decide when I leave it. I'm sure any fiancé of mine will understand that family is most important to me." She strode quickly from the room, Miranda pulled along behind her.

"I...but..." Her mother sputtered for a few moments before following them. "Your father better have a good explanation for this."

The carriage ride was torture. Normally, they wouldn't all fit in a single carriage but her mother insisted they ride together and so she had made the girls squeeze since they no longer cared to keep their dresses presentable. Her mother did nothing but mutter about her displeasure at the whole situation. She asked Miranda to explain three more times, but Miranda could only shake her head. Cordelia held her hand, gently patting it. It helped, but it wasn't enough to distract her from the explosion of what had just happened.

The kiss with Devin that had made her body feel things she'd never felt before. Made her knees weak. She'd dream about that kiss forever, there was no denying it. She hadn't intended to kiss him like that, either. Once her mouth had touched his, instinct took over. It had been thrilling, tantalizing. If she was only going to get one chance to kiss a rogue in a dark room, then she wanted to make the most of it.

It was probably sloppy and amateur, she'd been hasty and clumsy. Dragging him down over the desk hadn't been intentional. She had just wanted him closer, but her damn dress was in the way. Next thing she knew she was falling backward, and his arm had braced next to her and the sound he made...she had felt it everywhere.

She wished she could focus on the bliss of that stolen moment, but the threat hanging over her threatened to crush any solace she sought. Once again, Graves had undermined every facet of her strength. Her fear. Her worry. He had her trembling when Miranda knew she was strong. It was mortifying. And then her father and his rude comments...she'd just left Devin to fend for himself.

She had never felt worse than she did right then. Like her world was falling apart around her and she was utterly helpless to do anything.

The carriage arrived home, and Cordelia ushered her away from their chattering mother to her room. Lady Wilde took the hint and decided to wait on their father for more information, allowing Miranda to retreat with Cordelia.

"We can await father here," Cordelia said, "I'm not sure what's happened, Miri, but you have never looked so shaken."

"I'm not really okay to talk about it," Miranda said, she shirked off the full skirts and all the tedious layers until she was in just a chemise and curled onto her bed. "It was awful, Delia."

Cordelia flopped next to her and began to pluck pins from her hair, smoothing out the strands as she went. "Shh, I'm sure it won't seem as bad in the morning."

"I'm sure it will."

Cordelia laughed and Miranda sat up. It had been so long since she heard her sister laugh, let alone smile or visit her room or talk to her. Just last year they had shared each other's every confidence, now Miranda felt like a stranger, uncertain on what she should say or how to say it.

"Why have you been shutting me out all this time?" Miranda asked, and her sister's soothing gestures stopped.

Cordelia looked away. "I find...it's easier to not talk about it. And I know you, Miri, you'll only try and tell me how awful he is and how I should not marry him. But that would only make the reality all the harder, because mother and father are set on it and I...I don't have a choice."

"You can tell them, Delia, tell them you don't want to marry him."

"Oh, yes, it's so easy to tell our parents when we want our own way. You don't understand. You're their precious guardian daughter. The one with all the power who will continue with the grand tradition of guardians in the family. I'm their feeble human daughter whose only use is to find a good enough match to offset my deficiencies. You have been loved by all and paraded around your whole life. Everyone wants to know the society princess. I am the afterthought. No one remembers Cordelia Wilde, when there is Miranda."

Miranda wanted to shake her head and deny all of it, that her sister was not second to her, was so much more than a 'feeble human' but she realized with a sinking feeling that Cordelia was right. At least, about how the world viewed her and how her accomplishments had always been shadowed to the prestige of Miranda's blood.

Her heart broke for her sister, who she had always viewed as worthy, but perhaps, had not realized that the view from across the hall might be different from across the street. Even her parents, though Miranda wanted to believe they would never consciously hurt either of their children, were guilty of setting Miranda on a higher pedestal, with higher standards, with greater expectations.

"Don't fret over it, Miri, I'm...well, there is nothing I can do. I can't change what I am and I've found solace in—" A mischievous glint returned to Cordelia's eye, a spark Miranda thought long buried. "Well, let's just say I've found ways to cope."

"You could have come to me," Miranda started, guilt warring with everything else. "You're right, I would have rattled on about how much I think Graves is a snake and hardly appropriate to marry a slug, let alone my favorite sister." Cordelia's smile reminded her of how they often joked about favorites when it was only ever just the pair of them. "But if you had told me that is not what you needed, I would have stopped. I just wanted to be there for you and, maybe, you would not have had to endure all this alone."

"I suppose I was a bit closed off—"

"Closed off? You haven't spoken to me for nearly two months aside from pleasantries at the dining table or over tea."

"Well. I don't know." She pushed Miranda backward, and Miranda fell over, always allowing Cordelia to best her and feel stronger. Only, *had* she just pretended to fall? Cordelia's shove had grown more forceful and the shoulder she'd shoved twinged.

The sisters sat in silence for a few moments. As they had when they were children waiting for mother or father to come in and deliver the punishment for whatever they'd broken or causing a ruckus at the worst moments or locking nanny in the closet. They didn't say it aloud, but both knew that they would continue to grin and bear it.

Neither of them were very brave about standing up to their parents. Miranda was afraid they wouldn't believe her. Cordelia was afraid she'd disappoint them. Though, perhaps it was time to stop being scared.

Miranda knew her father had returned when she heard her mother's stern voice rising even from the lower foyer. Cordelia made a break for her own bedroom, kissing Miranda's cheek and whispering 'good luck.'

Miranda quickly buried herself in her covers. Hopefully, her father would allow her the small mercy of waiting until morning to scold her. She shut her eyes, feigning sleep, until she opened them again to a sky full of stars and a tense silence.

Miranda rolled onto her back to stare at the canopy of her bed. She was not going to find rest tonight. Instead, she leapt to her feet and pulled on the first dress she saw that she could do up herself. She had to make sure Devin was alright. And...her stomach flipped, a jolt of nerves rioting down to her toes. She was *not* seeking him out for any other reason than to check on him. It was *not* because she wanted to kiss him again. They could never kiss again, because that would mean admitting she found him even somewhat likable and Miranda hated to lose.

Though, she wanted to think he had enjoyed kissing her, at least. She may not be suited for him—he would surely look down on her innocence and circumstances—but it would be nice to know she hadn't made a fool of herself.

Like she had with Graves and her father.

Miranda opened her window and nimbly climbed down. So much had gone wrong, certainly the worst was behind her for the moment.

CHAPTER SEVEN

D EVIN STUMBLED INTO HIS apartment above the Black Heart, knocking over a side table and sending a stack of letters flying through the foyer. He didn't even have the excuse of alcohol. At present, he was miserably sober.

He retreated to his apartment in the Fells, craving familiar walls instead of lingering reminders of life's cruel tragedies. Tonight held enough cruel tragedies to contend with.

It was a bachelor's apartment, but large and expensive. The only personal touch he added among the pre-furnished fixtures aside from a bed, were special curtains to block out the sun. Servants were instructed to open them each dusk, as opposed to dawn.

He meandered toward the sitting room, not bothering to fiddle with the lanterns, and relying on the moon and muscle memory. It would be daylight soon. He could sense the sun pushing the moon from the sky. He needed a drink.

Tonight, had been hell. Crawling over the arm of a sofa with a groan, his face sank into the soft cushions, and he reached for one of the bottles that encircled the couch like a liquor moat. The staff was instructed to never move his collection, as he liked to have bottles on hand for nights just like this. His fingers closed around the cool glass, and he pulled it to his lips.

Fuck. Empty.

He tossed it to the carpet, and it rolled with dull thuds as he reached for another. Empty. Another. Empty.

He clawed at his face and hair, messing up his valet's attempt to make him presentable. It was laughable that he thought he could do this. And though he had plenty to worry about, it was not Graves's inevitable retaliation that haunted him just now.

Miranda.

Their embrace was supposed to be a chaste show to keep their true motives secret. Miranda was a lady! He would have bet his club that she was not the sort to explore passionate embraces with men in dark corners. All evidence suggested she was an innocent, a maiden. Yet, she'd kissed with the finesse of a savant, and he'd reacted like a virgin teenager necking for the first time.

The cynic in him boasted that working with her had been a mistake from the beginning. If he thought he was doomed after dancing with her, kissing her was a dive into insanity from which he couldn't charm his way out. Yet, what did he hope would come of continuing his acquaintance with her? He had only to listen to her father to understand his place in her world.

Lord Wilde had rambled on about honor and marriage and how dare he take liberties with his daughter. Devin had listened. Acknowledged the man's anger. Apologized. Assured him he would never see Miranda again. All empty platitudes. He was numb to the bombardment of emotions at that point.

But it had made clear one thing. He was not cut out for Miranda's world and he had no place in it.

Don't kid yourself. You *don't think you're good enough for her.*

Devin stared into the harsh shadows of his apartment. None of this mattered. The kiss was over. There was no need to muse over what-ifs. Miranda was gone, her father would never let her leave the house after this. She was better off. *He* may have slipped into a new tier of hell, but at least she would be okay.

Would she be okay? His thoughts spiraled to the look on Miranda's face while Graves had spoken of their past. Miranda, the confident and capable woman he knew, shrank to a stony girl desperately trying to hide her fear and shame.

It had taken every single shred of self-control he possessed to keep from tearing Graves apart as he listened to him carefully craft his words to threaten and sting.

Devin shifted, trying to get comfortable despite his legs still stuck up at an odd angle on the arm of the too-small-for-him-couch. With effort, he managed to flip onto his back, which was better, and Miranda returned once again as he closed his eyes.

This time the feel of her hands on him, pulling at his hair, her lips so willing and eager, how he had felt her in parts of his soul he'd thought locked away and crushed under the cruelty of the world.

He opened his eyes again. There was little use in pretending he'd ever have a moment's peace now, like he wouldn't see her every time he closed his eyes. He tasted her lips, knew the sounds she made when lost in pleasure, and no dream could compensate.

Was she home now? In her room, maybe, just as tortured and lost as he was?

Devin sat up and attempted to kick one of the bottles. He missed and the bottle merely tipped with an unsatisfying thud.

What was he even hoping for? That she'd look past his flaws enough to bed him? Is that really all he wanted from her? Physical satisfaction and then, what, he'd go back to pretending that she'd never strolled into his club and challenged the very fragile fabric of his reality?

Miranda is not coming back.

"I bloody know that," he snapped at the darkness.

This is why he avoided attachment. This is why he kept everyone at a distance. Or loss was inevitable.

His mother. Lost to despair and rejection while their meager loft literally poisoned her over the last seventeen years of her life. Trace exposure to iron had weakened her to illness. Devin might have realized sooner, but he wasn't affected by iron.

His fellow soldiers when Graves had ordered they retreat. They'd been outnumbered, trying to hold their position when Graves gave the command to run. Despite having better cover holding their position, Graves ordered them to surround him while he made a break for it. A barricade of bodies.

Devin had slipped in his friend's blood pooling on the grass. Felt it spray on his face as another fell. Heard their cries as they succumbed to injuries in the midst of the enemy with nowhere to turn. Graves had doomed them all.

Somehow, Devin managed to make it back to a friendly encampment, but he couldn't remember exactly how. And Graves spun the tale of that battle with his own narrative, one that painted him the hero who had done all he could to save his unit. The survivors were threatened and bribed for their silence. Devin included. Now, no one would believe him even though Graves had lost his leverage.

Graves needed the sort of justice he couldn't escape from. Permanent.

Devin released his clenched fists.

"Sir," a footman's voice sounded far away, but when Devin opened his eyes, the man was just in front of him, "So glad you're awake, sir. There's a woman here to see you, quite insistent, but I thought you'd prefer to get cleaned up first? At the very least, not to be found in...such a state."

Devin sat up, groaning a bit as his head spun. How long had he laid in that position? It left a terrible crick in his neck. When he managed to look at the footman, he instantly noted the glow surrounding him. An eager, grass green with touches of resilient amber and loyal plum. Devin had never had to decipher auras, always understood them intuitively. And he needed a drink.

Whoever was looking for him, it could wait till he had a drink. "Give me ten minutes," Devin murmured.

Wait...she? His heart stopped.

"Very good, sir. I'll send her—"

"Devin?"

The footman turned, startled and ready to shoo the person back to the door. But a blaze of color forced past the younger man. Her voice was equal parts thrilling and maddening.

What was she doing here?

She was here.

Before anyone could stop her, Miranda had pushed her way into the sitting room. It was the first time he'd ever seen her without the buffer of inebriation.

Miranda stood with her hair down, blonde waves swirling around her shoulders in brilliant contrast to the warmer tones in her skin. A modest dress hugged her curves, not even a cloak to cover her shoulders, as if she had rushed out in the first and simplest ensemble she could find. And the light coming from her was a proud and determined cerulean that traced her outline in a thin, but solid pattern. Surrounding the blue was a blaze of ruby passion and adventurous tangerine that erupted into the darkness of his apartment. Her aura was loud. Overpowering.

She was gorgeous.

"Devin." She ran to him and looked ready to hug him, but hesitated. A flash of doubt surged through the stronger colors of her personality. "I..."

"What are you doing here?" He asked, accusation feathering his words. He was elated that she was here. Giddy. But he was furious with her for leaving the safety of her home when Graves could retaliate at any time. Agonized that no matter what she was here for he *could not touch her*. His fingers itched to touch her. But he couldn't risk what it might lead to...his breathing grew ragged, desperate. *What would it lead to?*

"I had to make sure you were okay. I tried your...other house first, but when you weren't there I knew you'd be here," she started, innocently and naively sincere. "I hated leaving you with my father like that."

Devin looked away. The colors of her, the way they burned bright around her was proving too much for him. He desperately needed a drink so he could concentrate again.

"Your father did me a favor, though I'm not sure if he realized it or not." Devin crossed to a cupboard and threw it open, searching for a bottle that wasn't empty.

He pulled one free and yanked out the cork with his teeth. After a healthy swig—only enough to dull the colors of Miranda, rather than snuff them—he said, "Much better. Now. I appreciate the concern, love, but you shouldn't be here. And I think we both know it."

"I shall see her to the door, sir," the footman offered and went to gently guide Miranda, but she spun from his grip. The footman wisely made himself scarce. Devin almost ordered him to stay as a chaperone, if he thought it would help.

"No, I won't be escorted away like this is some unwanted social call. We have to discuss what happened."

"No, darling, we really don't."

"And you have a drinking problem, by the way," she yelled.

Devin's jaw hardened. "Yes, I'm well aware of my problems. Unfortunately, it's the only way I can pretend I'm not some abomination looked upon with either pity or disdain."

That gave her pause. "I don't..."

"You don't what? Look at me with pity for being a half-fae bastard? You may not realize it, Mira, but others do. I know people like your father like to think this city is built on tolerance, but I assure you, those of us that test that tolerance know the truth. People will never accept those that are different. They're too scared."

"I'm not scared," Miranda said, chin in the air. She was so sheltered, yet wanting so badly to be noble, it was almost charming. Except, it also hurt. "I don't look at you any different. I commented about the drinking because I don't want to see you hurting yourself."

"So, you'd be okay being seen with me in public? Fine with the looks? With the whispered comments? Content with losing valuable social alliances because you chose to associate with the notorious bastard who should never have been a lord in the first place? What happened at the ball was merely a taste of the ruin you'd face, and that's not even commenting on the dangers of you being here in the middle of the night."

Miranda was quiet, and Devin shook his head. "Listen, it's not your fault. This is the way the world is, sweetheart. You and I are just stuck with it."

"No, I want to be one of those that change it. That's the whole reason Unity exists. We're trying to overcome all this, and I know some people have latched on to the old ways of thinking, but they won't be in charge forever—"

He stepped into her space, crowding her with his height and broader build. She swallowed, but met his stare with her own resolution.

"Your ideals are admirable, but they won't matter in the end. You and I are not suited," he said each word slowly, nearly whispering.

"I never said we were suited," she said, matching his rigid stare. He was too close to her, but once he had started toward her, he hadn't been able to stop.

"Then why are you here, Miranda?" His hand reached out, feathering down her arm.

"To make sure you were okay," she said, eyes fluttering till they nearly closed. Her lips parted with shallow breaths.

"Liar."

Her jaw tensed. Steel consumed the wistful daze in her eyes. She teetered on her feet, but did not retreat. He chanced moving that much closer, fighting to keep his hands at his side. His fingers played at the fabric of her dress, biding their time, waiting for him to finally give in.

"I was also...curious," she said, then she chewed on her lip as if uncertain. "You're likely the only chance I'll have of...well, kissing. Was it bad? Or was I..." she licked her lips, and he watched the motion like a tiger stalking prey, "Good at it? Did I do it right?" She looked away, starting to fidget.

He would have laughed. He wanted to. Nothing was more ludicrous than Miranda Wilde standing in front of him like a siren calling to a man on the last fringes of control and thinking she was lacking.

"It is taking considerable strength not to devour you where you stand," he managed, "And you doubt your capacity to please?"

Her eyes went wide. "I didn't think...but I didn't know what I was doing—"

He lifted her chin with his hand, now so close they were pressed together, her breath warm on his lips. "Mira, you are going to have to say no or I'm afraid I'm not going to stop."

He felt her shiver. He felt it like a surge of longing straight to his cock.

The green of her eyes softened again, and she shook her head. "Please, don't stop."

And that simple request was his undoing.

Miranda was molten as Devin kissed her, knees nearly buckling except that his arms had wrapped around her, holding her upright.

Her whole body screamed *yes*.

But it wasn't enough—she wanted him closer. Once again, she was not herself. Some other Miranda was wrapping her arms around his shoulders, air forced through her nose so she didn't suffocate as she enjoyed each delicious glide of his mouth on hers. A soft gasp eased up her throat. In the study, she'd almost believed he'd hated kissing her, the way he seemed to merely react. Now he was kissing her fervently, like she was air and he was drowning.

He backed her toward the couch and before her legs bent in submission, Miranda maneuvered so that Devin fell onto it instead. He stared up at her for a breathless minute, eyes wide.

She had not intended to be rough as she crawled into his lap, squeezing either side of his hips with her thighs to hold him in place, the way she might with an enemy she wanted to subdue. Her fingers twisted in his collar, like she was pinning him in a fight instead of tasting the lingering bitterness of alcohol in his mouth. She was fueled by instinct, but she'd never let desire guide her before. A part of her still wondered if she was doing this right. Her body was singing, thrumming sensations both sweet and exhilarating. A blooming, consuming hunger that she was desperate to feed. But did that mean he felt the same?

Whatever his opinion on the matter, he uttered no complaints. Unable to move anything else, Devin's hands began to explore her body over her clothes, trailing fire where his fingers pressed or squeezed, like he knew exactly where she wanted to feel pressure. When her breath caught in her throat, his fingers lingered.

He only stopped the evocative search when his hands reached the swell of her breasts. He waited, teasing at the seam of fabric in her dress but never crossing. It was like he was tentative, unsure how far she was willing to go. Which, honestly, she had not expected.

Truly, she hadn't known *what* to expect, but Devin respectfully awaiting her permission before fondling her breasts as she pinned him to the couch and his tongue explored her mouth was not it.

She let her teeth scrape at his lips as she pulled back.

"Do it," she commanded.

His palm covered her through the dress and she shook her head.

"No," she whispered, and her fingers turned to claws on the back of his neck. "I know you're holding back. Don't."

"Fuck, Miranda," he hissed, but he obeyed and worked down her dress, exposing her breasts to the cold air of his apartment. She moaned into the darkness as his fingers danced over her taut nipples. A combination of the sensation and the thought of him touching her created a heady mix of tantalization and desire, made her desperate for something she didn't understand. Her hips started to move, craving a friction she couldn't satisfy while still. She stopped once she felt the hard length of him through her undergarments.

Devin choked on air, his hands flying to her hips and squeezing. For a moment, she was absolutely still.

He didn't attempt to push her further or to move her as she accepted the idea that this was really happening. This wasn't just a kiss, this was an intimate exploration of places normally secretive and hidden. She had looked through books and illustrations with Lydia, so she knew the basics. But a lady was not supposed to know what was in a man's trousers, let alone that grinding against it created the most amazing friction that radiated an even more intense pleasure than his kiss or his hands on her breasts.

It was intoxicating.

She ground her hips into him again.

Devin's head fell backward as he sucked in a breath through his teeth. His fingers squeezed hard enough to bruise. The sound of him unraveling egged her on, confirming that this was pleasurable for both of them. She continued to rock and adjust until she found the rhythm her body needed.

"Shit..." His voice was rough, strained. And delightfully erotic. His hands left her hips, clawing over his own face as he kept his head back, facing the ceiling instead of her. He was still holding back.

"I won't break," she breathed.

"I know that," he whined, desire and restraint smothering the smooth, confident air he always boasted. "You're fucking incredible and restraint is *killing* me."

"Then don't use restraint," she ordered as she continued her even, rhythmic movements.

"You don't know what you're asking," he said, as he bit down on his tongue. "I could ruin you or worse. I could hurt you or scare you or push you too far without realizing...There are so many ways..." His hands skimmed her hips. He locked them behind his head. "I want to..." His gaze aligned with her chest, watching her breasts sway up and down from the corner of his eye before he snapped them shut. His breathing grew ragged.

Miranda liked it. Watching him struggle to keep his hands away from her, *wanting* her with such intensity yet resisting was its own thrill.

His words were stilted, said between breaths, "And, Miranda, my control is wearing very thin," he swallowed, opening his eyes again, but avoiding the temptation of her chest to glare up at her face. "Very...very thin."

She bit her lip, excited by the idea that she might make him lose that control. Perhaps it was her turn to be the irrepressible rake. She leaned down so that her hair fell over her shoulder in a gentle wave, never ceasing the slow rock of her hips. "I am literally throwing myself against you," she ground her hips harder before adding in a sultry whisper, "And now you're going to disappoint me, Devin?"

With a growl his hand snaked behind her head, fingers tense on her neck as they speared through her hair and positioned her head to kiss her roughly, both of them desperately balancing lips and tongues and gasps for air.

She hooked her own hands around the back of his head to steady herself against his aggressive assault of her mouth. She couldn't name why his ferocity echoed through her, heightening the friction where she was grinding against him. Or why the harsh crash of his mouth bordered on painful, but she would have killed him if he stopped. She was chasing something that she couldn't name, desperate to reach it.

"I'm so close," she whispered, not knowing what other words to use.

"Fucking hell." He ripped away from her lips and drew his tongue over her exposed nipple.

"Holy fuck—" All at once, the sensations overwhelmed her. Her eyes shot open, unable to speak or think beyond the pleasure thrumming *everywhere*.

Her arms began to shake, her eyes wide open but she saw nothing as every single sense she possessed was consumed by the erotic combination of the rough scrape of his mouth against her sensitive skin and the movement of her hips. Her grip tightened, dragging him closer until he couldn't move his head away if he wanted. A muffled moan was her only indication that he was okay with her use of force.

She was clinging to him, her entire body unmoored except for where he touched her.

His tongue worked over the tender skin, lapping at her nipple until it was suddenly too much. She was about to shatter into pieces. The couch creaked and protested, the wood frame splintering.

And then she was there, finally, riding waves of pleasure somehow even more powerful than anything before. Her movements turned erratic, stuttering. Her nails dragged through his hair and down his neck to grasp for the support of his strong shoulders. Only as the last tendrils of pleasure stole from her limbs did she begin to loosen her grip.

She leaned on him more. The caress of fabric was electric on her heated skin and she adjusted so she was no longer in danger of brushing against his still hard erection.

Her hair fanned around her as she finally leaned toward him, her forehead resting on his.

She couldn't see his face, her eyes closed in lazy stupor. She feared she'd see a smirk of victory if she dared look.

"Are you alright?" He asked, when she had been silent for too long.

She opened an eye.

No smirk. His irises were still more black than blue, desire lingered in his gaze, but the rest of him was thoughtful, almost serious. Not what she expected. Maybe gloating, but not reservation.

"I..." She found it almost funny, humor taking over her mouth and threatening to make her laugh—not with derision, but with genuine mirth. "I suppose I understand the draw of coupling now. It's quite addicting."

He did laugh, but she didn't feel mocked. "*That*, was merely fore-play. A taste of the possibilities." He used a finger to sweep some of her hair behind her ear. It was an oddly sweet gesture, completely unfitting the brash rogue he often exemplified. "Had I not found my last shred of decency I'd show you exactly what could be accomplished if, for a start, I stripped you of every piece of these cumbersome garments."

Her body tingled as he spoke, thrilled by the possibility, but then...what possibility? Was she going down the path of fallen woman who gives in to lust with no promise of marriage? *Was* this love? No, it was attraction, certainly, and...well, he had his moments. But Miranda had no plans to get married and settle down. She just wanted...she didn't know what she wanted. To play this game a little longer? To enjoy the hunt and mystery and danger, but also maybe see what other pleasures Devin could show her, because it was far too late now. She wanted to explore everything. Screw his decency. However much the sentiment made her appreciate him all the more, her body wanted the unscrupulous cad.

His smile turned somber as she grew quiet. She was nestled in his side, his arm hooked around her in an embrace almost romantic. He just kept surprising her. She thought he would be unbearable at her weakness. She had just given in to his flirting and charms, succumbing to his allure. Yet he had kept her in control the entire time, allowing her to decide how far things went. Resisting her to the point of pain if his expression had been any indication.

Miranda was struck with the urge to kiss him again, but, not out of lust or desire, the urge was more tender than that. She wanted to kiss him because...because...she didn't know why. Or maybe she did and she just didn't want to admit it, not even to herself. But it was dangerously close to a need for affection.

"I'm still new to this," she started, and normally she would be loath to sound so uncertain and unsure, especially to someone like him, but in this area she did concede that he was the expert and she the novice. She had no plans to marry, but given how enjoyable it was to share intimacy with a man, she would not be opposed to other attachments in the future. Perhaps from less annoying suitors. And, whatever her ire with him during the day, she felt safe enough to continue. "So...was it, were you—"

He silenced her with a soft, gentle kiss. Her shock kept her from reacting with more than a giddy smile. Maybe he liked her more than she suspected. Maybe his flirting and banter wasn't just show. Her heart started racing. If she was right, did that change anything? Did she—maybe—want to try?

"If you're doubting your utter prowess in satisfaction again, I'm going to have no choice but to prove how very proficient you are."

A blush bloomed on her cheeks, but she liked the implications. It felt less like a jest and more like admiration.

He stared into her eyes for a moment. No smirk. No mask. He gazed at her with a tenderness that sparked something inside her, not her lust or carnal desires, but her heart. He looked at her and her heart answered.

Heavens, maybe she did like him. A little.

The moment grew heavy, the stillness around them suddenly too still. His finger began a slow dance up and down her arm, though not in an evocative way. Affection. Tenderness. These were not words she had ever thought would describe him.

Maybe she was more than a skirt to chase, maybe he liked the whole aggressive and impulsive side of her. Did just the parry of words thrill him as much as it did her? Surely, he was too experienced to be affected by such a trivial exchange. Yet, nothing about what they just did suggested he was indifferent to her. Her heart lurched again, her mind carrying her down fanciful daydreams that she didn't dare ponder for too long, lest he speak and burst her indulgent bubble.

"Mira," he said, soft and with a tremor of uncertainty. Did she make him nervous? He made her nervous. And her stomach flitted with butterflies when he called her 'Mira.' No one had ever done so before and it felt like a secret for only them, hidden from the rest of the world like the bruises his fingers left on her hip.

She tensed, waiting, but whatever he had wanted to say was not to be shared. The immortal she'd passed in Devin's home, came crashing into the room.

"Drake," the man started, then threw up his hands and averted his eyes as Miranda jumped up and adjusted herself. Blood bloomed so fiercely in her cheeks she feared they'd catch fire. "Damn it, Devin." He pinched the bridge of his nose.

"We're clothed, you prig. What the hell is it?" Devin stood, moving so he blocked her from view.

Jack uncovered his eyes and started, "It's..."

He was cut off by a racket of thuds and bangs. Screams.

Devin ran for the door. Miranda followed on his heels. Perhaps it was a fight between patrons? She glanced at the sunlight streaming through the windows. It was morning? Her parents would have gone looking for her by now. She had to get home or she'd never be able to explain her absence. She was a terrible liar.

"What's the situation," Devin asked as they flew down the stairs, taking two at a time. Jack moved with little effort, like he was walking a leisurely pace instead of full out sprinting down several flights.

"It came out of nowhere. There's a group of them just stormed the door. They were inside before anyone could blink. They're wearing all black, no identifying markings of any kind. Is this Wraith? A message?"

"Graves." Devin's voice was cold steel. "Jack, get as many out as you can. Patrons. Servants. All of them."

"Security is already trying to hold them off," Jack commented before disappearing like smoke to his task.

"Mira," Devin called as he stopped at the bottom of the stairwell. He took her hand and pulled her focus to him. She bobbed on her feet. Ready for whatever awaited. "There is a back exit. You head that way and go home. Do you understand?"

She almost nodded, too full of adrenaline to listen clearly, but then she caught his meaning and tore her hand free of his clutches.

"What? No." Who was he to tell her what to do, anyway? "Not a chance. I'm staying *and* I'm helping. I've trained for this. I can handle myself."

"Damn it, Mira, I can't bloody argue with you right now. I can't focus on what I need to if I'm worried about your safety."

"Then don't. I'm stronger than you," she countered.

"You're impossible. Stubborn. Infuriating. Bloody temptress who can't listen to reason to save your damn life." He sounded seconds from stomping his feet on the ground. "I don't care how capable you are, this is not your fight. I am telling you, *go home.*"

She narrowed her eyes, hoisting up her chin in defiance.

"Don't," he ordered. "I know that look, Miranda."

And in a battle of wills, she had a feeling hers would win. He met her stare, holding on longer than anyone else might have.

"You can't tell me what to do," she said through her teeth. There was nothing he could say that would stop her. She was not going to leave him, *again*, to fend for himself. Not when she could help.

He hung his head. "You are going to be the death of me."

She brightened, fluttering her lashes coyly. "Promise?"

"This is not a time for jokes, Miranda. These are likely Graves's assassins here to kill me. And you're begging to be in the crossfire."

"I know," she snapped, shaking her head. "If you just shut up and let me help you, we might have already finished this."

"No, no, sweetheart." He held up a finger. "We are not finished. Not in the slightest. As soon as this is over, we're having a long chat about needless heroism and you thinking you're in charge of every waking moment when, in the real world, you control very little."

She rolled her eyes and that made him seethe, his jaw clenched so tight she heard his teeth grinding. "If you're done lecturing me, can we just do this?"

He ran a hand through his hair. "*Fuck.*" He closed his eyes for a moment, possibly trying to recover some of his composure. He rounded on her with force, adding, "Swear that if anything happens to me, you'll get out of there. Immediately. Don't worry about the damn building or saving me or getting even. You get out of there."

She locked gazes with him again. This time, she was the one who retreated. It was a fair enough request, since she didn't plan on allowing that to happen. "Fine. I promise." She pushed past him and out the door that connected his apartment to the club.

"No, please, after you," she heard him grumble as he followed her.

They entered a room where people dressed in black continued to destroy and smash everything they could see. Miranda's heart stopped at the destruction and chaos. This was a message. They'd gotten too close to Graves.

Devin followed Miranda into mayhem. The door led to the gaming room, where he first saw Miranda days ago—*had it only been*

days?—most of the sturdy, green felted tables were destroyed. The chairs tossed about like a child's toys.

Clothed in black, their faces covered, Graves's enforcers tore apart everything. At least a dozen, if not more if the noise from the other room was any indication. Devin's home, the one thing he had built for himself or took any pride in, was being ripped to pieces.

He must have stood silent much longer than he realized, because the next thing he knew Miranda had yanked him from the path of flying debris.

While Devin found his footing, Miranda rushed forward without a thought or care, brazenly approaching one of the masked enforcers and punching them square in the face.

Devin shook off his stupor and focused on the enemy. Focused on stopping them from doing further damage, instead of fixating on what was already too late to save. He unsheathed a knife from his boot as he ran for Miranda, enforcers converging on her.

"Your left," he said, swinging the knife. Miranda slipped out of range and Devin caught an incoming punch with the blade. It slipped between the fingers of the enforcer's fist and out the back of their hand. They screamed. Blood sprayed. They took the damn knife with them as they jerked away.

Miranda was grinning, her cheeks flushed. She wiped at a bloody lip.

"They're strong," she said, dropping low and sweeping her leg out to knock another enforcer to the floor. Once their face was at the right height, Devin kicked straight into it, bone crunching under his heel. "Very, unnaturally strong," she finished.

She shared a look with him that he understood. These were Graves's new soldiers. The experimented fae who were now fueled by the blood of the Divine. And if the Divine's blood made humans equal to fae when they created the guardian subrace, then these fae were currently the most powerful beings in the city. He must have been further along in his research than the note suggested.

A pair of enforcers charged. Miranda used her foot to flick a fractured chair into her hands like a shield and rammed it forward into the attacker so the fragmented legs pierced the enforcer's chest with a sickening squelch. Blood dribbled from their nose as they slumped to the ground.

"Strong, but untrained," she commented as she tossed the skewered enforcer aside.

Devin had used the other enforcer's momentum to thrust them up and over, landing them on the last intact table. He winced at the destruction to his property. Things that had taken months to procure all destroyed in a moment.

"Behind you," Miranda shouted.

Devin side-stepped and caught an arm with an incoming blade—*his* blade—and with a slight twist he brought the arm down on his shoulder, breaking it at the elbow.

Miranda dove in front of him. Caught the blade as it fell and twisted into the slide until she was on her feet to thrust it into the eye of another.

Devin straightened his shirt as, for now, there were no new enemies to dispatch. "We seem to work well together, Mira."

"Don't let it go to your head." She grinned, twirling his knife in her skilled hands and his thoughts drifted toward a better use for those skills.

He swallowed.

Was it wrong to be turned on right now? Probably. It's not like he could sweep her in his arms and kiss the smug look off her face. And now that he'd had a taste, his body was screaming at him to indulge. If he thought her mere temptation before, she was close to irresistible now.

He avoided locking eyes with her, too afraid he'd see the same spark of desire mirrored back at him. Would she force him into a wall, hands like claws in his shirt or down his back, nails just starting to bite at his skin as she kissed him? This was hardly the time to imagine Miranda ripping through his clothes like paper, pinning him with her body or commanding him exactly where she wanted. The same way she'd been forceful and commanding a mere hour ago, taking her pleasure with a ruthlessness that made his blood run too hot.

His eyes landed on her. Unable to resist.

And lust bloomed in her gaze.

He could forget the loss, forget that the damage around him was devastating, for just one more stolen moment to hear her breathing hitch as she came undone against him.

More commotion from the other room broke the tension. Devin glanced around, a shield of numb emptiness settling over him as they moved to the next room. Miranda tossed him the knife and he caught it, but barely.

"You need the protection more than I do," she teased before entering the rooms devoted to his clienteles' baser interests. This room was normally cast in shadows and dim, warm lighting. But that was during club hours and the sun was rising fast. The softer touches of velvets and satin were in shreds. Enforcers threw benches and chaise lounges into a heap. Another doused the growing pile in a clear liquid.

They were going to burn the place down.

Miranda grappled with an enforcer, no match for them in strength, she was easily tossed aside. Devin started forward, but hadn't a chance to move before she nimbly rolled into the fall and snatched an end table as she stood.

Once again he was riveted to how her lithe body moved. How she smashed the solid table into the enforcer's side, sending shards of wood flying through the room. The enforcer was unfazed by the blow, but her intent had been to get close enough to leap and toss a leg around the enforcer's shoulders.

Using the momentum of her jump, her thighs twisted around their head before using her entire body to offset their balance and send them both crashing to the ground. Miranda popped to her feet and slammed her foot down on the enforcer's head. For a moment, Devin's only thoughts were of her thighs clenching around *his* face...

Devin tore his eyes from Miranda. She hardly needed his assistance and there had to be something productive he could do aside from standing there gawking. Though, it was now clear that adrenaline was tunneling his thoughts, blocking out the greater picture, and intently focused on Miranda tearing a slit in her dress so she could roundhouse an enforcer into a wall.

He had barely taken a step when the bigger picture started to put itself together. An enforcer flicked a match and tossed it into the sopping wreckage. They were burning the place down now, *right now*.

Time was up.

He ran for Miranda.

Devin was behind her when she dodged a punch that hit him square in the shoulder, sending him spinning onto the floor. Devin opened his eyes to an unbalanced ceiling—or perhaps that was just his vision that was unbalanced—and his shoulder burning.

Miranda helped him to his feet and every movement sent waves of hot acid through his arm and chest. His shoulder was out of alignment.

"You're hurt—"

"Doesn't matter...move," he pushed her forward with his good arm, urging her away as flames erupted behind them. With all the wood and the amount of starter fluid drenching things, they'd be engulfed in minutes. The enforcers stopped fighting and started retreating, their work done. Miranda didn't leave his side, instead letting him lean on her as they cleared the room and he guided her toward a back exit.

Once outside Devin was blinded by the sun. His propensity for the moon made it all the more painful to stare daylight in the face. He got himself to a crate of supplies, stacks of them lined the back alleys of the club, and closed his eyes to the throbbing in his shoulder.

Miranda approached, tentatively looking without getting too close to him.

She pursed her lips. "It's misaligned. It's happened to me a few times." She hovered in his face, his eyes barely open because of the sun and pain. "Just focus on me and it'll be fine in a moment."

Shit. He knew what she was going to do and he steeled himself.

In a flash, she adjusted her body and applied pressure at just the right angle until his shoulder gave with a horrendous *pop*. He doubled over, but the radiating agony was subsiding. He started to catch his breath.

"You'll be sore for a bit," Miranda added. Devin kept his eyes on the ground. As the pain subsided to a dull, but tolerable roar, his senses began to clear. His club was gone. Ruined. Beyond repair. Everything he'd built, gone in a blink.

"Devin, I'm so sorry," she offered, and pity and concern replaced her normal fire. "Maybe there's a way to repair the damage."

He could hear the crackle of flames taking root fast. The loss was more devastating than she could realize. She could lose her house and still have her place in the world, her wealth. This wasn't just his livelihood, this club was the proof that he had something more to offer than drinking his life away and a fruitless hunger for revenge.

"It's time you went home, Miranda," he said, standing upright.

In the sting of daylight, with so much devastation heaped on him over a single night, he had nothing left. The servants and his security had been gathered outside by Jack. They were mingling just ahead, near a different exit. Together they could keep the flames down and maybe save the structure, if not the contents.

"But..." She reached for him, and he pulled away. There was nothing more she could do aside from confusing his already frayed sanity. He didn't want comfort. He wanted to lay down and not get up. He wanted to throw and smash what was left, because what was the point? More than anything, he did not want to hurt Miranda or let her see that he could fracture, too. It was getting very difficult to hide his weakness. He wasn't about to allow himself to fall into her arms and let the warmth of her soothe his desolation. She had to leave. He was going to break.

"Of course, you're not going to listen," he said, voice gruff and harsh, "Fine. Don't listen. I'm not your keeper." He walked past her and tried to ignore the hurt in her eyes that pierced him like a spear. He kept walking.

"What is wrong with you?" Her voice followed him, a harsh yell that drew attention. Jack twitched like he'd heard, but kept directing those left with water and sand toward the fire.

Devin stopped. "Does the princess take offense to being ignored? Pissy about not getting your way for once?"

He regretted snapping the moment he'd done it, but it was too late.

"Fuck you," she spat, getting in his face. "You're a miserable, self-destructive, asshole hiding behind bravado."

Fine, if she wanted to throw around harsh truths, he had a few of his own. "And you're an entitled pain-in-the-ass who can't handle not being in control of every situation."

"Why do you work so hard to ruin everything?" She was getting closer, so he stepped away, determined not to let his body's draw to hers pull him back into her clutches. Her hands were working with her temper, fists clenching, hands slicing through the air to enunciate her words.

"You knew what you were getting into, sweetheart."

"Forgive me for thinking you could grow up for two seconds."

"Grow up? That's a laugh coming from you, who's never left her own backyard until a few days ago. What do you know of growing up, Miranda? Of hardship or suffering? Ever hold a dying friend as their aura snuffed out?"

Her jaw tensed. "No. I—their what?"

"Of course you haven't. You're protected and sheltered. As it bloody should be. You don't need to debase yourself with lowlife's in the Fells." *You deserve better than tarnishing your light with my darkness.*

She growled, reaching for his face like she wanted to squeeze the life from him. "I can't believe I was starting to fall for—" Her jaw snapped shut, but Devin's anger pivoted on her last words. She stood straighter, raising her pretty chin in that way she did whenever she wanted to be braver than she felt. "Forget it."

His jaw hung open, because there were very few ways to finish that declaration. He must have misheard her. Miranda turned away and ran.

Devin watched her without moving. Speechless. Until he felt Jack nudge him with an elbow.

"You're fucking stupid, boss," Jack said, his tone droll.

Devin glared at him.

"Just saying. If a girl that gorgeous was willing to be alone with me in a dark room, I'd not blow it the very next morning, you know? Savor it a bit."

Jaw clenched, Devin said through his teeth, "You'd never find a girl to be alone with you, Jack."

Jack nodded. "Yeah, that's fair."

"Put out the fire and take an assessment of the damage. And shut up while you do it."

Jack chuckled, no humor reaching his face as his features retained his signature scowl. "Yes, sir." He mock saluted and disappeared. Or, rather, he moved so silently and quickly it often appeared that way.

Devin turned away from the club, away from Miranda's retreating form.

Was he an idiot?

Maybe he had just lost something that he was only starting to realize he wanted to keep. But that was exactly the problem. He couldn't keep Miranda. And now his damn heart was starting to pine for something completely unattainable. The moment his walls threatened to crack in her presence, he'd pushed her so far away she might never come back. It was better that she was gone.

She was out of reach.

Forbidden.

She was seeping into every fiber and facet of his being and there was nothing he could do about it.

CHAPTER EIGHT

MIRANDA CLIMBED THROUGH HER window, numb and drained. With any luck, her parents had decided to sleep in and hadn't checked on her yet.

She began to undress, slipping out of her clothes—now torn and rumpled and full of memories that made her blush—until she was bare to the cold air of her room. She stoked the fire in her hearth, only embers remained from when the maid had lit it before heading to bed for the night.

Miranda needed to scrub the day from her skin. She stepped in front of the mirror as she grabbed a towel and sloshed it into the water basin beside it, then rubbed in a healthy lather of soap. If she asked for water for a full bath, her parents would know and they'd come interrogate her. Right now, she just wanted to be clean.

As she set to scrubbing and rinsing, Miranda took assessment of the damage. Bruises were setting in, a few purple ones on her legs and arms from taking hits. Her eyes lingered on her hips, where Devin's hands held her, grasped for her, burned into her skin like a brand.

She lifted the mirror and turned it around. She was determined not to think about Devin Drake. Or his hands. Or his blue eyes. Or his wicked, annoying, pleasing mouth.

That didn't last long.

There was a knock at her door.

"Miranda?" Her mother's voice. *Ugh.*

"Yes, mother, give me a moment." She hurried to throw a dressing gown over herself. Miranda barely secured the ties before her mother burst inside.

"Where the hell were you?"

Oh, no. If her mother swore, that was a very bad sign. Just past her mother's shoulder was Miranda's father—he'd at least waited to make sure she was decent before barreling through the door.

"Well?" Her mother said, crossing into the room like she was on the attack. "Where were you?"

Miranda swallowed, too tired to answer or pretend or lie. Her misery must have showed on her face, because her mother softened. Her father, however, did not.

"Tell me you weren't off seeing him again," her father said, not masking the accusation in his tone.

Miranda couldn't meet his eyes, but that answered the question well enough.

"Damn it, Miranda, you've been reckless before, but never like this. I *should* challenge him so that we don't appear complacent in his corruption. Your entire future could be ruined if word of this got into the wrong hands. *He* may not understand what such a scandal could do to your life, but *you* know better." Her father narrowed his eyes, spine straightening further. "Or. I could solve everything if I killed him with my bare hands. That sounds good, too."

"James," her mother warned.

"Don't..." Miranda took a breath, her weak outburst caught both her parents' attention and Miranda sighed. "I've been trying to find information on Yarrow Graves that will end his engagement to Cordelia."

She expected exasperation. An overflow of outrage. Insisting this was a lost cause, that there was nothing to find, and how could she do this to her sister? What about Cordelia's future? It was such an amiable match.

However, her parents were silent.

They exchanged looks, their postures shifting.

"James, get the door," her mother ordered. Her father obeyed without a word. Her mother's nose flared and urgency replaced anger. "Does he know?"

Miranda must have been delirious. She could hardly process what her mother asked. "Does...who know?"

Her mother rolled her eyes, mirroring Miranda for the first time in recollection. "*Graves*. Does he know you've been investigating him?"

Her father hung his head. "Of course, that's why they were in his private office. They were spying."

"Miranda Olivia Wilde. How could you do something so foolish?"

There it was. The disbelief. The denial. They would never believe her, and she felt so lost and hopeless and tired. Divine above, she hadn't slept more than a moment for two days. Hot tears trailed over her dusty cheeks. Her sister was in danger and there was nothing she could do. If Graves wasn't vengeful before, now he would make sure she never got in his way again. Her parents would never trust her or believe her again. And, even if it wasn't *love*, Devin had broken her heart.

The sobs started quiet, slowly building until her body shook.

Her mother rushed forward and held her. "There, there, darling. I'm sorry if I sounded harsh. I'm scared. Graves is so dangerous and I feared the worst."

Miranda choked on her tears.

What?

"It's not looking good, Cicely. Graves knew why she was there. He'd have done heaven knows what to Drake if I hadn't intervened. Thankfully, I was truly angry and in need of a private word with the rake." Her father let out a breath, squaring his shoulders. "We'll have to keep a guard on her. Make sure he doesn't find her alone."

"Infernal blast it, James, I told you this was too dangerous. Your investigation is over. We can hardly keep up the pretense of this engagement now. Who knows what he might do if he thinks Miranda has found him out?"

Miranda followed the exchange like a child who hadn't learned words, and could only sense tone and infer meaning. Was it possible she was wrong about her parents?

She stood up suddenly, shaking her head like that would shake reality back into place. "Wait, you both knew he was evil?"

"Of course, dear, do you think we're so easily manipulated?" Her mother urged her to the bed, petting her hair and easing the tangles free. "Your father intended to get close to Graves to find enough evidence to see him discharged as alderman. When he offered for your sister, well, I was against it, but we thought we could manage the leverage and with luck he'd be taken care of well before any ceremony."

"We didn't tell you because Graves has True Sight, it takes a special way of wording and intent to fool him. I grew up in politics. I'm very good at hiding my intentions and careful enough with my wording that I'm rarely telling an outright lie. Your mother, well, she would put me to shame."

"Enough, it doesn't matter now. We're going to stop this whole thing and find a way to keep both of you girls safe. Alright, my darling?" Her mother gently wiped her cheeks. "You're so strong, I forget you can be fragile, too."

"But..." Miranda was having trouble following the conversation. Retracing every interaction they'd had so far to find the truth of her parents' words. How her mother had never allowed Graves to be alone with Cordelia, even to talk in a corner. There was always an excuse to keep them apart. Her mother had been the one to suggest the flowers that were out of season that would delay the wedding. Miranda was unraveling. "But why did you let her suffer over these few months? You had to know Cordelia was miserable. Why didn't you stop it then or just tell her?"

Her mother's eyes filled with tears and anger. "I had not known Delia would react so...defeated to the news. I thought she'd hate it, yes, but not to...I hated seeing her that way. But there was no turning back once we started. If I called it off, our plan would be ruined. If I told her, there was no way your sister would be able to hide her true intentions from Graves's Sight and we'd have been worse than lost. My only solace was that I knew this was not real. That for all Delia's withdrawn sadness, I knew she would never have to marry that man."

"Your mother was right. It had been a mistake to involve you girls at all. Graves's power was growing and I feared something...something much worse than simple social climbing was coming. I wished to stop it before he got that far."

Her father did not know how right he was. Graves could create fae more powerful than any of them. Even Miranda would struggle to hold off a properly trained fae with that kind of strength. She considered telling them what she found, but stayed silent. They had kept so much from her, and while she was grateful that her assumptions had been wrong, that didn't change the undercurrent of betrayal sticking like a thorn amidst the relief.

"Why didn't you trust Graves, Miranda? I knew you didn't like him, but going so far as to scheme and put yourself in danger to investigate his doings all to save Cordelia? What aren't you telling us?" Her father asked the one question Miranda was afraid to answer. She considered not telling him, continuing her silence. She had been so scared they wouldn't believe her and now...

They patiently waited for Miranda to speak. Which was saying something as patience was not a family virtue. Control or restraint when needed, yes, but not patience. Her father was itching to get an answer, she could tell as he refused to sit, his every muscle strained. Her mother soothed her hair, a distraction to keep her from pressing Miranda. Did she dare break their hearts all the more?

Miranda took a breath. She had been silent for long enough. They deserved to know.

"Last year, Graves found me while I was getting some air during the Fairchild ball." She swallowed, the full details catching in her throat as she held her parents' rapt attention. "And, well, he...he proposed, in a way. Asked if I would consider marrying him."

Her mother's jaw flexed, like she was straining from speaking. Her father hadn't moved. Neither looked away from her. Images and sounds...the sensation of hands on her skin...she had to close her eyes to keep it from spilling from her chest. Panic welled in her heart.

"When I refused...he grew angry with me and made threats. He, um, tried to attack me." She pieced through the words carefully, selecting the tamest truth she could find. "Then I ran."

"Why didn't you tell us immediately?" Her mother clutched her chest like her heart was breaking and she was trying to keep the pieces together.

"I would never have let that leech near you if I...we knew he was dangerous, but not this. Infernal take him." Her father's anger threatened to slip from his control. Her story still felt like a lie, but the solace she felt at their anger was enough.

"Oh, Miranda, I am so sorry." Her mother hugged her. "I'm so sorry you had to live with this alone." Even her father stepped forward to wrap his arms around her. Miranda's tears fell faster, with relief as much as from sharing even a tempered version of the truth.

They stayed that way for a time, the chasm that had been forming between them finally had a bridge.

As the tears stopped and exhaustion began to take a firmer hold, Miranda settled backward on the bed.

"There's..." She took a breath, but if there was one thing her parents were better equipped to handle, it was her debt to Wraith. "There's one other thing. I did promise a large sum of money to Thaddeus Wraith for some information. I...I only had so much allowance saved, and I owe him more."

Her mother opened her mouth, the storm of indignation and worry simmering in her eyes.

"I'll take care of it." Her father stepped to her mother's side and set a hand on her shoulder. She speared him with a look and after a silent moment, she turned away, lips sealed shut. "I will take care of it, Miranda."

That was one weight lifted. Though, perhaps it was the lightest that was weighing her down, it was enough for now.

"Does that have anything to do with Drake's role in this?" her father said, though she sensed he was trying to be understanding.

"It's not my place to say," Miranda said, voice hollow even to her ears. "Just...we were working together. But, I don't think he'll want to see me anymore. Graves already burned his club to the ground."

"What?" Her father's stance opened, like he was prepared to fight Graves right there in her room.

"Miranda you should have started with that. James, what do we do?" Her mother hugged her tighter to her side.

"Calm down, we still have a few advantages that buy us some time. Miranda will not leave the house again, for now. We'll have a guard at her door. And make sure she has weapons hidden throughout the room, should she need them. It'll be fine, Cicely."

"It better be," her mother warned.

"Between the pair of us, Graves won't be able to get close," he said, then he stared at Miranda. "And a guard for the window, I suspect."

Miranda wanted to curl into her mother's side and sleep for a week. She didn't know what would happen next, but suddenly she was ten years old and perfectly content to let mommy and daddy handle everything. Sure, she would come back to her senses in the morning, but her eyes began to close as her parents rambled on. Her body had reached its limit, forcing sleep on her. She wasn't about to let them shut her away in her room when she had come so far. But, at least, she knew Cordelia would be safe. That was enough for now.

--

When Miranda opened her eyes, it was nearly night again. She ventured from her room and found two guards waiting outside the door.

"Sorry, we're not allowed to let you leave," the first said, Miranda didn't recognize her. She motioned to a tray set on a side table. "This was brought up for you, but you've been asleep all day."

Jaw clenched, Miranda retrieved the food and slammed the door. A guard? Really? She bit into a piece of her roll as she located her guardian uniform. They were not going to keep her locked up like some princess in a tower. Miranda slipped on the pieces of her uniform with practiced precision as she shoveled the cold chicken and seasoned potatoes into her mouth.

She swiped the crumbs from her lips as she searched her bedchamber for weapons. Her father wanted her to be armed in case anyone got through his defenses, which suited her well enough. She tucked knives into hidden pockets—slip blades along her calves, dirk along her thigh, and an arsenal of throwing knives on her hips.

Miranda went to her window and went to pop the latch, but her eyes stopped on the large, heavy lock. "Honestly, like this would stop me."

She fiddled with it for a moment, considered shattering the glass—but that would alert the guards at her door—before deciding the only option was to find one of the guest rooms.

Thankfully, her parents did not know about the passage leading to the spare room next door, or the one connecting that to Cordelia's bedchamber. She got to her hands and knees, her memory of the opening in the wall was that it was much taller, but then, she'd been fifteen the last time she used it.

Crawling through to the adjacent room, she found it guard free. With a flick the latch on the window popped free and the glass swung inward. She stepped onto the ledge and peered down.

There was a tree near her window that aided in her coming and going, but here she'd have to scale the meager recess and ledges created in the uneven lay of brick—an aesthetic choice by the architect that she was infinitely grateful for in that moment.

Miranda paused, not sure what her plan was, except that sitting in her room was not an option. Her first thought was to seek out Devin. The idea had made her smile and her heart flutter, until she remembered that they were no longer working together. Or, rather, he no longer wished to work with her.

The happy flutter twisted like a blade and she harshly swiped away the brim of tears in her eyes. It had been a hopeless infatuation, anyway. Devin was never going to remain in her life, so better to end it sooner rather than later.

Sitting on the ledge, Miranda realized she had no plan. The information was still tucked safe in her pocket and she took it out to look over the looping characters of the illegible words. Then at the bottom she noted the address Kylin had mentioned. Looking at it now, the format was obviously an address, and the street name had been written out in common characters. Miranda pursed her lips. She also knew the Faery numbers through ten...

This wasn't over. This address was her only lead. Cordelia was safe. But whatever Graves was planning would hurt more than her sister. This had been her mission, and while her motivations had changed, the end result was the same. She would stop Graves and see him properly behind bars where he could do no more harm.

Resolved, she swung her foot down to dig her toes into the first lip of exposed brick and the next, her fingers hooked into the cracks as she eased her way down. On the last step, when she lifted her foot to jump the last few feet, her boot slammed into something solid.

"Infernal blast it—"

"*Devin?*"

Devin opened his eyes to a full moon, drifting clouds, and a sense of pain sprouting from his...everything. His shoulder, in particular, was screaming at him. His memories shifted for a moment as he tried to recall what he had been doing before finding himself on his back in dewy grass.

Last he remembered, he drank a good deal. More than he usually required to limit his Aura Sight. He was trying to erase all the lingering reminders of Miranda. The scent of lilacs on his shirt—he'd thrown it into a corner. The scent of her arousal on his pants—he'd torn them off like they burned, afraid what the visceral scent would do to his already frayed senses. He fought to free his brain of each whispered moan and sigh that replayed when he closed his eyes.

Nothing worked.

She was everywhere.

And he'd been wrong. Not wrong in turning her away—it was glaringly obvious that he did not deserve her and so letting her go was the best thing he could do for her—but wrong to speak so harshly after her first time. There would be no peace for him until he assured her that she was not at fault.

He'd stumbled from his home more drunk than he'd been when his mother had passed. His addled brain had decided there was no time like the present to offer Miranda a most deserved apology.

But how did that lead to him on his back?

"Devin?"

Oh yes, in his attempt to find the servant's entrance—not wanting to chance asking at the front door, afraid Lord Wilde would skewer him on the spot, even inebriated Devin had the sense not to push him on that score—Miranda's boot had caught him in the face.

The pain was sobering, at least.

Miranda pulled him to his feet, lifting him easily. "Are you okay?"

He didn't feel blood, but he was surprised to meet concern instead of her fists. "I've had worse," he said.

"Oh, good." Then she pushed both hands into his chest full force. His back slammed into a tree so hard he thought his spine was done-for. All the air whooshed from his lungs as his knees hit the grass and he wheezed. "What the *hell* are you doing here?"

He waved a hand in the air, which was all he could manage at present. From his peripheral he noticed her boot tapping with impatience.

"I can't believe you're skulking around my house like a thief. You know my father has guards posted?" She hadn't waited for an answer, rambling on while slowly his breathing returned. "And why would you come here? You were quite clear that we didn't 'suit.' The audacity to show up at my house in the middle of the night. I hope it wasn't for anything..." she paused, her stance shifting. Devin got to his feet as the remnants of her blush started to fade. "I assure you, I am not the sort of woman who lets men sneak into her room at all hours. Kissing you was a one-time mistake. A lark. Curiosity, more than anything else. It was nice and all, but nothing I would miss."

Ouch. Nothing stung his pride quite like her casually dismissing what, in his opinion, had been one of the more euphoric experiences of his life. The shots at his character were one thing, insulting his ability to please a woman was entirely uncalled for. She had hardly given him a fair chance. That was one night and he'd been holding back for her sake. Given ample time and the freedom to act without fear of crossing a boundary, she might not be so dismissive. Hell, he didn't even need a bed. He'd have her screaming with just his knees on the floor and her legs on his shoulders.

But that was not the point and hardly appropriate for an apology. He was here to make amends for taking advantage, not promise to do it better the next time.

Because there could be no next time.

"I know I behaved less than chivalrously—" She scoffed, loudly enough to interrupt. "I am here," he continued, pointedly, "To apologize. After what transpired in my apartment, to push you away like that was...particularly, insensitive."

"I don't need an apology. I'm fine. Like I said, it meant very little." The quick dart of her eyes said otherwise.

"Regardless. You deserved an apology."

"I don't want it."

"That is your choice," he said through his teeth. *Impossible woman.*

"Fine."

"Fine."

He shook his head. This was hardly the place to be having this conversation. They were standing in the gardens behind her house, the space cut off from neighbors by a tall fence. Immaculately tended bushes of flowers and gravel pathways created a serene environment and an ill-fitting backdrop for the tense atmosphere. If her father had posted guards—and rightly so, Lord Wilde must know more than he let on—then Devin was not eager to be found here with Miranda.

"Where were you going?" Devin asked, glancing up at the window he assumed she'd climbed from.

"Not your business anymore," she snapped. Without another word, she turned and marched for the gate. He darted after her, slipping through before she could slam it in his face.

"The guards will hear," he warned just as she was about to let it fall closed. Miranda growled as she caught the gate and let it gently click into place.

"Don't follow me," she hissed, turning on her heel to continue toward wherever she planned to go at such an hour. Perhaps he had been right in assuming she regularly traversed the city at night.

"Miranda, stop." He stepped in front of her. She appeared to consider a full-on collision for half a moment—a collision that he would see the worst of—and he braced.

"What? What do you have to say?" She stopped just shy of running him over, but made sure to back a few steps away so that they were never too close. He'd made her angry before, but there was something about her anger now that unsettled him. Beneath the anger she hid genuine hurt and he was the cause. He flinched as she crossed her arms and looked away from him.

He may have come here drunk, but between her boot in his face and her eyes stabbing through his chest, his inebriation had dulled considerably.

"You don't have to accept my apology, Mira, but, I need you to know that my behavior had nothing to do with you." He looked away, more angry at himself than she could possibly be. "I did not..." he cleared his throat, "I do not regret anything nor was I trying to give you the impression that bedding you was my only aim—"

She raised an eyebrow.

Fuck, he was floundering. He'd never had to apologize for his behavior. This is why he avoided virgins. He was loath to toy with a woman's genuine emotions or take advantage of their innocence. "It was not my aim to take any liberties with you, or even to kiss you."

"*I* kissed *you*, I believe."

"Yes." He did not need the reminder right then. Did not need a reminder of how willingly she had jumped him. Nor her ardor as her nails had cut into his neck...the firm command in her voice...

Do it.

Now you're going to disappoint me, Devin?

He shook the lust from his thoughts. Divine above, he thought it impossible to resist her *before*. He kept his breathing even as he continued, "I meant, that it was not my reason for associating with you. I was determined not to cross any sort of line with you for the duration of our acquaintance. And then I did, and I lashed out unjustly."

She let out a breath, her posture easing, but she stayed silent.

Devin had never cared to gain the favor of someone he had wronged before. It was easier to just let the relationship end. But right now, he cared about nothing more than Miranda's forgiveness and how much he craved just one more chance to lick the sweat from her skin.

Frustrated, he changed the subject.

"Where are you planning to go at this hour, Mira?" He knew it wasn't to see him. Her anger had made that clear. Perhaps planning to knock on Graves's door and finish what she nearly started in the study? As ludicrous as the idea sounded, he would not have put it past her.

She bristled at the nickname, but otherwise ignored him.

He considered how to word his concerns without getting slapped. "Graves will be looking for a way to get you alone. Traversing the streets at night without an escort is the exact opening he needs."

"I'm not stupid," she snapped. "I know he's going to retaliate. But I'm not going to let my parents lock me in my bedroom while I wait for it to happen, either. I worked too hard to let someone else fix my problems. I'm the one who found what Graves was really planning. I get to decide what I do with it. He decided to marry my sister the last time I pissed him off, I can't imagine what he'd do to me now, but I'm not going to mope about while he decides."

Anger flared as he asked, "What happened the last time?"

Her eyes went wide, vulnerable. She shook her head. "I don't have to tell you."

She moved around him, continuing on her path down the block. There were very few places she could reach inside the city on foot. Devin came up behind her and guided her toward a shadowed area nestled in the overgrown foliage of one of the houses and out of the streetlight's glow. There was hardly any fight as she shrugged his arm away.

"Tell—" he started to order, but then stopped when he didn't even recognize his own voice. Whatever she had to say, he both wanted to know and feared hearing it.

Resigned that the only fair way to know what happened was an equal trade, Devin spoke first, "I served under Graves in the war. He was nobility, I was a sixteen-year-old who'd lied about my age so I could have access to food and a bed. One day our unit was caught in an ambush. We were hunkered down under cover, safe for the moment, when Graves ordered that we retreat.

"I argued against it. We were pinned down, but holding our position well enough. His cowardice became clear when he ordered us to cover him as he made a break back for friendly territory. All the members of my unit, friends and allies, were little more than his shield." He didn't go into more detail. Not to spare her the horror so much as to spare himself. "Only three of us made it back."

She was still. Some of the fight lifted from her shoulders, her posture easing. "I'm sorry...I can understand why you hate him."

"Hate is putting it mildly. So, if you ever feel like no one else understands what Graves is capable of, just know I'm not among them. I know he wronged you, Mira, but...maybe it's best if I don't know the details. I've reason enough to kill him, I don't need to be tempted to make it slow and painful as well."

She considered a moment. The street was quiet, the Garrison properly silent and empty at such an hour. They were a few houses away from Miranda's home, tucked into the darkness of some noble's flourishing front garden. When she spoke, her voice was quiet, almost hard to hear over the slight breeze stirring the trees.

"I was at a ball. My mother had been pushing me on bachelors all evening and I was done with the whole thing. When I went outside for some peace and fresh air, Graves followed me. At first, he was nice, charming. He commented on the night and the party. All polite enough. Except, we were outside alone and from the moment he showed up I felt uneasy." She hugged her arms around herself, never once looking into his eyes. Devin let go of the breath he hadn't realized he was holding.

Devin spoke with barely restrained anger. "Tell me he didn't..."

Miranda didn't meet his eyes. "Well, he didn't succeed. Not..." Tears welled in her eyes, then slipped down her cheeks as her vision grew distant. Her mind taking her somewhere else, somewhere worse.

"I refused his offers, and that angered him. He told me that a woman of my age, nearing spinsterhood, should have been glad to accept such an offer. He wasn't charming anymore, no more pretense. And he wasn't alone. I was held by two of his followers while—" Miranda's voice wavered and he wanted to tell her to stop, beg her not to finish her story, but he couldn't bring himself to speak. "I'm trained to handle every enemy, even those physically stronger. I knew exactly how to break their hold and free myself, but—in the moment I was so...confused. So scared and shocked that I forgot everything. I couldn't react as he tore at my..." She covered her chest with her arms. "My dress, and started to bunch up the skirts. His hands on my skin is the single most repulsing moment in my life. He said that if I were compromised, then I wouldn't be able to refuse him."

Her tears were a cascade, streams down her cheeks and dripping onto her dress. Each new detail left him more hollow, more...devastated.

She swiped at her cheeks and caught her breath. "Then my senses returned. I kneed him in the stomach and broke the hold on my arms. Then I ran." Brave Miranda raised her chin, tougher than the memories, even as her lips trembled.

Devin's fists vibrated with restrained anger. He had suspected that Graves had wronged her, noted how she had squirmed under his gaze, but he chose to ignore the implications out of self-preservation. He didn't need more reasons to hate the man. His animosity could not possibly grow any stronger. And yet, here he stood. Ready to shred the man into pieces, so that he didn't die right away but felt every tear and rip of himself the way he tore and ripped at those around him. For the first time since revenge had blackened his heart beyond repair, he considered that death might be too merciful an end for Graves.

"Damn it, Miranda—" Devin paused, his tirade halted in his throat. Her eyes were open, exposed. Begging for something that he feared he wasn't capable of giving. Hearing the words from her own lips had him struggling to keep his hands to himself.

Not to *touch* her, but to offer comfort in a way he did not understand. The only comfort he'd ever received was from his mother, whose touch rescinded further and further from him the more sadness weighed her down. He had been hugged as a small boy, but over time her affection had receded as the shadows in her eyes grew, until her touch wasn't even a memory.

Devin's hand found Miranda's arm, fingers gently curling around her wrist, waiting for her to pull away.

She didn't.

He looked into her green eyes, searching for...what? He didn't know. His heart maybe? He was unraveling in front of her again. If he wasn't careful a wall might budge, weakness might show, he needed to regain his composure. Instead, he stepped close enough to smell lilacs, overpowering the fresh blooms all around them, and his hand shifted from her arm to her back.

The steel in her spine softened, her guard dropping. He could only breathe and feel her breath against his chest. It occurred to him that he was taking comfort as much as he was trying to give it, and the idea threatened to unnerve him.

He tore his eyes from her face, from her parted lips and evocative eyes, so that he stared into a well-sculpted hedge instead. There were thorns among the dark green foliage, the leaf edges lined in severe points that would jab a finger if one attempted to touch it. A plant that was well guarded from predators. Like Miranda. Only, *he* was the predator snaking his way through the thorns.

He stopped short of letting his lips trail over the soft, loose tendrils of her hair.

"We should move, it's not smart to linger," he whispered.

"Yes...we should," she replied.

He held her now, their bodies couldn't be closer, and yet something else burned between them. Something—inexplicably—worse than passion.

He eased back, gently ripping his senses free of her. There was no part of him that wasn't vulnerable to her, that wasn't ready to lay down and submit. To end this game and just let the consequences be damned. Devin did not think he could hold himself back any longer. The last of his will had snapped and Miranda had no idea the danger she was in now, how very thoroughly he could ruin her should she say the word.

And he would not hesitate. All he needed was the *barest* hint that she wanted him again and he would lock her away until he could satisfy her every carnal desire.

For now, he continued to breathe, the scent of her making him drunk all over again. "Where were you planning to go, Mira?"

"The address on the paper."

"Well, if you're amenable, I may have a safer option. An old comrade of mine is currently captain of the Watchmen, one of the few to make it out with me."

She was quiet. He expected her to argue with him. Instead, she nodded.

"We should go, then, Mira," he said, drawing his knuckles along her cheek. She closed her eyes, leaning into his touch. The hand on her back clenched, pulling her tighter, closer. "Say the word, Mira, and we'll go."

"Yes...go."

He grinned.

She was going to be his.

And if he was going to hell, he was going to make sure he *thoroughly* deserved it.

CHAPTER NINE

WATCHMEN HEADQUARTERS SAT IN a hulking building connecting a Garrison cathedral and a Sanctuary hostel. On one
side, the cathedral with stained glass and elaborate carvings of the
Divine while the hostel had subdued dark stone and no windows.
Patrons came and went at their leisure, but not from the cathedral.
Thralls and blood donors used the hostel as a gathering place or to,
occasionally, interact with their hosts on more neutral territory.

Devin held the door for Miranda. His eyes followed her incredible
figure as she passed, her attention too focused on their surroundings
to notice. The door swung closed behind him as he paused to admire
her silhouette against the ambient lighting. It was dim, but the heavy
shadows made her all the more tantalizing. He was merely biding time.
Her only salvation would be to resist him, which, for her sake, would
be the wiser course.

But if she did not.

His gaze grew dark. Focused.

A sprawling interior expanded before them, the main chamber
open to high ceilings with sectioned rooms and offices acting as a

perimeter on the upper floors. It was tiered, with levels of cubicles and desks scattered or in rows, there was no observable pattern he could detect. The moon shone through elongated windows rising high into the rafters, with streetlamps set up in a grid-like system for extra light.

There was an industrial feel with brick and metal utilized in unique or practical ways offset by the scattering of thrift-style furniture. Pipe work holding rustic planks and stacks of books directly beside worn, whitewashed shelves or rusted filing cabinets. At this time of night, the place was nearly empty. The noise and bustle had to be spectacular during the day.

A secretary sat near the entrance and looked up from a book as they entered, hidden behind protective glass, he had to lift a vent to be heard.

"Can I help you?"

Devin tore his eyes from Miranda. "Is Blair still here?"

A nametag read Jones, who shook his head. "He went out about an hour ago. Can I take a message?"

"What about Rachel Stone?"

"Ah, yeah, she's still here." Jones's smile was strained. "She's always here late." Devin would bet anything that Gideon had slipped out drinking or to charm some woman into lowering her standards for a night, leaving Rachel to clean up whatever mess he left behind.

"We're old friends," Devin continued, "Could you tell her Drake is here?"

Jones considered, then with a long sigh he rose and headed past the barricade intended to keep civilians out.

"Where do you know Rachel?" Miranda asked, her tone uncharacteristically casual. She didn't meet his eyes.

"We served together." Was she jealous? His grin was predatory.

"Oh." Her words were clipped.

Devin drew closer, though he made sure to keep careful distance as he crossed his arms. "Do I detect jealousy?"

Her eyes snapped to him, burning straight into his soul. Infernal take him, he was half hard already.

"Of course not," she defended, though it was much too forceful to be true.

"Jealous or not, Rachel is merely an old friend. I assure you, she has more interest in proper table settings than she does in me and she abhors frivolous rituals. So there's no need to worry." He took another step, encroaching on her territory as he leaned in to whisper, "I am entirely yours, Mira."

She pushed his shoulder—the bad one—and he reeled. Pain hissed from his mouth. "Please. You're dreaming if you think you can charm me into letting my better judgment slip again. I told you, that was a singular mistake that I won't make twice."

The pain had done wonders to cool his ardor, though he was hardly out of the game yet.

She looked away. "But...sorry. I forgot about your shoulder."

He rotated his arm, but it still throbbed. "Who said I was trying to charm you?" He met her stare, grinning as her jaw fell open. "Mira, I will make you a promise, I'll not push or pressure you into anything you're unwilling to do. No more riling you. No more goading."

She raised her chin. Her tell that this was more bravado than anything else. *She was a goner.*

"Perfect. Thank you."

"However," he continued, eyes dangerous and his voice saturated in unbridled intent, "Should *you* give me even the smallest indication that you want me to continue, should you attempt to push at boundaries, know that I will no longer be exercising restraint." Her eyes grew wide, her teeth sucking in her bottom lip. "I will not hold back." He watched her thighs rub together, just the barest hint of movement, but it was more than enough. "And I will not stop until you are entirely spent."

She swallowed, drawing his eyes to her throat.

He could hear Jones returning and his smile shifted to a jovial grin, his sinful focus masked behind a chipper veneer.

"Yeah, she'll see you." Jones unlocked the door to allow them through. "Up the first stairs on the right, she's in the Captain's office."

Devin's tone was bright and airy as he gestured with a bow. "After you, Miss Wilde."

She did not move for several moments.

"Is there a problem, Miss Wilde?" He pressed. "Anything you wish to request, perhaps?" Her eyes rounded on him as she stalked forward and he raised his arms in submission. "Only an innocent inquiry, I assure you."

He followed her through the door.

Inside Captain Blair's office was a blonde woman with pale skin and sharp blue eyes who was grumbling as she shuffled amidst a sea of papers, garbage, and various clutter.

"Rachel, he does not deserve you," Devin started, fixing himself in the doorway to lean against the frame.

Miranda was not sure what to make of the new I'll-not-tempt-you Devin. She was wary, of course, because he was an ass who tended to be his own worst enemy. But his apology at her house had felt real and, while she had bristled and sneered, she'd believed him. She was beginning to see new facets and depth that peeked through whenever his defenses were down. The romantic whose hands stroked her arm and asked if she was alright. The honor hidden beneath swagger when he'd waited for permission before testing a boundary. And the pain he worked so hard to hide.

Still, while his promise had sounded genuine, she knew he intended his choice of words to lure her back into his arms. He made the offer thrilling, enticing, and hard to resist. And while the sensible voice in her head had cheered at his promise to behave, her body had purred. Hummed. She felt his words in places she now knew could be so exquisitely pleasurable. It might not have worked, except that she very much wanted to be lured.

He had not made a single comment on the walk up here and his eyes—which she had felt crawling over her skin like a trail of fire since leaving her house—had not once wavered. But did she dare tempt *him*? Did she dare test his promise to not hold back?

Miranda pulled her eyes away from Devin with a sigh.

Did she dare risk falling deeper?

"Hello to you to, Devin. And I'm not cleaning after him. This," Miss Stone hands righted a stack of uneven, lopsided papers. "Is his mess and he can get himself out of it. It's not my business. I'm just looking for my report on the recent Night Hawk sightings, which he was *supposed* to review two weeks ago, and now I have another three pages to add." She took a deep breath. Her hair was done in a simple bun, a style women could do without a maid and the soft blonde color matched the paler hue of her blue eyes. She had a calm presence, reassuring. Miranda liked her instantly.

"Oh," she stopped her search of the desk when she noticed Miranda. "New friend?"

"This is Miranda Wilde," Devin introduced and Rachel's eyebrow shot up. "Yes, of those Wilde's."

"Cordelia is my sister," Miranda clarified.

Miss Stone gave her a sympathetic nod. "My condolences, or," She turned to Devin, "Does she know?'

"It no longer matters," Miranda pressed forward before Devin could answer. "The marriage will not take place, so, that is the end of it."

Devin shot her a look, clearly thrown by the little detail she had neglected to mention, but in her defense he had hardly left her the space for it.

"Then why on earth are you here?" He directed the accusation at Miranda.

Miranda sighed. "I'm here for me. I lived my entire life preparing for a fight I was never meant to see. My sister may be free, but the city is not."

Miss Stone shook her head. "You're talking about Graves?" Her face remained impassive, the only hint to her feelings on the subject pointed to exhaustion, more than anger. "You roped her into your vendetta?"

Devin frowned. "I hardly roped her, she was insistent."

"Please, the pair of you sound as bad as Gideon." Miss Stone pushed around the desk, collecting garbage on the way and tossing it in a bin. She motioned toward the wall, where it wasn't in view of the open windows. A giant map of the city took up most of it, each line and street labeled or covered with pinned pictures and scribbled notes. "Gideon's 'idea' board. But it never gets anywhere."

She set her hands on her hips. Dressed in a Watchmen uniform, though she had removed the jacket and rolled up the sleeves on the black undershirt, Miss Stone exuded a unique femininity Miranda could relate to, though not common where Miranda grew up. A femininity that stemmed from assurance and physicality. From knowing that she was a woman who could handle herself.

"He has all this and still has not found a way to put Graves away?" Miranda took in the board, feeling a little sick. This looked like years of work and study. What if her evidence wasn't enough?

Miss Stone shrugged. "Graves is too smart. And we're greatly restricted by red tape and rules. We can't figure out which of the officers are on his payroll and anyone higher than Gideon thinks he's a champion of the city."

"That's why I maintain that it was insanity to join up with the Watchmen." Devin's comment earned a harsh glare from Miss Stone.

"Better than drinking away our feelings." She took a deep breath, arms crossing over the mess surrounding her. "What brings you here in the middle of the night, anyway? You didn't come to chit-chat towing a guardian noble behind you."

"No, we were hoping to speak with Blair."

Miss Stone's eyes hardened. "That won't be possible until morning. The Captain doesn't get here till at least nine. *And* he'll be hungover. Begging me to do the shift briefing while he holes up in here to sleep another few hours. Meanwhile, I've been up half the night trying to make heads or tails of this sty he calls an office when I know he's just going to come in here and mess it all up again." She took a calming breath and Miranda sensed there was a special sort of history between the Captain and Miss Stone.

"I was about to head home, but you're welcome to wait for him. I trust you not to go unlocking criminals in the cell bay or tamper with evidence or, honestly, I don't care enough to stop you. There's a few cots set up in the back offices if you need sleep." She eyed Devin and then Miranda. "Separate offices, if that's the preference."

"It is," Miranda insisted, but a little too forcefully. Miss Stone sent Devin a look that was both critical and knowing.

"I'm sorry I can't offer a chaperone. That matters to those upper ring types, doesn't it?" Miss Stone asked, but not unkindly. "There's

Watson over in dispatch, but…" She cringed. "You'd need a chaperone for *him*, if you get my meaning."

"It's fine," Miranda insisted, ready for this whole topic to be over.

"Alright then, goodnight," she said guiding them out the door.

Miss Stone descended the stairs, locking Gideon's office behind her and leaving Miranda and Devin in the upstairs hall outside it. Alone.

He may have said he would no longer attempt to sway her into anything untoward, but she did not fully trust herself to abide by her part of the bargain and, in truth, she hadn't decided if she wanted to. She was already curious to learn what he could show her, to feel that rush again, to bask in the impropriety of just one more night.

Devin watched her, arms crossed over his chest. He wore perfectly fitted black everything with a black vest and sleeves rolled up his forearms. His dark hair was roguishly tousled, just a hint longer than was fashionable. If she stared at him any longer the decision would be made for her.

She risked meeting his eyes, but she did not find desire. He was merely watching, waiting, she supposed, to see what she would do next. What was she going to do next?

"What'll it be, Miranda?" he asked, voice brushing through her body like satin. Two voices warred in her thoughts.

You don't have to be curious, you can find out for yourself.

And if he pushes you away again?

Would it be worth it?

Can your heart take the hit?

Miranda had lived so much of her life on the right and proper side of the rules. Though she had always been mischievous and her mother liked to deem her a rebel, she had never actually crossed any line that couldn't be uncrossed. Sneaking out to Lydia's house. Childish larks. Running in her dresses. Saying the wrong things. None of it compared to this. If she gave in, if she allowed how very much she wanted him to do all the wicked things his eyes had once suggested, then she was choosing a path and destroying another. The future her parents had wanted, the hovering threat of marriage and children and wasting away all the training as she carried on the family legacy, it would not be possible. She could never settle once she knew what awaited her.

She had expected the idea to terrify her, that her future might be suddenly thrown into flux on this one decision.

You made your decision long ago. It's already too late.

It was already too late.

Miranda swallowed as she responded, her chin rising into the air, "What do you mean? I plan to find one of those offices and bar the door."

"I promised not to pursue, so there's no need for bars."

She nodded and then turned on her heel. Heading down an open hallway, one side against the walls of offices, the other a railing that looked out over the entire lower floor, she found a row of rooms with the doors partially ajar. Inside were tables and shelves full of cleaning supplies and two cots each with folded blankets and a pillow. She imagined that officers needing a place to sleep between longer shifts might find refuge here for a few hours. Miranda paused. There were three rooms in front of her.

"Which will it be?" Devin's voice was far behind her, as if he dared not get too close. And his tone held no trace of promise or flirtation. He simply asked. Still, she flinched.

"It hardly matters." She stalked toward the first open room and stopped in the doorway. Sparing the barest turn of her head. Her breath caught.

Devin *watched*.

Whatever mask he'd been wearing while attempting to keep his promise had slipped completely. His gaze seemed to hinge on her every motion. Her finger twitched and his eyes darted to her hand before returning to her face. Heavens above, there was no mistaking his intentions now. With a fluttery breath she turned away and closed her eyes.

Then she made a choice for herself. Freeing herself of a future she hated for the excitement of uncertainty. Her future was hers to discover. Though, a minuscule part of her—tucked into her heart—hoped that Devin would still be with her when she found it.

She proceeded into the room and fiddled with the lantern so light bloomed to ease the darkness and then crossed her arms. She glanced back into the hall, where Devin waited. *Watching*.

She swallowed.

"You haven't closed the door," he said.

She had not closed the door.

Miranda returned her focus on the room, to the furnishings or the...

Her fingers trembled at her sides, but this was not with fear or frustration. She tried to keep her motions minimal as she clenched her thighs to the pulsing want that begged her to put her pride aside and forgive him.

He stepped closer, inches from the room.

"Close the door, Miranda."

She met his gaze. He waited, ready to pounce.

Waited for *her* to give the command.

The thought was thrilling and empowering.

He stepped into the doorway, but did not enter. "Mira, close the door."

She stepped forward and put her hand on the door handle, like she intended to close it on him. The loss and rejection were instant, his eyes filling with panic. But he did not move or speak. He was going to let her decide. He was so easy to tease.

Miranda reached out with her other hand and hooked a finger into his vest.

"Oh, you have made a very grave error in judgment," he hissed as he walked into her grip, not even waiting to be pulled, and shut the door as he towered over her, eyes dark and full of wicked promise. Darkness descended on the room and her eyes adjusted to the softer glow of the single lantern.

Miranda chewed her lip as she stroked the finger hooked in his vest up the soft linen of his shirt. Her head tilted and she rose up on her toes to say against his lips, "I hope so."

I hope so.

Devin sealed his mouth over her words and, as before, the spark between them ignited into a blaze. Miranda's passion was rooted in combat, driven to conquer, to overpower. She was climbing him, wrapping every leather clad contour of her body over him, her lust warring with the instinct to take him down.

And he would have eagerly submitted. But he had intention this time, and she was not going to rush this. She bared her teeth as he pulled away, a primal reaction that ratcheted the pounding of his pulse to deafening, but he was determined to resist.

Miranda had a taste, a sample, but she had no idea the possibilities that awaited. Devin was not the sort to deny a lady her conquests, in the sexual sense, but he would much rather her know the options before placing her order.

"I thought you promised to show me what I was missing," she said, still wrapped around him without need of support. He eased her hands from his neck and her legs dropped to the ground.

"I know what I promised," he said, hands now free to trace the skin above her collar, attempting a more relaxed pace. He needed clarity to properly unearth her intimate desires. "What I promised, was to not hold back." He undid the first hook of her uniform. "Which I am not."

She shivered, completely entranced.

Good.

That was the only way he'd keep her from throwing him to the ground and destroying all his meticulous plans—which was an equally tempting option. His body screamed to let her have her way, to set her loose on another erotic journey of discovery. Let her learn what felt good by taking whatever she wanted.

But oh, how he *wanted* to show her. If he was a rake and a rogue and a villain for wanting to be the one to show Miranda Wilde what made her body sing, then…well, he was going to burn for this anyway.

"I intend a more thorough exhibition of what was lacking in our last assignation." His hands nimbly unhooked and freed ties, letting his fingers drag or stroke along her body as he worked down. "I believe I promised not to stop until you are entirely satisfied." His face hovered near hers, watching how his words affected her features. All her longing clear in her parted lips, lidded gaze, and sharp breaths.

She was practically purring in his hands, and while he had not intended to kiss her again so quickly—he had anticipation to build, a mood to craft—he also could not resist a moment longer. For now, she was content to let him lead, allowing the slow, languid tease of his tongue, delving to meet hers in a sinfully controlled dance.

Miranda moaned, a low guttural sound and his concentration slipped. His fingers fumbled and he advanced on the space between them, nearly bending her backward as his blood roared to take her.

Willpower ready to snap, he managed to resume removing her uniform. It had never been difficult managing his reactions to his partner. A moan, a sigh, a gasp—they were tools to let him know when he should linger or move on, if she preferred his lips or the pressure of a fingertip, all part of the arousing puzzle that he needed to solve. Miranda was a puzzle he'd been desperate to work out for far too long—how could it have only been mere *days?*—and each piece he unlocked kept hitting him like a brick.

Miranda's every note of satisfaction cracked his careful control all too easily. His breathing turned uneven. What was it about her that continued to unravel everything he knew?

He tore his lips from hers, skating over her jaw—always lifted in maddening defiance—down to her neck as he worked her arms from her uniform. His hands hit something hard when he reached her hips and he paused.

"A knife. There's...seven." She pulled away a fraction as she slipped knives from her person, tossing them aside with a resounding clatter. Her arms were free of the leather uniform, her breasts covered in only the thin material of her chemise.

She let the last knife dangle from her fingertips and then drop. Her eyes boldly met his. Another thread of control tore and he caught her around the waist roughly and stripped away the rest of her uniform.

Her gasp and quiet whisper of, "Yes," echoed in his thoughts.

Yes. Yes. Yes. He had to feel her skin, to feel every part of her or he'd go mad.

Miranda's head was thrown back, her body blessedly liquid and willing. When his tongue raked over the dip above her clavicle, she latched onto his bicep and her body arched into him.

There.

He adopted a more rugged pace, fueled by her body's every signal that it was what she wanted. She wanted his teeth and rough hands and aggression. She bit her lip and groaned as he ripped the last thin barrier of her chemise down and let it fall. Clenched her thighs when he squeezed, fingertips leaving imprints in her skin. Bruising.

Miranda did not like gentle.

"Yes," she breathed again, her hands pressing up the length of his chest.

He paused, set his forehead against the warmth of her neck, not wanting to discourage her, but not sure how to keep from breaking something as her fingers began unhooking the buttons on his vest and pushing it over his shoulders. Then she started on his shirt.

He let her undress him while he breathed in the lilac on her skin and focused intently on remaining still. When her hands reached his pants, he stopped her. If she started undoing the ties, he would not last.

"Patience, Mira," he rasped, hoping his desperation wasn't glaring. His hand halted any protest, teasing and caressing her freshly exposed breasts, careful to give equal attention to each firm nipple grazing his palm. She was liquid again, lost in his touch.

He attempted to ease her onto her back, opting for the table over the cot—it was higher and provided a better angle—when she reflexively adjusted her stance to switch their positions.

He was *almost* caught off guard again. But he was prepared now, overcorrecting her maneuver and tossing her onto the table before she could stop him.

When she seemed about to protest, he drew his mouth over her breast, now at a better vantage to reach, and any argument she had died in a choked moan.

Though his mouth never stopped, his hands hesitated again. He set them on her knees, drawing slow circles on her skin. He wanted to tease and draw out the moment, but that is not what had him stalling.

He was nervous. Afraid that his control might snap to the sheer *want* to have her. His control was precarious as it stood.

Swallowing down the hesitation, he let his hands move up her thigh. Her back stiffened, noting his intent, but she did not try to stop him. No, her hands were working his hair into a lather as she moved his head over her breasts, forcing his mouth exactly where she wanted it.

Driving him absolutely insane.

He did not want to plow into her with his fingers and scare her, not for her first time, but each clench of her nails in his scalp, each time she forced his head to the right or left, his need swelled all the harder and he *ached* to be inside her, even if he had to settle for his fingers at the moment.

His breathing grew stuttered, hands clenching and unclenching against her inner thigh. If he wasn't careful, he'd end up making her giggle rather than come.

Pull yourself together.

She's just a woman. And you know what women like. Give it to her.

He drew his right hand down the heated, saturated center of her pleasure.

Oh shit.

Forced to remove his mouth from her breasts and break her hold so he could get some air, Devin undid the top laces of his pants and eased some of the pressure. If this continued, he'd finish well before they got started. But fuck, he had not expected how much the evidence of her want could unravel him, how just the lingering scent of her arousal on his fingers had him fighting to keep from touching *himself.*

"What? Did I do something wrong? Is...am I not—" He halted her words with a gesture of his raised hand—the one not occupied. Hardly tactful, but right then he was seconds from going feral.

"You are perfect," he managed, though he had to breathe through the words, focused on quieting the voice urging him to push her down, let his pants fall, and *take*.

His hands rested on her thighs, both to hold him upright and to assure her. Divine above, he'd never struggled so much with wanting someone. She was like a holy being designed for his distinct torment. He looked into her eyes, the green still darkened by lust, but also so earnest and enchanting. "It is agony to temper my desire for you," he said, lifting a hand to run his knuckles along her jawline, "Divine torture."

Before he could understand why, his pulse raced. Thoughts spiraled. His hands grasped at his hair, the ends so distressed by her vice grip that they stood on end. Shoulders moving with the weight of his breath. Practically frantic. Gaze shifting to stare into the darkness over her shoulder.

And I have no fucking clue how I'm ever going to recover from you. If I can ever go back to before or if you have ruined me forever.

He felt her move, but did not look.

He dared not look at her, naked and wet for *him*.

How was he supposed to perform when reality was nonsense? When Devin Drake was undone by green eyes and the mere suggestion of arousal?

She scooted forward, enough to lock her arms around his back. An embrace. A hug?

His breathing relaxed, but his pulse continued to race.

"So," her voice came light as a feather, bright as a sun in the darkness, "You're saying I'm pretty good at this?"

Devin looked into her eyes, aghast. Floored.

She was smiling. She was dazzling.

Gods above, was he swooning?

She reached up with her head to kiss him, gently. He leaned into her, tethered by the push and pull of her lips. Devin actively worked against sentiment in his pursuits. Resisted affection with every fiber of his being, yet now that it was being offered by Miranda he couldn't muster a shred of resistance. There was no calculation in the kiss, no focus on her pleasure or his. He drew his fingers along her cheek, a kiss from the happily-ever-after in a fairy tale that exposed some new, raw piece of him buried so deep it might never have existed at all. Then her fingers teased at his waist, dipping suddenly so her capable fingers drew down the length of his cock.

Holy hell.

"Mira," he started, but she grasped him through his pants and his every muscle tensed.

"I'm not sure what to do but," she licked at his jawline, "Seems to be working."

He clenched his teeth, shaking his head. *Yes, it was more than working.* "You were not supposed..." His head fell against her shoulder, fist clenched on the table. Her fingers traced and explored, not in any discernable pattern, but it was doing the job well enough. He was getting much too close to finishing than he liked, not when he'd barely started on *her.*

If she was going to turn this into a power struggle, he was not going to lose easily. And there was *one* thing he craved almost more than her teasing, probing touch.

Her thighs squeezed when his hand returned to the warmth between her legs. He wasn't playing fair. As good as her amateur exploration felt, he knew what he was doing, parting her with intentional circles massaging just above where he longed to sink his fingers. Her grip faltered and he seized the opportunity to ease her back, body splayed across the table.

Free of her touch, he did take a moment to admire the view before dropping his mouth to the taut muscles of her stomach, working his way down.

Miranda's body locked again. Devin glanced up to see her eyes wide, her mouth hanging open. He grinned into each kiss over her hip. While he intended to gently guide her legs further apart, she'd parted her thighs on her own, as if she wanted this as much as he did. This was a victory he savored.

Normally, he might have worked up to the moment, built anticipation as he dropped to a knee. But, honestly, he was way past finesse. He pressed his mouth against her core first as a kiss, a gentle reverent slide of his lips to let the shock reverberate for a moment before truly savoring the taste of her, working tongue and lips in equal parts pressure and pattern. His hands were locked on the edge of the table, knuckles white. He wasn't surprised when she clawed into his scalp, when she squeezed with her thighs, and used her strength to move him to her liking.

Fuck. He was not going to last. He had been close enough when she was touching him, but the wanton, brazen way she was grinding into him, was more than even *his* stamina could endure.

He lifted her hips for a better angle and the reward was her not-at-all-quiet-curse. When her breath hitched and her body clenched, and he felt the waves of her release start and then slowly recede, only then did he allow himself relief. It didn't take much. Not even two pumps of his hand and he finished just in time to save his clothes.

Out of breath, Devin swiped a rag from one of the lower shelves and cleaned himself. He fastened the draws of his pants as he got back to his feet. As the stupor of her climax began to lessen, he attempted to fix the cold, rather unromantic setting. He lifted her from the table and set her on one of the cots. He was lost for a moment, captivated by the disheveled mess of her hair, the glow of her skin, the smile of satisfaction on her lips.

Light haloed her body. The stronger colors of proud and determined cerulean, passionate ruby, and adventurous tangerine held a shimmer of canary yellow bliss wafting like the tendrils of her hair in a breeze. Normally, his Aura Sight would send him reeling for a bottle, seeking the quickest way to snuff it out before he could dwell on it for too long.

"What?" She asked, her smile growing, though she shifted her arms as if to cover herself. He fished his shirt from the corner of a bookcase and handed it to her.

Words escaped him. For the first time, there was no impulse to goad or jest, no insistent need to hide himself behind flirtation and false confidence.

"You're being a little too quiet for comfort," she said, a spark of nervous violet streaked through the more grounded colors. Moving faster than intended, he channeled the one certainty he could find amidst the chaos into a kiss. Her arms hooked around his neck and yanked him over her, a tricky feat on the narrow cot. He supported his weight on the wall and on a knee pinning the canvas.

The attempt to maintain their balance forced them to pull apart awkwardly and holding in his laughter was impossible. In seconds, they were both laughing, limbs and arms tangled and bent and not sure who's hand was where.

After a time, when the laughter had died away, Miranda fell asleep. The warmth of her body kept the flood of thoughts at bay long enough for him to doze, though fitfully, until he was jarred awake.

Distant noises. Innocuous alone, but startling in current circumstances: doors and metal and scraping and talking. Without the buffer of alcohol, Devin felt the loss of the moon even through the brick and concrete.

Slipping free of Miranda, he stumbled to the door. He opened it a fraction and Gideon Blair was at the base of the stairs, talking with Rachel. The entire walkway to the office was exposed to the lower floors. They risked being seen if they left together.

Miranda shot upright. "Oh shit, it's morning?"

"It would appear so," he said, wincing.

She blinked, looking at the mess, the evidence of their indiscretion. He tried not to read into the pulse of garnet panic or how she pulled his shirt tighter over her shoulders, like she wanted to hide. He searched for shame or regret, but just because he couldn't see it didn't always mean it wasn't there.

She would never admit to you, she'd rather hide than let them know your dirty hands were on her.

"Here." He began to scoop up her clothes, forcing the doubt in his head down. Her panic was not unreasonable, given her social status. *Not unreasonable because you are beneath her social status, lower in every way.* He closed his eyes as he said, "I'll head him off. Follow when you're ready."

She threw his shirt, hitting him in the face, and dove for the floor. Devin only had to return two layers and comb his fingers through his hair to tame what Miranda had pulled. There was a clear difference between disheveled and sex teased, and Blair would spot the difference easily.

Checking quickly to make sure Blair was still occupied, Devin slipped from the room and sprinted for his office. He kept away from the railing, but the Watchmen below were too occupied by their own conversations and morning routines to notice. Devin dared check only once, blinking against the kaleidoscope of colors that spanned in front of him. It had been so long since he'd used his sight he couldn't remember how to control it and with the onslaught of color came the bombardment of the various meanings.

He shut himself in Blair's office, grateful for the moment of peace. His brain was functioning with more clarity than it had freedom to in recent memory. And while that voice continued to taunt him and needle at his insecurities, something new warred with his self-loathing.

He couldn't name it yet, never having given too much thought to emotions he *was* familiar with, this was entirely other.

Blair's stock of brandy caught Devin's eye, drawing his attention. Yesterday, he would have already taken a sip. Today, he remained rooted to the spot, staring down temptation until the Captain himself burst through the door.

"Shit, it's way too early for this," Blair groaned. "Rachel didn't think I could get here early. Well. Who's wrong now?" It couldn't have been long past sunrise, Devin had only just started to feel the sun before sprinting over here.

"Long night?" Devin asked, squinting against Gideon's strong navy band of confidence and dedication and a fuzzy restless streak of obnoxious vermillion with the barest thread of anxious violet weaving through.

"You could say that," Blair said, crossing to the brandy. He lifted a glass in offering.

Take it, Miranda is a road to misery and pain. She does not want you, only what you can give her.

Devin stared at the offered glass, hands at his sides.

You're already miserable, what does it hurt to try?

Devin declined. Relief and terror flooding him as the offer rescinded.

"Suit yourself." Blair tossed back a glass and then fell into his chair and balanced the empty tumbler on his forehead.

He'd declined a drink. With Blair's aura slapping him in the face with its obnoxious glare. Why on earth would he do that?

"So—" Blair started.

Miranda's small knock interrupted, drawing Devin's attention and the sight of her eased the flood of doubt.

Her. It was all her.

Blair fumbled to catch the glass as he sat upright. A strong, crimson pulse of desire flared through his aura. His drawn, overtired frown vanished instantly, replaced by the charming grin he threw at every pleasing skirt in his vicinity. Gideon smoothed some wayward strands of his hair, charm exuding from him as he went to meet Miranda at the door.

He took her hand in his, kissing it gently. "You must be Miss Wilde."

And Devin's fury was immediate, focused, and drowned out everything else.

CHAPTER TEN

M IRANDA RACED TO GET dressed. She searched for her chemise, dismayed when she noticed that it had been torn and stretched to the point of ruin. She groaned, but she knew well enough how to dispose of evidence, and she had plenty of others. For now, she had to make do. She hopped around stuffing her limbs back into her uniform and trying to undo the tangled mess Devin's hands had left in the laces of her boots.

Color heated her cheeks and warmth fluttered in her belly. She would happily relive every moment again later, when she had the time. Or maybe she could orchestrate another moment? And another. Her pulse raced as she calculated all the ways she might seek him out unnoticed. She could go to his apartment in secret and—

Guilt crushed her excitement. She hadn't even asked if his apartment survived. And even if it had, he might be too busy salvaging his livelihood to indulge in clandestine meetings. At least he hadn't pushed her away this time, though he had been uncharacteristically quiet. She would ask him about that later, for now she had to focus on why she was here in the first place.

Adjusted, composed, hair hastily thrown into a...whatever her awkward fingers could manage—if she could use a blade to style her hair, then she'd be proficient, but she rarely dealt with the thick waves on her own. Using whatever she could find in the storeroom to wash the sex from her body so she could be somewhat presentable when she talked with the Captain of the Watchmen.

Miranda eased the door open. While, logically, she knew that Devin had slipped away several minutes ahead of her and was unlikely to have drawn notice, it still felt like a spotlight followed her every move, screaming to the overfilled headquarters that she had debauched herself. And every lesson of etiquette and decorum drilled into her said she should feel very ashamed, ruined beyond redemption. Yet, her steps had never been lighter, almost a saunter, and a wicked grin alighted her features.

Perhaps, she was always meant to be a fallen woman. Scorned and outcast from the society she was expected to serve. And if she'd known how damned good it felt, she may not have resisted it so much. Before, she had been too afraid to take any bold step away from the future she dreaded. It had always felt an inevitable certainty. Yet...maybe it wasn't. Maybe all she had to do was choose to follow her heart. It might devastate her parents, they might be pressured to cut communication with her if anyone found out about this indiscretion. Would she still be able to speak to Cordelia?

Miranda pushed the uncertainty aside as she drew closer to the Captain's office. Two of the sides were entirely glass with curtains that could be drawn if needed, but allowed him to overlook the officers below. She watched Captain Blair offer Devin some sort of liquid in a clear glass, liquor of some kind.

She huffed. Devin drank too much. While she sensed there was some dark reason, it seemed to her like he was trying to drown himself. She suspected it was the same reason he used to cover his ears.

Devin raised a hand to decline the offer, shocking her. She stopped for a moment. Why did he decline? She had never seen him without some hint of alcohol on his breath, what changed?

Me.

Miranda shook away the thought. It was the height of egotistical to assume she had anything to do with his choice. She continued forward, chewing her lip. But...maybe?

Something formed in her chest, something stronger than lust and desire. She walked a little faster, though she could hardly talk to him when she reached him, not when they weren't alone, but the Something pushed her faster and she almost didn't wait to be invited after she knocked on the door.

Her eyes were for Devin, focused on how all the doubt she'd been trying to bury evaporated, and so when Captain Blair swooped in to greet her, she nearly jumped.

"You must be Miss Wilde," he said, voice deep and soothing, "Rachel mentioned you stopped by last night but neglected to mention your beauty." She watched him with uncertainty as he took her hand to kiss it, which was technically the proper way to introduce himself, though he had missed a few steps that hinted he was not as practiced or had picked it up late in life, rather than born to those standards.

He was handsome, his athletic build perfectly displayed by the fit of his uniform. Black hair trim and neat. His smile would have had many a debutante blushing and giggling, crawling over each other to be on the receiving end of that smile, but the over-the-top flattery and performance had her choking back a laugh. "Captain Gideon Blair, at your service."

Captain Blair had barely straightened when a hand descended on his shoulder and ripped him backward.

"She gets it," Devin growled, jaw tense. Devin met her eyes with an intensity that made her entire body shiver. He was jealous. No one had ever been jealous of Miranda. No man had ever wanted a second dance with her, let alone to seek her out in the middle of the night to apologize to her or fill an entire night unlocking her every wanton, improper desire she hadn't known existed.

The Something grew ever stronger in her chest.

Devin cleared his throat and glanced away, as if he wasn't sure if his actions were wanted, but the impulse had been too strong. He spared one more glance before turning away from her to face Captain Blair again, though she noted his shoulder was positioned to block her from the flirtatious captain like a shield.

"Ah," Captain Blair raised an eyebrow at Devin, "I wasn't aware she was spoken for. My apologies."

Devin shifted on his feet, head turning but not quite enough to look at her. He stayed silent.

"I speak for myself, actually," Miranda said, crossing her arms and moving so she was shoulder to shoulder with Devin. She kept her eyes on the Captain, but made sure her arm brushed Devin's as she moved. "But your apology is accepted."

Captain Blair laughed, looking between them as if he were trying to get a read on the situation and found it amusing. "Fair enough. But if you ever tire of his insipid melancholy my door is always open. I'm infinitely better humored." He winked, and Devin took a step like he might attack, though he never left her side.

"I think you mean laughable," Miranda retorted, and she waited for the reprimand. For the scoff and disdain of the Captain that she dare show humor and wit or for her mother to somehow manage to scold her from halfway across the city.

Instead, Captain Blair nearly doubled over laughing.

Devin's tone was unamused as he said, "He doesn't take himself too seriously."

"She is *completely* out of your league, Drake," he said, wiping at his eyes, "And I've never known a society Lady to make jokes." The Captain's flirtation evaporated to genuine amusement.

"Maybe you just haven't been listening," Miranda quipped, fueled by his laughter.

"Ha, that's putting it mildly," Rachel's voice carried into the room as she stomped through the open doorway without knocking, "If Gideon ever gave a woman true, genuine attention that would mean hell's frozen over and he'd never give his mother the reprieve."

She continued straight past Devin and Miranda, like they didn't exist, to get to Captain Blair's desk. Devin's hand caught Miranda's back, gently guiding her out of the way. He let his hand linger for a moment before removing it, balling his fingers into a fist. The gesture sent butterflies loose in her stomach.

"I'm not doing the briefing," Rachel snapped as Captain Blair returned to his desk.

"Rachel, please, I'm in a meeting." Captain Blair waved her away, when she didn't budge, he added, "Look, you didn't think I could show up on time, but I got here, didn't I? And I can hardly give the shift briefing when I'm otherwise occupied." He gestured at Devin. "Besides, you're better at it than—"

She slammed a folder in front of him, sending papers flying like leaves in an autumn breeze, her stare just as chilled.

"You were supposed to sign off on this report *weeks* ago. Lottie can't file the reports if you don't. Sign. Them. And then it all stacks up here and no one can find their case files when they need to."

The Captain rolled his eyes. "Nonsense. I have my own filing system." He motioned to the papers still floating to the floor. "You just cost me months of careful organization, by the way. I won't be able to find anything now."

"Get a fucking drawer." She set her hands on his desk, glaring down into his face with a ferocity that even Miranda would be hesitant to challenge.

"I have a secretary, I don't need a drawer," he countered casually, eyes narrowed, but they didn't hold the same fire as Rachel's.

Rachel crossed her arms. "And where is she? She's supposed to be here even earlier than you, and somehow she's conveniently absent, yet again."

Captain Blair looked away, shrugging. "She asked for the day off."

"She hasn't shown up in two days. She missed half of last week and hasn't stayed until the end of her shift since she started." Rachel pressed her face into her hands, clearly on the last shred of her patience. "You hired her because she's pretty. You always pick the pretty ones and they never work out. They either don't know what they're doing, or you somehow manage to convince them they're 'not like the others' and then they're too heartbroken to stay. She's got you giving in to her every demand despite her being entirely unqualified for the position."

"Maybe not the *secretary* position..." The Captain was barely audible, but a silence descended that blanketed the room.

Devin's fingers curled around Miranda's elbow and he leaned in close to her ear. "Best step back," he said, lips lingering a touch longer than they had before, his fingers lightly drawing patterns over her sleeve before retreating.

Rachel's jaw clenched so tight Miranda feared it would detach.

Captain Blair waved away her palpable anger. "Fine. Fine. I'll fire her, if you'll just leave me in peace about it. Go hire that other one. The...married one. That should appease you."

"It would if I knew that would stop you."

He shrugged.

"You're an unscrupulous moron," she yelled, "And do not fire her, do not go near her. *I'll* do it. Divine knows you'll only find a way to prey on her vulnerability after learning she no longer has a job."

"I actually hadn't considered, but the idea isn't half—" He lifted his hands as she speared him with a look that could have drawn blood. "Okay, okay. I'll stop. Happy now, Emmy?"

Miranda cast a look sideways for clarification.

Devin shrugged. "Hell if I know. Sometimes he calls her that, but he's never shared why."

The use of the name, however, seemed to have made Rachel more irate. Her tone was lethal as she leaned in close. "I will be hiring the next secretary."

"I should get final approval—"

"Like hell you will."

"It's *my* secretary."

She stomped from the room, slamming the door so hard more papers were dislodged of their place and cascaded toward the floor.

"That's another two months of organizing you cost me!" The Captain yelled after her.

Miranda watched Rachel's angry path through the window, hiding a laugh as Rachel held up her middle finger before descending the stairs. Miranda wasn't sure why, but it felt like she'd just witnessed something private, like a voyeur to an intimate exchange between lovers.

"He must have slept with someone last night," Devin murmured, dipping so that only she would hear him. "It always sets her off."

"Why would..." Miranda closed her mouth. It was hard to imagine that any of that was because Rachel harbored romantic feelings for the Captain.

Devin filled her silence with confirmation. "For as long as I've known them."

Miranda had a new appreciation for Rachel Stone. Miranda would not have been strong enough for such restraint. She looked up at Devin, his smile kind and conspiratorial, his hand still casually finding ways to brush against her. No, she would not have been strong enough.

"Oh, right, you're still here," Captain Blair said, his tone drawn and defeated. "Well, get on with it. What do you want?"

The back of Devin's hand skimmed over hers as he moved past. What was this? They clearly weren't courting, but somehow they were no longer mere acquaintances either.

The casual touch, the shared looks, it reminded her of her parents, the way they always seemed to read each other's thoughts or how her father would stop and kiss the top of her mother's head while he was on his way out.

"I thought you'd be happy to hear we've uncovered evidence of Graves's crimes," Devin started. "Since you came knocking specifically for help with this case, I thought I'd share what we've learned."

Captain Blair eyed him, though he'd slunk into his seat and looked as if a long night and harsh morning was catching up with him. "By all means, pin it with the others. I'm sure it's nothing but more dead ends."

"How about a record of experimentation on fae that resulted in at least fifteen deaths? Signed by Graves." Miranda fished out the documents she'd carefully folded and slipped into an inner pocket of her uniform. She flashed the page, the Captain's eyes following it with curiosity, though he stayed slouched in his chair. "And proof that these experiments involve injecting fae with Divine blood."

Miranda sensed he was hesitant to believe her. If the board behind her was any indication of his fruitless diligence over the past few years, she didn't blame him. "You can't just inject the Divine's blood into fae. You can't *get* Divine blood. It's not a pill or some witch's potion you can pick up in the black market."

"It could be extracted from the source," Devin added, stepping behind her. She felt the heat of him through her uniform.

"But..." The Captain balked, looking at the pair of them like they were speaking a different language. He held out a hand. "Can I see this evidence?"

Miranda felt like she was losing to let it go, but it was the reason she came here. With a breath, she released the signed experiment and her copy of the drawing from Graves's desk.

Captain Blair studied the pages as he rose to his feet.

"This address..." He pushed around the desk to the giant map holding his notes. His finger hovered over the far east of the city. The Garrison and the Night Court bracketed a shipping yard where Unity bordered the Great Sea. A series of commercial warehouses stored various exports to the other cities of the Realm that honored the Accords.

The Captain ran his finger down the row of warehouses before stopping at one that held a red pin. He tapped the building twice.

"That's it. I've had my eye on this for months, certain that Graves was connected, but he's not on the lease or shipping registry. He must be using a false name or even a dummy investor. But it's the same address written here." Captain Blair held up the paper, but his eyes never left the board.

"So this is proof. Can you stop him?" Miranda asked, though she felt more defeated about passing off her mission to the Watchmen than she anticipated.

Captain Blair pinched the bridge of his nose. "No, you see it doesn't matter. This isn't...I need something more concrete if I'm going to bring this up to the commissioner. Parliament believes Graves to be one of their peers. They were already questioning my suspicions and

I've technically been ordered to 'stand down.' There're ordinances I have to tip-toe around and warrants and—"

"Graves suspects we have this information. He might already be covering his tracks," Devin said.

The Captain chewed on his tongue, concentrating on the board of clues, all leading to nowhere. "Or..." He turned on his heel, a smile that was both sinister and overjoyed distorted his handsome features. "*You* are not bound by red tape."

"What are you playing at, Blair?" Devin crossed his arms, obviously knowing the Captain well enough to piece together his intentions faster than her.

"If you are telling the truth, then time is of the essence. Even with this, I can hardly organize any sort of retaliation before Graves has ample time to destroy evidence. It could be days if I'm lucky, weeks if I'm not."

"We don't have that long—" Miranda started and The Captain's manic eyes turned on her.

"No. We don't have long at all. But if I had a reason to storm the building before Graves could bury the evidence, some...solid, unquestionable catalyst that would force my hand? Let's say, two civilians were caught up in this mess, snooping where their noses didn't belong, and somehow ended up way over their heads. In fact, they are attacked by the very monster they hoped to uncover. And what am I to do when they call on the Watchmen for aid?"

"You're not using us as bait—"

"We'd be the perfect bait—"

Miranda met Devin's eyes and she saw his refusal clearly. 'This was too dangerous, they could get hurt, there was no telling what awaited them if they went inside.' She could hear the tirade of reasons not to do this, but it didn't matter if the reasons were valid, it wasn't what was right. She would go alone if she had to.

"I can give you a moment, if needed," Captain Blair said, and a glare from Devin had him retreating into the hall, shutting the door behind him.

Devin's hand hovered near his mouth, worry radiating off him. "I'll do it alone. There's no reason for you to be—" He huffed as her chin started to rise, like he knew he already lost. "Fine. Together."

"You know as well as I do that *we* need to do this. It's your chance to get Graves and make it look like an accident or self-defense. You could get your revenge and avoid hanging for it."

"And what about you? Is your sister still set to marry that leech?" Miranda didn't respond, but that was answer enough. "Then why continue with the charade?"

Miranda worked her lip between her teeth, suddenly nervous. There was something about his eyes that clutched at her heart, like he was asking because his life hinged on her answer.

"I...I wanted to see this through."

He looked away, withdrawing. "Ah. That tracks, I suppose."

She set her hand on his cheek and forced him to turn back, to meet her eyes instead of retreat. "*And*, I was hoping you'd come to your senses."

He said nothing, just breathed and leaned a fraction further into her touch.

"As you said, we work pretty well together." She kissed him quickly, blushing. Though, why she would be blushing after all the parts of her *he* had kissed, she didn't understand. Dare she hope that this would all work out? That she'd be useful, to save the city from whatever Graves was planning and finally have someone who didn't try to control her? Who seemed to admire her and delight in her harsher side? She had not thought a future with Devin was possible, but that was because she hadn't wanted it. Not before.

Captain Blair opened the door. "Time's up, we got to move on this."

Devin shook his head.

"We'll do it," Miranda said.

"Thank the Divine." He shut the door. "It should go without saying that this plan does not leave this office."

The Captain flagged down a passing officer—since his secretary had the day off—and sent for Rachel.

Rachel's face didn't so much as twitch while Captain Blair spoke, his entire body animated.

When he finished and he looked at her expectantly, her features finally softened. "Don't get your hopes up, Gideon. You'll be putting your friend at risk and there's no guarantee it will lead anywhere." The gentle probing of her words was the first time Miranda could see her affection clearly. Rachel cared how Captain Blair might feel, offered a soft voice of reason when it was clear he was too consumed in his plan to see beyond the details.

"Drake will be fine, he's been through worse." The Captain waved her concern away, but Miranda watched the fear fill Rachel's eyes, how her gaze lingered on the back of Captain Blair's head while he stampeded through his thoughts unaware.

Devin's fingers intertwined with Miranda's, squeezing gently and she wasn't sure if he was trying to comfort her or himself. She leaned so that her weight pressed into his side, but only barely, hopefully not in a way that would draw notice. Although, with Rachel focused on Captain Blair and Captain Blair focused on his plan, she doubted they would.

"If anyone asks, you came to me with these accusations, but I didn't believe you. So, the pair of you took matters into your own hands." The Captain had pulled more maps from a shelf—which took several minutes of searching, though Rachel did not comment—studying them as he spoke. "You two will have to find your own way inside, shouldn't be hard. Not with upper class guardian training." Miranda suspected he hadn't intended to call her out in front of everyone, but she felt self-conscious all the same. Guardians from families outside the nobility went to a public academy for their training, and only for certain times of the year. It was not as rigorous or intense as her instruction had been.

"From there, I just need one of you to find a way to give me a signal that I can use," The Captain continued, "An explosion. A body falling out a window. Screaming. Something that one of my officers could find, react to, and then call me."

"I'll station Singer and Solis on the marina. Solis has sharp eyes and will notice any disturbance and Singer has a habit of stumbling into trouble, so if there's something to notice, she'll find it," Rachel said, her tone clipped.

Miranda suspected that, as much as Graves had wronged Rachel too, she didn't agree that it was worth the risk.

"I just need to work out a way to get a battalion of Watchmen ready without making it obvious. Maybe I'll start a training exercise, so they're all armed up? Or I can...I'll figure it out. You two okay with your side?"

"Get in. Make it obvious. There's not much to work out," Devin answered.

"Perfect, I'll—"

"Sir?" An officer came to the door.

Gideon huffed. "What? What is it?"

"Oh. Uh, your sister's, um. Here."

Captain Blair froze. As literally as Miranda had ever seen someone go from motion to statuesque. He wasn't even blinking.

"Is he okay?" Miranda asked, resisting the urge to wave her hand in front of his face.

"Yeah, he'll be fine," Rachel dismissed with a wave. "Thank you, Miller, he'll be down in a minute. You two should get started if we're short on time. If I help, I should be able to get everything in order by tomorrow, is that too soon?'"

"No, I'll be ready," Miranda said, knowing that she would have to return home and dreading it. Her parents might tie her to a chair after all the sneaking around she'd been doing lately. But she had been wrong when she thought they wouldn't believe her, maybe she could convince them that she needed to do this, for herself.

Captain Blair resumed breathing, the pencil in his hand snapping in two. He spoke loudly enough to be heard even as she and Devin left the office.

"Where is she?"

"A holding cell," Miller supplied, his wince audible.

"Fuck, not again."

Miranda turned to whisper to Devin, "Why is his sister in a holding cell?"

"Let's just say they took very different paths processing their trauma," he whispered and Miranda liked how he stayed close to her, how he hadn't let go of her hand, how their whispered confidence felt intimate, shared. It was the same sort of comradery she'd felt with Lydia, only she had never wanted to pull Lydia into a dark corner to act on indecent impulses where no one could see.

As they threaded their way through the now bustling main floor, a familiar face stopped Miranda, and eye contact forced a different set of instincts to take over.

She bowed in greeting. "Alderman North," she said.

What was Alderman Kieran North doing at Watchmen Headquarters at this hour?

North returned the greeting, all precise motions and rigid manners. North had never been known for his warmth and, while she had never found him cruel, his callous disposition was often mistaken as such. "Miss Wilde, what a surprise to find you here."

"I could say the same thing," she retorted, then bit her cheek. She had spent much too long in the company of rogues and scoundrels. Even *she* would not have dared speak to Alderman North that way a week ago. His piercing, frosty stare was unforgiving of indiscretion.

He didn't seem overly concerned with her slip just now, however, his attention seemed to be drifting elsewhere. His icy grey eyes remained bored as they moved over her shoulder to Devin.

"A friend of yours?" He drawled, voice sending chills down her skin and not the good kind.

"Oh!" She nodded, quickly pulling Devin to her side and then regretting the intimacy of the gesture and pushing him away. Heavens, she was flustered. Two worlds were warring for control and she didn't know which to fight. "This is Lord Devin Drake. A friend. We were just leaving."

"Very well. Please give my congratulations to your sister on her happy nuptials or whatever the phrase."

Miranda nodded and then froze. "What?"

"We're expected to wish others well in marital endeavors, no? I've assumed wrong before." He sounded as if he cared very little if he assumed wrong or not.

"No, no, it's...Cordelia isn't *married*." Miranda almost laughed, because the idea was...unthinkable. He had to be mistaken. "Nothing was planned until months from now."

His harsh brow furrowed, "Strange. I read only just this morning that the pair eloped."

Miranda's heart squeezed and the blood drained from her skin. "She...what?"

Alderman North continued as if his words *hadn't* knocked the wind from her. "Elopement. The announcement was in the papers this morning. I don't forget and I'm rarely wrong. Though I'm surprised you weren't aware, as her sister. Perhaps a long night has kept you from your family?" His gaze slid to Devin, and there was no smile or sneer, but somehow she was certain he knew what had kept her away the previous night. If she were not in the midst of panic, she might have cared.

"I..." she reached out to steady herself, for a wall, a chair, anything. A warm hand caught her and Miranda fell into Devin's strong, solid body.

"Thanks, North, was it?" Devin interrupted, drawing a sharp look from the Alderman, "It's been a pleasure, but I think I'd better see the lady home now." Devin's voice was clipped, impatient.

Miranda's legs weren't working properly. She felt wobbly. Unstable. Devin guided her out of the building and began to hail a cab for them with his free arm, his other remained wrapped around her waist.

"It's alright, Mira. We'll get to the bottom of this. It has to be a misunderstanding."

"Or, Graves has found a way to kidnap my sister without raising suspicion." Her chest felt hollow, raw. Had she eaten today? Her head started to swim, the world blurring into a mess of colors.

"Mira?" Devin caught her as she swayed. "Mira, hold on."

He lifted her, tucking her against his chest like she was fragile. She wasn't fragile...but maybe she could be for the moment. She set her ear against his chest, soothed by the sound of his heart that drowned the rest of the world. Devin's voice was muffled and indistinct. She sensed him lift her into a cab, sensed him cradle her in his arms, his cheek on her head and his hands attempting soothing, stroking motions.

Had she eaten today?

Miranda's last conscious thought was of Cordelia, and the overwhelming fear that she was too late to save her.

CHAPTER ELEVEN

T HE RIDE THROUGH THE Garrison was hell. It wasn't the fear of losing Miranda that tortured Devin with each sway and dip of the carriage, it was how scared and useless he felt despite being certain that she would recover. She was breathing, whole, her aura strong as ever—though a muddied panicked shade of violet was coiling around her like an oil spill in clear water.

It was likely just the overtaxing of her emotions combined with little sleep and no breakfast that caused her to collapse into his arms. All Miranda needed was some water, a hearty meal, and to check on her sister. With any luck, North had been misinformed and Cordelia would be happy and well when they arrived.

Yet, there was a tremble in his hands and dread had locked around his heart, squeezing with each frantic pulse. What was he supposed to do?

He held her. That much was simple. He tried to soothe her, but aside from a gentle stroke of his hand he didn't know what else he could offer her.

When the driver had asked for the destination, Devin briefly considered giving *his* address in the Garrison. A brief, selfish impulse to keep her to himself, as if he were responsible for her welfare and he alone held the right to her care—however out of his depth. But it's not where she needed to be. Miranda would want to check on her sister. She needed to go home. And he was her only means to get there.

Biting out the words, he had supplied her address and tried to keep calm. In a practical sense, there was nothing he could do. But in an emotional sense his body was shooting out adrenaline that settled in his limbs as nervous energy with no outlet. And he cared, so much more than he thought possible, that she opened her eyes again.

He didn't know where they stood with each other, not with any certainty. The words that would label his relation to her were murky, unclear, and who-the-hell-knows. Though, the words that might fit *his* attachment were closer to consuming, maddening, and too-deep-to-recover.

For as long as he could keep this going, he wanted to be with Miranda. It was pointless to pretend otherwise. Somehow, she had twisted her knives into all his buried, locked away pieces and pried them free with as much care and force as explosive powder excavating a mine. If he lost her, or *when* he lost her, there would be nothing left but gaping holes and he didn't think he was strong enough to attempt to patch them this time.

All through that blasted meeting with Gideon he'd had to stop himself from taking her hand or pulling her closer. Touch, as he knew it, had always been a tool for either violence or sex and the idea of wanting to feel her skin just for the warmth of it, because that warmth trickled into him and somehow made the ache lighter, soothed the doubt and self-deprecating voices of his inner demons, was as foreign to him as tea services and dinner parties.

Her aura had been steadfast in Gideon's office and his touch had only elicited colors of comfort or joy. But even his Sight could be misleading. His mother had always burned with one singular, solid color over all others, a maternal pink that flared whenever she was with him. But it wasn't enough. Her love for him never wavered while all her other colors grew muted, dull. Her care and ability to show him affection weren't stronger than the weight of everything else.

And colors of emotion could be fickle. Strong one minute, gone the next. Even a strong emotion might be ignored or pushed aside if they conflicted with someone's goals or ingrained beliefs. As a teenager he'd watched auras pulse with desire for him, even as they sneered and mocked him. Or a stranger's snap of pitying cyan before pretending they hadn't noticed him. Gideon was a master of changing colors. Crimson-indigo-vermillion-violet. He could whisk through several fleeting emotions in the span of a moment.

Devin's heart ached to hope.

The carriage finally stopped outside her home. He felt her stir and called to her softly to no answer. Oh well, looks like it was the front door then. He steeled himself for the rage that was sure to hit him when he knocked on the Wilde's door with their run-away daughter unconscious in his arms.

He kicked the door in the pattern of a knock, since his arms were occupied, and the butler answered with a look that suggested he did not appreciate his master's door being kicked, no matter how practical.

"Can I hel—" The butler's eyes landed on Miranda and a burst of alarming goldenrod blinded Devin for a moment. "Miss Wilde!"

The butler leaned, reaching out as if to save her from the scary villain, but Devin pulled away. Villain he may be, but he refused to let them take her inside and shut him out. He intended to be there when she opened her eyes, whether the Wilde's wanted him or not.

"Call for her parents. I'll ask you only once to step aside." Devin's tone left no room for argument and goldenrod turned to crimson anger.

With a huff, the butler allowed him to enter and Devin sought the first room he could find with a couch. He eased Miranda down as gently as he could, moving the hair from her face so it fell in gentle waves over the pillows. Like a princess in a fairy tale waiting for a prince to kiss her awake. He lingered for a moment, her hair still caught in his fingers.

Villainous rogues didn't kiss princesses.

Devin tore his hands away, wanting to linger where he could feel that she was still warm and breathing, but not wanting to be found touching her when her parents arrived.

"Miranda!" A woman pushed him backward. Familiar shades of ruby and blue—complimentary to her daughter's—dotted with worried plum purple flooded his vision and forced him to step back. "Miri, by the Divine, what happened? What—"

Lady Wilde set a hand on her daughter's cheek and when she felt warmth and the movement of breath, she collapsed at her daughter's side, not even attempting to mask the sobs that shook her whole body.

Lord Wilde followed on his wife's heels encompassed in a swirl of controlled, gallant white and authoritative royal blue, marred only by the same worried shade as his wife. But...another color caught Devin's attention as husband neared wife. A red link reached from her aura to his, a binding thread of color.

Two souls woven together.

He'd seen these threads before, but in the Fells, the bind of real love was hard to find. Though he tried to resist, afraid to see nothing, his gaze locked on Miranda, searching.

"What happened?" Lady Wilde got to her feet, advancing on Devin with purpose and fury. "What happened to her?"

Devin nearly tripped over a footstool, unprepared for Lady Wilde's aggression. He could not say for sure if she was a guardian, but he was not about to test the theory. She looked ready to start tearing limbs. Lord Wilde put a hand on her shoulder, reigning her back.

"Cicely, let him explain."

"Cordelia is gone and Miranda wasn't in her room. She wasn't..." Lady Wilde ground her teeth, hot angry tears streaming down her cheeks. "And now she's here and not waking up and *what happened*?" She directed the last question to Devin, growling as she advanced.

"She fainted. She'll be fine in a moment," he assured, "When she heard about Corde—er, the younger Miss Wilde," he corrected as two pairs of eyes narrowed on him at the familiar use of the sister's name, "It...I think she was just overwhelmed and in need of a decent meal."

"She was in need of her home!" Lady Wilde's aura was blazing, flickering flame red and blinding sunburst fear. "The girls need to be home."

"Miranda is here," Lord Wilde soothed, his hands holding her as she trembled, the red thread entwining their bodies. Devin looked away, eyes landing on Miranda, who was beginning to stir. He crossed around the inconveniently arranged furniture until he was at her side.

Her eyes fluttered and her smile allowed his heart to beat again. There was no red thread connecting them. Aura Sight didn't allow him to see his own aura, but he was certain the frayed edge of a red strand reached unrequited for Miranda.

Her smile vanished as she looked past him and bolted upright. "I'm home."

Lady Wilde reached for Miranda, hovering near Devin though careful not to touch him.

"Cordelia?" Miranda looked between her parents. Their looks were answer enough. Miranda shook her head and pushed through him to stand. "No! It was supposed to be me. He wanted *me*. She was...she isn't strong enough for this..."

"We've only just learned of the news. We had assumed both of you were safe in your rooms. There were no signs of capture in either of your chambers, so I can only assume that bars would be needed to keep the pair of you contained." Lord Wilde gave his daughter a pointed look.

"Cordelia climbed out her window?" Miranda asked as if the observation was ludicrous, which struck Devin as amusing considering how often Miranda herself seemed to abscond from windows.

"Or she was taken from it, though no evidence suggests she was forced," Lord Wilde said, "Then we saw the papers this morning and...we're working on getting her back. If we knew where to start that would be one thing, but she could be anywhere."

Miranda stopped pacing, turning on her heel to address the room. "I know where she is."

"Where?" Lady Wilde asked, desperation in her voice and aura.

"I had evidence of Graves's plans to use guardians to inject fae with Divine blood—"

"*What*?" Her parents interrupted together.

Miranda continued without acknowledging, talking as if her parents already knew this information—though their faces said otherwise. "In fact, that may be exactly why he had wanted me in the first place. What better source of guardian blood than a wife who he could control? But...Cordelia's human. He would have no use for her, other than as revenge for what I did. Or if he thinks that because of her family, maybe she still has traces...it doesn't matter. I'm going to get her back." Miranda lifted her chin.

There'd be no stopping her now.

She turned to Devin with a confident smile, focused aura, and...blatantly ignored her parents. Devin tried not to notice their aghast expressions, or how Miranda's clear intention to include him despite present company only ensnared him all the tighter.

"Devin and I have a plan, that doesn't have to change. We'll just move faster than Rachel anticipated. Captain Blair can just have the Watchmen ready sooner. Tonight." At present, Devin would have followed her into an active volcano, she had but to ask.

"No," Lady Wilde interjected, pushing through the furniture, her dress sweeping delicate decorations to the floor leaving a wake of broken trinkets, until her daughter was forced to look at her. "You are staying where you're safe. I'm not having both my girls lost in the city."

Miranda took a deep breath and then hugged her mother. When she pulled away, she said, "You're going to have to physically restrain me if you mean to stop me."

"I...Miri, it is much too dangerous and..."

"And what have I been training for? I'm not helpless. Cordelia *is*. I can get her back. I already had a plan to stop Graves, now I'll just make sure that I get Cordelia first. All I have to do is get the Watchmen's attention and I'll have all the backup I could need."

Devin stayed quiet, still not sure of his place. He knew where he wanted to be, beside Miranda.

Always.

Forever.

He was prepared to follow her down any foolhardy path, to stand beside her as she charged headfirst into trouble and to give whatever he had to offer if she faltered or got in over her head. If she allowed him to follow her. While there was still a whisper in his mind urging him not to trust her, it grew weaker every time she took his hand or smiled *because* of him or included him. But he was still hesitant to push into family matters. Her mother had a right to fear for her daughter, and Miranda did not need his help if her mind was set.

"Fine," Lady Wilde said, "Then I am going with you. James, you go down to the Watchmen headquarters and inform whoever is in charge of this...scheme our daughter has devised, knows the plans have changed. You make sure that whoever they are, they're organized and ready, or I will see to it they never work in polite society again." Lady Wilde went to the door, smoothing her hand over her dress, her eyes red and her cheeks still flushed. "I'm going to change. Hopefully..." She squared her shoulders, holding herself to her full height. "Hopefully, my uniform still fits."

Lord Wilde rounded on Miranda, his eyes slipping toward Devin. "I'll wait with you until your mother returns."

Miranda blushed, not meeting her father's eyes and Devin cringed. If her father had doubts about their relationship, his daughter blushing as she looked at him was proof enough.

"Lord Drake, you will give me a moment with my daughter."

It wasn't a negotiation, but still Devin looked to Miranda for the okay before leaving. The door slammed behind him and he sighed into the too large, too empty foyer.

Her home was just as grand and stately as Devin's late father. Ornate and decorated. Family heirlooms and the lingering presence of generations tucked into corners and the more intricate details. His eyes swept up the grand staircase, wondering which direction would lead to Miranda's room.

It was a better fantasy than reflecting on their conversation. He could imagine Lord Wilde was not happy about Devin's role in his daughter's recent streak of rebellion. Logically, he knew that any father would be angry, but there was still a voice that wondered how much of his objection was for what she had done as opposed to who she had done it with.

Enough. She has given you no reason to doubt her.

She *had* pushed him away when Alderman North had asked who he was.

But there were plenty of valid reasons she might have done that, and none of them had to include her being ashamed of him. Had she not just openly ignored her own parents to include him? Or was she just worked up and acting on impulses she might regret later?

He sighed again, loudly. It echoed throughout the foyer.

Why couldn't he just...be happy? A good thing *finally* shows up at his door—doesn't even knock, but kicks it in and demands his acceptance, refuses to leave even when it is the only sensible course—and yet he was still trying to reason away her interest and overanalyze any hint of doubt.

The absence of some red line of fate in her aura could mean anything. Perhaps it only appeared after marriage or perhaps he and Miranda were too uncertain of the future. It had barely been two weeks since he met her, for Divine's sake.

If he died alone and miserable, he would have only himself to blame.

He stopped in front of a portrait of the current Lord and Lady Wilde with their family. It had to have been many years ago, as Miranda and her sister were still children, Miranda barely taller than her father's waist. What if this was what Miranda wanted from him? A portrait with children hanging in their home? Marriage?

All his life, he never gave a thought to marriage one way or the other. It just wasn't something that would ever figure into the sort of life he planned to live. He had no desire for the lasting attachment and sentiment necessary to say 'I do' and he actively pushed away anyone who ever tried to get close to him.

Why would he invite more of his tainted lineage into the world? What kind of father sired children doomed to hardship? Even if attitudes were changing, the damage was done. The fear was part of him, as much as the hope. His maternal grandparents were still alive somewhere, not willing to acknowledge his existence.

He stared at the painting, trying to fit himself into the scene.

It wasn't possible. No stretch of the imagination could make Devin the father in that painting.

He turned away, rubbing his face in his hands. He would follow Miranda into danger, but could he follow her into vows, if she asked?

Would she ask?

He stared into the never-ending sea of porcelain, wood, and ornaments, vision blurring the colors into a muddied mass. While doubts and uncertainty and what-ifs threatened to overwhelm him, a singular truth rose above the chaos with astounding clarity.

Devin had, against all reason and his better judgement, somehow fallen in love with Miranda Wilde.

Fallen, crashed, dragged kicking and screaming, but here he was and there was nothing he could do to stop it now. He would have whatever life kept him close to her. A portrait in a grand hall, husband and wife, perfectly squeezed into all the proper molds. It didn't matter how rare the chance that he had inherited a title, it still meant he fit the definition of "titled nobility." He *could* give her that life if she wanted.

Or, if she asked, he'd live cast from society and all the security it offered. The wealth and acceptance. The stability. She was rebellious enough that he wouldn't put the idea past her.

He spared a glance at the door as Miranda's voice grew louder. He closed his eyes to the limitless list of what she could be saying.

It didn't matter.

Only Miranda mattered.

Maybe that was why, now that revenge on Graves was finally within reach and the culmination of years of guilt and rage finally about to be sated, he was more concerned with a portrait on a wall.

Miranda's father moved through the room to slam the door and then returned with the agility of a breeze through trees, darting past furniture and broken glass. Her heart was pounding.

"I don't want details," he said, calmly. She couldn't meet his eyes.

She had always remembered looking up at him. As a child, as an adolescent, even as she reached adulthood he had always had those last few inches that required she crane her neck to meet his gaze. But she could see in her peripheral as some of his control faltered and he pinched the bridge of his nose.

"I was young, Miranda, I know...things happen. You're not the first to let your feelings run away with you, it's part of being young, though we all like to pretend to be above such indulgences. Your mother—" He cleared his throat. "Wait, what I mean—"

"What about mother?" She pressed, not giving him the chance to backtrack.

Her father was always careful with his words, always sure of himself. Now, *he* refused to meet her eyes, hands growing fidgety as he scratched at his cheek or his ear. "That's...nothing. It was nothing. I was going to say nothing. If your mother asks...I said nothing." He sighed, but his hands never moved behind his back and his posture never returned to its normal rigidity.

"The way he looks at you," He continued through his teeth, "It's not...dissimilar to how I once looked at your mother nor, I suspect, much different than how much I, well, *cared* for her, even before we were married—but we *were* married. Promptly. As was the expected course. I had always planned to marry your mother and waiting for what we already knew proved...impossible." He closed his eyes, taking another breath in and Miranda allowed him a moment to gather himself before continuing.

Her cheeks burned all the brighter. Infernal blast it, she did not want to hear *that* about her parents.

"And you," he took a careful breath before finishing, "I've never seen you so assured."

Wait, was this approval?

"Don't get me wrong, you have always been confident. Divine above, you were never lacking in spirit. But, it's clear now that even then you were holding back. Locking away part of yourself," his hand reached out and gently took hers. "But I saw it now. Your anger, your passion, your spark. You were confident in more than just your ability to take someone out at the knees, you were confident in *yourself*. The whole of you. Or you would never have spoken to your mother that way."

Miranda was not sure what to make of this conversation. Her father was always so controlled and disciplined. He followed the rules, never faltered from routine, saw good as black and white, and was not the type to overshare. And what did he mean she lacked confidence in herself? Miranda had always been confident in herself. She was secure in who she was...right? She caught her reflection in the broken glass of a decorative vase that had belonged to her great-grandmother. Her mother's dress had knocked it from its perch as she had ripped through the room, her emotions raw and unmasked.

Miranda always pulled loose strands of hair free to soften her features, to hide. She always *tried* to keep her voice from rising, to keep the bite out of her tone—even if she didn't usually succeed. She always *tried* not to step on toes or kick the boy who had thrown mud at her in the park or push the Lord who thought he could call her 'too much' or 'annoyingly quarrelsome.' Miranda had *tried* to not be all those things, because she was not supposed to be all those things. Even when all those faults invariably slipped through her attempts at control, the guilt that surfaced had always made her shrink afterward, made her question, made her doubt.

She had never had confidence in all of who she was, only the parts that were acceptable.

Until meeting Devin.

She was starting to embrace the parts of her that she'd been told to hide. Which had felt good and liberating, but...then why had her father's reaction sent unease rolling through her chest?

"I'll never hate someone who makes my daughter smile like she means it," her father finished, and Miranda felt no relief at his acceptance, if that's what this was.

Her heart started beating harder, crashing against her ribs. Was he giving her the okay to...to court Devin?

No, he was probably giving his blessing for an official marriage that aligned with all the rules and structure she was expected to set her life to, but that's not what she wanted. She wanted Devin, but marriage to him—he was a titled lord, even if some did not approve of the means and circumstances, he was exactly the sort of suitor her mother would push onto her at a ballroom—would mean trapping herself in that life she had hated. She thought choosing him meant giving that up, but if her parents approved...if he agreed to marry her, then her life was right back on the same path it had always been.

"Miranda?" Her father reached out to her, but she stepped back.

"I don't want to get married," she said, finally. Loudly. Her eyes glanced at the door, but she could only hope her voice hadn't carried.

Her father shook his head. "First, no one has mentioned marriage, so let's not get carried away. I don't hate him, that's still plenty of steps away from wanting the man who had my daughter out at all hours for a son-in-law. Second, if you intend to continue this...whatever you two have, what other option is there than marriage?"

She wanted to cry, because she didn't have an answer. She wanted to be with Devin, more than anything she'd ever wanted. He was the first person to ever inspire her to act, to venture from an abhorrent pre-destined future. She had wanted to continue to have adventures, to explore new things, to use her skills to help people and to have Devin with her while she did. Devin gave the impression that he cared little for her world, for society, but that had a lot to do with him feeling like they rejected him. What if...what if, when given the chance, he would leap at the idea of finally fitting in? Of marriage to a well-bred woman who could settle in as Lady Drake in his father's estate—the home he chose to live in, despite already having a home at his club? A club now destroyed and so allowing him the freedom to enter fully into her parents' world without attachment.

Her heart was starting to fracture, little fissures that ached with each beat of her pulse. Her heart wanted Devin, her *body* wanted Devin, but...she had been so close to freedom. Could she give that all up? Could she hop right back in line when she had finally, *finally*, run through the untamed wilds and found they suited her infinitely better?

"Miri, honey, what's wrong?" Her father stepped closer, arms reaching out to soothe her. She hadn't noticed the tears had started falling.

"I just...I don't think I can be the daughter you want," she wailed, louder than intended, but she couldn't help it.

"What are you saying? You will always be—"

"But I can't! I *can't* tell you that I don't want my sole purpose in life to be motherhood. I don't want to manage my husband's social calls and raise daughters to be just as caged and...and *bored* as I am. I don't want to be a society princess." She finished the last words with a yell, not sure if she was screaming at him or herself.

Her father pulled her closer. "Shh, my dear, that is not what marriage is, at all. But...I also don't make the rules. What you're suggesting comes with consequences that not even I or your mother can change. We don't have the luxury to live however we want."

"I know." She wailed, burying her face in his pressed, wrinkle free jacket and smearing her tears into the expensive fabric.

He let her cry. If he had planned to say anything more, he didn't get the chance. Her mother opened the door, her brown hair swept up into a tight, orderly arrangement to keep it out of her face and her uniform hugging her figure in a way her dresses had always hidden. Her father's jaw fell open and Miranda hated that—with her newly discovered freedom—she now suspected she knew what his look implied.

"Enough, James, it's not like you've never seen me in this," her mother huffed, still adjusting herself like she wasn't used to wearing such form-fitting clothing. On her hips were dual swords, smaller and not as heavy as the two-handed blade Miranda and her father preferred.

"Now." She finally looked at the pair of them, her expression softening. "Oh, my dear, I know you're worried about your sister, but we will get her back." Her mother turned to her father, eyebrows raised. "James? Are you going to stare at me all night or are you going to do as I asked?"

"Right." He blinked, stepping away from Miranda, but not before his hand brushed through her hair, and he gave her a paternal kiss on the top of her head. "I'll be off." He gave her mother a look and she rolled her eyes, staring back in some silent exchange that Miranda couldn't decipher.

"Now then, grab what you need and meet me at the carriage as quickly as you can. I'm eager to have my daughter back," Her mother said, leading Miranda into the foyer and, when Devin made to follow

Miranda, she caught the back of his collar. "You will come with me, thank you."

"But—"

"Ah, ah, I'm a mother. My child is missing. You don't want to test my good graces at the moment." She tossed him forward, sending Devin stumbling ahead of her with little effort. "Out you go." She pushed him through the front door and shut it behind them as she yelled, "Make it quick, Miri, or I'll have to send a separate carriage for you while Lord Drake and I get better acquainted in private." The tone of her voice carried a hint of threat that suggested Devin might not survive if left alone while her mother was armed.

Miranda raced to the armory where they kept weapons that weren't for training or ceremonies. This room held swords and maces and bows passed through her family throughout the generations, tools carefully maintained and polished to be used in real combat. She picked a sword that felt good in her hand, the balance just right, and attached the sheath.

She made an additional stop at the kitchen, filling a loose cloth with anything she could grab: some fresh fruit, bread, a selection of sandwiches leftover from tea, and the last few pieces of bacon from breakfast. When she returned to her mother, the carriage was just being pulled out front.

Her mother made Devin crawl in first, then herself, then Miranda. Tearing into a roll, Miranda sat and passed some of her collection to Devin. Her mother watched with a hawk's precision, clearing her throat when Devin's fingers brushed Miranda's as she passed over bread and fruit. A sharp tap on his shin if his knee ventured too close to Miranda's. His every move was guarded and reprimanded until he could do no more than breathe.

"Enough, Mother, your point is taken. There's no need to keep attacking him," Miranda snapped after swallowing the last bit of bacon.

"Nonsense, no one is being attacked," her mother said, her voice rising an octave the way it did when she meant to appease company. "Are you being attacked, Lord Drake?"

Devin speared Miranda with a look as he answered, "Not at all, Lady Wilde."

"There. You see?"

Miranda huffed and focused on the window. A mantra of "this is for Cordelia" kept her sane and kept her from wondering why Devin was still here. If he wanted his revenge on Graves, he didn't have to wait for Miranda or indulge her overbearing mother in the process. He could have left. Yet there he sat, silent, brooding, unable to move without getting chastised.

He didn't leave when Miranda was harsh or when she snapped at him or scolded or yelled. Miranda's heart cheered, screaming *finally* and beating for the chance that Devin could actually *love* all of her, but the elation was tainted by the conversation with her father, the fear that if she married Devin her life would not be free.

Her mood soured.

As the carriage continued through the city to their destination—a few blocks clear of the marina, so they could plan how they would enter—a tense silence threatened to strangle her, but her mother was a master of easing tension, even tension she created.

Once the silence teetered on hostile, her mother spoke, "Now that we are underway, I think it's time you filled me in on what we are up against."

"Graves has figured out how to extract the Divine's blood from guardians and he's injecting it into loyal members of the Night Fae," Miranda started, "They're strong. I could barely move them without effort, but they're highly untrained, relying solely on brute force. Although, I suspect Graves has his own private guards of altered fae that are sure to be well equipped to defend him."

Her mother listened, nodding along, but her face grew more drawn. "We should have a plan. Can Lord Drake handle himself or are we going to have to compensate?" She asked, as if he weren't sitting right next to her.

"He can hold his own. Though he's prone to distraction, he's also more strategic than me and there's a hesitation in using his left hand, possibly from an old injury," Miranda answered.

"Hang on—"

"You have always been impulsive, I've told you time and again you need to be more mindful. What's his preferred weapon?" Her mother said, cutting off Devin who followed their conversation with his jaw open and brow furrowed.

"From what I've seen, knives. But that could just be because it's all that was available."

"Wait a damn minute," Devin growled, forcing them to acknowledge him.

Miranda winced. Tactical observations were as ingrained in her as reciting her alphabet. And while observation of the larger picture and scene had always escaped her, assessing individuals was second nature. When her mother asked, she had replied automatically.

"First, I'm right here, Lady Wilde, should you have a question you only need to ask. Second, I am hardly prone to distraction." His eyes landed on Miranda and then he looked away quickly, "Mostly, not prone to distraction. And third, we were given swords during the war and that is what I trained with, but I've had to defend myself enough times without preparation that I'm more versatile with my hands."

Miranda's thoughts drifted, her eyes dipped to his hands, toward memories she'd rather not ponder with her mother present. She chewed her lip as she crossed her legs and tried not to let her improper thoughts show. If her mother noticed, she said nothing.

"I apologize, Lord Drake, Miranda was trained to assess her enemies and allies for strengths and weaknesses. I assumed you didn't have technical training to provide me what I needed. And, if I am honest, I am not quite myself. I...I'm worried about your sister, Miri. She has been missing for several hours, at least, there is so much that..."

"I know," Miranda said as she set her hand on her mother's and they were silent until the carriage drew to a halt. She hoped they weren't too late.

CHAPTER TWELVE

T HE CARRIAGE STOPPED WELL clear of the marina, but hints of brine and fish managed to laced the air even here. Or perhaps that was just sobriety.

Now that Devin wasn't suppressing his Aura Sight, all of his senses were returning to normal. Vision was that much sharper. Peripheral that much wider. Reactions quicker, stability that much sounder. He could smell each distinct note of perfume from the women beside him and somehow differentiate it from the scents outside.

Over the years, he'd adapted to the inebriation, found ways to compensate for what he lacked. His tolerance allowed him to function at baseline human levels. Without the alcohol, the parts of him that didn't conform to humanity were becoming glaring. He felt other again. He felt fae.

Lady Wilde set off ahead as soon as they stopped, not bothering to wait.

In a few moments, there would be no turning back. Their course would be set and whatever fate had in store...there'd be no escape.

Devin caught Miranda's arm before she could follow her mother. His hand lingered, not willing to release her, yet knowing that under her mother's stare and the grim circumstances he might not be able to touch her like this again. She didn't protest, but there was a distance in her gaze that had grown since talking with her father.

It didn't take imagination to guess what was said between them. The disapproval and objections, the outrage that she would choose someone like him to debase herself. The confident, bright colors of her aura were edged in the faintest, almost translucent shade of lavender doubt.

Doubt.

He steeled himself for the worst. Because there was a chance he would not survive this mission and there were things he wanted to say.

"I don't know if we'll get another chance to talk and," His hand eased her closer, instinctively, because he was lost at sea and her touch alone kept the waves at bay. "If the worse should happen, I..."

Her gaze was open, waiting. Hanging on his words and he knew there were seconds left to him before her mother noticed they weren't following. Yet the words died in his throat, trapped, choking him. Because this was all too new and he was afraid. There was no red thread connecting him to her. There was no certainty there ever would be one. And was it fair to stick her with a declaration that would do little more than tether her to a memory if the worst should happen to him?

"Yes?" She prompted, inching closer like she needed to hear him say it, like she knew.

He kissed her.

If he couldn't tell her that she made him *finally* want to live, that he found something that meant more to him than his blasted revenge, then maybe he could *show* her.

He poured all of himself into her, hand cradling her cheek, arm wrapped around her waist so his fingers could sink into the dip of her hip. It was a kiss loaded with promise, with the unsaid. He kissed her to say that if he survived this, he was never going to stop kissing her for as long as she let him. He kissed her to promise that if he saw tomorrow, he was hers forever.

He didn't stop kissing her when tenderness melted into carnal, or as her nails started to bite or as his mouth shifted from adoring to ravenous. He pressed his luck as their undeniable chemistry teetered on combustion.

Devin pushed fate until the fear of Lady Wilde tossing him into traffic won out. He pulled away to press his forehead to hers, lingering for only a breath of a moment before meeting her eyes. The uncertainty and doubt lingered. But she continued to hold him, like she was just as afraid to let go.

"We have to get my sister back," she started, "But after...we can figure it out, after."

He desperately hoped there would be an after.

"We should catch up to your mother before she kills me," he said.

He suspected Miranda had left her own words unspoken, but when he checked the lavender band of doubt it was starting to become translucent. The relief of it washed through him, easing the heavy dread that had been smothering him.

Lady Wilde was farther ahead than Devin anticipated. As he and Miranda rounded a corner and the marina opened before them—a U shape of roads with docks and tethered ships—he couldn't find her in the crowd, though he could make out the obvious patrolling routes of Graves's enforcers. Miranda motioned to a shadowed alley between two buildings. A crumbling wood fence with jagged holes and uneven boards provided some cover and a way to look out at the street.

Salt thoroughly saturated the air, he could almost taste it, and the distant crash of waves and incessant cry of gulls bordered on distracting.

"I will not ask what kept you," Lady Wilde's voice was clipped, just behind them. "But I will ask that you do not delay again." Her eyes locked on Devin and he matched her stare with his own.

He was not going to apologize.

She bristled, but continued, "Now, what is the plan?"

"We need to be sure Cordelia is inside before we make any move that we can't take back," Miranda whispered.

"Any ideas on how?" Devin said, "There's no windows within reach."

"The roof," Lady Wilde chimed, nodding toward the top of the warehouse.

It wouldn't be easy to reach, but it was tiered, one section higher than the other, and a series of vents lined the upper tier. Presumably, one could look through and see inside the entire warehouse.

"I don't see a better option and Miranda is right, we can't be discovered until we know that Cordelia is inside. I don't intend to waste my energy on needless combat," said Lady Wilde.

"What about procuring some disguises?" Devin suggested, preferring that to attempting to climb onto the roof without being noticed. "There's plenty of his enforcers around and they did us the favor of hiding half their face as part of the uniform."

"We should split up," Lady Wilde said. Though her voice was steady, her aura suggested doubt and reluctance.

"Are you sure?" Miranda asked.

"Of course I am," she snapped, then took a breath. "I'm sorry, Miri. I'm as sure as I can be. I know you can do this. You and Devin should get disguises and get inside. Whoever is in a better position to get to Cordelia, that is their priority. The other can signal the Watchmen."

"We have to be careful we don't alert Gideon too soon," Devin said, "Not while Graves still has Miss Wilde."

"You're right, a sound observation," Lady Wilde conceded, though it seemed to cost her great effort. She pulled Miranda into a hug and kissed the top of her head. "I trust you, my dear, because you're strong and capable. I know I've been hard on you, wanting you to settle down, but it's never been out of spite or necessity. Marriage to your father has made me the happiest I could ever hope to be, and that is all I want for you. A partner, a friend to share life with so you don't have to do it alone. You think independence is strength, but *love* is strength, Miri. Having the courage to tether your life with another's is the greatest risk we can ever take, but worth every second if it is with the right person." Lady Wilde speared a look at Devin, contradicting the implication of how her words might relate to him. He was thankful that guardians didn't have Aura Sight, or Lady Wilde might see his disappointment.

Lady Wilde attempted to blend with the burly crowd of workers, sailors, and enforcers. Even hiding her face and outfit under the cloak she'd taken from her carriage, it was obvious that she didn't belong there. Thankfully, no one stopped her and soon she was out of sight, looking for a way to climb to the roof unnoticed.

Devin's eyes kept shifting to Miranda, who had closed off at the mention of marriage and the lavender began bubbling over the other colors of her aura, darkening into almost purple. She was silent while they waited. Devin intended to follow her lead, but the colors churning around her were becoming alarming.

He opened his mouth to speak, but she cut him off.

"Now," Miranda said, "How do we get disguises? There are about twenty enforcers and they all seem to be in pairs or threes. We can't just grab someone and run off with them."

Devin pulled his eyes from her shifting colors. He needed to focus on what was happening in the present. What he wanted to do was pull Miranda aside and demand to know what she was thinking, because the guessing was driving him mad. She was not hard to read, even without insight into her aura. But that wasn't the same as talking or hearing directly what the hell was going on in her mind.

First, save her sister.

It helped if he kept repeating it.

He let out a breath through his nose, casting his gaze out at the street until he found two enforcers with auras that were thinner than the others, drawn and tired. The pair walked toward a secluded section of the marina, settling themselves to lean against some crates out of view.

"There," he motioned with his head. "Those two are nearing their limits. They will be easily overpowered and they're already positioning themselves out of sight."

Miranda squinted, trying to pick out who he was referring to. "How do you know?"

He licked his lips. The instinct to lie about his gift was still habit. But if he had any hope of building a life with Miranda, it couldn't start with lies.

"I have Aura Sight. Those two are exhausted and likely looking for a way to rest without getting caught."

"I knew it," she breathed, "I knew it had to be something. Is that why you were always drinking?"

"It is, but I've recently decided to quit."

"Why?"

He turned to her, heart on his sleeves. "After last night...smothering it just didn't seem so tempting anymore." A puff of pleased pale pink wafted through her bolder colors. Pride swelled in his chest at having caused it.

"Oh," Miranda said, her voice timid for the first time since he'd met her.

Devin cleared his throat, brushing off his confession by adding, "The Sight can be a blasted pain, though. I'm not used to it."

He turned away, because if he didn't he'd continue this entirely ill-timed conversation and there was still a sister to save.

They took separate routes toward the targets, to better avoid detection. The street was full of enforcers coming and going to various tasks, but these two held back, lingering far from the others. Overworked or just exhausted, it left them vulnerable. And even with their greater strength, he and Miranda had no trouble muffling their screams and pulling them quickly behind a stack of shipping crates.

In seconds, Miranda's enforcer was unconscious. Devin had grappled for a moment, almost allowing his target to cry for help if not for a quick hit against the enforcer's windpipe. Now able to get a proper hold, a few more minutes passed before the enforcer's arms went slack.

The enforcers wore cowls and masks to obscure their faces. Devin easily removed them, revealing two fae with body proportions that wouldn't quite align with Miranda or himself. Miranda grabbed the smaller of the two and started undoing the jacket. She had to roll the sleeve to compensate for the longer limbs.

Devin undressed the larger of the two, but fae women tended to have narrower builds and this one had less muscle definition than him. Miranda held a hand over her mouth to suppress her laughter as he fought to get himself into the jacket.

"Yes, it's very amusing," he said, tone droll as he twisted to do up the buttons.

The material bunched and sagged in places, squeezed in others, his body type was too human and too male. With an ungraceful sigh he fixed the cowl over his head and secured the mask. Hopefully, no one would scrutinize his attire too closely. Neither of them bothered with the pants or boots, their own clothes matched well enough.

"You'll have to stuff your hair into the head covering," he said, motioning for her to turn around. She did, but as soon as he pulled the first pin of her hair free, she rounded on him.

"What're you doing?"

Devin lifted her wrist and set the pin in her hand. "Hold this. I'm fixing your hair." He gently spun her again and freed the rest of the pins before twisting her hair into a few braids and repinning it so it would fit under the cowl.

When he finished, he could see the question before she asked, and he said, "My mother didn't have a maid, just a son who hadn't the heart to refuse her when she wanted to look like the Ladies in the park. I'm out of practice, so it wouldn't do in a ballroom, but it'll keep your hair flat inside the hood."

"Is that how you learned to dance?"

The question caught him by surprise as they lifted and dragged the bodies further away from prying eyes. They were secluded enough hidden behind large stacks of shipping materials, but it was best to be on the safe side.

"My mother wanted to be part of human society. I assume that was the appeal of my father, but they never married and invitations to ballrooms don't include addresses in the Fells. But yes, she had taught me the proper dances." He kicked the lid off a shipping crate and inspected it. There were remnants of whatever foul-smelling cargo it had once carried—likely a crate leftover from a fishing trolley—but the enforcers would fit.

"She sounds—"

Devin heaved a body into the shipping crate. "Hers is a sad story, Mira. Best to leave it for the moment."

"I'm sorry, I just meant that...it seems like she loved you. And you loved her." Miranda heaved the other enforcer into the crate and set the heavy wood lid back on top.

"I did," he said, "And she did, in her way."

"Is she gone?"

He set another crate on top, trapping the pair inside, before finally meeting Miranda's eyes. She wanted so desperately for him to have a mother who would climb a building to rescue him. But that wasn't his reality. His mother loved him, but it hadn't been enough.

Between the heartbreak from his father, the loss of her family, and slow iron contamination over years her ability to function eroded away, leaving Devin alone and wondering why he hadn't been enough. He didn't hate her, but he also found it hard to forgive her.

He looked away as he answered, "She was gone long before she died."

Miranda's arms came up around him suddenly and her head pressed into his back. He was still for a moment, both caught off guard at the gesture and wanting to crumble into her. Her arms stayed as she maneuvered around him, her face now buried in his chest and he caved, returning the embrace and fearing he wouldn't be willing to let it end.

Miranda pulled away, the whole exchange lasting less than a minute, yet she'd shaken years of repressed trauma free.

"Cordelia first. Talk later, but...I figured there was time for a hug," she said, as her arms eased away from him and they could no longer risk touching or they might give themselves away.

Devin took a breath, rattled and disquieted, but somehow lighter.

Graves's warehouse bordered the Great Sea, just one in a long row of identical buildings only set apart by the number above the door. No one questioned them as they approached or when they slipped into a line of enforcers entering the building through a bay door.

Once inside, they were assaulted by an acidic, chemical smell with an undercurrent of rot. Here, there were various workers whose faces weren't covered. Workers stacking boxes, or tallying with clipboards, or packing crates. There was a flurry of activity, as if they were trying to get a lot done in a short window of time.

The ground floor was a single open level and the ceiling rose up to the rafted roof. But dividers and stacks of crates obscured their view and gave the effect of rooms and separated spaces. Above were a series of open walkways that crossed above their heads to allow workers open access to the levels below. An open storage platform spanned one corner and a walled off office in another.

Devin followed Miranda's gaze, searching for her mother through the vented slats on the roof. Lady Wilde shook her head. Cordelia wasn't in view from above.

"We need to go up," Miranda whispered. "I'll bet anything she's in that office."

"Agreed. If we walk like we know where we're going, we shouldn't be questioned," Devin said.

They chose a path and tried to make their search for the stairs look purposeful. There were several sets of stairs but once inside the network of 'rooms' it was hard to see the entire upper floor and get their bearings. The first path led to a dead end, and before they could turn around a line of enforcers forced them to duck into the closest room to avoid notice. Miranda lingered by the entrance—there were no proper doors—and listened for the retreat of footsteps.

Devin's newly returned awareness shifted his attention to the room. Unease crept up his spine. Dread lay stagnant in the air like a fog.

This room was against one of the outer walls, the other sides delineated by crates on one side, the other by shelves, and another by cages. The cages appeared empty, sized to hold larger animals, and the barred doors were left ajar. Against the crates were a series of desks littered with equipment. Test tubes and beakers, stacks of papers, pens and cutting instruments. On the shelves were endless rows of vials, all empty. Waiting.

Devin's focus was drawn to the wall of cages and the single latched door near the bottom. A red tube snaked from the bars, ran along the wall and into a carafe on the desk. An aura, the faintest shade of desolation he'd ever seen, was more like a void than a glow. The color was so dismal his Sight couldn't find a name for it, but the feeling seeped into the room, seemed to reach out to him with clawed, weakened fingers, dragging him down into the source's despair. It was a Winter Fae talent to sense Death, but no one could mistake the heavy presence of Death that waited in the cage, biding its time.

"Mira..." He reached for her, but her focus was elsewhere.

Devin remained frozen, trying to find the will to take a step, to lift an arm.

"These are the same drawings, the same notes from Graves's desk." She picked up a sheet of paper and then crumpled it in her fist. Anger began to emanate from her, flickering waves of red hot anger.

He followed it, allowed her bold, vibrant colors to lure him into taking a step.

"Devin?" She left the desk, meeting him in the middle of the room, and when her touch reached him he heaved in a breath like he'd been drowning. "What's wrong? What is it?"

He fell into her, taking the support. "The corner," he growled, motioning with his chin.

Her eyes followed the motion, but she shook her head. "What? There's nothing there."

"You can't see, but there is most certainly a soul in that cage." He twined his fingers with hers. "May I use your hand for a moment?"

She nodded, though confusion creased her brow.

Devin used her touch as a lifeline, a tether, to keep him from sinking. Then he grabbed the red tubing, which was actually a clear tube currently filled with the steady trickle of blood. With his free hand he drew a knife and sliced through it, some of the sticky, hot liquid draining onto his hand. The figure in the cage was too weak, too far gone to do more than slump further over, their aura flickering for a moment, but not going out.

Miranda gasped behind him, though he didn't dare turn as he continued. His hand squeezed hers, grounding him so he could finish his task. He flipped the knife and used the handle to snap through the lock. It had not been a strong lock. There was no fear of attempted escape.

He eased the door open, hinges groaning from disuse, but opening it had been more for Devin's sanity than anything. Whoever was inside hadn't the strength to leave and Devin could hardly waltz out with a prisoner and risk the mission. Hard as it was, Devin would have to trust that Gideon would do the rest.

"Let's get out of here," he growled, voice thick with a righteous sort of fury.

After a few more dead ends, they found the stairs closest to the upper office. They were about to ascend, when the office door burst open and they instinctively retreated into the shadows under the stairs.

Above, they could only make out the shoes and movement through the slats of the flooring, but the voices carried with perfect clarity.

"Please, remind the Chaplain where his new roof came from, and that it can be taken away just as easily. In fact," Graves's voice was razor sharp, laced with anger, his careful performance forgotten now that he wasn't being watched, "Let him know that if I don't see him in the next half hour I will simply burn his church to the ground. Do you understand me? Am I speaking clearly enough? Because if I see you again without a chaplain in tow I'll use your corpse as kindling."

"Burn the church—" A timid voice, from a pair of flat, men's shoes, their steps light and jittery.

"Oh, the Divine can try and smite me if They wish, but by the time I'm through with my plans, They'll be little more than a nuisance. Remember who holds the power here, Yen. Who do you fear more?"

The flat shoes skittered away to their task, bounding down the stairs and then disappearing.

Miranda made to lunge, but Devin caught her wrist. She huffed, but settled back into a crouch while Graves returned to his office and shut the door.

"She must be inside," Devin whispered, "If he is planning to bring a chaplain here, then she has to be close."

"A chaplain to force her into marriage." Miranda ground her teeth.

"Look at me," he guided her chin with his hand, meeting the cold steel of her eyes, "We will not let that happen. Graves has been doomed since the moment you entered my club." He let his words linger for a moment, before adding, "He stands no chance against a fierce, capable guardian with a devilishly handsome rogue at her side."

Miranda rolled her eyes, but he could see the anger ease from her body, replaced with a surge of navy confidence. Her smile returned, if only because he was insufferable and he knew it, but it worked.

Leaving their shelter, they took the stairs to the top, but there was little movement up here. Perhaps because all the walkways were entirely open and exposed it was easy to keep watch for anything amiss. The office had two small windows along the walkways and a large one to view the warehouse below. They lingered just under one of them, crouched down to avoid being seen before they carefully eased up to peer inside.

Two enforcers stood like silent sentinels in the corners of the office while a young woman with light brown hair and wearing her night-clothes stomped a slippered foot against the floor.

"I told you already, I won't cooperate. Bring all the chaplains you like, kill me if you have to, but I won't marry you." Her voice was a touch higher in pitch than Miranda's but her tenacity no less prevalent. A sunny, cheerful yellow danced with ribbons of daring teal and turquoise valor.

"Don't think I haven't considered that, missy," Graves barked. "You and your sister have been more trouble than either of you are worth, but it's too late now. I'm not starting this whole ridiculous dance over again. I needed an alliance with a guardian noble to ease my transition and the tests on your blood will be finished soon. If they come back negative, then you won't have to worry about marrying me after all."

"You think I have the Divine's blood?" Cordelia asked, then she laughed, doubled over and cackling. "You think...but that's hilarious. If I had Divine blood do you think I'd be sitting in tea rooms while my sister gets to play with swords all day? I could have saved us both a lot of trouble if I knew that's what you were after."

Graves's stare was deadly, but Cordelia either didn't notice or didn't care. "There is a chance that trace amounts could be stored in your blood, as a multigenerational family. You're my first test of that theory, however, so we'll see what the results show."

"Well, good luck with that, but I won't cooperate either way."

"Oh, please do fight back, you spoiled little brat, then I'll have a reason to use force."

Cordelia eyed the two enforcers behind her. "These two brutes? Oh no, I'm so scared!"

Perhaps the younger Miss Wilde had a death wish, because there was no other reason for her reckless taunting that Devin could see. Miranda was tense beside him. She couldn't go rushing in, or they'd be overwhelmed in seconds. He stepped back a few paces to get an eye on her mother and gave Lady Wilde a nod, pointing toward the offices.

He returned to Miranda, but a hand descended on his shoulder and launched Devin into the outer wall like he weighed nothing. The entire structure rippled. He may have cracked a rib, the pain sharp and stabbing as he fell on his knees. Another enforcer held Miranda while she struggled in their too strong grip. She might have been able to fight them off, but not when they had surprise on their side.

"I recognized the pair of you from that club we burned," said the enforcer holding Miranda. Another came and hauled Devin to his feet. "You don't see matching auras every day." Devin glanced down and for a second, the colors of his aura flickered into view. Cerulean compassion? Ruby integrity? The only color that made half a lick of sense was tangerine mischief. The enforcer continued, "But the thread of crimson is what gave you away. None of us share that kind of link, except Dorria and Jem, but only Dorria is here today. Now hold still. Travers, get the boss out here."

Devin's attention snapped to Miranda, wincing through the pain as he got to his feet. He tried to find the thread and *there*, buried under the fiercer colors of her aura was a whisper thin line of crimson. How had he missed it? Was he just not wanting to see it? Whatever had allowed him to see his aura allowed him to see the thread tethering them together.

Even as he attempted to work out the implications while not ignoring their current danger, the image faded, until once again he could only see the colors of Miranda and nothing else. He barely had time to register what it meant before Travers had returned.

Graves exited his office, meeting them on the walkway while the enforcers hauled Miranda and Devin in front of him. Struggling against the enforcer's grip was like fighting with steel. They were obscured from the view of the lower floors by the office, there was no way to get a signal to Lady Wilde.

Once again, Graves was in Devin's reach, and the icy, burning need to squeeze the triumph from Grave's eyes returned. All the lives Devin carried with him over the years, his fury for Miranda, for the nameless aura locked in a cage, for all the fear and hurt and death. Devin's vision narrowed to one, singular target. Steely calm washed over him.

Graves regarded them with fully expressed agitation, rather than his normal mask of jovial civility. "Ah. Miss Wilde and Mr. Drake. Not heeded my warnings, I see."

"I just want my sister," Miranda growled.

Graves smiled. "I'm sure you do, Miss Wilde, but my bride is no longer your concern. In fact, nothing is going to be your concern for much longer. I've worked very hard these past years. Bided my time. Rose through the power structures carefully. Positioned myself in the ideal seat for a transition into total domination. I've even developed a potion that will change the entire world for my people. And you think I'd allow you to waltz in seconds before my victory and destroy all I've worked for? No, Miss Wilde, you are sorely mistaken. I am going to kill the pair of you, that much is clear. In fact," Graves nodded and the fae holding Devin began to drag him away.

"No!" Miranda's voice sharp and scared.

"He doesn't matter," Graves said, "A half-fae nothing." Then to Devin he called out, "You were never a part of any world, Drake. Not to worry, I'll make sure your father's estate passes on to someone more worthy."

The taunts settled over him. Filled his heart. His lungs. His blood. All his life, he had believed those words. Poisoned and hated himself because he had believed them.

He waited for the inner voice in his head to whisper, to agree with Graves, to remind him that he was worthless.

But his head was silent.

"Miss Wilde, however, I must dispose of more politically."

Devin had a single, frozen moment of clarity. He stopped struggling and instead angled his arm for the blade stashed near his shoulder. He gave the blade a quick twirl so he could plunge it backward.

The enforcer's hand flew up in defense. Devin spun and slashed, coming to a stop as the spray of blood rained around him.

And for one glorious minute, there was nothing between him and Graves. And in that heartbeat of time, the oozing, corrupted onyx and burgundy ambition that surrounded Graves held a tremor of pale, ashen fear.

CHAPTER THIRTEEN

M IRANDA FROZE.

The world froze.

Devin faced Graves like he was about to enact the worst sort of violence and enjoy it. It wasn't Graves's fate that made her heart stop. It was the enforcer who leapt to prevent Devin from reaching him.

Miranda shouted a warning, but her voice seemed to carry in slow motion, the sound muted to her ears even as Devin charged.

Graves flailed backward, falling over himself in a comical parody of an escape. His collected superiority lost the moment real danger threatened him.

But he was not Devin's target. Mid-sprint, Devin threw the knife in his hand, catching Miranda's captor in the shoulder and allowing her to pull free. With his forward momentum he slid, kicking out the legs of the last enforcer so that they toppled over the railing and fell with a scream and a horrid, echoing squelch. The scream would draw every available enforcer to them.

Dodging past Graves, Devin headed toward the office. To Cordelia.

And Graves seized the opportunity, fleeing faster than Miranda could blink.

There wasn't time to dwell on the effervescent emotions brimming in Miranda's chest.

Enemies charged for the stairs from every direction. On the farther end of the warehouse, Miranda's mother sent a stack of crates tumbling end over end. The thick crates bounced on each step as the heavy wood fractured and cracked and crushed all in its path, effectively blocking that staircase. Her mother was supposed to signal Gideon, but instead she had climbed from the roof and unsheathed her swords.

Miranda followed Devin to the office. He had already kicked the door in, but it was empty.

"No! Where did he take her?"

Devin pointed. "I don't think he did, love."

She followed his hand, noting a smashed window and, finally, taking in the chaos of the previously ordered office that suggested a struggle. Had they tossed her sister out the window?

Miranda ran to it, looking down for a sign of Cordelia's body, but there was nothing. Heart squeezing as, once again, she had no idea of her sister's fate, she glanced up at the crisscrossing walkways that comprised the upper floor.

Her eyes scanned for a moment before finding her. Cordelia, sprinting down a walkway toward the dangers below. Her nightdress was torn, but there was no sign of blood, only dirt smeared in the once pristine white linen.

Miranda didn't question. She raced to her sister.

"Delia!"

Cordelia turned and a wide smile spread over her face. "Miri!" Miranda embraced her sister, spinning her off her feet, then held her at arm's length to inspect for damage. "I'm fine, honestly. You can let me go now."

"How did you get away?" Miranda asked, unable to stop smiling. Her sister was okay.

"Oh," Cordelia shrugged. "I'm slippery when I wish to be, but more importantly is that *our* mother?"

Cordelia pointed to the woman, now on the ground floor, hacking through enforcers with her dual blades like they were mere weeds in her garden. Even after all these years her mother had not forgotten her training. When too many overpowered enforcers converged, her mother used her surroundings to compensate for the discrepancy, utilizing their makeshift wall system to create obstacles or uprooting shelves to divert their path. She wisely favored her agility to dodge their attacks, even blocking a blow from one of them might prove painful, and with the right timing a punch would miss her and hit their ally.

Miranda had watched her mother do a few demonstrations when she was younger and, factually, she knew her mother had gone through the same rigorous and thorough training as herself. Yet, watching her leap and twist, navigate the space with precision and purpose, and leave a wake of destruction and death was too jarring. This couldn't be her mother. She commanded tea rooms, not converging enemy forces.

Or, it seemed, Miranda had to accept that her mother commanded both.

"Watch out, Miri," Cordelia tugged Miranda to follow her. A group of enforcers had ascended the stairs closest to them.

"Stay behind me," Miranda yelled as she drew her sword. The walkway forced the enemy into a side-by-side line of two bodies at a time. Miranda looked for Devin, but he wasn't in sight. Did he go after Graves? She wouldn't blame him. If his revenge was what he was here for, then she hoped he got it. She already owed him more than she could ever return.

Miranda surveyed her surroundings as she met swords with the first wave of enforcers. Each time her sword connected, the power they wielded threatened to knock her weapon from her hands. She was not going to win this by normal means. She had to adjust, reconsider, and make use of her surroundings. Just as her mother was doing. Her only goal was to get Cordelia to safety.

A hard downward swing forced Miranda to a knee. Her sword tip sank into the wooden planks of the floor. A simple tug wouldn't free it.

On her left was the outer wall of the building and on the other side, a railing, and past the railing were parallel catwalks. The wall was bare, just a flat sheet of metal, but over the edge of the railing were ropes and pulleys for heavier cargo. Below was too far to jump, though in a pinch they'd survive it if necessary.

Miranda side-stepped an incoming blow, kicking at the enforcer's arm so their swing overcorrected and their weapon went spinning over the railing. Miranda took out a knife and threw it, the blade sinking into the enforcer's chest. It seemed there were endless reinforcements and she was running out of blades.

While Miranda struggled to keep the enemy from reaching them, their position was gradually losing ground. The enforcers kept advancing and Miranda kept retreating. They were nearing the set of stairs her mother had filled with shipping crates. Her mother.

Miranda searched while navigating attacks and keeping forward momentum, tugging her sister this way and that to keep her from harm.

Her mother was fighting her own battle on the ground floor. They locked eyes for a moment as Miranda looked to Cordelia and back, her mother followed the motions and signaled her understanding with a nod. If she could get Cordelia to her mother, they could escape easier from the ground floor.

Miranda took Cordelia's hand and put some distance between them and the enforcers, running instead of fighting.

Clear of their forces for a moment, Miranda kicked at the railing. Once. Twice.

The enforcers were gaining. Sweat started to bead on her forehead. She kicked again, the railing gave. The final blow and the railing broke with a screeching metallic groan. She pried the metal tube of the railing free just in time to swipe at an enforcer's face. Still, it had been too close, and she lost her footing as she desperately tried to keep herself poised between them and Cordelia.

Strategically, she realized there were too many variables limiting her. She was alone, guarding her sister, no resources, and little room for movement or cover.

Miranda might not win.

Her mind spun, ticking through options that now wouldn't include her own survival, all that mattered was Cordelia's survival. She considered pushing her sister over the newly exposed ledge and hope her mother caught her in time, because they were about to be pinned down and her metal bar was already starting to bend and dent and wouldn't hold much longer.

"Looks like you could use a hand, love."

Miranda's head whirled around, and there was Devin on a parallel walkway, in just his shirt and vest once again and how did he still look immaculate when she was covered in sweat and gore?

Or, maybe he only seemed perfect, because she had not expected him to return and yet she was not at all surprised that he had. The fact that he was here did things to her heart she couldn't explore right then.

He had somehow wrangled the thick ropes and he used the heavy, metal pulley mechanism to swing one over.

She took it, grabbed Cordelia, and jumped.

Devin caught her on the upper swing and held the rope steady with one hand, pulling her up with the other. The enforcers had already changed course, sprinting for the connecting path.

"We need to get Cordelia to my mother," Miranda said, panicked.

"Understood." Devin heaved the rope further onto the walkway, then started to force the thick, resistant cord into some kind of knot.

He was panting when he finished, but there was a loop in the rope now, and he tested it with his foot, pushing against it with his boot to see if it would unravel. When it held, he turned to her sister.

"Pleasure to finally meet you, Miss Wilde. May I?"

Cordelia looked to Miranda.

"You can trust him," Miranda said, earning a quick look from Devin. His brow raised incredulously. "With getting you to safety. Beyond that, who can say."

He smiled as he continued adjusting the rope. "Hate to be predictable."

Assured, Cordelia gave him a single nod and took his offered hand.

Devin lifted Cordelia with ease, hefting her to sit on the railing as he kept her steady. He aligned her foot into the loop and pushed the rope into her hands.

"Put your weight on your right foot, and do not let go. Can you do that, Cordelia?"

Cordelia looked stricken for the first time since this whole mess started. Her sister nodded, unspeaking.

"I heard you in Graves's office. There's not many who would speak to Graves like that. You're as strong as your sister. Which is why I know you can handle this." He winked, like an incorrigible scoundrel and Miranda was torn between throttling him for it and kissing him for putting her sister at ease.

Red bloomed on Cordelia's cheeks and her only response was to nod silently.

"Now, I'm going to let you go and work the rope from here to lower you down," he continued. "Is your mother ready?" Devin asked over his shoulder.

Miranda leaned over the rail and found her mother just as she pulled a blade free of an enforcer's shoulder, kicking at the body so it rolled into two more attempting to rush her.

With a sharp whistle, Miranda signaled her mother and Lady Wilde moved until her fight was beneath them. She sheathed one of her swords so she could grab the lower end of the rope and defend the area.

"Ready, Cordelia?" Devin asked.

Cordelia nodded, stars shimmering in the soft brown of her gaze.

Miranda rolled her eyes. He wasn't *that* charming.

Devin eased Cordelia away from the railing and supported her weight with the other end of the rope. Hand over hand he lowered her to the ground. Miranda glanced past him, noting the incoming enforcers.

"I'll cover you," she said, getting into position.

Her sword was still lodged in the floor somewhere and her metal stick would not hold out much longer, but she had the advantage of skill.

As she met the first line of enforcers, Miranda deflected blows and concentrated her own strikes on breaking their footing. She was winded after a minute, each block or maneuver requiring much more effort than she was used to, given their strength.

"Is she clear?" Miranda yelled, panting as she leaned on the railing to brace as she kicked out at an enforcer's chest. It barely made them stagger.

There was a pause before Devin answered, "Yes, your mother has her."

Miranda heaved a sigh of relief, then she made a tactical retreat.

She grabbed Devin's arm and dragged him behind her, racing for a path that wasn't full of enemies.

"I thought you went after Graves," she said, searching for a way to the bottom floor. All the stairs were either blocked or guarded, but there was a tower of crates that was high enough for them to land on and probably survive.

"It was tempting," he said, taking her hand as they leapt over the railing and landed on the tower.

They broke straight through the top crate, wood splinters exploding around them. Devin brushed slivers from his hair as he added, "But I managed to signal Gideon instead."

She got to her feet, climbing down the rest of the tower. When they reached the bottom, Devin straightened and his eyes snapped to her. She felt his stare in the awkward, stuttering beat of her heart.

"And then you came back?" she asked.

"I knew you'd be lost without me."

She wasn't even angry at the quip, because he had come back and he'd helped save her sister, instead of revenge. It was too chaotic to put into words how that made her feel, but it was significant. The warm, overpowering sensation in her chest told her that much.

Now that they were on the ground floor, there was ample cover and plenty of debris to arm themselves. They ducked into the first in-tact, sheltered area they found to regroup.

"The door is several feet to my left," she said as she fished around for a weapon. "With luck, Gideon will already be there."

This must have been a supply area, it was full of cleaning solutions and overstocked containers.

Miranda fished around the shelves, stopping when she reached the corner. Among the brooms, mops, and dusting tools was a shovel and a crowbar. She held them up. "What's your preference?"

"The crowbar," Devin said and when she tossed it, he caught it with an unnecessary flourish. "Shall we?"

Electric excitement coursed through Miranda, more than simple adrenaline. Her sister was safe, the mission nearly completed, Graves may have escaped but by the time they were done all his work would be evidence, which left her freer and lighter than she'd been able to feel in months.

Devin's dark hair was mussed, strands sticking to his skin with sweat, and he somehow made sweat attractive. His blue eyes were on her, despite the chaos. Always focused on her. Her body hummed with more than just the thrill of a fight or the righteous validation of stopping a horrible man from doing horrible things. The longer their gazes locked, the more the vibrating energy of battle wormed into her abdomen and between her thighs, stirring an intoxicating blend of desire and bloodlust.

Devin's smile shifted to confusion for a fraction of a second, her gaze reflecting just how depraved she'd become after only a few days of his acquaintance.

He yanked her clear of a sword's downward arc, pulling her into his chest. He didn't let go as he attempted to decipher what he was seeing in her eyes, brow furrowing. Then, his gaze darted around her, to her aura, for answers. And it clicked. The iridescent blue of his eyes heated to nearly black.

"I thought I was the one prone to distraction," he said, a low, deep hunger reverberating through his words and hitting her somewhere intimate.

Miranda maneuvered around him, twisting to drive the broad side of the shovel hard into a cowl covered face. The clang reverberated up her arm and she dipped, allowing Devin to swing the crowbar, catching an incoming enforcer's shoulder with the slightly hooked end and wrenching their entire body from that singular point. Their face slammed into the shelf of supplies, containers and solutions top-pling over and leaking viscous acids that started to burn through their leather uniform.

Devin stood very still and very close to her, not backing away as she rose to her full height, practically grinding against him. She could feel every scorching inch.

"You are playing with fire, Mira," he warned, once again pulling her from an incoming attack. "You were plenty irresistible *before*." His hand enclosed around her jaw, thumb sweeping her lips like he was marking his next target. "If we were anywhere else this wouldn't even be a conversation," he rasped, voice heavy with implication.

Miranda's eyes locked with his as she swung with the blade edge of the shovel. When she felt it connect with something solid just past Devin's shoulder, she jerked the handle back, ripping and pulling against a torso. Screams followed.

It was the way desire pulsed in his eyes every time she moved, like watching her slam a shovel into someone's face was the most erotic thing he'd ever seen, like her power was arousing, that heated her all over. That ignited the undercurrent of arousal tainting the adrenaline.

Together they twirled and hacked, arms threading to reach ene-mies, anticipating and reacting in flawless synchronization. A perfect-ly choreographed duet of destruction. And each time he pulled close or she arched her back into his chest or their hands brushed, was an exhilarating rush unlike anything she'd ever experienced. Her body was screaming, vibrating with the energy to attack and yet warmth was building between her thighs, her heaving breaths were not from exertion.

The exit was in sight and Miranda sent her shovel nose first over Devin's shoulder, spearing an enforcer in the neck. She didn't bother removing her arm, instead draping it over Devin's back as the enforcer wheezed. She bit her lip because she couldn't bite his.

Not yet, anyway.

They lingered, but she didn't detect any new enemy bodies in her peripheral. She did hear the barking of voices just outside the door. Reinforcements had arrived. Whatever enforcers remained, they must have decided it was more prudent to scatter, than continue the fight.

And, yes, this was hardly the time or place to hook her fingers over the back of Devin's head, nor was it in any way appropriate to part her lips over his. There was a very responsible part of her that was well aware of just how indecent it was for his hands to draw down her body. How scandalous it was for his fingers to dip into her skin before hefting her off her feet. No arguing with how sinfully wicked it was for the pressure of his arousal to coax unabashed moans from her throat.

The door—that had been just within reach—was kicked inward, hinges snapping.

And it took entirely too long for either of them to think about stopping.

"What the hell?" Captain Blair fixed them with an incredulous stare. "Look, I'm not one to criticize or judge inappropriate proclivities, but there is actual blood all over you."

Devin set Miranda on her feet.

"Not ours," Devin commented, but Miranda was just grateful that it wasn't her mother that burst through the door.

"Not sure it matters," Captain Blair countered, then he began to take in the scene. He sighed, shoulders rising and falling with the gesture. "Did you leave...*anything* intact? This is going to take weeks to sort out."

"Are my mother and sister outside?" Miranda asked.

"Who? Oh, yeah. Wait a minute." Captain Blair spun on the spot, narrowing his eyes at her. "He was *your* father, wasn't he? That damn noble who came strolling into my HQ with way too much knowledge of very secret plans. He acted like he was suddenly in charge of everything and half my officers were ready to follow him out the door without even bothering for my approval."

"Things had changed, we wanted to make you aware," Devin said with a shrug.

"Just keep him away from my investigation from now on," Captain Blair ordered. "I assume Graves got away?"

Miranda watched Devin, gauging his reaction. It couldn't be easy to face now, knowing he might never get the chance again.

But she loved him for it.

The word flitted so effortlessly through her thoughts, she almost missed it entirely. Her heart must have figured it out long before her brain, because it felt too natural, too easy. Like she had loved him for much longer than this moment.

She expected to recoil at the realization. After all, love would make it all the harder when this ended. She had been adamant that falling for Devin was the last thing she wanted.

Then why couldn't she stop grinning?

"Yes, naturally, at the first sign of trouble he ran," Devin said, biting out the words.

"Cowards never change," Captain Blair replied, before he started to order about his men to different tasks.

This was no longer Miranda's part of the mission and she took Devin's hand, leading him toward the door.

"There's a person in need of immediate care," Devin called back to Captain Blair, "They're caged in the far corner. Not sure how long they have."

Captain Blair adjusted his orders accordingly and Miranda and Devin retreated out into the waning daylight, the sky exploding in purples and oranges. There was notable chaos in the street. Watchmen fenced off the area, keeping the crowd at bay. Miss Stone directed officers, giving Devin and her a solemn nod when she noticed the pair of them. She didn't smile, but it was clear in how her eyes softened that she was grateful they made it.

Miranda found her mother and father wrapped around Cordelia, who stared past their shoulders with pleading 'help me' eyes. Miranda and Devin drew closer and he began to release her hand, but she squeezed his all the harder.

"Miri, thank the Divine. They haven't let me breathe for ten minutes."

"I almost lost you," their mother cooed, "For the last twelve hours I didn't know if you were alive or dead. You can hold your breath for a few more minutes."

Cordelia's gaze darted to Devin then away and she pursed her lips, but didn't argue further.

Miranda watched her family and it was starting to settle in her chest that her mission was over. Cordelia was safe. Graves, while maybe not captured, had been exposed and soon would lose all his power and influence. And, maybe this whole whirlwind of an adventure had only started a week ago, but Miranda felt irrevocably altered.

If there was anything to say to her family, it could wait. They had time. Right now, Miranda only wanted one thing.

But not here.

She pulled Devin away before her parents noticed or tried to stop her. He didn't resist. One look at his face and she knew she could have guided him off the edge of the pier and he wouldn't have uttered a word of protest.

Maybe this is what marriage felt like, knowing that someone would do anything for you, trusting them. Seeing your truest self reflected in their eyes. If Miranda could have that, maybe she could figure out the rest later. Or maybe it didn't matter as much. Because being loved for all the abrasive, hidden parts of herself was its own kind of freedom.

And, regardless, they had precious little time before she tore through his clothes in the middle of the street. One problem at a time.

CHAPTER FOURTEEN

MIRANDA DRAGGED DEVIN INTO the carriage behind her, his hand fumbling for the door. It was either seconds or minutes later when Miranda tore her mouth free, distantly aware of someone else speaking from outside. "Did you give the cab an address?"

Undeterred, Devin drew his lips down her jaw, her neck. The texture of his stubble scraped her skin, instantly soothed by his tongue. He was practically on top of her, their bodies entwined in a seamless blend of limbs. She had underestimated how satisfying it was just to feel the weight of him on top of her, all warmth and pressure.

"I suppose a carriage *is* less than ideal." His teeth caught the pulse point at her neck and bit down enough to spear straight to the hungry flutter between her legs.

Miranda sucked in a breath through her teeth and arched her body reflexively. His self-satisfied smirk was infuriating and, yet, her limbs were molten.

"Though," he continued, tone filled with triumph, "I could make due anywhere with the right motivation." His palm teased across her breast, but through the tight leather of her uniform it did little more than drive her insane.

"Er, you got a destination in mind, sir?" The driver called. Again. They had ignored him the first two times.

Devin sighed. He shouted his address in the Garrison and Miranda set a hand on his chest to keep him from muddling her senses for a moment.

"I never asked," she started, savoring her own small victory when his frown at being denied deepened to a pout. "How bad was your club damaged? Can you still live there? I know how important it was."

His eyes were still dark as he considered her question. Though he hovered at arm's length, the pressure on her palm indicated that, should she give him the slightest quarter, he'd pounce. *His* hands, however, were unrestrained.

"I'd prefer to talk about this," he plucked the first hook of her uniform free and the shock of it made her elbow bend, his body seizing on her weakness and pinning her arm between them. He hovered dangerously close to her throat. "For example, I can't quite recall if you preferred here." He kissed her neck, his head forcing hers to turn and bend, exposing herself to the attack. "Or here." He moved down, lips suckling on the skin above her collar bone, effectively coaxing out a long, throaty moan. "Ah, yes, I believe I remember now."

He worked reverently over the sensitive skin, not overpowering her, but lulling her into a blissful stupor. It wouldn't work to distract her.

He hummed against her skin, a gentle rumble that burst through her like a shockwave.

It was starting to work.

"Gods, Devin." Her hands came up, threading into his hair. His smile was all victory. But, somewhere in the back of Miranda's dazed thoughts, she knew there was something they needed to do first. Something important before she got swept up in his irresistible magnetism and she never recovered. And it was with great effort that she forced him backward.

His eyes were closed as he allowed her to maneuver him. At that angle and position, it would have been easy to use his weight and strength to keep her pinned. Instead, he caved to the barest pressure, and a little, tiny part of her clicked into place with a certainty she hadn't realized she needed until this moment. She trusted him. Unequivocally.

"I know we need to talk, Mira," he said, voice gruff with desire and something else. Pain? He started massaging her lower back, where his hand had been anchored to angle her hips just moments ago. "I want to, I *plan* to, but..."

"But, what?" she prompted, tracing her fingers down his cheek, until her touch hovered just next to his ear.

He tensed.

She paused, not moving her hand any further.

"But I'm terrified," he said slowly, his eyes still squeezed shut.

"Of me?"

He smiled, but it was full of whatever he was holding on to that plagued him. "Not quite." He opened his eyes, finally, and the broken ache in his gaze hit her harder than any physical blow. "I'm terrified of what you're capable of."

She nearly laughed, because the idea that she would hurt him was absurd. "I know I'm strong, but I'd never attack you. What do you think I'm capable of doing?"

He pressed his forehead to hers, and a sudden sway of the carriage forced him to catch her as she was jolted from the bench. Supporting her weight, he eased backward into the seat, drawing her with him, settling her across his lap.

"Destroying me."

Miranda caught up to his meaning and her own fear threatened to surface again.

He shook his head, the words tumbling out. "I don't mean this to pressure you, Miranda. Whatever happens, it's not your job to hold me together or to worry about me. My sanity is not your problem. I've been destroyed before." He chuckled but it was borderline unhinged. "I survived. I'm nothing if not resilient. I didn't even think there was anything left *to* break. Whatever had lingered after the world was done with me, I had no issues mangling further. I don't think anyone hated me, more than me." He was talking fast, breathing sharp and quick. Miranda hated every second, but she remained tethered to the moment, unable to do more than take it in.

"And if you leave..." He swallowed, as if saying the words were tantamount to living them. "But, Gods, I did *not* want to say all this. I didn't want to influence you to pity me or to choose me out of charity. Whatever you decide, Miranda, whatever future you see for yourself, I'll be fine whether I'm included or not."

The way his voice faltered on the last sentence made her inclined to think it was a lie, that he would not be fine without her. But he gallantly wanted her to make her own choice.

"I think, if I loved you even a fraction less, I wouldn't be so close to falling apart," he whispered, "Your response might not be so terrifying. And I might be able to stop talking and allow you to respond. But, as it stands, your hold on me is beyond my ability to handle gracefully. So on I blather, half hoping you'll interrupt me and dreading that you'll tell me this is entirely one-sided."

She waited. He stared at nothing, clutching her with a ferocity and gentleness that broke her heart, equal parts push and pull. Because she hadn't given him an answer and so he looked to hover between hope and despair.

"I promise, I can handle rejection, Mira," but his voice was almost non-existent, so quiet she only heard it because they were entwined together. "Whatever the blathering, idiot part of me says, I will handle it."

She wrapped her arms around him, pressing her face into him.

"Letting you go is the last thing I want and this is far from one-sided," she said, and he immediately gave in to pull with a breath of relief she felt in her soul, "I thought I hated you for the longest time," she tried to speak around his roving mouth, alternating between soft, chaste kisses and nuzzling, each touch tingling through her skin and making her grin. "You were incorrigible, arrogant. Insufferable. Infuriating..."

She could feel the smile against her skin, his attention never wavering from reaching every inch of her face and neck.

"You have a very cruel way of saying 'I love you,'" he said from somewhere near her ear, where his tongue had driven all coherent thought from her mind.

"Maybe that's not what I was saying—" He set his teeth against her skin, alternating bite and suction until her skin bruised. Her fingers clenched against his shoulders, ruffling his shirt. "Fine. I give."

"It's not like you to concede so easily," he moved to the undone clasp of her uniform and worked another hook free.

"Well," she heaved, breaths coming in short gasps as pleasure danced through her limbs, "I wasn't quite done...or, rather." She was boneless and stiff at the same time, melting and tensed. He needed to stop or she would never finish her thoughts. "I still had something to say that we should, probably, talk about before we reach your house...because once we arrive there will be no more talking."

"What more is there to discuss?" He pulled away, an act of mercy, and Miranda fought to gather her thoughts and errant body parts into focus. "You're hopelessly in love with me and have been since you first saw me that night at my club. I returned your affections, you didn't immediately change your mind despite your salacious desire to argue with me, and so what else is there but to celebrate by indulging in carnal gratification until morning?"

As tempting as his words were, she wouldn't be deterred so easily. "Typically, we're on the sort of path with a singular destination." She huffed. "My father hinted marriage was our only option."

She watched him carefully, not sure what she was expecting, but he gave no indication of his opinion on the subject.

"What do you want?" He asked, finally.

She sighed, shifting on his lap as she got into the flow of her thoughts. "There aren't a whole lot of choices for people like me. If I don't marry you, and anyone finds out even half of what we've been doing, I'd be ruined. It would ripple out to affect my entire family. Cordelia would have a hard time finding a husband, if that's what she wanted. My mother and father would lose valuable social connections—"

He set his finger on her lips, effectively stopping her tirade, and then asked, "What do *you* want, Miranda Wilde?"

Her heart beat hard, pulse roaring in her ears. "I want you."

He grinned, and a touch of mischief reached his eyes, her stomach fluttered. "You already have me, Mira, entirely. Now. You've given me the future your father wants and the future that would hurt your family. But, again, Mira, what do *you* want?"

"I want to make my own future. I want to do that with you...and, at first I thought that meant that I couldn't get married. Marriage was my mother's happy ending, but I didn't want to sacrifice my sword for a tea room. But now, I think my mother chose to do that, she wasn't forced to. Did...did you honestly see marriage in your future?"

"No, but I didn't see myself falling in love before I met you, either, yet here we are."

"So, you're saying that whatever I want, you'll do? You have no opinion?"

"I'd prefer not to run away and join a circus. I've never been very good at juggling."

"But seriously, does this mean that, if I were fine with it, you'd be fine with it?"

"What is this 'it' we're discussing? But yes, probably, if this 'it' made you happy."

"The 'it' is marriage. A whole formal thing where I become Lady Drake and you suddenly become society's prince."

He sneered. "I'm sure they'll find ways around calling me that, given their contempt of me. And, no, I had never thought I would marry, but I know one thing." His tone grew serious, somber. "I'm not keen to put any potential children through my experiences. I won't be able to help that they'll be part fae, but being legitimate still matters to this world. I don't want to be the cause of closed doors when every door should be open to them."

"Do you want children?"

He stilled, but she couldn't exactly read the emotion in his eyes. "I had never considered. It was just assumed I wouldn't since I had no plans to marry and no desire to taint a new generation with my mixed lineage."

"And now?"

He locked eyes with her, remaining silent.

"I don't care about half or part or whole. Fae or human or guardian. The fact that you hate that part of you, makes me want to love it all the more *for* you." Her hand went up to his hair again, stopping just before pushing the dark strands away from his ears. "May I?"

He looked away, but his hand settled over hers, guiding it forward.

She pushed his hair back and, while it wasn't quite as prominent as the full fae she had seen, whose ears extended a good inch more than a human's, there was a clear point to the shape. She pulled his face back to her and kissed him. A long, deep kiss that melted all the tension she sensed building in his shoulders. "You should wear your hair shorter."

He let out a breath, still not quite ready to laugh about it, though it was clear that her approval had mattered. She traced the outline with her finger idly as she added, "And...maybe children would be nice. I don't want my sole role in life to be mother and wife, but I don't think it would be that way with you."

"I'm sure I could find other roles for you to play," he said, eyes growing dark again.

She swallowed. She was still settled across his legs, and it only took the suggestion before she was warming all over, desire snaking its way through her thoughts, whispering scandalous suggestions to her body. Like the suggestion to glide her thigh across him as she repositioned, so he was enclosed in her legs and responding with a gratified groan.

His hand splayed across her back to align her hips with his, the motion of the carriage creating a broken, scattered sort of rhythm. At some point she had wrapped around him, the transition into kissing becoming more familiar, not so much a choice but just unconscious habit. She could kiss him forever. A very small possessive part of her thrilled at the idea of being the last and only person who would get this pleasure.

He was hers.

The carriage drew to a halt with a substantial lurch that had her clutching at the roof to keep her balance. The driver called out that they arrived.

Between leaving the cab and entering Devin's house Miranda had no actual memory and she wasn't sure if her feet had ever touched the ground.

She was just coherent enough that when Devin called to the butler to draw a bath, she breathed, "Not enough time," against his ear.

"Wait an hour—" He started, addressing Haversham.

"Longer," she hummed.

"Never mind, I'll send for you."

And then she was in Devin's bedchamber and he set more of the hooks on her uniform free.

"This is the first time I've ever done this sober," he started, drawing his nose down the line of her jaw, "I can smell your arousal from here." He was breathing like he wanted to inhale every trace of it from the air. A thrill rippled through her. "And your aura is pulsing with colors that I can't even process fast enough. I can see every single sensation."

He eased the front of her uniform open. "Like the difference between this—" His hand slipped through the opening and he filled his palm with her breast, fingers working in a kneading pattern and drawing out soft, blissful sighs. "And this—" The top of her uniform hit the floor, and he sealed his mouth over her nipple through the already battered remains of her chemise. When he pulled away, his eyes traced the outline of her body with a satisfied smirk, the thin cotton sheer and pasted to her skin.

He removed the rest of her stained, battered uniform, guiding her toward the large bed. She stopped him with a hand, moving her fingers to undo his shirt before he could question and when she reached his pants she hesitated. Not afraid, but also, this was vastly different from pictures in a book...

"We don't have to—"

"I want to." She hated being coddled. And she loosened the ties until there was nothing keeping up his pants except her hands. She let go and took a step back.

He surpassed every crude illustration she'd giggled over with Lydia. The real thing was far from funny and it wasn't laughter that heated her skin as she admired the sight of him. She stepped closer and eased his hair back from his ears so she could admire the whole of him, even the parts he hated. Divine above. He was beautiful.

He didn't speak, but it was clear that his sanity hinged on her reaction.

Instead of words, she grabbed him and pinned him to the bed in a fluid motion that he was entirely unprepared to block.

She had liked it like this before and he had seemed to enjoy it as well.

The unmasked desire in his eyes was her only affirmation of his opinion on her use of force. And when she started to crawl up his body, stopping and sitting back on her heels, legs straddling his thighs, with Devin completely at her mercy, it felt erotic and powerful.

She did not plan to be merciful.

When her hand reached out for the hard length of him, he hissed, fingers clawing into the comforter.

He had tried to stop her last time, but he wasn't in charge anymore. Her hand moved and explored until she found the motions that seemed to draw the most reaction out of him. He'd thrown an arm over his eyes, breathing in a very focused, even pattern. With his eyes covered, Miranda felt the daring urge to lean forward and swipe once against the velvety tip with her tongue.

"Fucking hell." His words were drawn, ragged. So exquisitely *raw*.

Fuck. Shit. Fucking...shit. Devin couldn't put a single thought together. He had anticipated his bold, daring Miranda to explore him with her hands. However much a maiden, she was hardly squeamish. And he'd focused very, very intently on not coming all over her hands mere seconds after she'd started.

Then, Gods—fuck—the warm, wet glide of her tongue on his cock had sent him to another plane of existence. Mostly because he had *not* expected it, though, in hindsight, he should have.

Emboldened by his reaction, or just because she was a ruthless vixen, she'd lapped at the underside of him while her hand pumped up and down.

And fuck.

He wasn't going to last much longer.

"Mira," he tried, hating the agony in his voice, but he was determined not to finish all over her mouth—no matter how tempting—when she might not even be aware of what she was doing. He dared looking at her again, watching the boldest red strobe with each sweep of her tongue. And words slammed through him with each shimmer of color. Lust. Need. Bliss. Crave.

He was so close. If he didn't act now, there was no turning back.

Even though his body was rioting with protest, Devin twisted her hair in his fingers and pulled.

Devin's grip on her hair snatched Miranda's attention. She looked up—murderous at being stopped when she thought she was doing a decent job—and followed the not-quite-gentle but not-quite-painful pull on her hair until she was level with Devin's face.

And when he kissed her, there was an undercurrent of threat that shivered through her. Touching him had been arousing enough, but with his fingers still entwined with her hair, he used the free hand to slip down her stomach, reaching the building warmth between her thighs.

The noises that rose up her throat were almost animalistic. Low breathy moans and sighs that she couldn't have silenced if she wanted. Each slow stroke or intentional sweep, twisted and coiled as she chased that delicious release.

Slowly his fingers untangled from her hair and settled on the small of her back, pushing her forward. Miranda walked with her knees as she allowed him to guide her. Further and further until he had to move the arm filling her with the best sort of tension back to his side because the angle was too steep. She was straddling his chest and he continued easing her forward until she was kneeling over his face.

Oh.

And *holy shit*.

It was amazing before, but there was no doubt that using mouths for pleasure was at the top of the list of what she preferred. There was something captivating about his new position, something undeniably *best*. And she had soared from building pleasure to almost there in seconds.

And then he used his hand to rock her hips back and forth.

And that was all the encouragement she needed. Using the slow undulating motions she knew her body craved, Miranda chased her release on Devin's face. The power and pleasure shot lightning through her body. Every muted note of *his* pleasure vibrated against her core and thrust her higher, closer, speeding toward ecstasy.

And it took no time at all for her to come crashing down, catching herself on her hands to avoid crushing him as wave after wave liquefied her limbs.

And, once he'd untangled himself from her wobbly legs, it was clear in his eyes they were far from done.

Desire was persuasive as fuck. Devin had fully intended to end things here. Miranda haloed in blissful canary yellow and sprawled out on his bed where the scent of sweat and arousal nearly overpowered the traces of lilacs. But something snapped.

And he was not entirely himself when he maneuvered on the bed, kissing up the slope of her shoulder until he reached her neck. Gods, her neck. She must have used some sort of perfume there because that delicious floral scent was stronger.

"You're so beautiful," he breathed, and he didn't know if he'd ever seen anything as beautiful as her warm, tawny skin basking in the glow of release, and the long, blonde waves of her hair cascading over his sheets.

She turned so that she was on her back, eyes half-lidded with satisfaction. Perhaps he should stop here.

She bit her lip. "Are you going to fuck me now?"

And in the realm of possibilities, Miranda asking if he planned to fuck her while sprawled out on his bed after riding his face to orgasm should not have been anywhere close to possible.

He closed his eyes and spoke very, very carefully. "Not if you wish to stop."

Her fingers tapped at his cheek and he tentatively opened his eyes. "But you want to?" It was a challenge, a tease. She was goading him. Taunting him. Tormenting him.

"You have no idea," he replied with barely restrained control. "But what I want is irrelevant..."

Her head tilted, eyes narrowed. "Can't you read what I want in my aura?"

He breathed through his nose, because *yes* he could intuit what she wanted from her aura, he had been reading the very clear take-me amaranth for the better part of this conversation and it was driving him absolutely *insane*, but it wasn't enough. Those were emotions, unfiltered and fickle.

"I can."

"And what do you see?" she purred.

She was toying with him. His eyes were pure intent as he leaned down, pressing her into the bed. "I still need to hear you say it," he said.

"I thought I did."

His smile was dark, menacing. A burst of fuck yes ruby indicating she liked it.

He said, "No. You asked if I planned to fuck you. I need to hear you say you want me to."

Her breathing grew heavy, her breasts crushed beneath his chest. Now who was doing the tormenting?

In a move he had no time to block, no presence of mind to counter, she had pinned him beneath her once again.

"Fine," she said, angling her hips so that when she rocked, her still very wet center glided up the length of him, "I want you," another jerk of her hips, "Devin," he was choking, dying, "to fuck me," she ended as she eased the barest inch of his cock into her and then he truly was gone.

Saying the words had worked some kind of magic. At first, as she lay on Devin's bed, body still humming with a sweet sense of contentment, she thought it wouldn't be easy to find that place again.

She had been very wrong.

Her crude, sensual declaration had not just worked for him. She had felt each wicked word with such heightened intensity that she was already reaching for a second release.

She had moved carefully, easing herself into the unfamiliar. Each time she rolled her hips she felt him press that much further into her. And it should have been so many things, but what it felt like was *right* and then the same rhythm she had chased before wasn't even close to enough.

Back arching until there wasn't a whisper of space between them, Miranda rolled her hips faster. Harder. The pace wasn't even or controlled, but the sensations rippling through her took a breakneck pace and she had no idea how long she had been moving—it could have been minutes or hours—but she was coming down again, riding out the blissful friction until she couldn't move anymore.

And with some uttered word she couldn't hear, Devin squeezed her to him. Buried his face in her skin as she felt him shudder. She ran her fingers through his hair, hoping he'd felt as good as she had.

Miranda caught her breath, still wrapped in hazy satisfaction as they fell onto the bed fully, together. Maybe there was more to say, but Miranda couldn't keep her eyes open a second longer. In no time she had given in to the sweet pull of sleep.

Devin woke sometime after dawn. He knew because the sun was peeking through the curtains and giving him a piercing headache. The last thing he wanted in the world was to leave Miranda, who still slept soundly beside him, but that sliver of light had to go.

Waking up with a woman was not something he'd ever done intentionally before and, usually, came with a panicked hunt for his clothes and a quick retreat out a window. But as he drew a finger along her shoulder, the only word to describe how he felt was: happy.

Desperately in need of a bath, Devin called for Haversham and had one prepared. He planned to be quick so there would be time to set up clean water for Miranda. He also ordered food. Lots of food.

The room had an adjoining dressing room, with a tub set up for privacy. There was a door that would, hopefully, keep him from waking Miranda. In the main room, aside from the large poster bed with heavy drapes, was a fireplace and some furniture. A chaise lounge sat at the foot of the bed in lush velvets and awful oversaturated pink.

Once clean and dressed in fresh clothes—he'd had a collection of his things stored here, mostly for when he'd spilled too much drink while half-asleep, but this was an undeniable improvement—he settled in one of the fine armchairs near a small bookcase. The food was wheeled in on a cart and Devin thanked the servant as they shut the door and the room returned to a peaceful silence. A moment. A quiet moment.

Devin devoured the first plate of pastries. He wasn't a morning person, certainly, and once his basic needs had been met he'd waited for Miranda to wake.

He had intended to allow himself the moment to think, but he ended up drifting into a heavy sleep upright in the armchair. The sound of Miranda waking, her body stirring and her breathing altered, had his head jolting out of an impossible angle against the plush backing. He checked the clock, it was approaching evening and his...everything hurt.

He stretched and rotated his arms to ease out the kinks in his muscles. While Miranda rolled to look for him, her hand reaching out among the sea of sheets, he quickly rang on the bell to signal he was ready for fresh food and warm water in the bath. He thought he'd never get used to having others serve him, but he couldn't deny that right now, it was immensely convenient. It meant he didn't have to leave her.

His movement drew her attention and she sighed, like she had expected him to cut and run on her. Then her eyes landed on the table.

"Is that food?"

"Yes, but I've sent for fresh—"

She leapt from the bed, completely bare, the blankets fluttering forgotten in her wake. She bit into a scone. "This is the best thing I've ever eaten."

He raised an eyebrow, because there was no way a half stale, cold scone was that delicious. But she scarfed it down and was already on to the next.

"I've got to start remembering to eat," she groaned, crumbs littering the table like the carnage of battle. "How long have you been up? You're already dressed and smell good."

"There's a bath waiting for you, too."

She squealed in a delighted, girly pitch and raced for the adjoining chamber. Devin did consider following her, but he hesitated. She deserved a relaxing bath after everything and if he went in there, he'd start touching her, and then kissing her, and shit, he was already hard at the idea of stripping down and joining her.

Instead, he closed his eyes. He could hear her slipping into the water, the contented sigh, the gentle lap of water as she adjusted her limbs.

He closed the adjoining door, but his hearing was no longer inhibited by drink and he couldn't trick his lust into thinking an unlocked door was an adequate barrier.

That wasn't going to work either.

The only way Miranda would be able to bathe in peace was if he left temptation entirely. Devin intended to take a brisk walk down the stairs and back up. Twice.

Only, the door was already wide open. A servant would have closed it and the tray was still full of half-eaten food.

A gut feeling of warning was the only thing that saved him from being speared from behind. A blade sank into the armchair instead.

Devin whirled around and cold, Divine fear rooted him in place.

Yarrow Graves loomed as if he were another fixture of the room, positioned between Devin and the adjoining room with Miranda. He did not dare glance at the adjoining door and risk drawing Graves's attention, but reaching it first was his only priority.

"You didn't think I was going to let this go that easily, did you?" Graves's voice was full of venom, dripping with malice. He made no show to hide his intentions. There was no one left who would believe the performance anyway. A void of ebony oozed around Graves's form. The color of cold-blooded evil intent. "No, no, no. You and that fucking cunt have stolen my victory. I have nothing. *Nothing*. As soon as I'm done with the pair of you, I have to leave Unity for good."

Devin didn't speak. Didn't move.

He only cared about getting to Miranda first. He was calculating the quickest path and possibly distraction, when a single enforcer materialized beside Graves from the shadows.

This one didn't bother with the cowl and mask. A Night Fae with pale, almost grey skin and eyes. Then, his form shimmered and once again he was little more than a shadow. It had to be the reason they were able to get this far without drawing attention. Some Night Fae could cloak themselves, a trick with light that rendered them invisible. But now that Devin knew he was there, it was easier to detect the shimmer. Even the man's aura was concealed by the illusion.

The shimmer walked to the chair and, even though he was not built any different than Devin—on the leaner side even for fae—when he pulled on his weapon, he took the entire chair with it, tossing it free with a flick of his wrist so the once solid piece of furniture thudded against the wall.

"Devin?" Miranda.

His heart squeezed.

"Oh, is she here?" Graves's laugh was manic, terrifying. "How fortuitous that I get to kill two pesky, annoying little birds with one stone."

"Avery, if you please."

Devin heard the footfalls on the carpet, his reflexes still sharp. He dodged, picking up the pot of tea and slamming it into Graves's face. The wild cry of pain was followed by a flurry of curses and barked orders, but Devin had slipped in the adjoining door and locked it behind him.

He turned, expecting to find Miranda still oblivious in the bath, but instead she was just behind him. And wearing his clothes while brandishing a fire poker in her free hand. He should not have been surprised. She must have dressed in seconds, the fabric was sticking to her dripping skin. But even his steely, amazing Miranda's hands were trembling.

"I heard him," she said, voice hollow.

"We're going to—"

The door shattered, bursting into a thousand splinters and fragments over the floor. Devin took a small risk, diving away from Miranda to throw open the drapes that blocked the window. The sunset blasted into the room, and Devin felt it like a slap across the face. He didn't care about weakening himself, only the other two Night Fae. And, as he hoped, there was no turning invisible in sunlight. Besides, the most dangerous person in the room was entirely unaffected by the sun or moon.

"Fuck!" Graves stepped into the shadows. The sun was hardly dangerous or toxic, but so much so suddenly was bound to throw them off.

Avery, now no longer invisible, hadn't needed time to recover and advanced. Miranda lashed out with her fire poker, striking him with the hooked end. Blood sprayed, but the wound wasn't deep enough to deter him.

"Nice try." Graves recovered and took out his own weapon, though Devin suspected Graves would wait until Avery had weakened them enough to eliminate danger.

"You get Graves," Miranda shouted, easily ducking and dodging every attempt to corral her. "Devin, move, now's your chance."

His body felt like it was full of lead, like he couldn't have lifted a leg if he wanted to and it had nothing to do with the sun. Graves raised his arm to throw the blade, to stop Miranda who was currently the strongest force in the room, and the trance shattered.

Devin caught Graves's arm, grappling with him until the sword fell with a clatter. Graves kicked at his chest, knocking the air from his lungs.

"You worthless piece of trash," Graves spat, "How your mother could bear the thought of creating you, I'll never understand."

Devin knocked Graves backward, then lunged for the sword. As he lifted it, blade poised to slice through Graves's throat, the man's demeanor instantly shifted.

"Don't. Please, I beg you," Graves groveled.

And just as Devin was about to drive the blade home, Miranda cried out behind him. He turned, searching for her, fear squeezing his heart.

Pain erupted in his side.

"NO!"

The world blurred at the edges, and something wet and hot and sticky began to trickle down his side. Devin lost his balance.

Where was Miranda? He could hear her.

"Devin? Devin!"

He needed to find her, but he—

Miranda watched Devin sink to his knees. She screamed, but it wasn't enough. He still hit the floor, eyes flickering closed.

And there was not a force on earth that could have stopped her.

Evading Avery, Miranda leapt clear over the tub.

Graves started to back away. The knife slipped from his shaking fingers. His fear understood it didn't matter. No weapon would have saved him.

Miranda stalked closer. She used a foot to flick the fallen sword into her hand. She prepared to strike.

"Now, hold on." Graves held up a hand. "I let your sister live, isn't that...Avery! Avery, what the fuck am I paying you for? Stop her—"

Graves's back hit the wall. He held up his arms.

The start of a word formed on his lips. But his final sound was a guttural sputter.

And she did not stop stabbing.

Again. Again. Again.

Blood sprayed in her face and colored the pools of water from where she had left the tub without drying.

Hack. Hack. Hack.

She had to be sure he would *never* move again.

For her sister. For herself. For Devin.

Only when her body grew tired, did she stop. Then she turned, sword poised and drenched in gore, to Avery.

He held up his hands. "He can't pay me if he's dead. I'll see myself out."

And he disappeared. Miranda didn't care.

She let the sword go and raced to Devin's side.

He had to be alive.

She felt a pulse. He was breathing.

But for how much longer?

CHAPTER FIFTEEN

M IRANDA HAD NEVER KNOWN true terror.

Not before this moment. Devin was unconscious, too much blood oozing from the wound in his side, soaking his clothes, leeching into her. Water dripped from her hair to dilute the puddle gathering beneath them. Dread seeped into her very bones as she screamed for help. For those first precious seconds while she held him, the icy reality threatened to break her. He may not survive this.

She could lose him.

After that, time passed differently. Miranda lifted Devin to the bed. Servants were drawn to the noise and one of them sent for the Watchmen. Another sent for a doctor, hopefully a Healer. There weren't many Day Fae with the gift of healing, even less that sought to use that gift for others, but even as she was desperately trying not to think it, she feared magic was the only way to save him.

She couldn't lose him *now*.

Not after everything. Not when things were finally going right. She defeated the bad guy. She stopped the evil plot. She rescued her sister. This was supposed to be the happily ever after part of the fairy tale.

She was going to marry him and live a life of adventure and maybe someday have children with pointed ears and aura sight who she could love with every ounce of her heart so that they never grew up hating who they were. And she would love Devin. She did love him.

All that couldn't just be...over.

Miranda knew a little about dressing wounds, her training had always been on how best to keep her body functioning during battle. But there were limited supplies here. Only sheets and clothes and towels. She hadn't thought to ask the butler or ring for a footman for aid. She hadn't thought of anything in the last hour beyond her fear that he might stop breathing. Her first aid was amateur, but she was able to keep him stable. Pressure. Keep the wound clean. Monitor him until help arrived.

She paced at the edge of the bed. Why couldn't she just...attack this problem? There should be a way to fight Death. She would win. She was too fueled by the absolute terror of losing the person who had become her everything.

Voices outside the door drew her attention, the muted tones of an argument just outside.

"Nonsense, I'm sure it's fine," Captain Blair's voice carried over all the others, "We're his only friends, damn it."

"Miranda is in there, Gideon." Rachel's voice, softer but she must have been close enough to the door for it to carry anyway.

"And? Does she have dibs on his final moments because they're hooking up?"

A thud.

"What the hell was that for?"

"Just lower your voice."

"But I may have a way to help, did you even consider—"

Miranda threw the door open and Captain Blair turned, mid-word, from Rachel to her.

"You have a way to help?" Miranda didn't bother with introductions. This was a time to be rude.

His eyes darted away and he raised a shoulder. "I said...*may*. As in, maybe. Or, rather, depends on what we're looking at."

"May we come in?" Rachel asked, kindly.

"If you think you could help." Miranda moved out of his way.

"What happened?" Captain Blair searched the room, investigating. He stopped when he reached the bed, eyes lingering on Devin.

Devin let out a shallow breath and the Captain moved on.

He examined the door—splintered, destroyed—then leaned past the doorframe where Miranda's bath waited, cold and stained crimson. "What in the fuck happened here?"

"Graves stabbed him," Miranda said, not bothering to look anywhere but Devin. She set her hand on his chest gently, waiting until she felt the slow, feeble rise of breath.

"Where?" Rachel kneeled on the bed. She was already unwrapping Miranda's attempt at a bandage.

"He's lost a lot of blood and I'm worried that something internal was damaged. We're always taught to protect that area of the abdomen, because a strike there could be fatal. My hope is that we got lucky."

Rachel craned her head, hands already smeared in blood—Devin's blood. Miranda froze, icy fingers of dread squeezing her heart until she thought it would burst.

Rachel looked back up from the wound, her eyes soft with compassion. "I...I'm not a doctor."

"But?"

When she met Miranda's eyes there was a sadness in them that said more than her words. "But I don't think we got lucky."

Miranda got up and punched the wall, the plaster and parts of her crumbling to the floor.

"I was afraid of that," The Captain said, ignoring the gory scene in the other chamber. He crossed his arms, looking down at his friend. "We found a lot in that warehouse. All of Graves's research into the potion intended to give fae Divine blood."

"What does that have to do with Devin?" Miranda snapped.

The Captain raised his hands in surrender, but kept talking without a change in his demeanor. "Just that what we learned so far is that the potion isn't permanent, the effects wear off after a few hours, a day or two at most. There's a high risk of death, though. Even after they got the potion stable, it still risked killing the subject when first injected.""Again. Why the fuck does this matter?" She took a threatening step toward him.

He sighed. "Apparently, that first injection accelerates everything. Cell growth, metabolism, a bunch of other shit I can't remember the name of. It's like adrenaline, but times ten. That's the part that kills you, but if you survive it then you become the strongest race in our world. And there was one case," Now, Captain Blair addressed Miranda directly, with a mixture of pleading and despair in his dark eyes. "*One* subject was recorded to have healed, very quickly, during that phase."

Miranda felt like her heart could finally beat again.

"Why are we waiting? Did you bring any?"

"Because it's *one* case in hundreds of trials," Captain Blair said, "And it could kill him faster."

"I don't think it matters," she tried not to sob mid-sentence, but she had not expected hope to enter into this so easily. There was a chance. A real chance. "Either he dies without it, or he maybe dies with it."

Captain Blair turned to Rachel. "Is that it? Do you see any new angle or are we down to untested psycho lab potions and nothing else?"

Rachel was trying to wipe her hands clean with a napkin from the food tray. "I'm afraid so. Unless you want to wait till a doctor gets here to confirm."

"I don't think he has that kind of time. We can't sit around discussing this!" Miranda yelled.

"She gets a say, Gideon," Rachel said, both of them completely ignoring Miranda.

"Says who? We barely know her. We don't know what their relationship was. For all we know, she wants him dead and this is just a convenient way to keep her hands clean."

Had this been a different situation, Miranda might have responded to the accusation reasonably. After all, Captain Blair had known Devin first. They were friends. He did not know Miranda or her intentions.

But she was not in the mood for bullshit.

"She's going to hit you and I'm not going to stop her," Rachel murmured just before Miranda grabbed Captain Blair by the collar.

He was taller than her, and probably equal in strength, but he was no match for her fury or the all-consuming fear that tunneled her vision to one goal. One drive. Devin's survival.

"Where is it?"

"I thought she would hit you," Rachel's voice again, and she made no move to protect her superior officer.

"I'm not really the type to respond to force or ultimatums. And, for the record, I feel like I'm being unjustly attacked. I don't want to leap straight to a last resort when there might be a less lethal solution in front of us. I don't want him to die, either."

Miranda forced him against the wall, and he winced, but otherwise didn't show any sign of losing his composure. "There isn't time. And he *can't* die, do you understand? If he dies because you were trying to tick off boxes on a checklist you won't look much better than Graves."

"*Holy shit*, is that Yarrow Graves?" He glanced at the adjoining door to the crime scene in the dressing room. "You didn't leave much to identify him by, visually anyway."

"The potion, Blair. Where is it?" She pressed him harder into the wall, distantly aware that he wasn't putting up any sort of fight. But she didn't care about logic or reasoning. Devin might be dying.

Rachel's hand closed on Miranda's arm. Her grip was firm, squeezing, but her eyes were sympathetic as she said, "He's not trying to be insensitive. He's just like this. And I'm afraid I can't let you kill him." She did not remove her hand until Miranda let go.

Captain Blair adjusted his collar, like her iron grip had made it uncomfortable. "I can't give away evidence in an investigation. There're rules. I'm the captain. It's not like I can just do what I want."

"Then I'll get it myself."

He sighed, crossing his arms and pinching the bridge of his nose. "Look, if you were going to steal it, then you shouldn't have mentioned it to me. But..."

Miranda stopped, but she didn't turn around. She would hurt Captain Blair to get what she needed.

The thought left her cold. She would hurt him for the chance at saving Devin. The reality of it was starting to trickle in, covering the blinding fear. She took a steadying breath.

"But, there's another option. Emmy, you were with me when I was reading all those notes." It took Miranda a moment to figure out who the hell 'Emmy' could be, but Rachel was the one to respond.

"You fell asleep face first in those notes. I briefed you when we got the call about an attack at Devin's home."

"If Emmy read it, then she remembers." Captain Blair's attention had returned to Miranda, who was having trouble following his erratic trains of thought. "Which means we know how to *make* the potion." Back to Rachel, "Possible with the limited resources in this house?"

"Aside from the blood, I could manage," Rachel responded.

Miranda whirled, trying to follow the track of thoughts until she finally caught up to the Captain's intentions. "You mean Divine blood. The blood of a guardian."

"Yeah, but there's three guardians in this room, blood won't be the issue." Gideon gestured to the three of them, as if volunteering the blood donation of everyone in the room was his right.

"I'll do it," Miranda said, instantly. With absolute certainty.

"Alright, then. Emmy, get one of the rookies to help you get whatever you need," Captain Blair said, this time to Rachel, "And let's get an officer in the other room starting on a report. Get, uh, who's the least squeamish?"

"Morgan."

"Yeah, make sure he's primary. Get Holden to assist you. And if you see the doctor on your way, make sure he knows to get up here and maybe we can get in a more official prognosis before we poison the guy."

Rachel disappeared and a heavy silence settled over the room. The only noise was Devin's slight wheeze as he breathed, and listening to him struggle was tantamount to peeling off her own fingernails.

"I apologize, Captain. And thank you," Miranda offered, staring at the bed as she counted each second. She had been tempted to help Rachel gather supplies, just for something to do, but leaving Devin even for a second was impossible. She needed to watch him breathe or she'd go insane.

"You can call me Gideon. We're not so formal outside the Ring." Gideon slipped his hands into his pockets. "What was your name again?"

"Miranda," she answered as the helpless task of waiting settled over the room. She stood shoulder to shoulder with Gideon, watching Devin for any sign of a change in his condition. The dread of sudden stillness hovered like a ghost over their shoulders. Each ragged breath a blessing.

"You don't look like a Miranda," he murmured, then he started pacing. He kept reaching out to touch things. Shifting a book. Toeing at an errant boot on the floor. He picked up the knife from the food tray and wiped it clean of butter before twirling it around his fingers. "So. Graves is dead."

"Yes."

Gideon stared at the bed, knife twirling in his hand. "Self-defense. Perfectly reasonable."

"Yes."

"He attacked first."

"Yes."

"He broke into the house."

"Yes."

"Makes sense to me. The reports should reflect the same conclusions."

He finally glanced at her, a charming grin lighting his features and Miranda could see why other women liked him. "You *butchered* him. I'm impressed and a little jealous that it wasn't me who got to do it, but I guess that idea sailed the moment I joined the Watchmen. Can't go hacking up enemies beyond recognition, no matter how much they deserved it."

"It wasn't intentional. I just...I lost a bit of control."

He shrugged again, twirling the butter knife around and around with deft motions of his fingers. "It happens. I closed the door on my dying mother's pleas for help as she succumbed to disease."

Miranda's jaw fell open.

"If you knew her, you'd get it. I got my sister out of there before we caught it too and never looked back."

"I'm...sorry?"

"Don't be. It was the best day of my life."

He delivered the information so...casually. Miranda almost found it chilling, except as she watched him, knife twirling and twirling and twirling, faster and faster at the mention of his mother, it was obvious the detachment was more for his own protection than cruelty. She couldn't imagine hating a mother so much that you were happy they would die. But then, if nothing else, the past couple of weeks had shown her that the world held a lot more misfortune than she understood.

Rachel returned from her tasks after what felt like an eternity, but by the clock only a few minutes.

"I got Pen and Rose questioning the staff. Morgan is on his way to the scene now, but there's no door to shut, so we'll have to keep our voices down. Holden should be right behind me with the last of what I need."

Miranda checked on Devin again, Rachel had wrapped the wound tighter and cleaner, using proper supplies from a kit she thought to bring. His pulse was steady. Slow, but not gone.

"You realize this could be a painful way to go," Gideon said to the room, but mostly to Miranda.

Rachel moved the food tray and started to set up various bottles and containers.

Miranda ignored him, her eyes fixed on Devin.

"I only skimmed the files on it, but there were some pretty horrific descriptions in there. And there was no indication or pattern to explain what caused the subject to kick the bucket. At the current stage in testing, it was you either lived or it boiled you from the inside," Gideon continued.

"He'll be fine. He'll live through it," Miranda said.

"Why so sure?"

"Because he has to," she said, tone final, like she could will it so with enough confidence.

"Ready," Rachel said as she drew a knife from a hidden sheath on her thigh and held out a hand to Miranda. "Are you?"

A blue liquid simmered in a tea pot, ingredients scattered around the table. She had brought a small cook top, a crystal used to super heat whatever touched it. Some fae element Miranda didn't know the name of. Nothing about the scene looked medicinal.

Swallowing her trepidation, Miranda sat down and Rachel wrapped a torn strip of cloth tight around her arm. She examined Miranda's forearm for a moment, then carefully used the tip of her knife to create a tiny gash. Then she twisted the limb so the blood could collect in a measuring cup from the kitchen. Miranda didn't look at her arm, but kept her eye on Devin. Only taking a breath when she saw the gentle rise of his chest. Each one a few seconds slower than the last.

Once she finished, Rachel bandaged the wound and Miranda cradled her arm to her chest. It didn't hurt, but the idea felt precious somehow. She was literally giving him the blood from her veins. This was the sort of thing immortals did, not her. Yet, she'd have done it again. She'd have given all of it, if it saved him.

Rachel worked quickly, pouring the contents into a glass jar and heating it separately from the tea pot. Miranda only distantly watched as Rachel worked with the blood until a few silver drops bubbled to the surface of the coagulating mess in the jar. Carefully extracting the silvery beads, Rachel added them to the rest of the potion. The liquid inside shifted from blue to deep purple, shimmery threads of grey swirling near the surface.

Miranda cycled through all the warnings Gideon had given her. Trembling as Rachel pressed a clean cup of the potion into her hand. She wasn't trying to make this worse, but she didn't see another way.

Not when it had taken so long for anyone to get here in the first place. The doctor still hadn't arrived and finding one might take more time than they had.

Miranda eased Devin's head into her lap. She stroked his hair back from his forehead where sweat had pasted it to his skin. Easing his lips apart, she hesitated.

"The whole thing?"

Gideon raised his shoulders. "If you're going to do it, might as well do it. You don't want to risk it only half working."

"But I could ease him into it, see how he responds?"

"I don't have the answers, Wilde, this is a highly untested bottle of fucking *Divine* blood in there. We're talking gods and magic. He's also part human, so there's always a chance that could make it worse or better. We can flip a coin about it. But the fact remains, you wanted to make this choice, then you gotta make it."

Miranda closed her eyes.

She had no idea what the right call was.

She started to pour the potion into Devin's mouth, and when he sputtered, she pulled it back. He'd only swallowed half the contents. Was that enough? Would it be enough?

The room was pin-drop silent as everyone watched Devin for a sign that something was happening. And then he sucked in a loud, full breath, eyes flying open and screamed.

Miranda prayed to the Divine she hadn't just made a deadly mistake.

Devin's entire body was boiling. An excruciating blaze snaked through his veins and set his insides on fire. If he wasn't dead, he might have preferred it.

It lasted an eternity.

Then suddenly ended.

Devin took a slow breath in and out. His lungs were no longer on fire.

When he opened his eyes, he felt the moon like a physical presence, enveloping him with energy and calm. Soothing. Odd that he felt it so...much. His connection to the moon had always been distant. Maybe he had been too inebriated to notice before.

He sat up, blinking as the room spun and then snapped into crystal clear focus. Despite the heavy shadows and darkness, he could see everything in perfect definition. He would have noticed a pin dropping in the farthest corner. And he recognized this room. It was the bedchamber furthest from the master suite, meant for illustrious visitors like dukes and kings, back when those were a thing. It was the room he used when he spent the night here, if he didn't fall asleep half drunk in the study. The room where he'd brought Miranda and...

He had died.

The memories of last night were scattered, vague. The one thing he knew with certainty was that he had thought he'd breathed his last.

A sound to his left drew his attention and he nearly fell out of the bed. It was the loudest breath he'd ever heard. The source was Miranda, curled up on a couch that hadn't been there before. She was breathing gently, peacefully. Why did it sound like he was inside her lungs, rather than half a room away?

And her aura was *brighter*. If it blazed before, now he saw a sun and he had to shield his eyes so she didn't burn his retinas.

Taking careful breaths, Devin opened his eyes to Miranda's corner of the room, this time he shifted his focus. Concentrated on the sleeping Miranda, on her half-parted lips, her cheek squished against her hand. As he took in each new detail, the brightness of her aura dimmed until it was a faint shimmer in the background. Shifting his focus was the key to muting the colors. He'd have to learn how to do it subconsciously in the future.

Wait.

The full sequence of events caught up to him all at once. Miranda. Graves. He was stabbed.

Devin scrambled out of the bed, reaching for his side. His fingers slipped over a bandage saturated in blood and his heart stuttered. Was he a ghost?

He tore the bandage away—whoever wrapped it had done so thoroughly—until he reached clean, unmarred skin.

Was he dead or not?

He didn't *feel* dead. Actually, relatively speaking, he had never felt more alive.

"Devin?" Miranda stirred, blinking sleep away and squinting into the darkness. The only moonlight hit the bed, highlighting bloody, empty sheets. "Devin?" She stood, eyes searching, but passing right over him. "Devin!"

He *was* a ghost. Oh fuck. *No.*

She stared through him as she continued to scan the room. He was on the far side of the bed, shrouded in heavier shadows behind the curtains, but when he drew closer and into the sliver of moonlight, she screamed.

"What the fuck!" She scrambled back to the couch and drew her hands across the food tray, fingers closing around a fork. She held the fork like a dagger, pointing it at him.

"Who's there?" She demanded, staring into the room. Her eyes were on him, but she wasn't *seeing* him.

"Mira—"

"Oh my gods, Devin!" She dropped her weapon and attempted to get to him, feeling out with her hands for the bed, then the chaise, then working her way around the front of the room. He was about to call out, but she was already stumbling over his discarded pair of boots.

She fell in slow motion and he was there, catching her neatly before any part of her hit the ground. She folded into him, tucking herself as close as possible, burrowing into the folds of his shirt, under his shirt. When her hands reached skin she stopped, then her fingers trailed to his chest, resting above his heart.

"Did something happen? Why can't you see?" Devin pressed, disturbed and concerned that she might have been blinded in the fight. She set her forehead against him, breathing heavy.

"I can't see because it's pitch black in here," she said, pulling back until he could see her smiling through a cascade of tears. He swiped at her cheeks with his thumb and she nuzzled into his hand. "I thought you were gone. We hoped when you survived the first ten minutes that it worked, but then you just slept. I'm not sure how long."

He held her. "Seeing in the dark is not my gift, though. Are you sure it's *that* dark?" He looked around and the room was in the same sort of clarity as if the lanterns were lit.

"I mean, there's the barest gap letting in *some* moonlight, but it's one of those tiny quarter moons, so it's not enough to see by. Why? Is something wrong?"

He shrugged. "Wrong, in that I've never been able to see this well in just a fraction of moonlight before. Not wrong in that it's not exactly a problem, per say, but I don't understand how it's possible. I knew I was snuffing the edge off my natural senses all these years, but even as a boy I don't remember seeing this well in the dark."

Her eyes went wide and then her smile turned devious. "Pick me up."

"Pardon?"

"Just, lift me. If you can."

Devin rolled his eyes. "I've lifted you before, you're not—" He went to scoop his arm under her legs and nearly launched her across the room. If she were any other woman, she might have landed face first on the floor. Instead, she cartwheeled to land perfectly on her feet.

Miranda remained still for a moment, eyes wide, but she was grinning. "I...did not think that through."

"What just happened?"

She felt for him again, moving slowly to avoid tripping, and he caught her hands to guide her. "It's fine. It's fine. There's...so there's a lot to explain. You were nearly dead."

"I remember that part."

"Well, there weren't many options to save you. It was a lethal blow."

"Again, not surprising. How did I just lift you like you weighed nothing?"

"Fine, long story short, Gideon learned that the potion Graves made might heal you. So, we made some and you drank it and that's probably why you can see so well right now, too. But it's temporary. The effects should wear off by tomorrow or so."

He followed along, but he felt oddly detached from the information. "And Graves?"

Miranda winced. "Dead."

Devin nodded, and he was surprised at how okay he was with the news. Even though it hadn't been him to do it. "It was you, I assume."

She gave him a conspiratorial wink. "Gideon was quite impressed. I may have gone overboard, but he *did* nearly kill you. Plus, there was a lot of pent up rage to get through."

"Ah, stab therapy. And how do you feel now?""Oh, much better, thank you."

There was a lot to process. He didn't know how to wrap his mind around it all just then. It felt like he'd been out for days, not a few hours. He could process later.

Devin lifted Miranda again, this time carefully and with hands under her thighs so she could wrap her legs around him.

"I can't even see…" Her voice was full of laughter, dots of turquoise humor peppering her aura.

He kissed her. A slow, deep kiss.

"*You* don't need to see," he murmured, intending to lower her to the bed until he noticed the state of it.

"Oh, we hadn't wanted to move you, it's a mess and—"

"Mira, this house is full of beds and they all belong to me. We can use them all if you want, start at one end and work our way down the hall, defacing the hallowed chambers of my ancestors."

He kicked in the door to the adjacent bedchamber. "You said we have until tomorrow before this wears off?"

She nuzzled into his neck. "Can't say for sure."

"Then better to make the most of it while it lasts," he moved with a grace that he couldn't have achieved before, but with how light Miranda felt in his arms, he could walk and maneuver her body without effort.

The things he could do with this kind of strength. He could see how the power would be tempting, though his intentions were a fraction less sinister than what Graves had planned. But only a fraction, since his intentions for the still unmarried Miranda were, in some circles, considered contemptible.

And, by the end, the bed was beyond repair. Three of the four posts holding up the canopy were cracked and sagging toward the floor. The frame was on a dangerously uneven slant and the wall would need to be re-plastered.

Miranda was catching her breath as he enjoyed the sight of her with renewed clarity. Her tawny skin glistening with sweat, the sheets twined with her toned arms and legs. And that yellow shade of utter satisfaction pooling around her body. He was going to chase that color every single day.

"What are you staring at? Can you see my aura right now?"

He nodded.

"Is it weird to want to know what color it is?"

"I wouldn't know about weird, I never conferred much with other Night Fae on the subject. But it's not just one color. And each of those colors has a meaning. The same color, but on different people, can have an altered meaning."

"How do you know what they are?"

"Intuition, I think. The meanings just come to me."

"And...what does mine look like?"

"Yours is a solid band of proud and courageous cerulean. But dancing outward, like you are trying to light the world, is a passionate ruby red and adventurous tangerine. Then, occasionally, if you experience a strong emotion or feeling a new color can show up."

"Is that why you're staring at me?"

"Well, it's mostly because you're beautiful, and I plan to stare at you whenever I can, but you've got a shimmer of sated yellow which is my favorite color so far. It's a nice visual confirmation of my unquestionable prowess at satisfaction."

She lightly smacked his shoulder, but even the sore one felt entirely new. Her playful slap had all the pressure of a butterfly wing, but the message was clear. "Your admonition has lost its edge," he commented. "Could it be that you're warming up to my insufferable charm?"

"Never."

He started to crawl over her, head looming closer to hers. "I'm willing to bet that you have. In fact, I'd wager that you actually *love* when I'm a scoundrel."

She twisted so she was flat beneath him. "Don't push it. You may be stronger than me, but remember," She brought up her knee where he straddled her, her aim just slightly left of doing damage. "It's only temporary, and I'm not above delaying my revenge."

He bent like he meant to kiss her, but then changed his course at the last moment, teasing at the peak of her breast with his lips. "I'll give in if you admit it."

She squirmed, thighs squeezing together. "Not a chance."

"Suit yourself."

His lips were feather light, barely even a graze, and when she tried to press her body closer, he was able to pin her with a hand on her stomach. He was careful about the pressure, watching her for signs he might be pressing too hard, but Miranda's eyes were squeezed shut, every part of her wiggling and tensing with mounting frustration as his mouth whispered over sensitive skin. "I have plenty of patience, Mira. Endless patience."

"Shut up," she hissed.

He chanced the barest, infinitesimal flick of his tongue.

"Ah, fuck." Her hand speared through his hair. "I love when you're insufferable. I love when you're a rogue and you're annoying and I love how you pretend like you're the hottest thing in any given room." She yanked and, even though he was now more than strong enough to remain unmoved, where she summoned, he would go. "I love *all* of you. But if you don't fucking touch me I'm going to hurt you."

He was gentlemen enough not to deny a lady when asked so politely.

This time he went slower, taking his time until Miranda shuddered around him, body once again blooming in that perfect yellow. The bed, which was beyond repair before, was now little more than scrap.

"We should move to the next room," Devin breathed into her skin, bracing his arms to lean over her. His body didn't seem to tire, ready to go another round when not even he possessed such stamina in normal circumstances.

Forget violence or world domination, this potion could save every marriage in Unity in a single night.

"We should also get some sleep," she murmured, fingers tracing patterns on his bicep.

"You may have to insist on it, because I feel like I could do this for weeks."

"That's the potion talking."

"I suppose." Devin rolled next to her, testing to see if he could find a way to relax when he had never felt stronger, like his muscles were begging to be used. "Gideon better hope none of those fae got a taste for it. And that he confiscated it all. This stuff...I can see it becoming a problem. If I didn't possess such tremendous willpower and strength of character enough to resist addiction, I'd want more."

She tensed, then craned her head so she could meet his eyes. "You definitely don't have any of those traits, so now I'm concerned."

"Mira, you're my only addiction at the moment, and one is plenty. And since I have no intention of fighting this particular vice, you've no need to worry."

She sighed, but settled back down into the twisted knot of sheets.

"Ever?" She whispered.

"Miranda, I love you." He moved so that he could reach her face with his hands, holding her cheek. "If you're going to doubt it, then we're going to have to get married all the sooner."

Her eyes went wide. "What?"

"Miranda, I can't have you thinking that you'll ever be rid of me, not by any choice of mine. The way I see it, the best way to silence your doubts is to make it official. The sooner the better."

He knew the argument was coming, but her eyes were smiling, her lips were fighting a grin. "But...I...did we even officially decide?"

He kissed her. "Will you marry me, Miranda Wilde?"

She paused, for several seconds.

He may have once doubted at her hesitation, found ways to twist her silence into *his* failure. But he didn't doubt. He knew her well enough to know that, when it came to emotions, she was not nearly as quick on her feet as she was with a sword.

When she nodded, he wasn't surprised.

And the rest could wait. Her parents, her sister, the fallout of the most beloved Alderman in Unity dying in his home. None of that mattered now.

What *did* matter was finding an intact bed, letting Miranda get some rest, and praying that this potion lasted until morning.

EPILOGUE

T HE EXPLOSION WAS A surprise. Miranda crouched to retrieve her sword, staying low and out of sight. The building was destroyed. Whatever remained intact during the fight had been reduced to splinters. The larger debris provided cover, and Miranda peeked around what remained of a table. Devin met her eyes across the battlefield—a small tavern in the Fells now unrecognizable. The only clue to its origins was a mountain of broken glass where bottles had been stored.

The Day Fae in the center of the room continued to spit fire; the unrestricted blaze must have caused one of the barrels to ignite. Miranda's gaze returned to Devin.

"What's the plan?" he mouthed, giving the barest slant to an eyebrow.

Miranda surveyed the choices, returning a scrunched look to convey, "Do we have any devices left?"

He searched around him, then held up a fae contraption devised by Gideon's sister, Seraphina. Over the years, as the Watchmen looked to create a specialized task force to deal with the influx of Divinity in the population, they'd developed a few tricks. Miranda couldn't recall whatever fancy name Sera had given the device, but this one was designed to subdue Day Fae. Some mix of moonstone and night lily? Didn't matter. What mattered was that if used correctly, the device would knock the target out cold.

Their first few attempts had not landed, so they were down to this final device. Miranda was in charge of the Task Force assigned to these cases, though...technically, she was on leave and therefore not supposed to be working, let alone taking missions in the field.

But Miranda was nearest the scene when the call went out. She couldn't stand back while people were attacked. Devin was, of course, furious about it, insisting that she wait for her replacement before charging in headfirst. But she'd been cooped up for seven months now. She was getting bored.

Miranda gave Devin a nod and his eyes narrowed with frustration. He was going to be very cross later.

But when she leapt from cover, drawing the fae's attention, Devin seamlessly used the distraction as planned. He slid the device between the fae's legs, released the catch, and waited. The mechanism opened and a light burst from a compartment. The beam had no effect on Devin, since it was designed to inhibit Day Fae, but the fae hurling fireballs from their palm suddenly screamed in agony. The target crumbled to the floor when the device let out a small popping sound and gas poured into the room.

Devin stood above the noxious cloud, covering his mouth with his sleeve. The first part of the trap was specific to the fae target, but the gas would knock out anyone caught in the initial burst.

"The team should be here soon for clean-up and processing," Miranda said as Devin used his boot to shut the device, then bent down to restrain the target. People hopped up on Divinity required specialized restraints specific to their race, the fae kind were laced with iron to keep them from breaking through it. "Which means I won't be staying out at all hours with reports. And no bending to pick up evidence. Is that better?"

Devin stormed to her side. "*Better*, would be if my very pregnant wife didn't throw herself into danger in the first place." He crossed his arms. "You promised Allura."

Miranda winced. "Does she have to know?"

"How are you going to keep this from her? You have—" His face went white. "Mira, you're bleeding."

"What?" She looked down. "Oh, it's just a scratch—"

"It's more than a scratch. No more arguments. We're going home." He swept her into his arms and Miranda rolled her eyes.

"You're overreacting."

"Allura won't agree."

"Ah, fuck. I can't hide this, can I?"

"It's your own fault."

In their carriage—which they were *supposed* to use to attend an important political dinner with Lord and Lady Wilde when a commotion on this side of the park drew Miranda's attention and then, well, no dinner party—Devin tied off Miranda's leg at the knee. It would slow the blood oozing from the gash on her calf.

Her parents would understand. They didn't approve of her career, but she hadn't needed their approval and she learned that, when pushed, they chose to love her more than cling to their traditions. Devin said nothing as the carriage rattled along, bobbing on the uneven dirt streets until they transitioned to the cobbled roads of the Garrison. Once they reached their home, he threw the carriage door open and then spun to lift her before she could attempt the two steps to the sidewalk. Up the stairs to the door, he kicked at it with his boot.

"Why does this feel so familiar?" He asked, partly seething, partly amused.

She snuggled into his arms, not willing to admit that getting off her feet felt amazing.

Haversham answered the door and merely stepped aside with a nod. They had not even made it through the threshold when a nine-year-old girl marched down the stairs. Long, pointed ears stuck out from dark silky hair and her eyes—a soft, human shade of brown—narrowed with anger.

"How could you!"

"Sweetheart, it's really—"

Their eldest, Allura, pointed swiftly and silently toward the sitting room in a manner that brokered no argument. She followed Devin with a huff and glared as her mother was nestled into the couch, her leg propped on the table. Allura heaved a case from the corner, the one she kept stocked with all manner of first aid and various emergency supplies. She opened the case and, with the silent calm of a surgeon, began to tend to her mother's wound.

"You promised no more missions in your condition. What if something happened to the baby?"

"I know, but I was careful and your father—"

"Daddy agrees with me, so I know you did that thing where you look at him funny and he does whatever you want."

Devin crossed his arms, nodding in agreement, then he frowned. "Hang on, that is not how it works, Allie."

Allura rolled her eyes as she slipped on gloves and began cleaning with gauze and some concoction that bubbled when it hit the open wound. Miranda winced, but did her best to hide her discomfort.

"Wait," Devin hung his head. "Where's the nanny?"

Allura ignored him.

"Damn it, Allura, you've got to stop locking them up. Where is she?" He stuck his head out of the room. "Never mind, I'll follow the yelling." He set off to find wherever his daughter had stashed her current caretaker.

"Maybe you should hire competent nannies," Allura murmured as she focused on the needle and thread in her steady hands. She deftly speared the needle and set to work on the stitches. She'd had a lot of practice cleaning wounds over the years. Her first patients were her dolls and then her baby brother—which was promptly stopped by Devin and Miranda. Babies are not test subjects, they'd had to reiterate more than once.

"The nannies are not for you," Miranda scolded, though it was without any sort of authority.

Allura had never responded to scolding. Or rules. She always did just as she pleased, but with such well-reasoned, indisputable logic that it was impossible to argue with her. According to Devin, children didn't usually have an aura. Or if they did, it was fuzzy and constantly shifting. A strong emotion might create some color, but nothing that lasted until their personalities were more settled. Allura had developed a defined, rigid wavelength of 'sensible azure,' as Devin called it, by the time she was three.

Devin returned with a squirming toddler in his arms. A smiling boy with blonde hair and tawny skin. His eyes were a sparkling shade of lavender.

"What happened to mommy?"

"She was reckless and irresponsible—" Allura started, but Miranda quickly cut her off.

"I'm okay, Finn." Miranda sent Allura a glare that silenced her for the moment, at least.

"That's a lot of blood," Finn said, craning his head to see the injury. "Can I see?"

"No. You're too young," Allura snapped.

"You're not the boss."

"I am when I'm with a patient."

"Mommy's the boss."

"And...I think it's nap time," Devin said, turning with Finn in his arms, who twisted to stick his tongue out over Devin's shoulder. Allura was oblivious to the insult.

Devin bounced Finn a few times on his shoulder, a flurry of giggles filling the room. "You didn't fall asleep in the library again, did you?"

Finn spoke through his laughter, "Maybe."

Devin's sigh could be heard even as he ascended the stairs.

Allura finished and Miranda began to clean up the mess. Allura was brave and proud, but she was also nine.

"Darling, you know I'm the strongest person in the world, right?" The little game Miranda had started once Allura was old enough to understand Miranda's work for the Watchmen. The dangers had been a hard subject for Allura to grasp. They had joked that Miranda was the strongest person in the world, so she would always come home. Allura figured out the lie about a year later.

"The strongest in the world," Allura repeated.

"And I will always do whatever it takes to come home to you." Miranda held out her arms and Allura finished reorganizing her case and snapped it shut. Looking at the floor, Allura climbed onto the couch and snuggled into her mother's side.

"I know."

"But you still get scared?"

"Yes."

Miranda started to stroke her long dark hair. "That's understandable. My work is definitely scary. But it's also what I need to do. And it's not your job to worry about me, darling."

"I worry about lots of things," Allura said, voice tiny.

"I know. Do you want to play that game? The distraction game we talked about for when your worry gets too big?"

Allura nodded. And together, they both searched the room for things that would be the grossest to eat or make the best weapon or that would make the silliest hat.

It wasn't the same sort of childhood as Miranda's. Her children were given freedom to be themselves. And though they received the same education as the other children in the Garrison, Miranda didn't enforce the lessons and her children's manners were not what the social elite would consider 'up to standards.'

She still wasn't certain how much of her guardian blood was in her children. Their strength had never seemed greater than any other child. But she still sent both of them to training three days a week. Allura hated it, but Miranda wouldn't be swayed from the necessity of learning how to defend herself. Finn loved every second, showing a real flare for combat despite his clumsy toddler bearings.

But most importantly, they were accepted. Kieran North and his wife had made significant improvements to the city's infrastructure, inclusive measures to help ease the transition into ending the boundaries between races.

Devin was not particularly liked by higher society, but Miranda maintained that it was mostly because they had gotten to know him that caused their contempt, not his past or lineage. The peerage were quick to overlook his ancestry and birth when the truth of Graves had been exposed. They were not quick, however, to overlook his inappropriate comments or ill-timed jokes.

The children, however, were social peers with every door open to them. Whatever they wanted was in their reach. And Devin and Miranda had smothered the children in as much love and confidence in themselves as they could manage.

Miranda hobbled up the stairs to the nursery. Inside, Devin sat in an armchair snoring lightly as Finn flipped through the pages of a picture book.

"Daddy fell asleep."

"I see that, darling."

Finn used his tiny blanket to cover Devin's chest and planted a wet, sloppy kiss on his cheek. "Night, night," he whispered as he climbed down.

Miranda giggled as Devin wiped at the wet spot with his sleeve, eyes still closed but grinning.

As Finn raced closer, she carefully scooped him up. "Why don't we let daddy rest?"

"Yeah, he says you wear him out."

Miranda pursed her lips. "Oh?"

"And that you'll be the death of him."

"Traitor," Devin mumbled.

Behind his shoulder, the moon shone through the window. Their mid-day. They kept a Night Fae schedule as a family. The children showed clear preference for moonlight from infancy. Sometimes the strange hours caught up with Miranda, waking at odd times or her stomach rumbling during her previous luncheon, now the middle of her sleep cycle.

At the moment, however, she was always hungry.

"Well, I'm starving. How about we do family picnic?" She asked.

Finn nearly jumped from her arms and Miranda was forced to set him down, her hand protecting her stomach from his flailing legs. "Picnic! Picnic!"

"Cook hates when we do family picnic," Allura said, appearing in the doorway. But she was smiling.

"Well, I'm sure a small bonus will ease her frustration. Now. To the kitchen!"

The children raced ahead and Miranda held out her hand, Devin took it, and they followed at a slower pace.

"I'm starving," she started, already imagining what she would pack.

Devin chuckled. The children always pretended to gag and over-act throwing up while Pregnant Miranda arranged the strangest concoctions of food he'd ever seen.

Hands full, basket bursting, and the kitchen thoroughly raided of anything edible, the Drake family set out blankets in the back garden under the moonlight and settled on cushions swiped from the sofa.

Devin had hated this home once. It had filled him with regret and bitterness. He didn't feel like he belonged to its history.

So he had emptied it of every piece of furniture and artwork and portrait. He wiped the slate of the Warner legacy clean, and filled the house with a new legacy. And in the front hall, a grand portrait of him and Miranda and two children hung over the fresh coat of paint—their wild, energetic poses best suited to each personality was unlike any other portrait ever painted, if the artist was to be believed.

RETURN TO UNITY IN BOOK II

"Life-is-a-mess" Seraphina Blair unravels Kieran North's meticulously structured world...

COMING WINTER 2026

Acknowledgements

T HANK YOU TO EVERYONE who made this book possible.

My scrib friends who critiqued like champions. This book might have existed without you, but it'd probably be a lot shittier. Critiquing the first rounds of this book and enjoying it even when it was in it's worst stages gave me the confidence to continue. Wish I could give you all the karma.

MK and Trix, you were both invaluable to this process. Looking forward to returning the favor, so get writing!

My husband who doesn't know shit about creative writing, but was always there to say "it's good" whenever I babbled about scenes. He never let my play by play descriptions of 'is this possible??' adult scenes get awkward. And for working so hard so I could pursue my dream.

My daughter. Kid, you're amazing and talented and I love you more than you know. Thanks for playing alone more than either of us liked (sorry, but you still can't have a brother) cause I can only stop mid-scene to open bottles of water or play impromptu pretend vet so many times before the flow is completely broken. That said, a hammer is not a surgical tool, all your patients are dead.

To my pets. I love my mini menagerie, but not one of you actually helped to make this happen. However, you do provide endless entertainment and cuddles so you get a mention.

My parents, in all their forms and iterations, thanks for the support and encouragement. I hope to one day soon be able to tell you 'I did it.'

And I think it's fair to thank myself. Cause I wrote this thing and I never imagined I'd be able to call myself 'author.' But I did it. I wrote and wrote and edited (gods did I edit, I can't read a word from this book again) and did the steps. Now it's published and that was really hard. So for that, go me.

ABOUT THE AUTHOR

L UCI BRIAR LIVES IN Florida with her family and too many pets. Five cats, two dogs, a snake, blue death feigning beetles, a jumping spider, and a pac-man frog. She enjoys writing romance, reading romance, watching romance, analyzing romance, and observing romance. All her life Luci has found charm in Regency tales and fantasy settings, combining all her passions into her books. Always with a touch of humor and plenty of spice. All her characters are assured to get their HEA because reality is hard enough and books are her happy place.

When not writing she's doing her best to keep a small human alive and, hopefully, help her to grow into a functional, well-adjusted version of a big human. Luci also enjoys board games, video games, cottage-core vibes, and not being outside.

Check her out online at Lucibriarbooks.com

TT @lucibriarbooks

IG @lucibriarbooks